THE
Celestial Bed

By Irving Wallace

Fiction

The Celestial Bed
The Seventh Secret
The Miracle
The Almighty
The Second Lady
The Pigeon Project
The R Document
The Fan Club
The Word
The Seven Minutes
The Plot
The Man
The Three Sirens
The Prize
The Chapman Report
The Sins of Philip Fleming

Nonfiction

Significa (Coauthor)
The Intimate Sex Lives of Famous People (Coauthor)
The Book of Lists 1, 2, and 3 (Coauthor)
The Two (Coauthor)
The People's Almanac 1, 2, and 3 (Coauthor)
The Nympho and Other Maniacs
The Writing of One Novel
The Sunday Gentleman
The Twenty-seventh Wife
The Fabulous Showman
The Square Pegs
The Fabulous Originals

Irving Wallace

THE
Celestial Bed

DELACORTE PRESS / NEW YORK

To
Ed Victor
friend, literary agent, true believer

Published by
Delacorte Press
1 Dag Hammarskjold Plaza
New York, New York 10017

MANUFACTURED IN THE UNITED STATES OF AMERICA

FIRST PRINTING

Library of Congress Cataloging in Publication Data
Wallace, Irving, 1916–
    The celestial bed.
    I. Title.
PS3573.A426C45   1987   813'.54
ISBN 0-385-29556-1
Library of Congress Catalog Card Number: 86-24129

In 1783 one of the most popular attractions in London was the Temple of Health, promoted by an amiable Scot named Dr. James Graham. The main feature of the Temple was the canopied Celestial Bed, supported by twenty-eight glass pillars and attended by a live nude Goddess of Health. Male visitors were invited to recline on the Celestial Bed for fifty pounds a night with the promise that this treatment would lead to a cure for impotence.

I

As he was driving home for dinner, having parted from his visitor and locked up his clinic, Dr. Arnold Freeberg decided that this was one of the best days—perhaps *the* best day—he had enjoyed since establishing himself in Tucson, Arizona, after having left New York six years earlier.

All because of his visitor, Ben Hebble, Tucson's most successful banker, and Hebble's announcement of an astonishing gift to him.

Freeberg recalled the essence of the corpulent banker's visit. "It's because your sex therapy cured my son," Hebble had said. "Timothy was a mess, and we both know it. Afraid to be with girls, because he couldn't get it up till his psychiatrist sent him to you. Well, you did the job, all right. In two months, you did it. After that, Timothy played the field for a while until he fell in love with a pretty young lady from Texas. They tried living together, and it was such a success that they're getting married. Because of you, I expect to be a grandfather yet!"

"Congratulations!" Freeberg had exclaimed, remembering how he and his sex surrogate, Gayle Miller, had so patiently worked to bring the dysfunctional banker's son to sexual adequacy.

"No, it's you, Dr. Freeberg. You're the one who deserves the congratulations," Hebble had boomed out, "and I'm here to thank you in a very practical way. I'm here to tell you that I'm setting up a foundation to supplement your own clinic, a foundation that will enable you and your staff to help cure dysfunctional patients who can't afford to hire you. I'm talking about guaranteeing you one hundred thousand dollars a year toward this end for ten years. That's a million dollars to give you a chance to broaden your work and lend a hand to other unfortunate victims of impotence."

Freeberg recalled that he had felt faint. "I—I really don't know what to say. This is overwhelming."

"Only one condition attached," Hebble had added briskly. "I want this set up in Tucson, and all your work must be done here. This city has been kind to me. I owe it something. What do you say to that?"

"No problem. None whatsoever. This is most generous of you, Mr. Hebble."

Freeberg had parted from his benefactor in a daze.

Now, reaching home, opening the front door, he was humming to himself when he saw his plump wife Miriam waiting for him in the entry hall.

Cheerily, Freeberg kissed her, but before he could speak she whispered to him. "Arnie, you have someone waiting for you in the living room. The city attorney, Thomas O'Neil."

"Oh, he can wait a minute," Freeberg said, putting an arm around his wife. He and O'Neil were casual friends, often on the same committees together to raise money for local charities. "Probably just some more community business. Now, listen to what just happened to me at the clinic."

Quickly, he told her about Hebble's offer.

Miriam exploded with excitement, hugged her husband, and kissed him again and again. "How marvelous, how truly marvelous, Arnie. Now you can do everything you ever dreamed of."

"And then some!"

She took Freeberg by the arm and directed him toward

the living room. "You better find out what Mr. O'Neil wants. He's been here ten minutes. You shouldn't keep him waiting forever."

Moments later, having entered the living room and greeted the city attorney, Freeberg sat down across from him. Freeberg was puzzled to see that the city attorney looked uncomfortable.

City Attorney O'Neil was apologetic. "I hate to break in on you during your dinner hour," he said, "but I have several appointments this evening, and I felt I must speak to you as soon as possible about an—well, an urgent matter."

Freeberg continued to be puzzled. This did not sound like the usual charity fund-raiser.

"What is it, Tom?" Freeberg asked.

"It's about your work, Arnold."

"What about my work?"

"Well, I've been officially informed by—by several other therapists that you're using a sex surrogate to cure patients. Is that true?"

Freeberg squirmed uneasily. "Why, yes, it—it is true. Because I've found that it's the only means that works with many dysfunctional patients."

O'Neil shook his head. "It's against the law in Arizona, Arnold."

"I know, but I thought I could cut a corner or two, if I did it quietly, to effect cures for my more drastically troubled patients."

O'Neil remained adamant. "'Illegal,'" he said. "It means you're pandering, and the woman you're using is playing prostitute. I'd like to close my eyes to what you're doing. We're friends. But I can't. Too much pressure is being put on me. I can't ignore it any longer." He straightened himself and seemed to force out the next words. "What it comes down to is your losing your job or me losing mine. This has to be resolved immediately—and strictly according to the law. Let me tell you what you have to do. It's the best proposition I can make to you, Arnold. Are you ready to listen?"

Pale faced, Dr. Arnold Freeberg nodded, and he listened . . .

Later, after City Attorney O'Neil had gone, Freeberg sat moodily through dinner, picking away at his food, unaware of what he was eating and totally lost in thought. He was conscious and grateful that Miriam was distracting Jonny, their four-year-old son, while he himself sought to recover from the knockout blow and to think out the consequences.

Freeberg had worked so hard and long, against such constant opposition, to achieve his success in Tucson and Hebble's magnificent offer. And now, suddenly, the edifice of success had crumbled to dust.

He thought back to the start. The start had actually been when Freeberg graduated from Columbia University in New York as a psychologist. Once he opened his own practice, the results had not been satisfying. The preponderance of his cases dealt with intimate human relationships, mostly involving sexual problems, and for many reasons, the psychological approach had not worked effectively, at least not for him. The patients who came and went, left him perhaps with more understanding of their problems but with little of use in the way of practical solutions.

More and more, Freeberg had begun to investigate other forms of sex therapy ranging from hypnosis to assertiveness training to group efforts. None of them impressed him enough until he attended a series of classes where a Dr. Lauterbach demonstrated the use of sex surrogates in therapy. The method, and the favorable results, had appealed to Freeberg at once.

After an in-depth study, Freeberg subscribed unconditionally to the idea of using sex surrogates. At one lecture, he met a warm, delightful young woman named Miriam Cohen, a successful department store buyer, who had been there seeking answers to her own problems and who had been one of the few females in the room who agreed with him on the value of sex surrogate therapy. Soon, Freeberg had found he had much more in common with Miriam; he began to date her regularly, and finally he married her.

At last content to continue his practice as a psychologist, but now planning to employ sex surrogates when required, Freeberg looked forward to carrying out this promising treatment.

Miriam had become unwell, suffering diminished lung capacity, which was diagnosed as a severe bronchial condition. Miriam's physician, seconded by a pulmonary specialist, advised an immediate move to Arizona. Freeberg had not hesitated to close down his affairs in New York and set up shop in Tucson. Miriam had fared well. Freeberg had not. The use of sex surrogates was strictly forbidden in Arizona.

Freeberg had soon established his new practice in Tucson. But once more, insight treatment as a psychologist was not fully effective with patients suffering serious sexual dysfunctions. In desperation Freeberg had decided to gamble. Secretly, he had trained, then employed, a female surrogate to use undercover. When five out of five of his patients suffering sexual dysfunctions had been fully cured, he knew true professional satisfaction.

And now, suddenly, this evening, his means of usefulness had been stripped away. In effect, he had been handcuffed and rendered helpless by the law.

There seemed to be no choice but to go back to being a limited and often ineffective talk therapist. He could continue making a livelihood in Tucson. But he could no longer cure.

It was impossible, yet there was no choice.

Then the realization came to him that there might be a choice, after all. There just might be.

First, it would require two telephone calls. And luck.

Freeberg looked up from his half-empty dinner plate and pushed away his chair.

"Miriam, Jonny," he said, rising, "why don't you both keep busy with television for a little while—I think there's a circus special on—while I go into the library and make a couple of important phone calls? I'll catch up with you soon."

Closing the door of the library, seating himself at the telephone, Freeberg called his wife's physician in Tucson. Freeberg had a question to ask. Then he waited for the answer.

Once that was done, Freeberg direct-dialed his old friend and onetime Columbia University roommate, Roger Kile, attorney-at-law, in Los Angeles, California.

Freeberg hoped Kile was in. He was.

Disposing of the amenities quickly, Freeberg got right down to it. "I'm in trouble, Roger," he said, unable to hide the urgency in his voice. "I'm in trouble, real trouble," he repeated. "They want to run me out of town."

"What are you talking about?" said Kile, plainly confused. " 'They'—who are 'they'? The police?"

"Yes and no. Actually, no. It's the city attorney and his staff. They want to put me out of business."

"You're joking! Why?" Kile wanted to know. "Did you commit some offense? Is there a crime involved?"

"Well . . ." Freeberg hesitated, "maybe in their eyes . . . Maybe . . ." He hesitated once more, then blurted out, "Roger, I was using a sex surrogate."

"A sex surrogate?"

"Don't you remember? I explained it to you once."

Kile was clearly bewildered. "It seems to have slipped—"

Freeberg tried to contain his impatience. "You know what a surrogate is. A person appointed or hired to act in the place of another. A substitute. A surrogate is a substitute." Then, more emphatically. "A sex surrogate is a substitute sex partner, usually for a single man, a man who doesn't have a wife or cooperative girlfriend, a man who is suffering a sexual dysfunction, has a sex problem—so he uses a female sex partner to help him, a woman supervised by a sex therapist. The team of Masters and Johnson started it in St. Louis in 1958—"

"Yes, I remember," Kile interrupted. "I read about their

use. And now I remember that you were considering using sex surrogates in Tucson. Well, what's wrong with that?"

"One thing," said Freeberg. "It's against the law, Roger. The use of surrogates is okay in New York and Illinois and California and a few other states, but in the rest of the states, it's against the law. That includes Arizona. Sex surrogates are considered prostitutes."

"I see," said Kile. "And you used them?"

"One—I used only one," said Freeberg. "But apparently one too many. Let me explain." He seemed to recover some balance in his voice. "I told you it's illegal here, so I started doing it underground. I *had* to, Roger. Talk therapy doesn't work in certain cases, the worst ones like impotence and sometimes premature ejaculation. It's essential to use a trained female partner to teach, to demonstrate, to give guidance. I found such a person, a great young lady. I used her to work with five difficult cases. All five were cured. One hundred percent cured. But somehow word got out. The therapists are very conservative here—and maybe jealous. . . . Maybe they resented my success. Anyway, word got to the city attorney, and he came over to see me at home, maybe an hour ago. I was pandering, he said, and using a prostitute, and that was against the law. Instead of arresting me, putting me on trial, he offered me an alternative. To avoid wasting time and money to prosecute me, he advised me to shut down my surrogate operation. Then he'd let me continue practicing as an ordinary therapist."

"Will you?"

"I can't, Roger. I can't be helpful to certain patients who come to me without employment of a surrogate. Look what happened to Masters and Johnson when they were forced to give up the use of sex surrogates in 1970. Until then, using surrogates, their success rate was seventy-five percent. Once they gave up on surrogates, their success rate dropped to twenty-five percent. I can't let that happen. If I did, I shouldn't be in this profession. Yet I want to be in this profession. It's not a question of making a living. It's more. It's getting crippled people, sex cripples, healthy and virile. I don't want to sound Boy Scoutish. But that's it. And that's why, much as I hated to bother you, I decided to call you tonight."

"I'm glad you did," Kile said assuringly. "But, Arnie, what can I do for you in Tucson?"

"You can get me out of here," said Freeberg simply. "I remembered something you once said, when I was first moving to Arizona. You said, Why not come to southern California? You said it's freer country than anywhere else. You said you'd heard of a number of therapists who used sex surrogates in Los Angeles and San Francisco."

"Did I? I guess I did. Anyway, it's true."

"I resisted only because Miriam's doctor in New York had been adamant that Arizona was the best place for her bronchial condition. That was six years ago. Now her doctor in Tucson—I just phoned him—feels she's better and could fare as well in southern California."

"You mean you'd consider moving here?"

"Yes," said Freeberg. "There's no other choice." He swallowed. "Roger, California is unknown country to me. I need your help. You're a Californian now. You know your way around. You could be of enormous assistance, if it's not asking too much."

"It's asking very little. You know I'd do anything I can for you, Arnie."

"I'm not rich," Freeberg went on. "I have everything invested in my clinic here. No big thing getting rid of it, once I have a real estate agent put the building on the market. It's a valuable property. I'm sure I can sell it in no time at all and come out your way with sufficient money to set up another clinic in southern California." He swallowed nervously again. "But I do need help. I'll pay you for your time, of course."

"Cut it out, Arnie," Kile said with a pretense of annoyance. "This is friendship. What are friends for, anyway? I'll tell you what. If I ever run into trouble myself—can't get it up one day—you can pay me back by contributing your services and loaning me one of your lady surrogates. So you've got a deal. What do you want from me?"

"A promising location in or around Los Angeles. A

building I can afford and can remodel as a clinic. I'll send you details tomorrow. Photographs of the two-story place I have right now. And I'll let you know, in round numbers, how much I can afford to spend."

"You've got it," said Kile. "Let me start making inquiries right away. Once I have your specifications and limitations —well, give me two weeks, Arnie. I'll call you when I have something for you to see. Meanwhile, give my regards to Miriam, and I look forward to meeting that little boy of yours. It sure will be good to see you again."

Freeberg was reluctant to hang up. "Roger, you're positive I'd be welcome there? I mean, with sex surrogates and all?"

"Not to worry. I'll double-check the criminal code, but I'm absolutely certain it's not against the law. Arnie, this is freedom land. I guarantee it. Now, let's get going."

It worked. It went smoothly. Every aspect of the move worked out.

Today, four months later, Dr. Arnold Freeberg could sit comfortably in his high-backed leather swivel chair behind the wide oak desk covered with a custom-fitted black felt blotter and listen to the muffled sounds of hammering outside the entrance downstairs. The workmen were putting into place the blue and white sign that read, in block letters: FREEBERG CLINIC. The sign was being mounted over two glistening glass doors that led to the reception area.

Today, too, early this afternoon, Freeberg would be briefing the five new sex surrogates he had selected out of the six he would be using. He wished that his sixth surrogate, his most experienced, the one he had employed in Tucson, could also be here right now. Gayle Miller had agreed to join him, go on with him, in a few weeks, after she had graduated from the University of Arizona. Then she would apply for graduate school at the University of California at Los Angeles to get her masters degree and doctorate in psychology. The imminent appearance of Gayle Miller gave Freeberg confidence. He was certain the new surrogates would be good, but Gayle was a gem—young, attractive, serious, and experienced. She'd been his sex surrogate on all five cases in Tucson, and she had been faultless. Every problem male had been discharged to go forward with a normal sex life.

Absently gathering his notes together, notes he had jotted down the past few days to remind himself of points he wanted to cover in addressing the new surrogates, Freeberg's gaze roamed around the walls of his spacious office. There was still the pungent, stinging smell of the fresh paint on the walls. The oak wainscot had been stained deep brown to give it a rich paneled look. Hung from the walls, in cream matted frames, were Freeberg's impressive panoply of idols: Sigmund Freud, Richard von Krafft-Ebing, Havelock Ellis, Theodore H. van de Velde, Marie Stopes, Alfred Kinsey, William Masters and Virginia Johnson.

On the nearby wall, there was a decorative mirror, and Dr. Arnold Freeberg's eyes came to rest on that and on the reflection of himself. Sheepishly, he inspected himself—high comb of wiry black hair, somewhat stiff and unruly; thick horn-rimmed spectacles over small myopic eyes; hooked nose; full dark mustache and short beard encircling his fat lips. Fleetingly, closed in by his predecessors, he felt embarrassed. He didn't measure up to them. Not yet, not yet. But one day soon, perhaps. He believed and he would try.

His eyes moved to the silver-framed photograph on a corner of his desk. His wife, Miriam, attractive in her mid-thirties, and their smiling son, Jonny, a delight. Freeberg became conscious of his own years, his late fortyishness, late to have a first child. But not really, not actually.

Giving his head a shake, he drew his notes closer and tried to concentrate on them. Quickly, he skimmed them, then pushed them aside. He knew them all by heart and would not need them for reference when he spoke to his new surrogates.

He still had fifteen minutes to spare before his five surrogates appeared, and almost as a relaxation, he began to review the events of the last four months that had brought him to these moments. He relived those four months in the present.

Within two weeks of Freeberg's initial phone call from Tucson to Roger Kile in Los Angeles, Kile had finished his investigations and found the location. Not in Los Angeles proper, as it turned out. Los Angeles was too heavily populated with sex therapists, Kile had learned, and furthermore, centrally situated properties were overpriced. But following expert advice—Kile had always been a clever investigator, even in law school at Columbia, and although a tax attorney his knowledge and interests were widespread —he had found the community in which his friend might prosper an hour north of Los Angeles.

The community proved to be Hillsdale, California, a burgeoning incorporated city on the coast highway and close to the rolling blue Pacific Ocean. It was a sprawling city of three hundred and sixty thousand. There were plenty of psychiatrists and psychologists there, but not one sex therapist yet. Roger Kile had been assured, by knowledgeable contacts, that a practice would flourish for any reputable sex therapist who set up shop in Hillsdale with a team of trained and professional sex surrogates. Hillsdale, Kile learned from medical contacts, had more than a fair share of disturbed, troubled, and sexually dysfunctional persons.

After that, Kile found two well-recommended realtors, and they quickly led him to four small office buildings that appeared to be possibilities. Freeberg spotted the perfect building immediately, a vacant two-story construction abandoned by a clothing store chain and set in the middle of Market Avenue, three blocks off bustling Main Street. After that, everything fell into place rapidly. Freeberg hired an excellent young architect to remodel the vacant building along the lines of his Tucson clinic. Then Freeberg flew back to Tucson to divest himself of the old clinic. Meanwhile, Miriam got rid of their ranch-style adobe tract house, breaking even.

They went to Hillsdale four times in the period that followed. While Freeberg stood by to oversee the remodeling of his clinic, Miriam sought a new house and found a

wonderful eight-room one-story residence about three
miles from her husband's offices.

Immediately, Freeberg began to install the necessary
personnel in his clinic. Through an M.D. nearby, Dr. Stan
Lopez, a general practitioner that Freeberg had come to
respect, Freeberg was able to obtain Suzy Edwards as his
personal secretary. Lopez had been using Suzy as a part-
time second secretary and knew that she wanted a full-time
job. Freeberg interviewed Suzy, a solemn and interested
redhead of around thirty. She was eager for the job, and
Freeberg had already heard that she was trustworthy. After
that, he hired Norah Ames for his practical nurse and Tess
Wilbur for his receptionist.

Next, Freeberg sent personal letters to every medical
person around the country that he had met at conventions
and seminars, announcing the opening of the Freeberg
Clinic in Hillsdale, California, and offering intensive treatment and the use of female and male sex surrogates when
they were found necessary. While awaiting responses, Freeberg instigated his search for sex surrogate candidates. To
obtain applicants, Freeberg wrote personal letters to psy-
choanalysts in Hillsdale and to fellow therapists in Los
Angeles, Santa Barbara, San Francisco, Chicago, and New
York. Within a few short weeks, he received twenty-three
applications from those wishing to become sex surrogates,
and even as the replies came in, Freeberg received referrals
of patients who were in desperate need of his kind of therapy. From these referrals, Freeberg knew that he would
require five surrogates, four women and one man, plus the
services of Gayle Miller, who would shortly be leaving Tucson for Hillsdale.

As the surrogate candidates gradually arrived, Freeberg
began to screen them, interviewing each personally. Many
were short interviews, because the candidates did not qualify. If a candidate gave for her motivation that she thought
this would be interesting work, she was disqualified. Interesting work was not good enough—not motivation enough.
If any candidate showed the slightest concern about being a

candidate, or any hesitancy whatsoever, she was eliminated.

The longer interviews were given over to women who were well motivated. There were divorced women, with no children living at home, who'd had sexually inadequate husbands. There were women who'd had problems with lovers suffering sexual dysfunctions. There were women who'd seen sexual troubles in their parents, siblings, other relatives. All the candidates, no matter what their previous callings, were bound by a common desire to assist sexually crippled men in becoming fully normal males.

Always, in his interviews, Freeberg kept in mind something that a colleague had once remarked: "A good surrogate is sensitive, compassionate, and emotionally mature." A qualified surrogate was someone who was also comfortable with her own body and her own sexuality. Every female that Freeberg seriously considered, if she was presently unmarried, had to have had a normal sexual relationship, had to know that she was sexually responsive, and had to have confidence in her own femininity. Above all else, she had to burn with the desire to repair the sexually wounded among the male population.

In the end, Freeberg wound up with four highly promising female sex surrogate candidates—Lila Van Patten, Elaine Oakes, Beth Brant, and Janet Schneider. Once trained, they would make a perfect group to team up with his soon-to-arrive Gayle Miller.

Freeberg had required only one male sex surrogate. Male surrogates to work with dysfunctional female patients were not in demand. Freeberg had discovered that a male surrogate did not fit the value system of most females. It was the old nonsense, lingering into the 1980s: If a male had numerous women, he was okay, a cocksman. If a female had casual sex with many men, she had round heels and was a fool. Generally, having sex with a stranger—in this case, a male surrogate—was unthinkable by American social standards. Usually women, far more than men, needed time to build toward a satisfying relationship. But this was California. Times were changing. A little, just a little. Freeberg could see that there would be a female patient now and then, and so he would need at least one male sex surrogate. In Freeberg's screenings, a single applicant had stood out. He was a young man from Oregon, experienced, interested in his personal growth, thoughtful, warm, and with a real desire to help troubled and suffering women patients become normal. His name was Paul Brandon. Among the handful of male candidates, Brandon was the one that Freeberg selected for training.

The door to his office had opened, and Freeberg came out of his reverie. "They're here, Dr. Freeberg," his red-headed personal secretary, Suzy Edwards, was saying. "The surrogates you selected. They're seated in the all-purpose room, waiting for you."

Freeberg smiled and heaved his stocky body to his feet. "Thanks, Suzy. Time for the curtain to go up."

Dr. Arnold Freeberg shut down the piped-in music, left his office, and walked briskly to the far end of the all-purpose room—a thirty-foot room that resembled a sparsely furnished living room. Here and there, on the floor, lay mattresses, and at the far end was the sofa facing the five surrogates, who ranged in age from twenty-eight to forty-two. They were seated on folding chairs in a semicircle.

With a smile, Freeberg nodded to them, pleased to see they were all neatly dressed and alert. He knew that they were comfortable—his nurse Norah had already introduced them to one another—but on their faces were expectant expressions.

Freeberg sat down on the sofa, settled back, and crossed one leg over the other.

"Janet Schneider," he said as if reading a roll call, "Paul Brandon, Lila Van Patten, Beth Brant, Elaine Oakes—I'm so pleased to have you here. Welcome to the Freeberg Clinic. I am delighted to tell you that you are all, without exception, decidedly qualified, highly qualified, to become valuable and useful partner surrogates."

He observed their immediate and unanimous pleasure at the compliment.

"I am going to speak to you today about your training program, which will begin in this room tomorrow at nine o'clock in the morning. Your training will be entirely under my supervision, five days a week, for six weeks. Only in the final stages will I bring in outsiders. When we get to penile-vaginal contact, I will require the assistance of four males and one female recommended by the International Professional Surrogates Association in Los Angeles. These will be former patients—or clients, as some call them today—who once suffered their own sexual problems, have gone through full courses of exercises with reputable therapists and experienced surrogates, and have been pronounced cured and ready to deal with their own intimate lives.

"At this time, I am going to brief you on the training period that lies ahead of you so that you know what to expect. This will be a monologue. I will speak without pause. If you have questions, save them for when I have finished. Also, of course, I will shorthand the whole procedure, so to speak—just give you the highlights, since all of it will develop fully in your training period. Further, do not be concerned about any questions you failed to ask me today. You can ask them as we work from tomorrow on.

"Oh, yes"—he focused on Paul Brandon—"Mr. Brandon, since most of the patients we'll be dealing with in therapy will be males, I will address myself to the activities of our female surrogates who will work with them. However, almost all the procedures I discuss will apply to you, too, as a male surrogate working with female patients. Where there are exceptions in your treatments, well, we can take these up privately later when you are assigned to female patients seeking help."

Digging into his pocket for his box of cigarillos, Freeberg said, "I have no objections to any of you smoking if those around you do not mind, or even chewing gum or mints." Lighting his cigarillo, he saw Brandon pull an old briar pipe and pouch from his jacket pocket, while Lila Van Patten removed a package of cigarettes from her purse.

"Let's begin with the basics," Freeberg continued. "Why were you selected to serve as partner or sex surrogates? I selected you not because of your good looks or physiques or what I deemed to be your sex appeal. I selected you for more important overall qualities—because I saw in each of you the qualities of knowledge, compassion, warmth, and real concern for others not as healthy as yourselves. You all have in common an appreciation of giving, receiving, touching, and caring and a desire to share what you have to offer.

"Let's begin with Masters and Johnson, the real pioneers in the use of sex surrogates. William Masters came from Ohio, studied medicine at the University of Rochester, and eventually began a research program in sexual functioning at Washington University School of Medicine. Two years later, realizing that he needed a female associate, Masters hired Virginia Johnson. She was a Missouri farm girl, a divorcée and mother, who had taken some courses in psychology but had no college degree. They made a perfect investigative team, and as you undoubtedly know, they eventually married each other.

"As Masters and Johnson quickly learned, insight or talk therapy—free association, questions and answers—did not provide enough help for their more desperate patients. What their male patients needed, Masters and Johnson saw, was 'someone to hold on to, talk to, work with, learn from, be a part of, and above all else, *give to* and *get from* during the sexually dysfunctional male's acute phase of therapy.' I suppose that was how the idea of the sex surrogate was born in 1957. There were men with grave sexual problems who did not have cooperative female partners, married or unmarried, to come along with them to the therapy, and there were others who had no women friends at all. Were these men to be penalized for not having sex partners willing to join them in their therapy? 'These men are societal cripples,' Masters used to say. 'If they are not treated it is discrimination of one segment of society over another.' So to treat them, Masters and Johnson began to train female partners, sex surrogates, to work with them while under the guidance of the two therapists.

"And the new treatment was extremely successful. In eleven years, Masters and Johnson used sex surrogates to work with forty-one single men. Of these, thirty-two had their sexual problems resolved, fully overcome, through the use of sex surrogates. That's an impressive record. And I can vouch for the means used because, in my previous activity elsewhere, I had one excellent surrogate who worked with five seriously crippled and sexually inadequate patients, and in every case, their symptoms and failures were reversed and cured.

"In 1970, as you may have read, Masters and Johnson gave up the use of sex surrogates altogether. It was said that one of their female surrogates, unknown to them, had a husband, and the husband sued Masters and Johnson for alienation of affection. Rather than go to court, and fuel a scandal for the media, Masters and Johnson made a legal settlement out of court and, after that, simply gave up the practice of using surrogates. I trust this will not be my predicament. From what I could learn about each of you, while three of you are divorced, not one of you is presently married. The other thing that disenchanted Masters and Johnson was the realization that so many surrogates were not only working as surrogates but were also trying to behave as therapists themselves. Of course, this is something I would never permit.

"At any rate, as you know, sexual inadequacy is the greatest cause for divorce in the United States. William Masters discovered some years ago that of the forty-five million married couples in this country, half were sexually incompatible. The figures may vary somewhat today, but you and I know that something should and can be done to make troubled people healthier and happier."

Freeberg leaned down to pick an ashtray off the floor, stubbed out his cigarillo, and set the ashtray aside. This had served as a punctuation mark. He was ready to enter into a more specific outline of the training.

"Now to your actual training," Freeberg resumed. "Your

internship of six weeks will be under my supervision. You will be given a reading list of professional literature to cover. There will be added sessions in which I will question each of you more intensively on your earlier sexual experience and your responsivity to various adequate mates you've been involved with. I will attempt to teach you various counseling skills that you may need with your patients. You will receive thorough descriptions and demonstrations of male and female sexual functioning, to give you physiological knowledge and psychological insights. We will discuss, at some length, especially as it applies to poorly performing males, their problem in playing spectator roles to their own performances.

"But most important of all, you will each receive a complete course in surrogate sex therapy, learning and experiencing yourselves what your patients will experience. In fact, right now, without going into detail, I want to describe the steps, the exercises, you will be sharing with your patients.

"You will be meeting with each patient perhaps three or four times a week, each session loosely limited to two hours. What kind of sexual dysfunctions can you expect to encounter? Sometimes the problems will be simple—a patient with low sexual desire, a person who is naive and socially frightened and isolated, or even a person who is still a virgin. But more commonly, with male patients, you'll be dealing with a man who has erectile difficulties, one who is primarily impotent. You'll be dealing with a man who suffers premature ejaculation. You'll be dealing with a man who is unable to experience sexual pleasure. In the case of a woman patient, you may encounter a female who is nonorgasmic, one who cannot have a climax, even through masturbation. More challenging might be the case of a woman suffering vaginismus, which is a vaginal muscular spasm that makes sexual intercourse difficult or very painful.

"How will you go about curing all these human dysfunctions? It really comes down to teaching a patient to be in touch with his own feelings and to be comfortable with

intimacy. The client has come to you to be helped. The
purpose of your job will be to develop, nurture, and secure
an intimate relationship. It will involve sharing feelings and
behaviors. This can be done only on a gradual basis, to
remove the patient's inhibitions and make him more aware
of his sexuality and his partner's sexuality. Many patients
are in a hurry to get it over with, to get somewhere immediately. Many of the male patients are secretly saying to themselves, 'What the hell, why do I have to go through all this
preliminary nonsense? When will we get down to the real
business?' But no matter what the client's urgency, you, the
surrogate, will have to remember that it is going to take
time, and each patient must absolutely be made to understand that.

"The whole process begins and continues in this manner. A problem patient is referred to me for ultimate treatment. First, I see that the patient is examined by an M.D. to
be certain he has no physical disorders—for example, no
hormonal deficiencies, no disease. If the problem is not
physical, I meet with the patient and listen to his full sexual
history. Listening to this, I can usually pinpoint how things
went wrong with the patient. I will ask him questions such
as—when you were growing up, was nudity allowed in the
home? Was there much hugging, kissing, caressing, touching in your family? The answers to these questions are
usually no. Later, maturing, the patient has his first sexual
experience. It is usually negative. Then the patient is in
trouble. In speaking to him, I try to calm him by explaining
that fear and ignorance are strangling him, and that given
help and time he can be free and sex can be as natural for
him as breathing.

"When it is your turn to take over as surrogates, and lend
me assistance with the patient, you must understand that
the ongoing reasons the patient is in trouble are twofold:
first, he has difficulty communicating with other human
beings; second, he has low sexual self-esteem. To solve
these problems, you have to make the patient know you are
caressing him not because you want to arouse him and
bring him to orgasm but because it is giving you pleasure.

Since we are not a pleasure-oriented society, we don't often
allow ourselves to enjoy something nice unless we work for
it. Most of us don't experience pleasure for pleasure's sake,
without having to earn it or pay back for it. Your primary
goal with a patient is to enjoy yourself and, in so doing,
transmit the same enjoyment to another.

"I told you that I take the patient's sexual history and talk
things over with him. After that, I try to match the patient
with the one of you who might be most compatible with
him. Knowing the patient's age, education, social background, interests, I try to pair him up with one of you who
comes closest to fulfilling his needs. Then I personally brief
you on the patient, and then I arrange a private meeting
with the patient, the surrogate, and myself.

"After that, I turn him over to you. I expect the assigned
surrogate to give me a full report, usually on tape, sometimes in person, on each session as it is completed. Occa-
sionally, I will call a surrogate in to discuss the case, possibly make readjustments. Certainly I will meet with the
patient regularly to find out how he feels about what is
going on."

Freeberg paused and studied the surrogates seated before him and listening intently.

"All right," he said, "what is going on? What you are
doing with the patient is carrying out what you will be
trained to do in the next six weeks. You will be doing a
series of sensual exercises with the patient. We call each
exercise a 'sensate focus.'

"Your first meeting, and every one after that, will take
place in the privacy of your own home. This meeting will be
half social, half work. The social part is to put a frightened
guest at ease. You might offer the patient something to
drink. Preferably tea or a soft drink. No alcohol. No stimu-
lants. Remember, what you are trying to do is to tap into
the patient's own potential for exhilaration without outside
help. The two of you have your refreshments, and fully
dressed, you talk about—well, whatever you wish—food,
sports, current events. You tell the patient a little about

yourself and get him to speak of himself. Try to alleviate his anxiety.

"Finally, at that first session, you get to a hand caress. It is the least unnerving thing you can do. You are really focusing on the sense of touch. You begin by demonstrating a hand caress. You ask the patient to close his eyes, and you close yours. And you don't talk. We don't want any visual or verbal input to confuse the comforting hand caress.

"During the next session, you go to a face caress. You touch the various parts of his face, going smoothly, lightly, over every bump and crevice, fingertips on the face's bone structure, the skin, the fuzz on it. You do this to the patient, and then he does it to you. It is amazingly relaxing and sensual. Incidentally, exercises need not be in rigid order. You can modify or change the order according to the situation or circumstances.

"Anyway, at the third meeting, if all is going normally, you do a footbath. Literally a footbath. Clothes remain on, but feet are bared, soaked in warm water, and rubbed.

"Not until the fourth meeting do you get into the initial nudity. You each undress yourself, or if you both wish, you undress each other. Usually, this isn't a problem, but sometimes it's not simple. Lots of people are used to undressing in the dark. As adolescents, they usually had not been troubled by being naked in a locker room, although some had worried about other boys whose penises were larger or who were hairier or more muscular. And they don't worry about being naked with a doctor or a nurse. But once they put on street clothes, and then have to take them off, it can be more difficult. Usually, it isn't too difficult since almost all men are used to disrobing when they have sex, and no matter if it's good or bad sex, they are used to being naked then.

"So now you both have your clothes off. Now you do the exercise called body imaging. You, the surrogate, stand in front of a full-length mirror, allowing your patient to sit back and watch you, and you point out various parts of your body from head to toe and then honestly confess what you dislike or like about your anatomical self. Then your patient does the same. You learn a good deal about yourself and each other during this exercise."

Freeberg paused again to draw another cigarillo out of his box and light it. He glanced at his digital watch.

"I don't want to exhaust all of you unduly, so I'll go a little faster from here on. After all, everything I mention will be demonstrated to you in your training. Now, after body imaging comes the sensual shower—it can be a shower or a bath—together in warm water, and you lather each other and use soap as a lubricant. At the next session, you do a nude back caress. Just what that implies. After that, the exercise of the frontal caress without touching breasts and genitals. This is followed by the frontal caress including touching each other's breasts and genitals. But no big deal. Breasts and genitals get no more attention than touching the nose or the neck.

"At the next session comes nondemand genital pleasuring. This means what it states. You have your patient lie on his back and you caress his genitals. The goal is not to stimulate or arouse but to concentrate on giving someone pleasure, and they don't have to pay you back in any way.

"During the following meeting, you will be expected to try two things. One is the anatomy tour, and the other is something we call The Clock. We do the anatomy tour because most men, while familiar with their penises, have no idea what women's genitals look like. Usually, they climb into bed, grope in the dark, hope to find the right place, and then go at it. In the anatomy tour, you use a flashlight and speculum to show and explain to a male what is inside you. Then you do The Clock. You consider your vagina has a clock inside, with numbers one to twelve going around in there. You have the patient insert a finger and pressure you at one o'clock or six or eleven, so he can feel what it is like in a woman's vaginal barrel and see how she reacts differently to pressure in various places. Sometimes you might let the male keep his moving finger in your vagina until you experience orgasm, a real orgasm, so he can feel what happens inside you.

"At this stage in the therapy, you will clearly see that your patient is getting erections, partial or total. But even if his penis is almost flaccid, I assure you he is getting some kind of erection. When your patient has this, he is ready for his final exercises, perhaps the last two or three. If he is suffering premature ejaculation, you can control it easily by the famous squeeze method. We'll all practice it in your training.

"Anyway, we've now come to the ultimate act. The act, obviously, is penetration, successful sexual intercourse. Okay, here is how you go about that . . ."

Freeberg talked on for another ten minutes, aware that he had the avid attention of his pupils. His smoke had gone out, and he threw the cold cigarillo into the ashtray, found a fresh one, and stood up to stretch. Lighting the cigarillo, he smiled and said, "Now you can ask questions."

He dropped down onto the sofa again and lifted the palms of his hands. "The floor is open to you."

Lila Van Patten sought his attention. "Dr. Freeberg, can we tell our friends and acquaintances what we are doing?"

"Why not?" Freeberg countered. "You will never disclose to anyone else the identity of your patients. That is strictly confidential. But if you wish to speak about your own career work, what you do professionally, you can certainly tell anyone. However, I will caution you about one problem: public acceptance. There are some people who may regard you as a prostitute—women might be appalled that you can make love to a stranger for pay, and many men may think of you as an easy mark. You'll have to use your own judgment."

Beth Brant raised her hand. "What if your patient gets turned on and wants to go from step four to fourteen right away? What if he wants to skip the intermediate steps and get into coitus as quickly as possible?"

Freeberg nodded. "That happens frequently. The minute you touch your patient's genitals, he'll perceive that as an invitation to enter you as fast as possible. But that's his very problem, don't you see? His problem is he goes from step four to fourteen because he is too anxious to get there, and he misses all the richness and learning in between. Any such attempt should be aborted right away."

Janet Schneider was waving a pad. "I made notes when you spoke of the face caress. Is it just caressing? What if he wants to kiss you?"

"Nothing wrong with that. Let him do so and direct him. Lots of men don't know enough about kissing."

Consulting her pad again, Janet went on. "When he touches my genitals, I may approach an orgasm. What would I do about that?"

Freeberg nodded solemnly. "You just have it," he said. "You let it happen. Try to control your external reaction, if possible, because it might scare him and make him feel more inadequate. On the other hand, it might excite him and make him feel virile. Again, you will have to be the judge."

The single male surrogate's voice spoke up. Paul Brandon. "About the nudity. We work in the nude from the body-imaging point on?"

"Always after that," said Freeberg. "As a matter of fact, you'll get so used to being nude it won't mean a thing."

"Oh, I have no problem with that," Brandon replied quickly. "Just wanted the information."

"My turn," said Elaine Oakes. "At penetration, intercourse, well, is it safe?"

"The patient will have been examined thoroughly, I assure you. He'll have no diseases."

"I meant impregnation."

"Ah, yes. Well, you're probably on the pill. If you aren't, an alternative is the use of a diaphragm when it comes to coitus."

Freeberg waited. There were no more questions. But the word "coitus" had triggered a question of his own. He regarded his listeners briefly.

"Well, I have one last question," he began. "Now that

you've heard it all, have an overview, do any of you wish to withdraw from the program?"

The five facing him remained immobile. Not one of them stirred or spoke.

Freeberg smiled. "Good," he said softly. He came to his feet. "Tomorrow morning at nine o'clock, right here. Tomorrow you'll be on your way to becoming professional sex surrogates. God bless us, one and all."

II

Six weeks and a day had passed, and now Dr. Arnold Freeberg was seated behind his desk at ten minutes to two in the afternoon waiting for the last of his group meetings to begin shortly. Looking out the window, he could see that this day in mid-July was overcast, somewhat bleak, and he wished the sun were shining. Because he felt sunny inside. The grueling training period had been a complete success. He had a team of bright, warm sex surrogates, and he was eager to get them on the road.

As he waited in his office for the arrival of his surrogates at two o'clock, he thought about what he had accomplished in the morning. He had reviewed the tapes of his first four patients referred to him by colleagues. The patients had all been dysfunctional men. There had been no female patient set for Paul Brandon yet, but he knew that several were being considered by psychiatrists for referral, so Brandon would soon be busy, too. Freeberg had given Suzy the tapes to transcribe on her word processor.

Following that, Freeberg had met with Gayle Miller, his original surrogate, who had finally arrived from Tucson a week ago, after graduating from the University of Arizona and winding up her affairs there. He had not seen much of her during the week—except for one visit she'd made to his clinic when he had introduced her to his surrogate trainees—because she had been busy finding and settling into a bungalow in Hillsdale. She had also been busy preparing her application for graduate school at UCLA—seeking admission to the doctoral program in psychology—and her request for a fellowship or financial aid. She had delivered all this along with her University of Arizona transcript and three letters of recommendation to the university.

When she had come in this morning, to assist him with his send-off ceremony, Freeberg had been so delighted to see her, so reassured by her confident professional presence, that he had invited her to the Market Grill next door, the coffee and sandwich shop where they might lunch together. Following Gayle out of the clinic, and then into the street toward the grill, he had realized that she was certainly the most attractive of his surrogates.

As they seated themselves in a booth, Freeberg noticed once more how graceful and beautiful Gayle was, attired in a pink silk blouse, nipped at her waist by a yellow leather belt, and below the belt, a pleated silk skirt that clung to her thighs when she walked. Watching her, as she studied the menu, Freeberg enjoyed Gayle's pretty face. She had dark glossy hair trimmed in a gamine bob, encasing a countenance that resembled the features of an Oriental porcelain doll—behind her big lavender sunglasses were widespread green almond eyes, and beneath the glasses, a pert nose and a generous mouth with a full lower lip. The rest of her person, he recollected, was equally arresting. He had seen her nude several times six years ago in Tucson during her own surrogate training period. Printed indelibly on his memory were her smooth sloping alabaster shoulders; her protruding firm full breasts with their large brown nipples; her small supple waist, narrow hips, and ample thighs (one with a beauty mark); and her shapely legs. He tried to remember . . . She must have been, must be now, five feet four or five. And dim in his memory, there had been some kind of tragedy in her case record, something that had motivated her to undertake the surrogate work for him.

The important things about Gayle Miller, he reminded himself, were not physical. She had proved to be intelligent, adaptable, forthright, articulate, and possessed of a sweet and giving personality. The fact remained that she had enabled him to have total success with his most disturbed and seemingly hopeless patients.

At lunch, he had gone along with her in ordering a salad and a hamburger, and he had glowed at the realization that this experienced twenty-seven-year-old woman was the leader of his team.

But that had been earlier. Now, at his desk, Freeberg saw that it was two o'clock, and his new surrogates were beginning to arrive. He greeted each of them as they came in and informally took their places on the sofa before him and in the pull-up chairs. He shuffled his notes, deciding he would speak very briefly and then bring Gayle Miller in from Suzy's office, introduce her, and let her give them one last word of reassurance.

Freeberg did not stand up. He eased back into his leather swivel chair and surveyed his group.

"Welcome," he said to them. "You all had yesterday off, and I hope you've recovered from your training period. Actually, I missed you. We've been so close in the last six weeks that I feel we've become a family. I'm not here to address you once more. You got enough of that the day before the training began and during every workday of the six weeks we trained. I feel that you know your job now, and that each of you is dedicated to it and will do well. Just keep one thing in mind. With each of you, I've tried to build a bridge, a human bridge to help troubled people cross over from a place where they are—a bad place—to a better place where they want to be, a place that will make them whole again and alive, not only sexually but in their careers and in their personal lives.

"Remember this, the men who are coming to you want to learn something. They want to learn how to be loving human beings. They are coming to you with their disorders and their quiet desperation. They are in effect pleading with you, trying to say to you, 'Here I am, and I don't know

what to do about my disabling problem. Please help me.'
To them, you are their last resort.

"Anyway, tomorrow we begin. I've drawn up a schedule
for meeting with you and your patients tomorrow morning
and afternoon. The day after that, you will each be largely
on your own, except for your continuing reports to me.
Before you leave, I will meet privately with each of you to
discuss your first assignments.

"Enough from me. I'm now going to bring in Gayle Miller. She was the one surrogate I used, in Tucson, before I
trained you. You each met her the last week of training,
when she came by to say hello. But you had no chance to
talk to her. I thought it might be useful if Gayle spoke to
you briefly about her own experiences and gave you a
chance to ask any more questions that come to mind. Now
let me get Gayle Miller."

Just before leaving Suzy's secretarial office for Freeberg's
more imposing office, Gayle had hesitated to speak to the
therapist once more.

"What do I do?" Gayle had asked.

Freeberg had smiled. "Stage fright? You just go in there
and do whatever comes naturally. Sit down behind my desk
or stand next to it, as you prefer. Chat with them casually,
about your work. They're waiting there, friendly but apprehensive. Whatever I've told them is one thing. But to them,
I'm somewhat removed from the main scene. Whatever
comes from you comes from someone who's been in the
field. It'll make them feel more comfortable. Give them a
few minutes from the voice of experience, and if they have
any questions, simply answer them candidly. You can do it,
Gayle. Good luck."

Once in Freeberg's office, Gayle decided to stand behind
Freeberg's desk and talk to them. The five new surrogates
appeared alert, eager, receptive, and a bit curious, too.

"You all know the procedures," Gayle began. "I can only
tell you of my own experience in working with Dr. Freeberg
on five cases in Tucson. Two were cases where the men

suffered an inability either to get an erection or to maintain one. Two were cases where the men suffered premature ejaculation. One was a case of terrible shyness and lack of knowledge—I mean, for him the problem was not in bringing a woman home with him but, once he had her home, how to take the next step, how to get her from the living room or kitchen to the bedroom, then what to say, what to do. All these cases, I am happy to tell you, were resolved satisfactorily."

Janet Schneider interrupted. "Did you make love with all of them, Gayle?"

"Of course," Gayle replied. "You mean sexual intercourse? Yes, I eventually had it with each one. Therapists like to say that intercourse isn't the goal of the treatment. They like to say that teaching someone to get in touch with his feelings, learn to be intimate, learn to handle sex naturally is the goal. All of that is true. But the ultimate goal is successful intercourse. If a man who has been unable to complete intercourse does arrive at the point where he can do that and do it as well as almost any other man, then I feel the main goal has been achieved."

Janet Schneider's hand was up again. "One more thing," she said. "What about the transmission of the AIDS virus in our work? How much are we endangered?"

"Let me say frankly, you're in a high-risk job," Gayle answered. "The AIDS virus, as far as we know, is transmitted through bodily fluids or from the blood of an infected person. You can be infected with the virus through sexual intercourse or intravenous injection. You can't get AIDS merely by touching another person. The virus does not survive long in open air or after sterilization. But, I repeat, it can survive in your body fluids and bloodstream. Risky as your work is, there are things you can do to protect yourself. At a surrogates meeting in New York concerning AIDS, I joined a group that worked out a way of practicing safer sex. First, no deep kissing with patients—no exchange of fluids at any time. Second, permit no penetration without use of a condom by the patient. And let the surrogate doubly protect herself by using a spermicide." Gayle lowered her voice. "Confidentially, I don't insist on my patients using a condom, once I know they've had a blood test for AIDS and it's negative. To me, condoms are just too inhibiting for already inhibited people. Many therapists demand that a surrogate have a test after every penetration. That's a little antsy, and Dr. Freeberg agrees. He requires his surrogates to be tested only once every three months. Anyway, follow the safe sex suggestions I've made, and the odds are strongly in your favor that you won't have anything to fear."

Before Gayle could resume, there was another question, this time from Lila Van Patten. "I'm wondering about something else. How would you, as a surrogate, define a successful erection?"

Gayle nodded and replied, "The best definition was given by Masters and Johnson, and Dr. Freeberg concurs. If, after your treatment, a formerly impotent man can get an erection and keep it up in three out of four encounters, then he's okay, he's made it." Her eyes fell on the man in the group, Paul Brandon, and she said, "As for nonorgasmic female patients, we agree with Masters and Johnson who felt that two orgasms out of every four encounters was a sign of success."

Searching the others for more questions, Gayle heard none, so she went on.

"I've always told my patients that I am not a teacher. I am a partner . . . but a partner who knows a little more than they know and wants to help them. Some of my patients have been lawyers and computer experts. I've told them that if I had a legal problem or had to know something about computers, I'd go to someone knowledgeable to find out what I need to know. But my own specialty is sex, so if they have a problem in that area, it's reasonable that they should employ me to find out more about it."

"Have they always trusted you?" someone called out.

"Not always. Sometimes they resented me, because they needed help and felt dependent on me. Also, they often resented hiring a temporary partner they had to pay. They know they're paying Dr. Freeberg five thousand dollars for the course of treatment. They know that from that fee, he will be paying each of us seventy-five dollars an hour or one hundred and fifty dollars for a two-hour session. Sometimes patients don't like that aspect of it. One of my patients once said to me, 'You're on the payroll, Gayle. I can't see myself relating to you as a caring person.' But eventually he did, and so did the others. I learned that if they trusted Dr. Freeberg, they invariably soon trusted me. It's really not a big problem."

Then she went on again.

"The big problem is the inadequate male's attitude. Once he's had trouble, with every new encounter, he takes on the role of spectator during his own sexual act, with no spontaneity, just waiting to observe if anything will happen, if he can make it work. That's the real problem. As Dr. Masters said, 'An impotent male is traumatized infinitely more above the neck than he is below the belt.'

"I found out that most disorders began when the patient was young, perhaps in his teens. At that time, the young man realized he didn't need to give or receive any touching or caressing because he could get aroused quickly and could go right at it. He was usually able to find a willing partner who thought that was what sex was all about and was ready to reinforce his bad habits. But as our young man grew older, no longer nineteen but now forty-nine, he found that his poor training in foreplay was working against him. A woman's bare breasts no longer turned him on as they once did. Arousal and erection were more difficult to attain. Because he never depended on touching, only on what he saw and wanted, he ceased being turned on as fast. He began to panic. He began to look for younger and sexier women, and when that stimulus also ceased to work, the man's entire sexual system broke down. He became dysfunctional.

"All this can be changed, through the exercises, by getting the patient in touch with his feelings, so he enjoys the pleasures of intimacy. At no time are the exercises enough. You will learn, as I have learned, that you must communicate with the patient steadily—not as a technician but as a human being, through constant caressing, cuddling, and being sensual."

She searched her mind to see if there was more to say. There did not seem to be. From now on, for the surrogates, there remained the relationships and their actions.

"Tonight," said Gayle, "I will undertake my first case in Hillsdale. It will not be an easy one. Mine involves an adult young man who has a problem involving impotency that naturally is affecting his work. The patient's impotency, I am told, grows from an obsessive self-concern that his penis is too small."

"Is it?" Paul Brandon asked from the group of surrogates.

For an instant, Gayle stopped, startled. Her eyes held on the speaker, the one male in the surrogate group. She spoke to him directly, trying to keep her tone even. "Mr. Brandon, there is no such thing as too small. Certainly you know that. I'm sure my patient will, eventually, do as well as anyone—as even yourself."

Still annoyed, Gayle turned away from him to conclude with the others.

"Tomorrow, you all begin. I hope you derive as much happiness from what you will be doing as I have up to now. Dr. Freeberg has already wished you luck. To that I can only add, I wish you success."

At promptly three thirty in the afternoon, Suzy ushered Adam Demski into Dr. Freeberg's office.

Freeberg shook hands with the first patient who had come to his Hillsdale clinic several days earlier. He greeted the man cordially and pointed him to a comfortable chair across from his desk.

Returning to his own swivel chair, Freeberg was secretly pleased that Demski had arrived at all today, let alone promptly. After their first meeting, Freeberg had wondered if this patient, referred by a Chicago psychoanalyst, would go through with it and actually show up. In their first confidential meeting, Demski had been diffident, nervous to the point of being almost inarticulate, and only after the most artful questioning had Freeberg been able to learn the details of his patient's impotency.

At the end of the initial meeting, Freeberg had packed Demski off to get a physical examination from Dr. Stan Lopez, the general physician he trusted and intended to use in all his cases. The purpose had been to learn if Demski's condition was organic or the result of psychological factors. Demski's personal physician in Chicago had indicated that he had found no organic problems during earlier examinations. Still, Freeberg had to be doubly certain of this and had requested Dr. Lopez to reexamine the patient. If the problem did have some organic cause, Dr. Freeberg had expected to divert Demski to physicians who would treat his sexual dysfunction from a medical view. If, on the other hand, his visitor's problem were psychological, Freeberg planned to go ahead and apply sex therapy with the use of his most experienced sex surrogate.

This afternoon's second meeting was for the purpose of reviewing Dr. Lopez's report on Demski's physical condition and then introducing him to Gayle Miller and discussing with him the procedure that would be followed in surrogate treatment.

Through the thick lens of his spectacles, Freeberg could see that Demski was again exceedingly apprehensive. Demski, rather anemic in appearance, sat uneasily in his chair, his lanky frame fidgeting as he kept his gaze fixed on the carpet.

Running his fingers through his bristly, unruly dark hair, Dr. Freeberg then stroked his short graying beard as he once more scrutinized the results of Dr. Lopez's physical report.

Wearing his most engaging smile, Freeberg said, "Well, Mr. Demski, I think I can reassure you about one thing. Your disorder has no organic basis. That is something to be grateful for." He tapped the report on his desk. "Dr. Lopez seems to have done a very thorough job. I see he even had an excellent urologist, Dr. Gerald Clark, look you over."

Demski nodded. Then he said, "Yes."

"All right," Freeberg went on, "let's consider Dr. Lopez's findings together, just to be sure I've not overlooked anything."

Demski nodded unhappily. Somehow, Freeberg could see, his patient did not feel reassured.

Freeberg brought the physician's report up closer to his myopic vision. "I see you were tested for the possibility of undiagnosed diabetes. Such a condition could hurt your blood vessels and possibly make normal physical response difficult. But Dr. Lopez tells us you are not a diabetic. So we can rule that out. Next"—Freeberg's eyes ran down Dr. Lopez's report—"he looked into your vascular condition."

"Vascular?" asked Demski, puzzled.

"Like hardening of the arteries—the penile arteries—which would slow down the blood flow to the genital area and could obstruct an erection." Freeberg shook his head. "Not a thing wrong in that area. The urologist, Dr. Clark, confirmed that by testing the blood pressure of your legs and penis."

Demski nodded unhappily, apparently remembering with embarrassment that genital test.

Freeberg rattled the two sheets in his hand. "Everything else seems clear. You take no antidepressants or tranquilizers. You do not drink to excess. No mood-altering drugs, like cocaine. No amphetamines, barbiturates. No prostate or bladder surgery. No damage at any time to your pelvic area, genitals, or spinal cord." Freeberg paused. "Testosterone level, fine. You are in your forties, aren't you?"

"Forty-two."

"So your libido has not been affected at all. I see here that the urologist did not think a prosthetic implant was called for."

"No."

Freeberg dropped the report on his desk and gazed at the patient squarely. "Plainly, Mr. Demski, your condition does not evolve from an organic impairment."

"It—it comes from something."

"Certainly it does. But not from any physical cause. That has now been confirmed. Your problem, it appears, is a psychological one that continues despite your psychotherapy. Probably after your first failure, there were more failures and an inability to focus on your sensations. This is something I can likely reverse and normalize through diminishing your anxiety. It requires only your full cooperation every step of the way."

"I came here," mumbled Demski.

"You did, and that means you can be helped. As you know, insight or talk therapy can be useful, but often it is not enough. After you had such therapy in Chicago, it proved to be not quite enough. That is why your analyst recommended that you come to California to see me. I will work with you almost daily, of course, but I won't be alone. I will be assisted by a sexual surrogate, a trained woman who will guide you and teach you under my close direction. You know about these partner surrogates from what you learned at home and what you heard from me. You know the functions of a sexual surrogate, don't you?"

"I—I think so, yes," Demski said in a small voice.

"Very well. I've assigned my very best and most experienced sexual surrogate to you. Her name is Gayle Miller, a young lady you should find most agreeable and useful. She's prepared to begin your exercises with you."

"W—when?"

"This evening at seven o'clock at her residence."

Demski looked pale and stricken. "Tonight?"

"Yes. You're ready to start. Now I want you to meet Gayle Miller. She knows your case, of course. She's read the transcript of our first meeting, and I've elaborated upon it personally with her. She will join us, sit in on the rest of our meeting, as I explain to you precisely the program laid out for you and the exact exercises you will undergo with Miss Miller."

Freeberg picked up his receiver, pressed down the intercom button, and said, "Suzy, please send Gayle Miller into my office. We are ready for her now."

* * *

The afternoon had waned, and the surrogates, including Gayle Miller, had left for their homes. The Freeberg Clinic was all but empty, except for Freeberg himself, putting away his papers, and Suzy Edwards next door proofing the pages of case histories that she had transcribed from tapes.

Dr. Freeberg, his briefcase in hand, poked his head into his secretary's office. "How goes it, Suzy?"

She lifted her head from her pages, pushing the stray strands of red hair away from her forehead. "Almost done, Doctor. Just catching a few typos. I hear it went well with the surrogates."

"Very well, I think."

Suzy fingered the sheaf of pages on the desk before her. "I must tell you, Doctor, even though I knew what you were doing, I had no idea how difficult and fascinating your cases would be."

"I agree with you. They are fascinating. I never get tired of the human maze, the confusion, the conflict, even the suspense. Yes, they are difficult, every one of them, but I'm confident they'll all make out."

"I'm sure they will."

"Well, I'm off to dinner. When you've finished, leave the transcripts on my desk. Before you leave, be sure to turn on the alarm and lock up. See you tomorrow, Suzy."

"Tomorrow," she said.

After he'd gone, Suzy stared at the door he had closed. Tomorrow, she thought. Why wait? There was still tonight, a long tonight, ahead. Quickly, concentrating, she finished her proofing and checked her pages to see that they were in order. Then, without hesitation, she reached for her telephone.

The decision to call Chet had come to her while she had been proofing. Only when her hand was on the receiver did she hesitate. She considered the call she was about to make and tried to imagine how he might react, not merely to her call but to what could follow.

She thought about Chet Hunter, her new boyfriend, her best, and pictured him as he'd been the first moment she had met him. It had been a month ago, in the Hillsdale Main Public Library. She had been at a reading table, going through some medical magazines to see if she could learn more about Dr. Arnold Freeberg, her new boss. This fellow, probably in his thirties, surely no more than five years older than she, was carrying some books from the shelves, and the only spot open was the chair next to hers. Apologetically, he eased into the chair tight against her own. She had been taken by him at once. He was of medium build, receding neat brown hair, high forehead, soulful brown eyes highlighted by steel-framed spectacles set near the tip of a pug nose, his manner reserved but obviously an intellectual type.

They had exchanged occasional whispered talk, mostly bookish talk, and at closing time, he had accompanied her out of the library, casting sidelong glances at her and, as they were about to part, suddenly asking if she'd like to have a cup of coffee with him. She had wanted to, indeed, and they'd sipped their coffees and become acquainted.

His work had been unclear to her—and in a way, still was. Two years ago he had founded, and still ran, something called the Acme Research Bureau. He was a full-time researcher, he had explained, digging up facts from countless sources for free-lance writers, graduate students, magazines, newspapers. He worked on an hourly pay basis, poor pay, set barely at subsistence level, earning just enough to keep him in food, clothing, and a three-room apartment. She wondered what he researched and for whom. Just everything imaginable—who the only bachelor U.S. president was, for a political candidate; what the second highest mountain in the world was, for a travel writer; how advanced the process of cloning was, for a medical magazine; how many reported rapes there had been in Hillsdale and Los Angeles last year, for a Hillsdale attorney . . . She asked how he found his answers, and he explained that he did so by checking books in the library, corresponding with experts, interviewing specialists—why he had even studied and trained to become a police reservist in the Hillsdale

Police Force, to get closer to law enforcement material for many of his clients.

"A police reservist?" Suzy had wondered. "Whatever is that?"

"A part-time auxiliary policeman, a reserve police officer, the way a National Guardsman is a part-time soldier," Hunter had explained. "The police force needs added manpower. They take volunteers. Not easy to become a reservist. You're tested by a physician, then a psychiatrist, and if accepted you go to the Hillsdale Police Academy three nights a week for almost five months. Only two out of fifty of us graduated. At first I was a technical reservist, doing indoor work like taking reports at the police station. Then I studied for the line reserve and was trained in everything from use of firearms to criminal law. I wound up with a blue uniform and badge, a .38 Smith & Wesson pistol, handcuffs, and the rest. I work two eight-hour shifts a month and get fifteen dollars a month as pay. But I don't care about the pay. It's the firsthand research I'm interested in."

"You did all that for research?"

Hunter had considered Suzy's question. "Actually, there was another reason I went through it," Hunter had told her. "You see, this researching is only a stopgap, to keep me going until I can get what I want."

"What do you want, Chet?"

"I'm a born journalist, and I want to be one full-time. My one ambition now is to be a staff reporter on the Hillsdale *Daily Chronicle.* That's what I really want, really dream about. In fact, that's why I went through the whole heavy business of becoming a police reservist, to help get a lead on a big story and recognize it when it comes along. Otto Ferguson, he's the editor in chief at the *Chronicle,* he's not sure I'm ready yet. He feels I have to prove myself. So I keep trying and waiting, hoping for that big one. If I ever get it, I'm positive Ferguson will take me on." At this point, he had halted, embarrassed. "Forgive me, Suzy, for running off at the mouth like this. I haven't even asked you what you do. Are you an actress or something like that?"

She had blushed. "Of course not. I just took a job as a medical secretary."

"You could be, an actress, I mean."

Two nights later they had dated more formally. Suzy really liked him. He was the most interesting and darling man she had ever met. She had suspected he liked her, too. The night after that, after dinner, she had asked to see some examples of his work. She had gone up to his three-room apartment, and after two vodkas on the rocks, she had gone to bed with him.

In fact, since then she had gone to bed with him twice more, most recently last night.

She had definitely fallen in love with him, but there was also definitely a problem.

She felt more certain than ever that it could be overcome. She lifted the phone and dialed his number, hoping he was in.

He answered the phone. "Hello . . ."

"Hi, Chet. It's Suzy."

"Suzy, why I—"

"Chet," she said quickly, "if you're free tonight, I'd like to come over and see you for a little while."

"You mean that? Of course I'm free. Gee, Suzy, I guess I didn't expect to hear from you again after last night. You know how much I want to see you."

"Don't be silly. I want to see you, too. Can I come over to your place after dinner? Say, maybe between nine and nine thirty?"

"I can't wait, Suzy. I'll be looking forward."

After hanging up, she sat there staring at the phone. She thought, I'll be looking forward too. Tonight was important, really important. Her whole future was at stake.

Gayle Miller, her legs tucked under her, sat on the couch she had shipped from Tucson and sewed a button on her blue cashmere sweater.

The electric clock, set on the mantel of the fireplace across the small but cozy living room of her newly leased bungalow in Hillsdale, registered a few minutes before seven o'clock in the evening.

If he weren't too frightened, Adam Demski, her very first patient in Hillsdale, should be arriving in a few minutes.

Her mind held only the vaguest picture of him, although she had met with him and with Dr. Freeberg for nearly an hour after the surrogate meeting this afternoon. She retained the impression of a slender, tallish, slightly hunched man, maybe forty, with a hangdog expression. A cadaver type of narrow, sunken countenance. A tentative person in every way. With his concern over a small penis. Two women, a new girlfriend and then a prostitute, had mocked him for it. So he had been unable to get it up after that. Not up at all. He had buried himself in his work, accountancy in Chicago, and avoided women socially. Had tried dating a few who were kinder, but that hadn't helped. His penis had remained flaccid. And recently, his work, or rather his attitude toward it, had become flaccid, too. It was then that he had consulted a psychoanalyst, but verbalizing had not solved his erectile problem. Determined to help him, the psychoanalyst had referred Adam to Dr. Freeberg. Now Adam Demski was in Hillsdale to be resurrected among the living.

The doorbell rang.

Hastily, Gayle gathered her sweater and sewing kit together, stuffed them into the drawer of the end table beside the sofa, then stood up and appraised herself in the wall mirror. She fluffed her hair a little. Otherwise, everything in place.

She went to the front door and opened it.

A pale youngish man, somewhat taller than she remembered, and thinner, stood there under the yellow porch light. "I—I'm Adam Demski," he said, his voice constricted. "I don't know if you remember."

"Of course I remember." Cheerfully, she put out her hand. "And in case you forgot, I'm Gayle Miller. We have a date. I hoped you wouldn't stand me up."

"I wouldn't," he muttered, pausing there, staring at her, not yet taking her hand.

Gayle was used to this, the standing and staring, because it had happened to her before. This happened, she guessed, because the patients had formed their own mental image of what a sex surrogate would look like. In Dr. Freeberg's office, Demski had scarcely looked at her. Probably he expected someone more hardened and professional, and least of all a fresh, clean, soft all-American girl, one who might actually be a date.

She pushed forward her hand again, and this time he took it in a brief handshake. Her hand went up to the sleeve covering his forearm. "Come in. Do come in," she said, drawing him into the living room. "It's so good to see you."

He stood in the middle of the living room, a bit bewildered. What had he expected? she wondered. A red satin bordello?

"It's—it's very nice," he said. "Homey."

"Oh, it's not really decorated yet," she said. "I just rented it and arranged some of my own furniture that came from Arizona—the sofa, the chairs, and the bed are old pieces. But I've been shopping. More will be coming in next week. Look, make yourself comfortable. You can take off your jacket, loosen your tie if you'd like." She gestured toward the couch. "Have a seat. I was about to heat up some water for my tea. Would you like a cup? Or maybe coffee or a soft drink?"

"Whatever you're having, Miss—Miss Miller."

"Gayle," she said. "Let's be friends, Adam. I'm Gayle from now on."

Awkwardly, he sat down, then remembered to loosen his tie as she went into the kitchen.

Minutes later she emerged with a tray bearing two cups of tea and a plate of chocolate chip cookies. He had taken off his suit jacket and folded it neatly over the back of the couch. He was thumbing the pages of the latest *Vogue* disinterestedly.

Gayle settled down on the couch, not too close to him, and handed him his cup of tea. She noticed his hand trembled as he took it.

"You're from Chicago, I recall," she said.

"Born there," he told her.

"Where in Chicago? I've been there a few times."

"North side."

"You live alone?"

"Yes. I have an apartment."

"You have many women friends?"

He shook his head. "No. Not now. I'm very busy."

Gayle sipped her tea. "What do you do when you're not busy, Adam?"

"I don't know. Catch up on my reading. Catch up on movies. I belong to a videotape club. On Sundays, in season, I sometimes go to football games with some fellows from the office."

She considered how much she could push him. "Do you have any time for a social life, Adam?"

He blinked at her. "I—I don't know what you mean. You mean girls?"

"Do you go to parties? Meet women? See women for dinner?"

He gulped his tea and put down his empty cup. "I used to. Not much. I hardly do that at all anymore." He looked at Gayle sideways, tried to hold on her. "You—you know I have a problem. You were there when Dr. Freeberg discussed it. You know my problem."

She nodded. "Of course. Maybe half the men in this country have problems in that area; only they repress them, won't face them." She wasn't sure of her statistics, but it sounded right.

"Really?" he said. "Well, I guess I wouldn't discuss it either, for a long time. But when I realized it was affecting my work—I wasn't concentrating on my regular accounts, not going after new ones—I thought maybe there was a connection."

"You were right, Adam. There is a connection. If you are having sexual difficulties, it affects not only your love life but your entire life, the way you relate to people and to your career."

"I was having more—more trouble," he said. "I was having trouble sleeping. But I was too ashamed to try to get help until a fellow in the office mentioned a great analyst he was sending his son to. Well, I went, and this analyst, he helped me open up, speak about the problem, and finally recommended I go to California for a month to see Dr. Freeberg." He gave a shrug. "So here I am. I—I'm not sure anything can be done."

"Well, you were smart and gutsy enough to try. And, Adam, I assure you something can be done. If you work with Dr. Freeberg and me, go along with us, and don't get discouraged, I'm certain you won't know your old self in a month—less than a month. You'll be a brand-new person. You'll be wanting women all the time, and they'll be wanting you, again and again."

"It's hard to believe. You've done it for other men?"

"A number of times. With patients far worse off than you. Dr. Freeberg and I have never failed."

"When do we get started?" Demski blurted out, his chalky pallor more evident.

"Now. Right now if you feel relaxed."

"I guess I'm as relaxed as I'll ever be." There was a slight tic beside his right eye. He swallowed. "Do I—do I undress now?"

"No, Adam," she said seriously. "That would be rushing it. In due time, when we're ready, we'll both undress. Right now, some simple exercises, fully clothed, but important exercises. One is called the hand caress. The other, the face caress. We can start with the hand caress."

"Hand caress," he said. "What's that?"

"Exactly what the name implies. I'm going to focus on your two hands, focus on touching them, rubbing them, feeling them, to give you relaxation, a sense of pleasure, a minimal sense of intimacy. Adam, I'd like to sit closer to you to start this. Do you mind?"

"Of course not. Whatever you have to do, just do it."

Gayle lifted herself off the couch, narrowed the gap between them, and eased onto a cushion beside him, her thigh barely touching his. "It's a two-way thing, Adam. I'll take your hands first, because I want to demonstrate the exercise. I'll ask you not to talk, and I won't talk, either. I'll ask you to keep your eyes closed. I don't want any visual input confusing you."

Demski was clearly puzzled. "Visual input confusing me? How could that happen?"

Gayle thought of how she might explain the necessity for him to keep his eyes shut. Then she remembered something. "I think I can give you an example of what I mean," she said. "When I was in training in Tucson, learning to become a surrogate, Dr. Freeberg found me a male partner to work with while Dr. Freeberg guided me. Well, the first time my partner and I were nude, I was struck by how handsome and well built my partner was. Although Dr. Freeberg was trying to show me the point of sensate focus —concentrating on a back caress—I paid little attention because I wouldn't shut my eyes but kept staring at my good-looking partner, or at least what I could see of him. Dr. Freeberg noticed what I was doing. Immediately, he pulled out his large handkerchief, folded it, and blind-folded me so that I would stop focusing on the wrong thing and get in touch with my feelings about the caressing. Dr. Freeberg succeeded in doing that by shutting my eyes for me. Now you can realize the importance of that, Adam, can't you?"

"I—I think so."

"Something else to know. When I start touching you, it'll be for my own pleasure. When I'm doing that, I'm doing it for my own sake and therefore not putting pressure on you or on me to perform. I'm doing it for pleasure rather than performance. The effect of the touching is that it feels good, first for me, then for you. Good lovemaking is first loving yourself and then learning to share that love with another. Once you can learn to share your love for yourself, then you're on your way. Does that make any sense?"

"I'm not sure."

She realized further talk, at this stage, would do little good. Only through demonstration would she be able to define better what she had been trying to explain. "I think that as we proceed, it will become clearer to you and will make sense. The place to begin, I repeat, is the hand caress.

Right now, I want you to sit back and be comfortable and let me take your hands. When I'm through, I'll tell you, and then I want you to do exactly the same thing to me. You understand?"

"Yes."

"Sit back now, go limp, shut your eyes, give me your hands."

Demski did as he was told, shifting toward her slightly, extending his hands, which were trembling once more. Gayle took his hands and placed them in her lap. His fingers were long, knobby, the nails manicured. She released his left hand and cupped his entire right hand in her own.

"In your mind, just focus on the temperature of my hands on yours and how it feels when I stroke you. Now we'll be quiet."

Softly, her warm fingers stroked upward across his fingers and the smooth back of his hand to the hairs at his wrist. Gradually, she stroked downward, between the crevice separating his thumb and forefinger, between his bony fingers, then she slowly kneaded his entire hand. Slowly, she turned his hand over, palm upward, and resumed her light stroking and caresses.

Not until his right hand was limp and warm did she take his left hand in hers and begin to massage it on both sides.

Then she took both his hands together inside her own and cupped them warmly, moving her fingers, rubbing, stroking, kneading.

After perhaps twenty minutes she lowered his hands to her lap and released them.

"All right, Adam, you can open your eyes now, and we can talk a little." She met his eyes. "How was that—how did it feel?"

"I don't know exactly. What can I say? It felt sort of good."

Gayle moved her fingers over his left hand. "Were you aware of the different feelings when I touched your hand in different places? Did you feel pressures here on this bump, there on that crevice?"

"Sure, it was nice."

Gayle slipped one of her hands under his. "Okay, do the same hand caress to me. Close your eyes, and I'll close mine, and you do it to me the way I did it to you. For as long as you wish."

After a brief hesitation, Demski began to rub and squeeze her hands. He continued to do so with more and more intensity.

Nearly ten minutes had gone by when Gayle laced her fingers between his and stopped him. "Okay, Adam, that's fine. You can look at me. How did it feel? Did you get any special feeling from it?"

"Well, I guess so. It was sort of—sort of—" He couldn't find the right word.

Gayle tried to find it for him.

"Sensuous, maybe?"

"Yes, that's it."

"There was more," Gayle said professionally. "Did my hands feel soft or weak or firm to you? Did you notice I had even the tiniest callus? Were you conscious of my finger-nails, that they're not too long but they have nail polish on them? And the backs of my hands—were they smooth or chapped? To most people a hand is a hand is a hand, something to eat with, write with, shake with. But there's a lot more there. The purpose of this exercise, Adam, is to develop and heighten your sense of discrimination and focus. I want you to know more about your body, and my own. I want you to know shape and texture. Because if you do, you'll start creating pictures in your head, and the more sensual pictures you create, the more alive you're going to feel."

"I had sensual pictures doing it."

"Excellent," said Gayle. "The ridges of our hands, the smoothness of them, their texture, that can make you aware of yourself and of me as human beings. We get too accustomed to ourselves and others. But as we do more touching, you'll realize the richness and variations about your body and mine. You'll know how different it is when you touch the hairline of my neck, then the hairline of my groin. You'll stop being turned off from your body, and you'll become more alert and awake to every sensuous experience. Like the face caress. That should be next, and we have time."

"What is it?" Demski asked worriedly.

"Just touching each other's faces, the various parts of our faces in different ways, feeling the bone structure, the skin, the fuzz. I've always thought the face caress an exquisite experience. Some patients have told me it reminds them of when they were children, the tender way they were touched then, but they haven't been touched that way by anyone since. Let's try it, Adam. First, me to you, then you to me. Now shut your eyes."

He did so, and Gayle moved more closely to him, then reached up and began to massage his forehead softly, soon running the tips of her fingers over his nose and across his cheeks, flitting them across his quivering lips and down his chin.

She repeated this several times and finally finished by cupping his face in her hands. "All right, Adam." When he opened his eyes, she could feel his warm breath on her cheek. "Well, Adam, what did you feel?"

At first he was unable to speak, then he whispered, "Like I—I wanted to kiss you."

She stared at him. "Why not? Go ahead."

He pushed his face toward hers and brushed his lips against her lips.

"Was that what you wanted to do?" she asked.

"Yes."

"Or did you want to kiss me in different ways?"

"I—I don't know what ways."

"A woman likes to be kissed in other ways, too. On the eyelids, tip of the nose, cleft of the chin, hollow of the throat, and on her earlobes, in her ears, behind her ears. Have you ever done that?"

"No."

"Do it now, to me. Kissing can be almost as intimate as intercourse. Start with my eyelids."

She closed her eyes and felt his nervous lips flutter at them, then waited as he made small pecks at her ears, cheeks, nose, chin. She was tempted to grab him, press his mouth against her own, open his mouth and her own, and give him a tongue kiss. Just to loosen him up. But she didn't succumb to it. That would be going too fast, pushing it too hard.

When he was done, she said, "Now it's your turn to give me a face caress."

His fingers went over her face, tentatively exploring and rubbing every feature, for many minutes.

At last, she opened her eyes. "How was it, Adam?"

He smiled with less effort. "I liked it."

"So did I."

"Sort of—uh—sensuous," he added.

"That's what I thought." She sat back. "Well, there you are. First two exercises behind you. And nothing scary at all. Maybe you even found it fun."

"It was fun, I admit." He wriggled forward, reaching for his jacket behind him. "I guess I should go." He paused. "What—what do we do at the next session?"

"Footbath. Then"—Gayle was thinking—"maybe we'll move right into body imaging."

"Body imaging?"

"We both stand in front of a full-length mirror and tell what we like and don't like about our own bodies. We'll both be nude."

His expression did not hide his concern. "We'll undress? I thought you said that would come later?"

"Usually it does. A little later. But I was just thinking it would make it easier for both of us, definitely show more progress, if we were able to work together without anything on." She searched his face. "How do you feel about that, Adam?"

"I—I'm not sure."

"Well, let me discuss it with Dr. Freeberg first."

"If we do that . . . how will it help me?"
Gayle smiled enigmatically. "You'll see."

In the quiet of his computerized modern rectory in the
rear of his Church of the Resurrection—actually a suite of
rooms where the Reverend Mr. Josh Scrafield both lived
and worked—Darlene Young efficiently continued to go
through the routine of preparing her employer for his
weekly television broadcast.

As she secured Scrafield's clerical collar to his starched
white shirt, and helped him into the coat of his conservative
dark suit, Darlene was again conscious of her employer's
size and strength, which by now she knew all too well.
Scrafield was a powerful man physically, over six feet tall
and muscular, who considered his body a temple and who
worked out with barbells four times a week with a local
exercise coach. She knew, for he had told her so many
times, that his temple must be cleansed and strengthened
regularly, so that he could stand as an inspiration to the
weak and frail of his ever-expanding flock of followers.
Scrafield liked to say that he perceived the fears and lusts of
his followers, and it was only to understand their tempta-
tions fully that he brought himself—forced himself, as he
put it—at least once a week, to yield to her tender ministra-
tions.

When she had applied for the job as Scrafield's secretary,
and been hired, her double role of servicing had been
understood from the start. Nor had Darlene minded. Scrafield had been single, and Darlene herself long divorced. In
her late thirties, Darlene had wanted a man. Scrafield had
not been unattractive. His thick eyebrows over oddly
Mongolian eyes, fierce riveting black eyes, his pinched
nose, jutting jaw, and mesmerizing voice (a grandiloquence
of speech) had proved utterly seductive. She had been devoted to him, and to his generosity, and she had shown
qualities of cleverness that matched his own, and this had
gained her a promotion to publicist and television pro-
ducer and allowed her to hire a secretary for herself. By

then, she had become less enchanted with him, had tried to overlook his vanity, cunning, and what she suspected was a certain insincerity about his calling. Scrafield's real religion, she guessed, was his ambition to be Somebody.

Now that she had him neatly dressed, except for his trousers, she began to remove his trousers from the hanger.

"Not yet," he said, waving them aside. "You know I like to keep them pressed until the last minute."

With that, she knew what she had known the last several months. She knew what was in store for her.

Dressed, but still in his boxer shorts, Scrafield was walking to his gargantuan desk, large enough to satisfy a Mussolini.

"I want to run through the script for tonight one more time," he was saying as he lowered himself behind the desk, took up the script, and wheeled his chair toward her. "Do you mind listening?"

"I look forward to it," said Darlene.

"If any of it sounds wrong, you let me know."

"Absolutely."

"All right," said Scrafield, clearing his throat, "let's run through it."

She sat on an ottoman, near him, as he began to read aloud from the script in his deepened and more theatrical voice.

"Brothers and Sisters," the Reverend Mr. Scrafield began, "once more I have come upon new information about the latest threat that is quietly but inexorably setting about to destroy our families and the very foundations of the American way of life.

"This insidious and cancerous growth that has invaded the schools of our youngest—the schools our children attend, namely, grammar schools and high schools—is known as sex education. This blatant and provocative teaching is being pressed on our young and unformed heirs.

"Speak to anyone who favors sex education in our classrooms instead of in our homes, and more often than not you will find yourself talking to someone who also favors unrestricted abortion, dangerous gay rights, atheism, and Communism.

"Tonight, my Brothers and Sisters, I want you to listen to some facts—actual facts—that have come to light on the matter of sex education.

"According to the latest available statistics, for youngsters between the ages of thirteen and nineteen, there were over one million pregnancies in a single year—roughly half of them leading to abortions and half to births.

"Obviously, these unwanted pregnancies were provoked by the kind of sex education going on throughout the states of America—the teachings, by untrained or ill-trained instructors, on every sexual subject from the use of contraceptives to sexual techniques to orgasms. This, in the face of the facts produced by a recent Yankelovich, Skelly, White survey that eighty-four percent of parents of teenagers polled feel that it is up to them to inform their children about sexual matters, a responsibility that should be borne only by caring families and not by politicized schools.

"Let me reveal to you a horror story that has recently been exposed in our own backyard. In the high school of San Marcos, California, over twenty percent of the young girl students were found to be pregnant by the year 1984. When the school board learned that fact, the members were quick to reassess the school's sex education program and modify it sharply.

"When you learn the shocking statistic that forty-eight percent of the states have no guideline policies on sex teachings, and leave policy-making up to local school boards, then you realize that you must have a voice in the decision making by letting your school board know you have an eye on it and will hold its members accountable for sinful behavior they promote under the guise of education.

"We must all act in concert with The Women's Committee for Responsible Government, which has already sued the state of California for spending public money on subversive sex education in our schools. We must join hand in hand to stop this systematic corruption of the innocent. We, too, must become the God-fearing, God-loving moral majority of this wonderful nation."

Scrafield droned on and on, and Darlene Young dutifully and attentively listened.

When he had concluded, Scrafield set his script aside and looked up. "What do you think, Darlene?"

"Very good, very frightening," she said. "Are those statistics actually true?"

"True blue, you bet. You ought to know. You hired that researcher, Chet Hunter, to research it for me. He's got a reputation for accuracy."

"Yes, he's good."

Scrafield studied his wristwatch. "We've still got fifteen minutes or more before the limo comes by to take us to the television studio. I could use a little relaxation, I guess, before going on the air. You up to it, baby?"

She nodded with fake enthusiasm. "You know I am."

As Scrafield reached down to the fly of his shorts, she wondered fleetingly why this change had taken place a few months ago. It had always been his habit, in times before, and always before he went on the air, to take her to bed. He had claimed he needed loosening up. He would take her to bed for a quickie.

But lately, there was no more bed. There was only this. She wondered if, turning forty, she had become less attractive to him. Her blond hair bleached brighter, her face puffier, her large breasts drooping further, and a bit thicker around the waistline and hips. Or was it simply that he had tired of her somewhat, become more impatient, and had aged himself and wanted to be relieved more easily without having to work for it?

She could see that he had opened his shorts and bared himself for her pleasure.

Without hesitation, and with a set smile, she had come off the ottoman to her knees before him. She took his flaccid organ in one hand. As she did so, he muttered his favorite non sequitur she had heard from him before. "Like W. C. Fields used to say, 'I never drink water because fish fuck in it.' " Then he chuckled.

Skillfully, with one hand, she was arousing him. He responded quickly. She saw him close his eyes and lie back as she lowered her head between his legs.

In five minutes, he made a throaty sound and then exhaled a great puff of air.

Later, seated across from him once more, Darlene waited for him to fully recover. Scrafield reached out and patted her on the head. "Good, very good, baby. How was I?"

"Wonderful. I love to go down on you."

Scrafield frowned darkly. "You know I don't like that expression. I'm against that kind of talk."

She felt defiant. "Well, it's something. What is it?"

"Just loosening me up before the big show, that's all. It's just diddling, just diddling around."

"Sounds okay by me, whatever the name."

They both came to their feet. "Now, help me on with my trousers," he said. "Car should be here for us in five minutes." He picked up his script. "You don't think I sounded like I was against sex, do you?"

"Oh, no, Josh," she said. "Your speech was healthy. It was clearly just against immoral sex. Let me get your trousers."

When Suzy Edwards arrived at Chet Hunter's apartment door, he admitted her at once, welcoming her with an enthusiastic kiss.

She could see that he had the television set on and was eager to get back to it. "Make yourself at home, Suzy." He indicated the television. "I have to watch the end of this. It's almost over."

Unbuttoning her leather jacket, Suzy wondered what had riveted Chet to the television set. He was planted before it once more in his wide broken-down armchair. Throwing her jacket aside, she strolled over to see what he was watching. He patted a narrow place next to him on the seat, and she eased into it close to him.

Filling the television screen was a handsome man in his early fifties, with the beefy face of a Roman senator, broad shoulders, heavy arms, and wearing a clergyman's collar and a dark blue suit. Now he was pausing to take up a glass of water from a table at the side of the pulpit.

Suzy recognized him as the Reverend Josh Scrafield, the most popular evangelist on the West Coast, and immediately she scowled. "Chet, what are you doing wasting your time listening to that bigot?" she complained. "He's awful. I saw him once, by accident, and I turned him right off. He was doing a terrible number against sex education in the schools."

"That's just his usual routine," said Hunter, watching the television screen.

"But you don't have to spend your time—"

"Business," said Hunter. "He's one of my research customers. He assigns me to do an occasional poll for him when he's looking for issues to discuss on his weekly broadcasts."

Scrafield's booming voice began to fill the small room again, and Suzy wriggled out of the chair, jumped up, and shut off the television set. "I can't stand this any longer," she said. "We have more important things to do."

Hunter had begun to protest, but when Suzy returned and fell back into the big chair beside him, he shrugged, then smiled and wrapped his arms around her. "This suits me fine," he said. "I'm sure glad you came over."

Hunter's hand moved across Suzy's blouse, curving around her full-blown breasts. He began to undo her blouse. Suzy tried to stay his hand. "Listen, Chet, I wanted to talk to you about something first."

But his hand was already under her brassiere, his fingers searching for one of her nipples. "Make it second," he said. "I've got something else that's first."

"Chet, I'm serious . . ." Her voice drifted off as she felt her nipples harden and allowed him to pull her atop him. "Chet . . ." Then she felt his erection against her thigh and emitted a little moan.

He was taking off her blouse. "We can talk later, honey. I want to go to bed. This time we'll be great. Come on, honey."

Her resistance had gone, along with her blouse. Her brassiere came loose and she staggered to her feet, unzipping her dirndl skirt. As her skirt dropped to the floor, she whispered, "All right, darling. Let's."

She rolled down her panty hose as he quickly undressed.

A minute later she was on the bed, on her back, her legs wide apart. She watched as he knelt on the bed beside her. She could see that he was ready and her excitement grew.

She reached up for him, and he moved quickly between her fleshy thighs.

"Put it in, darling," she called up breathlessly.

He was bending over her, feeling for the mark, and then he found it and she groaned again.

He began to enter her when suddenly he choked, almost convulsively, and began to have an orgasm.

"Oh, God!" he exclaimed.

Suzy lay there, helplessly, her eyes fixed on his tortured face.

Premature ejaculation.

Again.

A minute later he fell back on his haunches ready to weep. Suzy crawled off the bed, rubbed his head, and walked out of the room. He heard the sound of the shower, and when she returned she settled down near him.

"Jesus, I'm sorry," he croaked. "I'm real sorry. I apologize. I'm as sick of myself as you must be of me."

She placed an arm around his hunched naked shoulders. "I'm not sick of you, darling. I love you as much as ever."

"How can you?" He shook his head. "I don't know what's wrong with me."

"Maybe I do," she said, trying to console him. "Maybe I know what's wrong. I know somebody who knows what can be done—somebody who can help. That's really why I came over tonight. To tell you I have somebody who can help us both."

He met her eyes, discouraged. "How? How can anyone?"

"Please hear me out, Chet. You know I took a new job as a secretary a short time ago—a medical secretary . . ."

"Of course."

"Maybe I told you who it was with or maybe I didn't because of confidentiality. Anyway, the man I went to work for is Dr. Arnold Freeberg. Ring a bell?"

"Faintly. Seems like I read—"

"He opened the Freeberg Clinic downtown not long ago. He's a bona fide sex therapist. He's trained six sex surrogates to start working for him, with him."

Hunter wrinkled his brow. "Sex surrogates? You mean the ones who pitch in to help men—men in—in trouble?"

"Exactly. Dr. Freeberg has just accepted four or five patients. He and his surrogates are going to try to cure them. I know all about it. I was transcribing the patients' case histories today."

She began to tell Hunter about the cases, one in particular with a problem precisely like Chet Hunter's own.

"Premature ejaculation," Suzy said. "Dr. Freeberg told the surrogate who will work on it, 'That should be easy. Those are the easiest to set right.' His surrogate is going to put the patient through exercises that should cure him."

For the first time, Hunter had straightened up on the bed. "Sex surrogates," he murmured, "right here in Hillsdale, actual sex surrogates in sweet little Hillsdale."

Suzy was puzzled. "What's so unusual about that?"

Hunter reacted surprised. Obviously, his mind was racing. "Don't you see, honey? Your run-of-the-mill conservative American family city doesn't have sex surrogates on its premises. It just doesn't. That's unheard of."

"I still don't understand."

Hunter jumped off the bed and began to pull on his shorts. "Suzy, it's a story, a big story. If I gave Otto Ferguson at the *Chronicle* a tip like this, he could put me on the story. And it could lead to my big break, to the job on the newspaper I've always wanted."

Suzy was on her feet. "Forget it, that angle of it, Chet. That's confidential stuff. Even if I broke my word for you, I'm still Dr. Freeberg's confidential secretary."

"I know. Not to worry."

She went to him and placed an arm around his waist. "I

told you all this because I want to help us. I can get you to
Dr. Freeberg. He'd take you as a patient. He'd set you right,
and there'd be no more problem."

Hunter nodded, kissing her. "Of course, Suzy. You're a
doll. I'll see your Freeberg . . . I sure will. If he takes me
on, everything will be rosy. Of course, I don't know if I have
enough money for that kind of treatment."

"Never mind, Chet. I can loan you enough."

"No, thanks. I can get the money on my own. Leave it to
me."

She started to dress. "But you will see Dr. Freeberg? I
mean, as soon as possible?"

"You know I will. I already promised it, didn't I? You can
depend on me. Now, let's have a drink to it. You and me
together, making it, making out very soon."

Having completed her first session with her first patient
in Hillsdale, Gayle Miller returned to the Freeberg Clinic in
midevening, locked herself in one of the three soundproof
small rooms downstairs reserved for taping reports, and
dictated into the cassette machine all that had transpired
with Adam Demski. After that, she left the tape on Dr.
Freeberg's desk, so that he could listen to it in the morning,
and then she went next door to the Market Grill for a cup of
coffee and a cheese croissant.

Now, seating herself at the only free table along the
picture window overlooking the street, she recognized a
familiar figure enter and search for a place to sit. The five
stools at the counter were occupied, and the rest of the
tables in the room were also filled. Observing Paul Brandon hunting for a table, Gayle was not certain that she
wanted him to sit across from her, remembering his annoy-
ing remark to her this morning. Then, watching him cool
his heels, she softened. For one thing, he was a fellow sex
surrogate. For another, he was damned attractive—about
five eleven, she guessed, well built but lean, with dark
mussed hair in need of a trim, and a gaunt angular face.

Good chin, shaven. He was wearing a gray blazer over an open-collared checked sport shirt, and faded denims.

Seeing him coming nearer, as he cast about to learn if any place would soon be free, she lifted one hand and signaled to him. When he saw this, she pointed to the empty chair across from her.

Realizing who she was, he smiled, nodded, and gave his order to a passing waitress.

As Brandon came up to her, she indicated the vacant chair again. "If you like," Gayle said.

"I like," Brandon said. "Thanks, Gayle. I wasn't sure you'd want me here, after our little exchange this afternoon."

"Oh, that. Forget it."

Brandon shrugged. "Well, you put me down, and I deserved it." He waited until the waitress had delivered his black coffee and spoon. "Anyway, I apologize for being a smart ass. It's not my style. I think I just wanted to get your attention."

She sipped her coffee. "Why? Actually, I had a feeling you somehow disapproved of me."

His eyes on her, he shook his head vigorously. "No, not at all. In fact, quite the opposite. I approve of you very much. For one thing, you were speaking mostly to the women, and I wanted you to know I was there and aware of you." He hesitated. "For another, I just . . . Well, observing you, I couldn't see how a girl as lovely as you, as desirable, was . . . I don't know—"

"Going to bed with different men?"

"I suppose that's it. I know that's foolish, after all my training."

"Yes. And you did work side by side with all our other female surrogates."

"Not the same. They're a nice group, but I found you younger, fresher, and just an unlikely surrogate. So when you mentioned that you had a patient tonight, I senselessly wanted to get your attention—maybe unconsciously I wanted to keep you from being involved with another man."

"Well, Paul, whatever your good intentions, I simply have no problem seeing and working with men. I do it because I feel that I'm accomplishing something, doing some good, making another human being whole."

He drank his coffee. "Okay, if you want me to feel ashamed, you've succeeded."

"I only want you to understand my motivation."

Brandon nodded. "I do, I think. I've thrown in the towel. By the way, how did it go with your patient tonight?"

"Routinely well. We did both the hand caress and the face caress. He's very shy, so I'm trying to get on some trusting basis with him. I just finished filing my first report for Dr. Freeberg." She nibbled at her croissant and sipped more of her coffee. "By the way, what are you doing here at this hour? You don't have a patient yet, do you?"

"No. And I don't have an apartment yet, either. I'm still staying in a fleabag hotel. I came over to the clinic to go through a list of rooming prospects Suzy had left for me, and then I got involved in reading a psychology book in the clinic library."

"Psychology book?" Gayle said with interest. "Psychology is my subject and goal. Is it yours?"

"I'm not sure. Maybe psychology. Maybe sex education. Right now it's a toss-up. Are you telling me your surrogate work isn't your goal?"

"That's not it, Paul. I've been in it a while, and I wouldn't mind going on and on. But there's a lot of stress in the work, as you'll find out, and I figure I'd better have a fall-back position once I'm a burnt-out case. Sex psychology would be perfect, if I can get a graduate degree and do it while I continue my surrogate work. I could go for a long time with the surrogate work, knowing I'm doing something necessary."

"You're making me feel more unworthy than ever."

"I'm only telling you how I feel," she said seriously.

"And I believe you." Brandon pushed aside his coffee and extracted his pipe. He held it up. "Mind?"

"Not a bit. There's something both contemplative and mature about a pipe."

Brandon laughed. "That's the point." He filled his pipe bowl and ran his flaming lighter over the top. He studied her. "I'm curious, Gayle. How did a cheerleader type like yourself become a sex surrogate?"

She smiled. "Lucky, I guess. No, I don't mind telling you the truth. You have an open face. In college, I had a few light affairs. I couldn't get going. I blamed it on myself and worried because I was nonorgasmic. So I heard of Dr. Freeberg, who'd just moved to Tucson. I went to him, and we talked it out. He directed me to try masturbation. I'd never tried that since childhood. Maybe I thought it was sinful. It wasn't. It was wonderful. It seemed to break the ice. In my next two sexual encounters, I was very orgasmic. No problem. Am I boring you?"

"I'm entranced."

"Then I fell in love with a classmate, a young introvert and history major named . . . My God, have I forgotten his name already? Oh . . . it was Ted, Ted whatever . . . He was as smart as could be—but a brooder. A very disturbed young man, but I didn't know to what extent at the time. He fell for me, too. We made it to bed, but that's all. No further. He couldn't perform at all. Another mother's victim. I tried my best with him. I think we went to bed six, seven, ten times. He couldn't get it up once. Anyway—I don't want to go into detail—one morning they found him dead. He'd overdosed. A suicide at twenty. I can't tell you how it shook me up. Anyway, I went back to Dr. Freeberg and poured out my feelings. Finally, I realized it hadn't been my fault, and I got on my feet again. Meantime, between that episode and my visits to Dr. Freeberg, a resolve began to form in my mind. I told myself that what had happened to Ted must never happen to anyone else again, if it could be prevented. I wanted to be useful, to assist in the recovery of other men who were sexually disabled. Dr. Freeberg had once mentioned the words 'sex surrogate' to me, and I asked him to tell me more. And he did. Then he told me he had been considering using a sex surrogate himself. He had some seemingly hopeless cases, and he felt working with a sex surrogate might repair them. He wondered if I was interested. I certainly was. So he trained me, and then I went to work for him. It was exhilarating—but it was also illegal. When this was found out, Dr. Freeberg was forced to leave Arizona for California. I was eager to follow him. He'll do well here. So will I. How's that for a long story?"

"Not long enough," said Brandon earnestly. "Some evening, when you have time, I'd like to hear more. You're an interesting lady."

Gayle ignored his verbal pass. She stared at him. "What about you? Why are you here?"

"You really want to know?"

"Everything. Like what were you doing and where were you doing it when you decided to move to Hillsdale?"

"I'll try to make it a short short story," said Brandon. "I graduated from the University of Oregon in Eugene. I took a B.S. in biology. I'd also taken some classes in sex education. After that, because of an involvement with someone, I spent a brief interlude in Los Angeles. Then I scurried back to Oregon and put in some time as a substitute science teacher at the secondary school level, all this while trying to determine what to do with myself. When I heard of Dr. Freeberg's need for a male sex surrogate, I applied. But I knew I couldn't make a living at that. So at the same time, I applied to the Hillsdale School District for a job as a substitute science teacher. I took and passed the California Basic Educational Skills Test. I've been teaching off and on since I got here, going through my surrogate training, and waiting for an assignment from Dr. Freeberg. There you have it, Gayle."

"Not quite," said Gayle, who had been listening intently. "I've told you why I'm in surrogate work. But you still haven't told me why you're in it. Why are you in it, Paul?"

He gave her a crooked smile. "Is this the honest hour?"

"Absolutely. I prefer you to be honest. Why are you a sex surrogate?"

He let out his breath, then said, "Money. I have a little savings. I didn't want it to drain away. I needed something to supplement my teaching salary. Sex surrogate sounded just right. It could help me make a living temporarily at what comes naturally. I mean, while having fun."

"Well, it's not always fun, as you'll find out when you get involved. Only money?"

"Only money," he repeated.

"You *are* honest."

Brandon forced another smile. "Right now I wish I weren't. I wish I had a loftier motive."

"No, you are what you are," she said. "It is just hard for me to see it the way you do. I really think I'm doing some good."

"And you are," he said, knocking the ash out of his pipe. "Your patients are very lucky. They're getting a very beautiful young woman . . . and a very devoted one."

Gayle gathered up her purse and check. Standing, she momentarily stared at him once more. "You know what, Paul? I'm not sure I believe you entirely, that you're doing this only for money, I mean. After all, you went into teaching, and that's a low-paying profession. You must want to teach for reasons other than money. Maybe because you also want to help young people. Which led you into surrogate work for the same reason." She looked at him questioningly. "Yes, I suspect there's more to you than meets the eye."

Rising, he grinned. "There's only one way to find out. See me again." He reached over and quickly pulled away her check. "If you pay for yourself, this is only an encounter. If I pay, it's our first date. What about our second?"

She came up beside him. "Call me up when you can. Suzy has my number. Then we'll see." She shook her head. "Two sex surrogates on their own time together? Sounds awfully kinky to me." She touched his hand. "But why not?" And then she walked out of the café.

III

It was morning, and in his Hillsdale clinic office, Dr. Arnold Freeberg was awaiting the arrival any minute of Dr. Max Quarrie, a medical colleague and psychoanalyst from Los Angeles.

Earlier that morning, after breakfast and before leaving for his clinic, Freeberg had received the unexpected phone call from Dr. Quarrie.

Following brief social amenities, Dr. Quarrie had settled down to something more professional. "Got your letter, Arnold," he had said. "So you're in business?"

"I'm in business," Freeberg had agreed, wondering.

"Well, I may have someone for you. It all depends. Do you have a trained male sex surrogate on your staff?"

"I do. I have one. Fully trained. A competent one, I believe."

"I was remembering the little talk we had at that sexual dysfunction seminar in Buffalo, and you were saying trained male surrogates weren't easy to come by."

"Because there's so little demand for them, Max. Lots of women with problems could use them, but as we agreed then, most women are understandably reluctant to have contact with a male stranger these days. However, from recent inquiries I've had from other doctors, I know that more and more women are accepting the idea, provided there is no risk involved. So I took on a male surrogate, and now he's fully trained. You have a case in mind?"

"I do, Arnold. A case referred to me by an M.D. friend. This young lady has a problem. I feel it can be dealt with. Not by me, I decided, and not by a gynecologist. I've tried that, too. But maybe by somebody like you. I think I'd like to see you, the sooner the better. When can I come over?"

"Why, right now, if you wish. I'll be free in an hour."

"I'll be there in an hour. Then you can decide if anything can be done. I'll bring the case history."

"Sure thing, Max. Be glad to see you."

Now Freeberg was in his office, behind his desk, and myopic, pudgy Dr. Max Quarrie was seated in a chair opposite, holding a blue folder in his lap.

With his free hand, he extracted a handkerchief and mopped his brow. "Damn humid out, and it's not a short drive." He pushed the handkerchief back in a pocket and held the blue folder in both hands. "Her name's Nan Whitcomb. Single. Never been married but not inexperienced either. In her late thirties. Plain. Physically sound. She was orphaned in her early teens, then taken in by an elderly aunt who looked after her. The aunt never had much money. About three months ago the aunt died, and Nan was left alone. When she'd almost used up the small amount of money she'd inherited, Nan realized she would have to find a job to subsist. She also needed companionship. She had a few male friends, but they came to nothing. Her female friends are all married and have families."

"So she needed a job and a home?"

"Yes, Arnold. She'd never held a real job before, except filling in as a cashier in various stores during every Christmas holiday season. She's good at figures. Anyway, she began to read the want ads for an opening as a cashier, found several but no luck. Then about two months ago she saw an ad for an experienced cashier in the main Hillsdale restaurant of a chain of eateries owned by a man named Tony Zecca. I've never met him. But I gather from Nan he's a Vietnam veteran, forty-five years old, a rough character whom Nan suspects has organized crime connections—a minor cog, but I'd guess those outsiders financed his restaurant chain. Anyway, Nan applied for the cashier's job at Hillsdale Mall, and late one afternoon Zecca himself interviewed her in his office. He's a short, bull-shouldered man, with hooded eyes, I gather. It was a long interview, mostly routine questions, and throughout it, Zecca kept staring at her.

"The way Nan tells it, at one point Zecca suddenly sat up, still staring, then shook his head and said, 'This is really weird.' Somewhat confused, Nan said, 'What is, Mr. Zecca?' He said, 'You. The way you look and sound like a girl I used to know. That was just before the army. Her name was Crystal. I was just getting to know her, nothing intimate yet, and kind of thinking I really liked her, when I got grabbed up for Vietnam. I got her promise to wait for me until I was discharged—then maybe we'd get married. She promised to wait. But she didn't.' She sent Zecca one of those Dear John letters, or whatever they're called now, saying she was sorry, but she'd met some other man, and they were getting married and moving to the East. Zecca was understandably bitter. He swore never to trust another woman. And then Nan came into his life. 'What's weird,' he told Nan, 'is that you're so much like Crystal. I can't believe it. It's sort of like she came back to me.' I think Nan said, 'I'm flattered you think I resemble someone you cared for.'

"Anyway, by that time it was getting dark, and near the dinner hour, so Zecca asked Nan if he could continue the interview while they dined in a corner of his restaurant. She was happy to do so." Abruptly, Dr. Quarrie handed the blue folder across the desk to Freeberg. "The rest is in there. At least the highlights. You can see for yourself. Take your time." Dr. Quarrie stuck two pieces of gum in his mouth. "Mind if I wander around, have a look at your facility while you read?"

"Please do."

Alone, Freeberg rocked back in his swivel chair, opened the case history of someone named Miss Nan Whitcomb—

and presumably, Mr. Tony Zecca—and began to skim
through the neatly typed double-spaced pages. Here and
there he lingered to read and reread more carefully.

It was Freeberg's habit, whenever he studied a written
case history, to recreate it as he suspected it had actually
happened in life. He went back to an earlier section, the
part recounting Nan's extended job interview and dinner
with Tony Zecca in the corner of his restaurant. Reading it
once more, Freeberg began to recreate it . . .

Seated in their booth, Zecca was uninterested in his food.
He was interested in his drinks. Nan nursed one drink but
observed nervously that Zecca was on his fourth Scotch.
His questions about her job qualifications were beginning
to repeat themselves, and his voice was starting to slur
slightly. He became less and less communicative, and he
stared at her more and more, at her nervous countenance,
at her rising and falling bosom.

Suddenly, breaking another silence, Zecca leaned forward, his eyes fixed on her, lowered his voice, and said,
"Hey, lady, are you a virgin?"

She tried to make light of it. "Is anyone over fourteen a
virgin these days?"

"Yeah, sure. Ever have any serious affairs?"

"No."

"I mean, ever fall for anyone in a big way?"

"Not—not yet," she said more nervously but a bit provocatively. She wanted that job. She needed it.

"Okay." Long pause. "Think you could fall for me?"

She was uncertain about how to handle this. "Maybe. It
depends."

"Depends on what?"

"Well, what you're after, Mr. Zecca."

"Tell you what I'm after." He was pressing closer against
the table so that it now separated them by less space. She
could see that he had a broad face, pugilist's nose, and that
his arms and chest were very large for a short man. Absently, he finished his fourth drink, and she could smell the

alcohol on his breath. "Lemme be frank with you. I don't believe in holding things back. I like to come straight to the point. That's how I got where I am—nice large house in Sherman Park, five restaurants, plenty of cash in the bank. By being frank. You be frank with me the same way, and we'll get along. You understand?"

"I think I do."

"Awright. Here's my proposition to you. I need a cashier —sure, a smart one, honest one, sure—but I also need a live-in friend. Somebody nice to keep me company. I'll take care of her if she takes care of me. Know what I mean? But there's one rule. She's got to be faithful to me one hundred percent. No fucking around. No cheating. Think you can take care of me like that?"

Nan was a little afraid and more than a little mixed up. She wasn't sure how much she really liked him—or if she liked him at all. He was crude, rough, maybe even mean, but maybe not. He was, in his way, being kind, too. He was offering her everything in the world she needed. He was offering security, safety, companionship, a home. He was also telling her he liked her and wanted her to belong only to him. There were virtues there.

"Whatdoya think, kid?" he was asking.

"I—I think I can take care of you the way you want."

His face broke into a satisfied grin. His teeth were yellow and uneven. "Good girl. Then you got nothing more to worry about. You got a home. You got a job. You got a boyfriend. You can move in tomorrow."

"I—I appreciate that, Mr. Zecca."

"Tony, from now on."

"Tony."

"What was your name?"

"Nan."

"Okay, and you better know you got yourself a real loverboy, Nan."

Rereading this meeting, trying to make it come alive in his head, Freeberg turned a page of Nan Whitcomb's case history and was arrested by the report of her initial sexual encounter with Zecca.

Nan had moved into Zecca's ten-room, two-story house with her few effects and been shown to her room by the housekeeper, whose name was Hilda.

It had been exciting, all this luxury, this wonderful cocoon that was now partially her own. She wanted to hold on to it and be as attractive as possible for her first dinner here.

Zecca had come home at seven forty-five, greeted her with a wave, seemed to be pleased with her well-worn tight-fitting jersey dress and long legs. He told her to be ready to eat at eight sharp.

Zecca had two drinks at the outset of the meal and buried himself in a newspaper. Except for a few words to inquire if she was settled and satisfied, he did not speak.

During the dessert, she wondered what would be next, what was expected of her.

After dinner, he beckoned her to follow him into the gaudily decorated modern living room. Settling down into an upholstered easy chair, he patted the footstool nearby for Nan to sit on, then aimed his remote control at the television set.

"There're two one-hour programs I got to watch every night—great action stuff. You'll like them."

She hated them. The violence was unremitting. Between shows, he ordered Scotches for her and himself. He finished his drink and called to Hilda, the housekeeper, for another. Nan made an effort to drink but couldn't. He paid no attention.

As the second show ended, her apprehension grew.

What next?

He swallowed his last drink, stood up, stretched. "Okay, kiddo, let's get down to it. Time for bed. I don't like staying up late. Come on, Nanny girl."

She knew that this was it. First payment on security and comfort. She trailed him to his darkened bedroom.

She had expected him to kiss her, caress her a little, get her ready. He didn't bother.

As he began to remove his shirt, he called over his shoulder. "What are you waiting for? Get out of your things. We're getting into the sack."

Hesitantly, she kicked off her pumps and began to unzip her dress. "Should I—should I put on a nightgown?"

"Naw." He snorted. "Who needs that kind of stuff? I like my ladies bare ass."

As she slipped out of her dress she turned to see him walking toward the king-size bed. At the edge of the bed, he stopped to throw back the blanket. He was naked, and she had her first real look at the man she would live with. He was muscular, all right—and not leastwise in the genital area. She couldn't make out if he was soft or hard yet. It looked like he was hard, but she guessed it was still soft and only looked the other way.

He crawled into bed, peered at her, then snapped, "What's holding you, baby? Let's get going."

With fumbling fingers, she unhooked her bra.

She heard his voice. "Not bad in the tit department."

Almost breathless, she pulled down her cheap nylon panties and pushed them aside with her foot. She had a large thatch of pubic hair and wished that it would cover everything, but it wouldn't and she knew that soon he would see the pink folds below. With wooden legs, she made for the bed.

He was on an elbow, his eyes riveted on her private parts. "Nice gash," he grunted. "Maybe I guessed right. Okay, let's find out."

She pushed herself up on the bed and wriggled toward him.

"Better, that's better," he said.

Momentarily, she closed her eyes, waiting for his kiss, his hug, his hands, the beginnings of foreplay. But opening her eyes, she could see there would be no foreplay.

"Tony," she implored, "put out the lamp."

"No way. I like to see what I'm doing. I like my money's worth."

She sighed, embarrassed, as he knelt over her, his hairy hands yanking her knees apart.

He had her legs wide apart, and she could not take her eyes off what was pointing at her. *Now* he had a hard-on. It resembled a blunt instrument.

As he came down between her legs, she prayed that it might be good, after all.

It wasn't.

His entry stunned her. She was still dry, but he shoved it in hard and brutally. He shoved it deeper and then began his thrusts. The pain made her try to pull away, avoid the pain, but he mistook her movement as cooperation. The thrusting became more savage and relentless. He was going on like an automatic pile driver. Her insides ached. Her thin buttocks ached.

It was endless, the punishment, and she thought it would never stop. Later, in the bathroom, she tried to tell herself that his mindless performance was due to his intense excitement. After this time, in other times to follow, he would be aware of her and considerate, and possibly in his manner a bit more gentle.

Reading the scene in Dr. Quarrie's case history, animating it in his own mind, Freeberg had found it not entirely unfamiliar. There were human beings in the world, and there were human beings who were still animals.

Freeberg resumed his reading of the case history, then Dr. Quarrie's summation of what followed.

This went on, the same pattern, for six weeks. Not only was Zecca insatiable in his desire for intercourse, but in each episode that came after the first, he was as thoughtless as before and increasingly brutal. According to Nan, the pain suffered during these couplings was almost unbearable. As the couplings grew longer, as they inevitably would, Nan was forced to bite her lip to smother protests, and she bit her lip until it bled. Finally, during each coupling, she began to scream. Given Zecca's utter insensitivity, he misinterpreted her screams for sounds of arousal, and he was as pleased as a child receiving a gift. He showed his pleasure by giving Nan a modest raise in salary, and after a month, he gave her an imitation gold necklace.

Recently, according to Nan, after finishing with her, he lay back puffing and mused aloud to her, "I like you. I sure do. I'm going to keep you for good. I wouldn't want you messing around with anyone else. None of that. I mean, if you did, I'd find out. I could easily kill you. I killed plenty of gooks in Nam. Killing is easy if someone tries to do you in. If I was ever double-crossed, I'd kill again. So you just behave."

Nan claims she said, "Of course, I'll behave. I'm with you, Tony. I'm yours."

He said, "Good girl."

Reading this, Freeberg reached out on his desk for his box of cigarillos, managed to free one, and lighted it. Smoking, he read on, waiting to come across the scene that he was sure would happen. Then he found it. He read and reread it. He dramatized it in his mind . . .

Two weeks ago, less than two weeks ago, it happened. They were in bed together at night. He tore her legs apart, and without any preliminaries, he drove his rigid instrument at her, ready to go into her as usual—only this time it didn't go in.

Shoving as strongly as he could, he tried to enter her. No luck.

"Hey, now, what the fuck's going on?" he wanted to know. "What's wrong there? I got it in the right place, ain't I?"

"Yes, yes, go ahead, Tony . . . Please go ahead."

Once more he tried, and again he was unable to enter her. He swore at his frustration. "You're locked up like a steel vault down there. What's going on?"

"I don't know. I'm not doing anything. I'm trying like always."

Determined, for the fourth time, he rammed himself between her legs. No luck.

"Lemme see what's going on," he muttered. He lifted

her pelvis, his hands clenched under her buttocks, high toward him. He took one hand and dug three fingers into her. "Seems okay now. Let's find out."

He dropped her on the bed and tried for a fifth time to force his way into her. He couldn't enter beyond an inch. "Something is sure haywire. How does it feel?"

"It feels tight, real tight. And it hurts a little. Maybe it's something organic."

"Something what?"

"Organic. Physical. Anyway, something is wrong with me. Maybe I can go see a doctor tomorrow."

"You got a doctor?"

"A gynecologist in town. He'd know."

Zecca humored her. "Yeah, baby, you do that. Find out what's ailing you. Get it set right." He looked down at his drooping instrument. "Now, what about tonight?"

"I—I can still make you happy."

"Yeah, you do that."

She reached out between his legs, to get hold of that thing and make him happy. But before she could take hold, one of his hands reached up behind her head and pushed it down between his legs.

Shutting her eyes, she opened her mouth and went ahead.

Finishing the page, reliving this scene from Nan Whitcomb's case history, Freeberg murmured to himself, "Poor woman."

He completed reading the last of the case history and put the blue folder on his desk to await Dr. Max Quarrie's return. To his surprise, Dr. Quarrie had already returned and was seated opposite him.

"Well, Arnold," said Dr. Quarrie, "what do you think?"

"Definitely a case of vaginismus, in an extreme form. I doubt if she's phobic about coitus. She's getting muscular spasms in the region to avoid any more intercourse with him."

"Confirms my own diagnosis and the gynecologist's,"

said Dr. Quarrie. "Question is, Think you can do something about it? I can't talk her into getting better. I suspect
it will take more."

"Yes," Freeberg agreed. He thought of his one male sex
surrogate, Paul Brandon, awaiting his first patient. Now he
would have her. Freeberg nodded. "It's made to order for
us, for a surrogate and myself working with her. I'm sure we
can help. When can I see her?"

"Right now," said Dr. Quarrie, rising. "She's waiting in
my car. I'll send her up."

Chet Hunter had been unable to get an appointment to
see Otto Ferguson, editor in chief of the Hillsdale *Chronicle*,
until late this morning. Ever since Suzy's great tip last
night, the big story—and big break—had been forming in
Hunter's mind, and he was eager to pitch it to Ferguson.
Bland as Ferguson seemed, cynical and negative as he was,
Hunter was positive he would go for this news lead.

After cooling his heels outside Ferguson's glass-enclosed
office, Hunter was finally shown in.

He could see Ferguson's bald pate as he bent over some
copy, marking it, and at last he lifted his head and focused
his baggy St. Bernard eyes on his visitor.

Nervously, Hunter had set himself on the edge of the
straight chair across from Ferguson.

"Well, Chet," said the editor, "what brings you here this
time? Want to sell us an exclusive lead from your police
friends? Or the Reverend Scrafield? Or on a poll you've
been taking?"

"I don't want to sell you any research," said Hunter.
"This time, I want to sell you a story, a complete story."

"It had better be something bigger than the stuff you've
been feeding us so far."

Hunter was emphatic. "It is bigger—this is bigger than
anything I've ever had. It's the biggest."

"Oh, yeah?" Ferguson's mask of skepticism remained.
"All right, young man. Go ahead. I'm from Missouri."

Hunter braced himself, then raised his voice as if it were a

boldface headline. "Exclusive in the *Chronicle:* SEX SURRO-
GATE OPERATION TAKES OVER HILLSDALE!"

"What?"

"Exactly. Found out about it last night. Unimpeachable
source. Trained sex surrogates from around the country
have gone to work today for a new sex clinic that just
opened in our fair city. You know what sex surrogates are?"

"Knew about them while you were still wetting your
pants." A flicker of interest had crossed the editor's face. It
was as if he were talking to himself. "Sex surrogates in L.A.,
Chicago, New York, to be expected. In pure little Hillsdale,
never. Are you sure you're sure?"

"I'm positive, Otto. And I can prove it."

"Tell me about it."

Excitedly, without revealing Suzy Edwards's name or position, Hunter told him about it, told Ferguson about the
new Freeberg Clinic, Dr. Arnold Freeberg, the six sex surrogates from around the country who had gathered here
and been assigned to work. "Right now in Hillsdale.
They're loose in Hillsdale. I say that's not a lead—that's a
super story."

"Could be," Ferguson conceded, "could very well be.
Depends. How would you go about getting such a story?"

"From the inside, by joining up. Becoming a patient.
Rapping with Dr. Freeberg as a patient. And rolling in the
hay with one of his paid female sex surrogates. Then I'd
expose the whole mess. You'd have headlines for weeks."

"A sting operation," said Ferguson, half to himself. "Yes,
that would be the way to do it. It could be big, no question." He considered it, then frowned. "Only I see some
problems . . . one in particular. If you applied as a patient, a professional therapist like Freeberg would see right
through you. You'd never get away with it if you faked it."
He narrowed his eyes on Hunter. "Or would you be faking
it? Maybe you know you'd qualify for treatments?"

Hunter's cheeks reddened ever so slightly. "Never mind
about that, Otto. Don't make me spell it out for you. Let's
say I could qualify. But frankly, I don't have the ready cash
to ante up and get treatments from a sex surrogate."

"What are we talking about, Chet?"

"Five thousand dollars on the line."

"That's a hefty amount for a fuck," said Ferguson.

"It's for our story, Otto. HIGHEST-PAID PROSTITUTES IN COUNTRY NOW IN HILLSDALE! How does that sound?"

"Anyway, money isn't an issue when there's a really big story."

"Well, then, let's go."

But Ferguson was hesitant. He fell back against the slats of his chair, thinking. "There's one more thing—another problem . . ." he began. "You know, Chet, that's a pretty raunchy story for a family newspaper like ours . . . unless—"

"Unless what?"

"—unless we could turn this from a smirking exposé into a newspaper's civic duty—a political issue and crusade to clean up fair Hillsdale." He mused aloud. "Prostitution is the world's oldest profession. Now we have the world's newest profession, the sex surrogate, who is also paid to give a piece of ass in the guise of a cure. If we could just make this into a community campaign. Maybe get your friend the Reverend Josh Scrafield interested, part of his ongoing cleanup campaign . . ."

"I could get Scrafield for you in a minute, Otto. Once he learns about this, he'll grab it and run with it."

"And then there's one more element, the wrap-up element that would make it possible for us to print this. If you could get Scrafield to storm in on the district attorney, Hoyt Lewis, and have him reveal the whole secret operation, and get the D.A.'s office to indict this Dr. Freeberg for illegal pandering under state law and grab one of his female surrogates for practicing illegal prostitution under existing state law—and then put them on trial—we could run with it from there. We'd have a criminal story, a political story, a virtuous civic story. Copies of every edition would race off the newsstands. But first, Chet, you've got to get Scrafield and Lewis behind you . . . and behind us. Then you've got to infiltrate that Freeberg operation and get the goods firsthand. Think you can do all that?"

Hunter was on his feet, pumping Ferguson's hand. "Can I? Otto, watch me do it. Faster than a speeding bullet. Watch me move. And start setting my byline in type!"

Not until early this afternoon, as he listened to Chet Hunter in the computerized office at the rear of his Church of the Resurrection, had the Reverend Josh Scrafield looked upon his part-time researcher with any real respect.

Until this afternoon, Scrafield had always regarded Chet Hunter with mild contempt, something of a frail grub and intellectual nerd, sallow and frightened of life.

About a year ago, when Scrafield had been planning to undertake his campaign against the insidious sex education then invading the public schools, Darlene had discovered Hunter and advised Scrafield that the young researcher might be useful in digging up facts. Reluctantly, Scrafield had taken on the library mole, the ferret.

But early this afternoon Scrafield had heard and seen another side of the grub. For Hunter, in revealing his knowledge of the pandering Dr. Freeberg and the sluts he sent out to corrupt the purity of Hillsdale, had shown a human side to himself. Like Scrafield himself, young Hunter had shown some understanding of lust and how it might come to destroy paradise.

Once he had understood what Hunter had in mind, and what his own role might be, Scrafield had been quick to arrange a meeting for both of them with Hoyt Lewis, Hillsdale's clever district attorney.

Now, towering over his informant, Scrafield led Hunter into District Attorney Hoyt Lewis's impressive office in the marble-floored city hall. Scrafield felt comfortable about this meeting. For one thing, the district attorney was a smart and perceptive man in his late thirties, as smart and perceptive as Scrafield himself. Despite his scraggly sandy-colored mustache and his tendency toward obesity, emphasized by his habit of locking his hands across his spreading paunch, Lewis was a man above the crowd and a man who was going places. In fact, he was self-assured enough to wear a black string tie. Lewis came from one of the better families in Hillsdale (they were said to have second and third homes in Malibu and Palm Springs), and he possessed a real comprehension of the needs and wants of the masses. Not unlike Scrafield, the district attorney could communicate with the peasants and was popular with them.

Hoyt Lewis had come to his feet, to shake hands with Scrafield and Hunter after they had entered his vast office, and was gesturing them to a button-backed leather sofa near his desk. After they had been seated, Lewis had drawn up a leather chair on casters and lowered himself into it, filling it to overflowing.

"Good to see you, gentlemen," Lewis was saying. His mustache rose to reveal his even white teeth, and he was as cordial as a host at a dinner party. "Well, to what do I owe the honor of this visit?"

While Hunter seemed to cringe inwardly, Scrafield was pleased with the thoughtful formality.

Scrafield glanced at Hunter, then at Lewis. "Let me kick this off, Hoyt. It's an important matter that, I perceive, requires your immediate attention." He jerked a thumb at his companion. "Chet Hunter here, he's an expert researcher, you know. I've seen his work firsthand. He came to me originally, out of civic duty, with the most appalling information about programs the liberals were instigating to infect our school system. This information proved to be accurate and has been something I've been able to employ effectively on my weekly television shows."

Hoyt Lewis bobbed his head. "My wife and I are regular watchers of your shows. They have done much to assist our office in keeping the community clean."

"Thank you, Hoyt. But now our enterprising Mr. Hunter has come up with something far more insidious and dangerous to our fair community. My fight against indecent sex education in the schools absolutely pales beside the foul pollution that Chet Hunter has uncovered."

Hoyt Lewis's curiosity was evident. "I'm eager to hear what you're talking about, Reverend Scrafield. Please go ahead and tell me about it."

The Reverend Scrafield nodded. "I think I would rather have Chet here tell it to you exactly as he told it to me. Go ahead, Chet. You have the floor. Don't hold anything back."

Hunter appeared to gird himself, determined to do it right with so much at stake. "What this is about is the recently opened Freeberg Clinic, about a half mile from here. Do you know about it?"

"I'm aware that it exists," said Lewis. "The latest medical building."

"But different," Hunter said emphatically, "different from any other medical building in our community. You see, Dr. Arnold Freeberg is a sex therapist. There's nothing inherently wrong about that . . . except Dr. Freeberg employs female sex surrogates as his assistants."

Hunter knew that he had the district attorney's full attention now, and he related what he knew, omitting no detail. Hunter had learned that Dr. Freeberg had been forced to leave Arizona for breaking the law and had seen free-wheeling California as a fertile field for his questionable practices. Freeberg had hired five women and one man, according to a reliable informant inside his clinic, to try to rehabilitate persons with sex problems through use of their bodies, ultimately offering sexual intercourse.

Somewhat breathless, Hunter concluded his lurid account while Hoyt Lewis listened with obvious surprise and fascination.

The moment Hunter had concluded his report, the Reverend Scrafield jumped into the breach as if to underline it. "Hoyt, what has come to Hillsdale is out-and-out pandering and prostitution, under the disguise of therapy, and what Freeberg is practicing every day with his brothel ladies is totally in defiance of our state laws. If you promise to prosecute this outrage, once you have the goods—"

"How do I get the goods?" Lewis interrupted.

"Through me," said Hunter hastily. "I can get it for you. I could enlist in Dr. Freeberg's surrogate program as a patient—"

"Would you qualify?" asked Lewis.

"No question," said Hunter. "Trust me. I could get in and observe and participate, and keep a running record of it, which I'd turn over to you. I could be your star witness."

"My star witness?" Lewis wrinkled his nose. "I don't know. Normally, this would require an undercover police investigation. We'd wire someone and put him in with one of those women, and then—"

"Mr. Lewis, I'm a bona fide member of the Hillsdale Police Force—I'm a reservist."

"He joined and trained to fulfill a civic duty," Scrafield said pontifically.

"And to help with my research," added Hunter openly.

"Police reserve," said Lewis, pushing himself out of his chair. "Let me see." He walked to his desk, shuffled through a few folders, found the one he wanted, and opened it. "When you and the Reverend Scrafield here made this appointment to see me, I didn't know anything about you. I decided to see if we had any kind of file on you. We did. I skimmed it, but I must have missed the police reserve aspect. Yes, I see it now—right here. You are, indeed, a de facto member of our law enforcement apparatus. Yes, as a reserve officer, with three years training, you could qualify to support us on any charges we made. You could be the key prosecution witness."

He tossed the folder back on his desk and returned to his chair. He sat lost in thought a few moments. "Before any criminal complaint and arrest warrant, I'd have to do a little research of my own through this office. This kind of matter is not new in California. I've read of sex surrogates being used throughout the state." He paused. "I wonder why they've never been challenged before?"

Scrafield snorted. "Because they mask themselves as legitimate aides to legitimate therapists. No one wants to get caught in that quagmire. Everyone's been afraid to tackle them. But there's no question in my mind that they should be arrested, booked, arraigned on misdemeanor and felony counts, and put on trial for defying the California Penal Code."

"Still, it's a little tricky," said the district attorney cautiously. "We wouldn't be dealing with a straight open-and-shut criminal case. We would have to redefine, reinterpret legally, both 'pandering' and 'prostitution,' maybe set a precedent in establishing a new point of law. Yet, it seems possible to do so. Even then, if I were convinced that this is a criminal offense, I'd want to put Dr. Freeberg on notice before acting further, give him an opportunity to cease and desist in his practice, once I had the necessary evidence."

Hunter refused to have his enthusiasm dampened by the district attorney's compromise statement. "In either instance," said Hunter, "if Freeberg gives up, it would be a victory for your office. If he refused to quit, you'd have a legitimate reason to take him to trial. All I can say is that if you do decide to proceed with criminal charges, I can get you all the evidence you need and stand up as key witness for the prosecution."

"Very generous of you," said Lewis. "Let me consider this a little longer before we proceed."

The Reverend Scrafield turned to Hunter. "Thanks, Chet. Do you mind stepping out into the corridor a moment? I want to talk to Mr. Lewis a few minutes alone. A private matter. I'll join you right away."

Hunter cast Scrafield a covert, hopeful glance, nodded agreeably, and hastened to leave the room.

After waiting for the door to shut, assured that the two of them were alone, Scrafield came to his feet and took the chair beside the district attorney.

"Hoyt," he began, "this is something I wanted to discuss with you in confidence. I hope you have a moment or two to spare."

"I'm at your service, Reverend Scrafield," Lewis said, leaning forward attentively.

"Hoyt, I wanted to speak to you about your future. I've always felt—and others of some importance in this community agree with me—that you are simply too big a man for this job you hold. I'm not denigrating your office, but you are overqualified for it. There are more important political jobs that could be yours for the asking."

"I appreciate that," said the district attorney with quiet

modesty, "but I assure you that I've never given a moment's thought to another job—or more important job, as you put it."

"Then you should, you should, Hoyt," said Scrafield urgently. "Hillsdale is a fine place to succeed. But the state of California is a finer one, and inevitably a larger role in California might give you a real role in the nation. Let me repeat, something bigger and better in the state could be yours for the asking."

"Suppose I were to be interested in something bigger and better. I hardly think it could be mine for the asking. I'm a local figure, almost unknown outside this relatively small community."

Scrafield tilted forward in his chair. "Exactly my point, Hoyt. Exactly. You're in a position to make yourself known, overnight, the length and breadth of this state. You could have the electorate at your feet."

Hoyt Lewis was genuinely puzzled. "How?"

"By getting behind Chet Hunter, getting behind what he's offered you and I've offered you," said Scrafield earnestly. "He's handed you a dynamite issue . . . no, even more—a public bombshell. The sex surrogate matter. Prostitutes disguising themselves as healers to invade insidiously and to undermine our society, young and old."

The district attorney had been listening intently. "You really think the public would give it that much attention?"

"Hoyt, take my word, trust my knowledge of the public out there. I know the raw nerve issues. I know what counts. I have an instinct for public concerns. That's why my audience grows larger every week, and my viewer ratings go up every month. Believe me."

"Oh, I do believe you, Reverend Scrafield," Lewis said quickly.

"Once Hunter gets the green light to go for the evidence, and gets it to you and the press, once I air the scandal on television, you can prosecute and you can't lose. We'll arouse the public in this community. Your name will be on everyone's lips. You'll have unanimous public support and widespread attention. This is not some murky, incompre-

hensible matter like tax deficits or budgets or some minor
corporate crime. This is sex surrogates—*sex* sluts—threatening every wife, mother, and girlfriend for as far as the eye
can see. This is the stuff of headlines and the six o'clock
news, Hoyt. This is the road to the big time."

"You're sure of that?"

"If I know what it can do for me, I'm twice as positive I
know what it can do for you. I've always seen you as a future
state attorney, and after that, governor, once you have the
springboard to catapult your presence to the capitol, and
the surrogate issue would do it. A vigorous prosecution of
those whores, and their medical pimp, has star quality written all over it. Think of it, Hoyt. You'd have me on the air
supporting you. You'd have Ferguson at the *Chronicle* with
his front pages backing you. And you'd have Chet Hunter
as your Trojan horse inside the enemy's bordello, getting
you the facts firsthand. And, Hoyt, I'll be at your side all the
way. Do you understand me?"

The district attorney sat silently a moment, absently staring down at the carpet with an air of gravity. He raised his
head, directing his gaze at the clergyman. "You can be very
persuasive, Reverend."

Scrafield's lips curled. "It's my business, Mr. D.A." He
added softly, "I know my business. I can't ever afford to be
wrong."

"Neither can I," said Hoyt Lewis, half to himself.
Abruptly, he rose to his feet. "Okay, Reverend Scrafield, I
stand convinced. I do believe, given all-out support and
with public sentiment on my side, we could prosecute and
win this one. I agree, it could be a big one." He stuck out his
hand, and Scrafield, also on his feet, grabbed it. "It's a
deal," said the district attorney. "You go out into the hall
there and tell Chet Hunter to get the evidence, firsthand,
and as soon as possible. Once I know I have it, you can
leave the rest to me."

IV

For Paul Brandon it was an afternoon of firsts.

First patient interview, first therapy session, and first day in his just-rented three-room apartment.

Brandon had suspected from the moment he had met Nan Whitcomb and listened to her case history with Dr. Freeberg in the therapist's office that it might be a struggle all the way. Brandon's immediate concern before meeting his patient was that she might be too fat. All fat women turned him off.

To his relief, Brandon had found Nan Whitcomb, despite her plainness, not unattractive. She had long chestnut hair held in place with a barrette, and hazel eyes. Rather than given to fat, she had appeared somewhat thin, with a skeletal figure, except for prominent helicoid breasts and broad hips. But Brandon's relief had once more turned to concern as he had heard her shyly recount her sex history, her relationship with Tony Zecca, and her vaginal problem. She had barely given Brandon so much as a glance as she had addressed herself to Freeberg in a voice a little above a whisper.

Trying to hear her, Brandon's initial concern about being able to perform sexually with her ultimately had evaporated. The difficulty here, he had seen, was one of trust. She had been so badly misused by one male that she might be resistant to responding to any male, especially a stranger, and unable to allow any rapport or closeness between them.

Definitely, Brandon had told himself, it would be an uphill struggle.

On the other hand, Dr. Freeberg had shown no lack of confidence and had been totally reassuring. "I've seen Dr. Lopez's medical report," Freeberg had told her, "and there is nothing organically wrong with you. This is certainly an episode of vaginismus, which I've already explained to you. This is something, given time, that we can treat successfully."

"Doctor, as I tried to tell you, I don't have that much time. If I come here too often, Tony will get suspicious."

"So you still feel it would be better to put you on an intensive treatment program?"

"Yes, two to three weeks at the most."

"Well, that can be done, I'm sure." He had swiveled toward Brandon. "Don't you agree, Paul?"

Brandon had tried to be reassuring before her. "Absolutely."

But he had still continued to worry that it might not be as easy as it sounded.

"All right, settled," Freeberg had said. "Let's begin treatment tomorrow. Let's say tomorrow evening after dinner at Paul's place, around eight—"

Nan had interrupted. "No, I can't."

Freeberg's brow had knitted.

"Evenings are impossible," Nan had gone on. "Tony wouldn't let me get away. Besides, how would I explain seeing an ordinary doctor at night?"

Freeberg had nodded understandingly. "You're right." Once more he had turned to Brandon. "Can you make it at three tomorrow afternoon, Paul?"

"Perfect."

But it had not been perfect from the instant of Nan Whitcomb's tentative entrance into Brandon's living room.

He had held out his hands to take her coat, and she had
shed it slowly, then stood there in her white blouse and
beige skirt, furtively taking in the room.

Brandon had seated her on his couch and made it a point
to sit several feet from her.

He had tried to make small talk, put her at her ease, but
essentially she had been noncommunicative.

"What are we going to do?" she asked suddenly.

"Hand caress and facial caress."

He had described the two exercises and the reasons why
they could be helpful.

"Is that all there is to it?" she had asked.

"That's all, Nan. Really very simple."

"Whatever you say. Okay, let's do them."

Sitting closer to her, Brandon had gently caressed both
her hands, although they were rigid. Then, in turn, he had
encouraged her to caress his hands. After that, he had
stroked her face with his fingertips and glided his palms
across her chin and cheeks and forehead. Her face had
been tight, as if she'd had it fashioned into a mask. Once he
had finished, he had closed his eyes and requested her to
do the same to him.

Upon beginning, her fingers had pressed rather hard in
and around his features, but gradually her hands had relaxed and massaged his countenance lightly.

He had opened his eyes. "Good, very good."

"That's all there is to it?"

"That's all, Nan."

"I guess there was nothing to be afraid of."

"Of course not."

"Will we do anything else?"

He had noted the time. They had used up only an hour
and fifteen minutes of the two-hour treatment session.
There had still been three quarters of an hour left to them.
He had wondered how to make the best use of it. Once
again he might try to talk to her. Often, with women, conversation was the most relaxing and effective approach.

Now, on the sofa, he said, "Why don't we talk a little?"

He made no effort to move away from her. "I'd like to know more about you, if you don't mind."

She seemed relieved, even met his eyes. "I don't mind."

"I'm curious about how you're going to handle your boyfriend."

"You mean Tony?"

"Yes, Tony Zecca. What are you going to tell him you're up to? I mean, if he asks?"

"He'll ask, all right. While we're having dinner."

"What are you going to tell him?"

"Not that I saw you or Dr. Freeberg. You can be sure of that. Dr. Freeberg already advised me how to handle it."

"How, Nan?"

"I'm going to tell him I'm seeing my gynecologist for a series of shots. To overcome a hormone deficiency."

"What if Tony wants to know the name of your gynecologist?"

"I'm to tell him it is Dr. Lopez, the one who examined me for Dr. Freeberg."

"What if Tony tries to check your story with Dr. Lopez?"

Nan gave the ghost of a smile. "Already taken care of. Dr. Freeberg alerted Dr. Lopez."

"Nice and neat," said Brandon, smiling back at her, sensing a few inches gained, the slightest start of establishing rapport. He became serious again. "Only one thing troubles me."

"What's that, Paul?"

"He might want sex with you tonight. Think you can deal with him?"

"If I follow Dr. Freeberg's instructions. No sex tonight or any night while I'm working with both of you. I'm to tell him I must finish the series of shots before—before we go to bed again."

"What if Tony insists on sex?"

She laughed for the first time. "Oh, he will—you can bet on that. But I won't let him. I'm to be very firm about saying no. Which will be easy, believe me."

"Maybe he'll force himself." To his surprise, Brandon

found himself feeling some apprehension for her well-being.

"You mean, like rape me? Let him try. You know my condition. He won't get anywhere."

"But one day, when you can, he will . . ." He wanted to ask her something, considered if he should, and then did. "Nan, have you ever thought of solving part of your problem by leaving him?"

"I've thought of it."

"Well?"

Her voice was almost plaintive. "Where would I go, Paul?"

"I see."

He was feeling sympathy for her, and sensing that she was more comfortable with him, he had an urge to make this initial session as intensive as it could be. He wanted her to progress quickly, so that she could feel safe.

Instinct told him what the next best step should be in their relationship. They should disrobe together, then stand naked with each other. If successful, this would eliminate her inhibitions, bond their relationship, and make everything that followed easier and warmer.

He looked at the wall clock. They still had twenty-five minutes left. So there was time enough to get something more intimate started. Dare he suggest it?

He cast an eye inward at his instinct signals. No green light showed. But there was something that resembled a yellow light, a yellow light that said, You can go, but go easy.

Try it, but slowly.

Body imaging—but she'd be much too frightened to strip and stand before the mirror. She was still a timid creature, not as timid as she had been when she had entered his apartment, but still a member of the walking wounded, the psychically wounded, and she would be afraid to strip totally before one more man, a man who might blur in her mind into another potential Tony Zecca. To reveal herself so totally might lose everything that had been gained this afternoon.

Then Brandon, drawing on his training, remembered Freeberg speaking of compromises that had to be made and could be made on the spot. If a patient was too inhibited, do what you have to do gradually.

Go slowly, Brandon reminded himself again.

He turned his head to look at her and found to his pleasant surprise that Nan had been watching him.

"You seemed lost in thought," she said.

"I was, Nan. I was thinking of something else we could do that would make the next sessions easier."

"What's that?" she wanted to know.

"Trying a back caress. Just to get it started. We can do it more fully next time."

"A back caress? How do you do it?"

"I'd like to take off my shirt. Not my trousers, just my shirt."

"I don't mind. I've seen men without shirts on the beach all the time."

"And I'd like you to take off your blouse."

"Take off my blouse?" The earlier fright appeared on her face. "I'm wearing a brassiere underneath. What about that?"

Yellow light. Careful. He was relying on his instinct completely—that and his little knowledge of her.

"Never mind about your bra," he said casually. "Leave it on. Just your blouse off and my shirt off. We'll stand up. I'll stand behind you. You'll shut your eyes and let me rub your back."

"Nothing else?"

"Just that."

He began removing his shirt as he watched her fumble to open and release her blouse.

He was bare chested, on his feet, waiting for her.

She was having trouble with her white blouse, but finally she pulled it off and stood up. She was stiff, self-conscious about the protrusion of the obviously new lace brassiere.

"How's that?" she said, almost defiantly.

"Excellent. Stand in front of me, Nan, with your back to me."

She stepped in front of him, then turned her back to him. From the rise of her square shoulders, he could see that she was breathing faster.

"What else am I to do?"

"Not a thing, Nan, except relax, if you can. I'll only caress your back, just rub and massage it."

"If you think it'll do any good."

"It'll help. Now, close your eyes. No more talk. Listen to my fingers. Feel my fingers."

He applied his fingertips to the curve of her back, above the brassiere band and below it, as if they were butterflies. Then more pressure, more friction. Minute by minute, her muscular constriction began to ease. Soon, she was almost relaxing, absorbing and enjoying the circular movements of his hands.

As he continued to caress her back, he could hear sounds, soft sounds of pleasure, that she was involuntarily emitting.

Then in a whisper, she spoke. "Feels wonderful, wonderful."

He did not reply. His hands spoke on her flesh, his fingers and palm now gliding upward, gliding downward.

For twenty minutes.

"All right, Nan," he said.

Her hands came back behind her. He thought she was reaching behind to touch his hands. But no, her fingers had darted to the hooks on her brassiere. She undid the hooks, let the bra come free, and then turned around and looked up at him.

She pulled off her brassiere and allowed her straight, high conical breasts to be revealed. He could not help staring at them. The ruby nipples were pointed. They were hard.

"I just wanted you to know," she said, "I'm not a prude and I'm not a sickie. Even though I've never had an orgasm with anyone, I'm sure I could be all right in the right hands."

"Thank you, Nan."

She looked down at her breasts, shook them a little, then looked up at him. "Not bad for somebody my age."

"They're lovely, Nan."

She began to cover them again with her brassiere, fastening the hooks on the band behind her. "That—that's for starters," she said, reaching for her blouse. "Next time, if you're just as gentle, you can see what goes with it."

Early that evening, Adam Demski sat on the edge of the living room sofa, with Gayle Miller completing his footbath exercise. Demski was in shirt sleeves and trousers, but his trousers were rolled up just below his knees, and his feet were immersed in a large square plastic dishpan filled with soapy tepid water.

Gayle, her hands in the water, finished rubbing and caressing his feet and then told him that he could take his feet out of the water and set them on a bath mat beside it.

"How was that, Adam?" Gayle wanted to know, picking up a velour towel and beginning to dry one of his feet.

"Pleasant, of course," he answered, wiggling his toes. He appeared considerably less tense than he had been at the outset of the exercise.

"It can be a delightful experience," said Gayle. "It actually gives you a good feeling about an often neglected but sensual part of your body. It puts you in closer touch with yourself. Unfortunately, most of my patients don't want to bother about doing it."

"Why not?"

Gayle continued to busy herself wiping his feet. "Because they are not interested in their feet. Each patient, I assure you, is interested only in his penis. He tells himself, 'It's my penis that's in trouble, not my feet. Besides, my feet aren't all that attractive. In fact, they're rather ugly, so why waste time on them?' " She peered up at him. "Did you feel that way, Adam?"

"Well, maybe I was wondering that a little, wondering if it wasn't a waste of time, sort of."

"It wasn't, Adam. Take my word for it. Feet can be surprisingly erotic. Also, caressing them gives us a chance to continue building a relationship. I mean, we get a chance to know each other a little better before we try to get closer."

"Okay, I let you do it." As she cast her towel aside, he added, "What do I do next? Do I do it to you?"

"We'll skip that."

"Should I put my socks and shoes back on?"

"No."

She had given the next step careful consideration. In fact, she had discussed it with Dr. Freeberg just before lunch. Gayle had speculated on going into body imaging during the last half of her second session with Adam Demski.

"Do you think he's ready for total nudity yet?" she pondered aloud.

Freeberg, who had been leafing through a transcript of Demski's case history, and then Gayle's report on their opening session, sat back to reflect on this.

"You seem to have made some real progress with him, Gayle."

"I believe I have. He was much more relaxed when the first session ended. More comfortable. Almost not scared of me at all."

"Though he may be reluctant about full nudity. Remember, once he takes his clothes off, you are going to see what he perceives as his real problem. He *will* be scared, feel threatened. On the other hand, from his talks with me, while he is not pressing to rush along, he really wants to get to his problem, focus on it. Despite his outward appearance of resistance, I have a gut feeling that he's ready to do anything, no matter how difficult for him, to overcome his problem. I sense he's determined. Yes, Gayle, I think you can undertake body imaging with him tonight"—Freeberg had hesitated briefly—"but be careful."

"What do you mean 'be careful'?"

"Don't hurry him. Talk him along. Chat about nude experiences. Ease him into it."

"No problem with that."

Freeberg had sat up. "Where do you intend to do the body imaging? In your bedroom this time?"

"God, no," she had said emphatically. "I still feel the same way I did in Tucson. My bedroom is my private retreat, never part of my surrogate work. I remember something you told me: once you ask a man to take his clothes off, if he's dysfunctional, his anxiety goes sky-high. He associates undressing with having to perform. Taking him into my bedroom would mean the same thing. I stopped using a bedroom with my first case, as you advised. I have my therapy room down the hallway of my new house. It looks like an office. I shipped everything from Tucson. A full-length three-sided mirror on one wall. A desk and file cabinet on another. Across from the mirror wall, a rather firm oversized couch with a pull-up armchair on either side. The floor's covered with a thick mat the size of a double bed. We'll do the exercises there. Except for the mat, the atmosphere is fairly austere and clinical, and that's where we'll work."

Dr. Freeberg had smiled his approval. "Good girl. Then go ahead. Do it."

So now, seated near Demski, she realized that she was at the brink of a crucial step.

She heard Demski speaking, a bit confused. "You said no? I'm not to put my shoes on?"

"No, don't bother," she repeated, springing up. She held out her hand to Demski, wanting him to rise. Once he was beside her, she added cheerfully, "As long as you have your shoes and socks off, I thought we might just go on from there."

"You mean undress?" He sounded as if he had a frog in his throat.

"Why not?" Still cheerfully. "We'll want to do that sooner or later. Why not sooner? It's necessary for body imaging, and it's healthy. I promise you, Adam, it's a big, big step."

"Did—did you talk to Dr. Freeberg about it?"

"I certainly did. I told him I thought you were ready for it. He agreed. He approves."

"*You* think I'm ready?"

"I do." She took him by the hand. "Come on, let's go in the back."

Demski resisted. "Where to? Your bedroom?"

"Oh, no, that's way down the line, if we use it at all. I'm taking you to a cozy room I have in the rear that I use as a part-time office. It has a special mirror I want to show you." She tightened her hold on Demski's hand. "Come along. Follow me."

She led him into the hallway.

"What's body imaging?" he wanted to know, his voice hoarse.

"I'll demonstrate it for you," she promised. As she walked ahead of him she went on. "You know, nudity is a very common experience. At one time or another, everyone is nude. When you were a baby, you were nude while your sister or mother diapered you. Around the country many kids go swimming naked in some cove on a lake. Or maybe they swim naked at the YMCA. Did you?"

"At the Y—once."

"You must have undressed in the locker room at high school before gym class."

"Yes, of course."

"You strip down whenever you have a checkup at your doctor's. Maybe sometimes, there is a female nurse present."

"That's true, but it's different."

Ignoring his remark, Gayle went on. "I remember that on some of your later dates, you tried to make love to women. I'm sure you undressed completely."

"I did. But I didn't like it."

They were standing before Gayle's therapy room, and she opened the door and waved him inside. The overhead fluorescent lights were already on. They were direct, businesslike, clearly not illumination that was low and seductive.

"You'll find this easier, much easier," Gayle said. She swung a hand at the furniture. "Sit down wherever you like, Adam."

He sat edgily in the nearest pull-up chair.

Gayle had gone to the full-length mirror to consider herself. She had purposely dressed down for this occasion. No turn-on clothes, not any garment that might be regarded as sexy. No see-through blouse or half bra or clinging skirt or sheer nylon stockings or boots. She was wearing a loose-fitting pullover sweater with a modest V neck, a light wool skirt, no stockings, and low-heeled shoes. It was a sexless uniform that could be discarded without much delay.

Still dressed, she pivoted from the long mirror to confront Demski.

"Let me tell you what body imaging is, Adam."

Then she explained the technique of body imaging to him.

When she had finished, Demski repeated, "Stand in front of the mirror?"

"With nothing on. Nude. And go through the same drill I've just done. Pointing to your various body parts and relating to me how you feel about them."

"Well, maybe I won't know how. I mean, I've never tried that."

"You'll know," Gayle assured him. "I'm not saying it's exactly the same when women and men body image. Women are likely to spend more time talking about their faces. Women are much more into makeup, cosmetics, and worrying about how they look to outsiders. Men are most often ready to skip their faces and go to what counts for them. A man may go straight to his penis and want to talk about that. Because his penis is all he's interested in talking about. But frequently, men will go from head to toe and go past their genitals without mentioning them. If they do that, I mention it afterward, then tell them they forgot their genitals and ask them how they feel about them. I'm not interested in asking why they skipped that area, because I don't need to know, and I have no judgments to make. But I do want them to get back to that area and talk about it. I mean, that's basically what this is all about. Do you understand the procedure, Adam?"

"I'm not sure. Maybe I do."

"Well, just imitate me. When it's your turn, do what I've done. You can do it, I'm sure."

"If you think so."

Gayle offered Demski a warm smile and said softly, "Now, you stand up, Adam, and let's both take off our clothes."

"At the same time?"

"No matter. Let's just undress." As he wobbled to his feet, she added in a kindly tone, "Undressing, Adam, doesn't mean you have to get an erection and jump into bed and make it with me. It means only what I've explained —we are undressing so that you can get in touch with how you feel about your whole body, because you've never thought about it that much, and to give me some information about your body and how you feel about it, and most of all, to give us an easier and closer relationship. Okay?"

"Okay," he said glumly.

She half turned away, as she began to pull her sweater over her head, and did not fix on his own fumbling efforts to undress so as not to inhibit further what he was trying to do.

She had her sweater off, then reached behind to unfasten her brassiere and tossed it on a chair, then unzipped her skirt, let it drop to the carpet, kicking it aside, along with her shoes. She could see, from the mirror, that she was naked except for her tight nylon panties. She slipped them down and stepped out of them. In the mirror, she could observe Demski undressing at last. His shirt was off, and his trousers. He was lingering over his polka-dot jock shorts.

"You can sit down again when you're through," she called out.

When she turned fully toward him, he was seated once more. She could not see his penis. Somehow he had covered it with his bare arms crossed over his bare thighs.

Not wishing to make him more self-conscious, she pivoted back to the mirror but could see him from an angle with his eyes wide and fastened on her entire person reflected in the glass.

Well, that was all right, she told herself. He had probably

never before seen a young woman naked in a bright light for so long. It might relax him a little. What surely would relax him more would be her own performance before the mirror. If she did it well, he would become engrossed in watching her and would soon forget that he himself was sitting there naked. He would, if she succeeded, become so entranced by her cool manner while analyzing herself that he would lose any sense of shame. And when his turn came, he might be less petrified.

But now it was her turn, her cue to start this off.

"All right, Adam, this is our body-imaging exercise," she began, facing the full-length mirror squarely.

"My hair," she said, fluffing the short bob. "I rather like it this way, and I like being a brunette. I never wanted to be a real blond and have that kind of pubic hair. There's something insubstantial, lightweight, about being a blond. A nice, cute brunette like me . . . you can always trust someone like me. Remember that, Adam."

In the mirror, she detected the tiniest flicker of amusement about his mouth.

Her forefinger went down to her nose. "Not bad, but not great either. The upturned nose has its point. Pun, Adam, get it? But in truth, it is a little too wide for my own taste. A narrower nose could be more appealing."

Her forefinger moved down to her mouth. "In romance novels, these are called generous lips. And they are. Men seem to like them, like their cushiony softness when they kiss, so I shouldn't complain. As long as you like them, Adam."

"I do, Gayle."

She placed her hands under her breasts. "How about these, without a bra to hold them up more firmly? What do you make of them?"

"They're beautiful," Demski said, a choke in his voice.

Gayle considered her breasts briefly in the mirror. "I don't know. I'm not sure. I always remember when I was a youngster, during puberty, and I had practically no breasts at all. I thought they'd never grow, and I'd be like boys, and boys would never care for me. Well, they finally came along, all right, and there was no question I was a girl, but I was never sure if young men expected and wanted more. I know breasts much smaller than mine look great on fashion models in the fancier women's magazines. But men are not interested in those shapes. They like what they see in men's magazines, the big boobs, the thirty-eights. Well, that's not me, and I'm not sure I'm happy."

"They're beautiful, Gayle," Demski repeated, "to me. Just right."

Her fingers patted her flat, firm stomach.

"No complaints here," she said. "My weight's fine, and I don't even have to diet."

Her hand went lazily down to her thatch of dark pubic hair. "Okay, my vaginal mound and my triangle of pubic hair. I'm somewhat ambivalent about it all, aesthetically. It's full and downy and soft, and I'm frankly pleased about that. Some women I've seen have pubic hair that seems as prickly as steel wool. Mine feels like a tiny pillow of the softest wee feathers. So why am I ambivalent about what I see? I'll tell you why. Maybe you can't see it very well now, but you will certainly see it when you're up closer to me. While my pubic hair seems thick enough all around, it isn't down the middle. It seems to thin out, and therefore you can see—anyway, I can see—my clitoris and, below it, the lips of my outer labia and vulva. I suppose there's not much wrong with it, their being exposed, but somehow I often think I'd like those vital parts kept hidden until someone has the fun of finding them."

Gayle glanced up at the mirror. She could see Demski hypnotized, swallowing, unable to speak.

She reached behind her and tried to grasp her buttocks in both hands.

"Definitely too much of a good thing. Nature was over-abundant here. I don't like to wear a girdle or have any restraints, so my ass is always out there wiggling in the wind. I don't like it. I'm unhappy with it."

After that, Gayle went to her hips, her thighs, her knees, her calves, right down to her toes, doing a commentary all the while.

Done, she wheeled slowly to confront Demski.

"Do you have any remarks to make, Adam?"

"Well, I—" His voice sank out of hearing.

"Come on, Adam . . . Well, what? Give me a break. Speak the truth."

"Uh, I think you have a lovely ass."

"You do?"

"It's not too big. Uh, and the rest—"

"The rest of what?" She could see where his eyes were focused. "You mean my vagina?"

He nodded vigorously. "You—you were being overly critical. You look good to me."

She smiled, pleased. "You're giving me close to a rave review."

"A real rave review," Demski said.

She clapped her hands with undisguised pleasure and walked right up to him. "You're a gentleman, Adam, a gentleman and a scholar." And she bent over him, one breast brushing his face, and kissed him on the forehead. "I thank you."

Then she reached down and gripped both his forearms hard, uncrossing his arms, lifting them away from his crotch, and pulling him to his feet. He recoiled a little, tried to twist away from her, but she held on to him, making him stand directly before her.

"Now, it's your turn to do the body image for me," she said.

Trying to escape her eyes, he half ran nakedly to the full-length mirror, as if to hide in the looking glass away from her, only his unprotected back to her.

Then, trembling, he stood erect before the mirror, and he could see that she had sunk down in his chair, her eyes on the reflection of him in the glass. His arms hung helpless at his sides. There was no hiding from her anymore.

Gayle settled back, never pretending not to look, her green eyes holding on the reflection of him in the mirror.

Not half bad, she thought. Rather tall, too bony and skinny, his ribs showing. Smooth thighs, knobby knees, sturdy legs. But the place she could not help focusing on was the understandable source of his trouble and fear. It *was* small. An inch and a half maybe. What made it seem even smaller were his balls, the bags hanging low and full, like an oversized frame on a mere miniature.

Yet, she felt challenged. It was not impossible, she knew. She was certain that she could make that miniature stand straight up to be counted, one day a source of pride, not shame, to him. She knew that it could happen. He had come to her with what he thought was a toothpick. If she succeeded, he would leave her thinking he was carrying a telephone pole. Yes, if she succeeded. She would try her damnedest to save him.

She hoped she could do it. Starting tonight. Oh, God, she would try.

"Okay, Adam, you saw me body imaging. Please do the same in the mirror for me, starting with the hair on your head."

Demski nodded but remained motionless as he considered himself in the mirror, and the reflection of Gayle in it off to one side. Almost imperceptibly, he changed his stance, leaning more on his left leg, then placing his legs apart. It was as if he were ignoring his shame ever so slightly.

Observing this, Gayle perceived what was on his mind. His attitude of relaxation had come as a sort of surrender. He was utterly naked; he could be seen from head to toe; his problem could be seen. There was nothing to hide anymore. She *knew.* Yet her expression was noncritical, perfectly accepting.

Exhaling, Demski reached for his upper hairline, patted his pompadour, and mumbled something about the fact that at least he had a head of hair. Maybe this was good because it was aesthetically pleasing; at the same time, it was bad because his hair probably deceived some members of the opposite sex into thinking he was virile.

He had no patience for discussing his various facial features, his rather pigeon-breasted chest, his flat but soft abdomen. He mumbled a short sentence or two about each of those areas, and then he did what Gayle had seen other men do when they had his condition. He went straight to the trouble zone.

He pointed down at his penis while watching himself unhappily in the mirror.

"Then there's this," he said a bit loudly. "You can see— no use kidding ourselves—it's too small."

Gayle sat up. "I don't think it's too small," she said decisively. "There's no such thing as too small. Tell me, Adam, tell me exactly what bothers you about it?"

"Like I said, it's too small. Fortunately, it's mostly hidden. I don't want any women to see it. They might laugh at me—or make some cracks about it." Before she could speak, he added, "You know it happened twice."

"I know. But those were exceptional reactions. The two women were expressing their anger against men in general. If one hundred women had seen your penis, I am sure ninety-eight would not have reacted adversely, would have been ready to go ahead with lovemaking."

"I don't think so."

She wanted to shake him. "Adam, you must believe me. I'm a young woman. I've had some experience with different kinds of men. If we undressed together to make love, I would not care if your penis were one inch long or two inches or ten. Anyway, it would more than double or triple in size once you're aroused. You must have seen that when you masturbated. Your size simply wouldn't matter. I would just want to hold you and know it would be all right and know what followed would be pleasurable."

"How could you, when you've seen—"

"Seen what?" she interrupted sarcastically. "I know what's bugging you, and I know you've been completely misled. When you were a kid in grammar school, junior high, high school, even college, wherever, and had to undress with other young men, you were conscious of the difference between your body and theirs. In your eyes, you were frail, puny, and your penis too small, and by contrast, all the others were muscular, hairy, and they all had big penises. And after that, whenever you went to a porno movie or peeled through a men's girlie magazine, all the men that were shown frontally nude had big penises, just as the nude women had big breasts. Because the idiots who cast those characters suspect that most of the ignorant male population equates a large penis with great sex. When, actually, one has nothing to do with the other."

"Doesn't it?" Demski said uncertainly. "Doesn't a female —doesn't she think something big inside her can be—can gratify her more than something small?"

"Adam, the female vagina is built to accommodate almost any size and get pleasure from it. You could put your little finger in my vagina, and my folds would close around your little finger, encompass it, and eventually lubricate it as I enjoy its movement. In the same way, the vagina can absorb and encompass four or five of your fingers. The vagina accommodates all sizes. After all, the vagina makes room for a nine-pound baby to emerge from it and be born. The vagina can handle any size penis and get equal pleasure from it. I speak from my own experiences."

Demski stared at himself in the mirror. "You mean, if I could get it up, it could make a woman happy?" He blinked at her reflection in the mirror. "It could make you happy?"

She smiled. "We'll prove it."

He appeared to be somewhat soothed but not ready yet to leave the subject of his penis and go to the remaining parts of his anatomy.

He wanted to be reassured once more. Gayle was willing. They discussed his penis, his dysfunction, the possibilities of sexual pleasure, for almost ten more minutes.

Gayle wound up by summarizing her thoughts about girlie magazines and their stories again. "Those sexy stories are great for erotic fantasy, but they give you a terrible sex education. In those stories, not only do the heroes have abnormally oversized penises, but once inside a woman, they can keep going all night. An impressionable and uncertain young man reading that nonsense believes it's the truth, and when he tries to emulate those heroes, he can't. So he begins to develop anxiety. I'm sure that's one of the negative things that happened to you."

"I guess maybe it did."

Now, somewhat satisfied, Demski turned back to the full-length mirror and went on to discuss his hips and legs and feet.

After he had finished, he still gave his attention to his penis. She thought that he was regarding it less as an abomination, more as a friendly part of himself.

Gayle came to her feet. "All right," she said. She walked toward him as he turned around to meet her. She knew that he was considering taking hold of her, but she kept her distance.

"Do you want to get dressed now?" she said nicely.

"Not especially." He laughed. His first outright laugh. "Of course, I will," he said, to prove he had been joking.

My God, she thought, handing him his jock shorts, he sounds like a human being at last. Not like a frightened rabbit.

My God.

She wanted to sing.

After Demski had left, somewhat jauntily, Gayle dressed carefully and went outside to her Honda in the driveway.

A half hour later, she had parked in the area allotted them next to the Market Grill, walked cheerfully to the clinic, and was surprised to find the lights on downstairs and upstairs and the front door still open.

Even though the reception desk was unoccupied, Gayle was sure that Freeberg and Suzy Edwards were still at work upstairs. But Gayle's mind was on completing her evening's assignment. She entered one of the recording rooms, removed her jacket, and sat down to prepare a tape for Freeberg on her second session with Adam Demski.

She dictated for twenty minutes and had just finished when the soundproof padded door behind her was pushed open.

Her visitor was Suzy Edwards. "If you're still working . . ." she said apologetically.

"All done," said Gayle.

"Well, if you don't mind, if you have time, Dr. Freeberg wondered if you could come by and see him."

"Only too happy to. One sec, Suzy. Let me reverse this tape and label it. You can transcribe it in the morning."

After Gayle had given the tape cassette to Suzy, she preceded her up the staircase to Dr. Freeberg's office.

It was as if Freeberg had been eagerly awaiting her. He sat tapping the end of a pencil on his desk blotter while he welcomed her with a cheerful hello and gestured her to a chair.

"Let me tell you what this is all about," Freeberg began. "It's about the possibility of your taking on a second patient right now. I know you're busy enough with Mr. Demski, but I wonder if you could take on another patient simultaneously? I could turn this over to one of our new surrogates, but the new case I have in mind is a premature ejaculation one. The very kind of case you had such success with when we were in Arizona. If it's not too much . . ."

Gayle had already made up her mind. She had great pride in her ability to retard premature ejaculation. It would be gratifying to get another lost soul on his feet. And the extra money would help toward her expenses if she were accepted by the Psychology Department at UCLA.

"It's not too much at all," she said briskly. "When do we start?"

"Tomorrow, if possible. It's to be an intensive program. The patient has limited time."

"I'm clear tomorrow afternoon."

"Good. We can have a preliminary meeting with him at nine in the morning. How's that?"

"I'll be here. Can you tell me anything now?"

Freeberg took a sheaf of papers from his desk and shoved it across to Gayle. "There's the case history. You can review it tonight." As she folded the papers and stuffed them into her purse, Freeberg went on. "He's a young writer, a magazine free-lancer named Chet Hunter."

"I don't recognize the name."

"He's still struggling. His dysfunction may be an obstruction to his work."

"I hope I can help. Is he a good writer?"

Freeberg shrugged. "I'd say this one needs some rewriting." More seriously, Freeberg said, "He's a little too fast and anxious. He even wants to hurry through our program, which is not unexpected. While you might move him along at a steady pace, still it wouldn't hurt to slow him down."

"If I can, I'll do it," said Gayle.

"I'm confident," said Freeberg. "At nine o'clock in the morning, Chet Hunter and I will be waiting."

Passing the Market Grill on her way to the parking lot, Gayle decided that she wanted a cup of coffee.

Inside, the restaurant was almost empty. She was about to sit at the counter when she saw someone waving from a booth. Then she recognized that the man signaling her was Paul Brandon. He looked as attractive as he had the last time she had seen him here—in fact, better in his sport jacket and turtleneck sweater—and she made up her mind to join him.

After calling out her coffee order, she strode over to Brandon's booth and slid in across from him.

"How are you, Gayle?" he asked.

"Never better. Busy. Hey, I hear tell that you're busy, too. Freeberg got you a patient. Is that so?"

"Oh, yes. A local lady. Very interesting."

The waitress delivered Gayle's coffee, and Gayle busied herself sweetening it.

Without looking up, Gayle said, "So she's interesting? Well, that's lucky." Gayle paused. "Is she pretty?"

"Not Miss America, but attractive in a plain way. She's rather shy, which lends her a certain charm."

"I see. Have you helped her overcome her shyness?"

"A little, I think." He appeared reluctant to discuss his case. "What about you, Gayle? How's it going with you? I know you have a case."

"Two, in fact." She sipped her coffee.

"Two?" He grimaced. "Isn't that a bit of a load?"

"No, not at all. I can manage. The first one, as you know, is impotency, the tougher of the pair, but we're well on our way. The new one is premature ejaculation. I'm rather good at curing that, if I do say so."

"Two of them?" Brandon repeated. "But how . . . ?"

She laughed. "Not together, silly. I'm going to do them alternately, if possible. There is some pressure, but it's a challenge."

He shook his head. "You're something. I'm barely able to make it with one. But two . . . I don't think I could . . ."

"You're a man," she said. "Ultimately, you have to get it up. So more than one would be asking a lot of you. With women, with me, it's not the same problem."

Brandon had become uncommunicative. Gayle sipped her coffee and tried to guess what was on his mind. Her mention of two male patients had upset him. Was he disapproving? Was he a competitive male before he was a trained surrogate? Could he be regarding her as some kind of chippy? No, that was impossible. Still, men were incredible in their expectations of a woman.

Another thought occurred to her. Could he be jealous?

That was impossible. He hardly knew her. He could not be remotely possessive.

Still, who could tell?

Taking him in once more, Gayle reaffirmed that he was attractive and that she was drawn to him. She wondered what it would be like to be held in his arms. To be embraced by him when both of them were naked.

This was ridiculous, she decided, and too quickly she changed the subject, launching into an account of her application to UCLA for a scholarship. Then she asked him how he was doing subbing as a science teacher.

"Well enough to keep my head above water," he replied.

"You may drown if most of your teaching has to do with sex education classes in the secondary schools. Does it?"

"It does. What do you mean by saying I may go under?"

"There's an evangelist here in Hillsdale—I think his name is Scrafield—who's been on television weekly ranting about sex education in the schools. I caught a bit of his show twice. To me, he was revolting. But maybe, to others, persuasive. He wants to give sex education back to the family."

"Which is like giving evolution back to the Bible," said Brandon. "That guy—Scrafield, you say?—is obviously a nut. I'm not worried about him. Sex education is in the schools to stay. So don't worry about my drowning."

When she'd drained her cup of coffee, she gathered up her purse and check. He tried to take her check from her. She held on to it. "No. This time we go Dutch." She started to rise. "I'd better be going."

"Me, too," he said, standing. "Do you happen to have a car?"

"Next door. Need a lift?"

"If you don't mind," Brandon said. "I should have my own car tomorrow. I bought a nice secondhand Chevy. They're still tuning the motor."

"Well, tonight you can be my guest."

After paying the cashier, they walked silently out to her Honda. She got behind the wheel, and he sat beside her.

"Turn right," he said as they left the parking lot.

He directed her to a five-story apartment building. He pointed at it. "My new digs," he said.

Gayle drew up at the curb near the front door and let her engine idle as he got out, then came around the car to her side.

He opened her door. "Why don't you park it and come up and see my new apartment? It's a nice one. Maybe you'd like to have a look?"

She sat unmoving, her hands on the wheel.

"You're inviting me to come up to your place?" she said.

"Why, yes."

"Then what?"

He was taken aback. "Why, I don't know. We—"

"I know, Paul," she said. "You want to take me to bed."

He stared down at her. "Now that you mention it, not exactly a bad idea. In fact, a very good idea."

He held out his hand for her, but she ignored it.

"Paul," she said, "let's get off on the right foot. First, if I went to your apartment, I'd go to bed with you. I'd want to.

But not tonight. Two reasons. One, I don't want you to think I'm a pushover. Two, I don't think I can handle three men in one week." She closed the door. He leaned toward her, but she said, "And no good-night kiss. That could ruin all my resolve. Let's save something for next time."

"Next time," he said, cherishing the words as if they were pearls.

"Definitely," she said, gunning the engine and then shifting into drive. "Don't call me. I'll call you."

And she and her car were off, as he stood looking after her, his heart beating harder and his person utterly flabbergasted.

V

It was during his interview and discussion with his latest patient, Chet Hunter, and the surrogate assigned to the case, Gayle Miller, that Dr. Freeberg received the unexpected telephone call.

At nine twenty-one in the morning, Freeberg's ICM button on his phone lighted up, and his secretary's voice came on. "Sorry to disturb you, Doctor," said Suzy Edwards, "but I have Mr. Hoyt Lewis, the district attorney of Hillsdale, on the line. He wants to speak to you."

Annoyed by the interruption, Freeberg flipped off the tape recorder and replied, "The district attorney, you say? I have no business I know of with him, and I'm tied up right now. Can't it wait?"

"I'm afraid not, Dr. Freeberg. Mr. Lewis insists on speaking to you. He says it's important."

Freeberg had been glaring at the phone, but then Suzy's message gave him a pause of apprehension. "Well . . ." he said, becoming less resistant. "Okay, Suzy, if it's so important, you might as well put him through." He lifted the receiver, held a palm over the mouthpiece, and apologized to his patient and surrogate. "Excuse me, Mr. Hunter, Gayle. You heard. The district attorney. I suppose I should be respectful."

Hunter and Gayle both indicated their understanding as
Freeberg brought his palm away from the mouthpiece and
drew the receiver closer.

"Hello," he said into the phone. "This is Dr. Freeberg."

"Ah, Dr. Freeberg, glad I could get hold of you," came
the voice from the other end, at once hearty and jovial,
"and sorry to butt in on your busy day. I'm Hoyt Lewis, the
city's district attorney. We've never met, but I've heard of
you."

"I've heard of you, too, Mr. Lewis. What can I do for
you?"

"We need to meet personally, Doctor. It's some local
matter that's come up. Nothing I can go into on the phone.
Just something I want to discuss briefly. The sooner, the
better."

"How soon?"

"Like today, if possible. Even later this morning, before
lunch. Can you make it?"

Freeberg had bent over to examine his calendar and appointments. "I'm just looking to see . . ." He nodded at
the mouthpiece. "Yes, I could schedule a meeting this
morning. I have a heavy work load in the afternoon. But
this morning I'll be clear from eleven o'clock on. Is that
satisfactory?"

"Perfect. Eleven is perfect."

"Where's your office, Mr. Lewis?"

"I'm in city hall," said the district attorney, "but never
mind. I'll just drop by and look in on you."

"Do you know where the clinic is?"

"I know," said the district attorney. "Looking forward."

Hanging up, Freeberg was not certain that he himself
looked forward. But the tone of the district attorney's voice
had carried no sign of urgency, other than the fact that their
meeting had some priority. Freeberg determined to put it
out of his mind for the time being. He cleared his throat,
apologized to Hunter and Gayle once more, and reached
for his notes. He realized that there were no notes because
he had been recording the discussion.

"All right," he said, "let's see where we left off." He

pressed the Rewind button on his tape recorder, then pressed Stop, then Play.

Freeberg heard his voice on the machine. "—so, of course, you may remember, we discussed surrogate therapy at length in our initial talk. You already have an idea of what it is and what it is not. I think you have the picture."

He heard Hunter's voice. "I think so, Doctor."

He heard his own voice again. "Now, the purpose of this session is not only to acquaint you with your actual surrogate, Gayle Miller, who will be working closely with you, but also to review the goal of the therapy, to be specific about it. Essentially, the goal is not just to make you feel better and to do better; it is to make you function better all around. So—"

At this point, Suzy's buzzer and voice on the intercom broke into the tape, and then there was no more on the tape because obviously, just then, Freeberg had shut the recorder off.

Freeberg stopped the machine, pressed two buttons to start it recording again, and swung toward Hunter and Gayle.

"Now we can resume," Freeberg said. "There was one thing I neglected to ask you, Mr. Hunter, in our first session. You felt, I gather, some discontent about your sexual dysfunctioning from the very beginning of any intimate relationship you had with women?"

"That's true," said Hunter.

"I mean, it is a problem that's worried you for a long time? It didn't happen yesterday and make you decide to do something about it? Perhaps it's been eating away at you for many months, even years?"

"At least three years," said Hunter, half addressing himself to Gayle.

She did not appear surprised, and nodded with understanding.

"And each time you tried to be intimate with a woman," said Freeberg, "you were uncomfortable, and your own anxiety continued to sabotage you again and again?" Free-

berg sat straight. "Mr. Hunter, did you feel your dysfunction in any way affected your work?"

Hunter seemed startled. "My work? I'm not sure I know
what you mean."

"You're a writer. You were a writer in New York before
you moved to California. All that time, you had this sexual
problem. Did you feel that this problem interfered with
your concentration, your creativity?"

"It was sure on my mind a lot," Hunter admitted. "I
would be trying to work, but I was also always worrying
about my—my failures."

"These so-called failures," said Freeberg, "did they result in an emotional, even a physical, withdrawal in your
behavior? What I mean is, did you date less often—and
when you dated, avoid intimacy more often—because you
were concerned with not performing?"

Hunter squirmed uneasily. "Well, you have a couple of
questions there . . ."

"I'm sorry. Can you sort them out?"

"Yes. I kept dating women all the time. I wouldn't give
up. But, yeah, you're right about avoiding sex. I mean I did
try, but when I kept ejaculating too soon, I began to stop
testing myself with women. I knew it wasn't going to go
well. After I moved out here, I almost became a celibate.
Not quite, but almost. Then I met a woman . . . and fell
for her. I fell in love with this young woman in Hillsdale. So
I felt that this could be a new start. If you're in love, and
want someone for real, want her so much, it has to go
good." He shook his head sadly. "But it didn't."

Freeberg was sympathetic. "So you wisely decided to do
something about it."

"Not easy," said Hunter.

Gayle, in a kindly tone, spoke to the patient. "In our
society, with all its pressures, your anxieties are fully understandable. However, your problem shouldn't embarrass or
humiliate you. What's happened to you happens to many,
many men every day, but they don't talk to each other about
it because they think they're the only ones suffering, and so
they suffer alone and in silence. Dr. Freeberg has assured

you that you can be cured, and for my part, I can assure you, too."

Hunter had been listening to Gayle with new interest.

Smiling, Freeberg resumed once more. "Now, let's review the design of your therapy, how we're going to work together."

The three-way session went on for another hour, as Freeberg probed into Hunter's background and sexual history and finally determined that Hunter could begin his first meeting with Gayle at her place later that afternoon. Further intensive sessions would continue the following day and the day after, once Freeberg was satisfied with the progress being made.

After dismissing his surrogate and patient, Freeberg was alone. Yet, in a sense, he was not alone. He realized that District Attorney Hoyt Lewis was still with him. He tried to give his latest patient more thought, but then he decided that Gayle was competent enough to handle this kind of case well and he put Hunter out of his mind. He was free to entertain thoughts of the district attorney once more.

On the surface the request for a meeting by Hoyt Lewis seemed sociable enough. Perhaps, Freeberg decided, the district attorney might only want to welcome Freeberg to the community or, more likely, to urge him to join in some community undertaking. But at once, Freeberg knew those ideas were absurd. Because behind the district attorney's seemingly bland approach, there had been a definite insistence on seeing Freeberg immediately.

This was not a social visit, Freeberg decided. Instinctively, as if seeking a refresher on his work, Freeberg reached down to the bottom drawer of his desk where he kept research notes for a paper he had long been preparing, and putting off, on the evolution of sexual therapy and the changes that had been wrought in the profession since the pioneering days of Masters and Johnson.

He was soon absorbed in reviewing his notes, and the next time he looked at his desk clock, it was nine minutes to eleven. Hastily, Freeberg pushed his notes aside and went to the bathroom. He washed up, dousing his face with cold water to make himself as alert as possible.

At eleven o'clock he was once more at his desk and ready for anything.

District Attorney Hoyt Lewis arrived at five minutes after eleven, and he was not by himself. Lewis, a large man sartorially impeccable except for a disconcerting string tie, pumped Freeberg's hand vigorously and then introduced the much smaller man who was accompanying him.

"Dr. Freeberg," said Lewis, "I hope you don't mind my bringing along an old friend and consultant, Dr. Elliot Ogelthorpe, from the University of Virginia, who heads up their Sex Education Department. He happened to be in town . . ."

"Not at all," said Freeberg, shaking Ogelthorpe's hand. "Pleased to meet you." Freeberg was not pleased at all. Not only did he dislike Ogelthorpe's appearance—he had beady eyes, an unsmiling mouth, a sharp affected Van Dyke beard (which made Freeberg ashamed of his own scruffy beard)—but he disliked the man for his reputation. "I've read your articles in medical journals," said Freeberg, "including your recent one on partner surrogates, 'The Newest Old Profession,' so I can say I know your work quite well."

"And I know yours," said Ogelthorpe, with no trace of friendliness.

Freeberg directed both of them to chairs across from his desk. As Hoyt Lewis took his seat, he was still assuming an air of sociability. "Normally," said Lewis, "when I meet someone on business, I like to invite him to my office in the city hall." He laughed. "It's more intimidating. But actually, today, I thought I'd stroll over and have a look at your clinic before seeing you. Very nice."

Freeberg still clung to Lewis's usage of the word "business." If the district attorney had a business meeting in mind, it could be ominous. "Glad you like our little place here," Freeberg said. "It's all new, and I'm rather proud of it." He suspected that Lewis had come here to look the place over—To look for what? Orgies?—and had been disappointed.

Freeberg waited in silence for what might be next.

The district attorney wet his lips with his tongue, straightened up, and dropped his air of sociability. He was plainly all business now. "I'm sure you're puzzled as to why I'm here . . . and why I wanted to see you as soon as possible."

Freeberg tried unsuccessfully to smile. "I gave it a passing thought."

"Dr. Freeberg, since you've settled down in Hillsdale," said Hoyt Lewis, "something of your activity has been brought to my attention by—well, by respected members of this community."

"My activity?" said Freeberg mildly.

"Yes, your work as a sex therapist, a perfectly honorable profession, and your use of sex surrogates . . . engaged in a somewhat more questionable profession. This has been brought to my attention and has forced me to look into the work that you and your hired surrogates do. I've done some extensive preliminary research."

"What have you found out, Mr. Lewis?" Freeberg asked quietly.

"That you may be involved, quite innocently, in an activity that is illegal, perhaps even criminal. I have been investigating the possibility that as a sex therapist you may be engaged in pandering and your sex surrogates may be involved in what might be construed as nothing more than prostitution."

"Oh, come on now," Freeberg objected, trying to make light of the accusation, "we're living in modern times, in the progressive state of California—"

"Ah, California," interrupted Lewis, fumbling in his jacket pocket for a piece of paper, which he then unfolded. "Let me tell you something about the law of California, which, as a newcomer, you may not know. California has two statutes on its books that specifically prohibit the work you and your associates are doing." He consulted the sheet of paper in his hands. "Here's a mention of 'pandering.' This means any action in which one person procures and provides another person for the purpose of prostitution." He looked up. "By sending sex surrogates out to work for you, there is little doubt that you are engaged in pandering. That, Dr. Freeberg, is against the law in California and in fifty states of this Union. It is a felony."

Freeberg started to speak, but Hoyt Lewis held up a hand to silence him and consulted his sheet of paper again. "And here we have 'disorderly conduct.' Meaning, a person who takes part in an act of prostitution, which includes any lewd act between persons for money or other consideration. That, too, is against the law in California, and a misdemeanor."

Freeberg felt his cheeks flush, and he tried to contain himself. "You haven't defined 'prostitution' yet, Mr. Lewis."

The district attorney was back to his sheet of paper. " 'Prostitution,' " he murmured, "meaning someone involved in professional sexual relations, especially for money." He looked up. "A prostitute is commonly declared to be a woman who engages in promiscuous sexual intercourse, especially for money. There you have it all. And from my investigation, it appears you are perilously close to, or totally engaged in, the practice of procuring women to engage in lewd acts with members of the opposite sex and to hire themselves out as prostitutes for pay. Now then—"

"One second, Mr. Lewis," Freeberg broke in. "Can we discuss this matter?"

"The very reason I'm here," said Lewis. "To discuss your activity and then to put you on warning."

"First, can we talk about the matter?"

"Absolutely."

"Because," said Freeberg, "you may have been misled in your researches and misinformed in your investigation. May I clarify a few things for you?"

"Go right ahead."

Trying to control himself, Freeberg began, "I think it is

essential that you know the vast difference that separates the prostitute from the sex surrogate."

"From my understanding of it, they are one and the same," said Lewis.

"Please, let me go on," Freeberg persisted. "After all, your understanding of what a prostitute is and what a sex surrogate is may be totally incorrect."

Hoyt Lewis shifted his bulk in his chair. "Very well, Dr. Freeberg. I'm listening."

"All right," Freeberg said, "let's start with this. Your average general practitioner in this country or any country knows very little about sexual problems, unless the problems involve something organically wrong with a patient. So whenever a man, young or old, has had a sexual problem, he's found it hopeless to consult his family doctor. If he was properly directed, he went eventually to some kind of specialized consultant—a psychiatrist, a trained therapist in sexual matters—and he tried to get to the root of his problem by talking it out. But early on, we began to learn that talk was not enough. As one psychologist pointed out, 'Sex is action, not talk,' and effective therapy had to be based on action. The first men of science to comprehend the necessity for something more than talk were Dr. Joseph Wolpe, who suggested that sexual partners be recruited to help the sexually disabled, and Arnold Lazarus, a Ph.D., who felt that sexual partners were 'necessary' to get anywhere with sexually dysfunctional males. But Masters and Johnson were the ones who actually coined the words 'sex surrogate' or 'partner surrogate' and put these so-called fantasy wives or lovers into their rehabilitation program. Now, Masters and Johnson—"

"Dr. Freeberg," the district attorney cut in, "if you're going to talk about Masters and Johnson, you'd better include my friend Dr. Ogelthorpe in your discussion. As you know from your reading, he's an expert on Masters and Johnson."

"I'm including you in all of this, of course," said Freeberg to the district attorney's companion.

"Then I have something to say to you," Ogelthorpe be-

gan, "and I think it should be said right up front. Masters
and Johnson saw from the very moment they got into this
therapy that prostitutes, real prostitutes, would make excellent surrogates and used them as such."

"Not true," Freeberg answered sharply. "You're distorting the facts."

"Am I?" snapped Ogelthorpe.

"Please allow me the floor," Freeberg demanded.

Dr. Ogelthorpe fell silent.

"I'll give you the facts about Masters and Johnson and
prostitutes. They never, not once, used a prostitute as an
actual sex surrogate. What happened was this: In 1954,
Masters, through movies and observation of seven hundred
persons, undertook research to learn what happens physio-
logically to the human body before, during, and after coitus
and orgasm. To accomplish this study, he needed female
subjects. So at the outset, he hired prostitutes. This proved
ineffective because the anatomies and responses of prostitutes were not like those of other women. So he dropped
prostitutes and used female volunteers from the Washington University School of Medicine to be observed and pho-
tographed. Then, after Johnson joined him, for their next
researches, they decided to study the usefulness of female
sex surrogates in therapy."

Hoyt Lewis stopped Freeberg. "Are you saying that Masters and Johnson never employed prostitutes as sex surrogates?"

"Never, not ever as sex surrogates," Freeberg told him
emphatically as he thumbed through his research notes. He
held up a piece of paper. "Allow me to have William Masters speak for himself on this matter." He read from his
paper, quoting Masters. " 'It should be emphasized that no
thought was ever given to employing the prostitute population [as surrogates] . . . . So much more is needed and
demanded from a substitute partner than effectiveness of
purely physical sexual performance that to use prostitutes
would have been at best clinically unsuccessful and at worst
psychologically disastrous.' " Freeberg put down his paper.
"So Masters and Johnson asked for ordinary women to

volunteer as sex surrogates. After careful screening, they found thirteen women from the ages of twenty-four to forty-three to work as their sex surrogates."

"And these women," Lewis reiterated, "were not prostitutes, although they performed the same role as common whores do?"

"Not really, not at all," replied Freeberg strongly. "A prostitute is in business to give a man quick gratification sexually. A sex surrogate—in Masters and Johnson's program, and in our own, as you must know—is anything but a sexual athlete. Her task is to rehabilitate an ailing patient. A surrogate is trained and employed to be a therapist's aide, as well as an observer, reporter, role model. In her relationship with a patient, the surrogate—through a series of touching and caressing exercises—tries to help a patient learn how to experience human intimacy. And it works. In the eleven years during which Masters and Johnson treated fifty-four unmarried men with sexual disorders, forty-one of them received help from trained sex surrogates. Of the forty-one men so treated, thirty-two had their sexual problems solved by use of surrogates, and twenty-four of them subsequently married and performed successfully."

Dr. Ogelthorpe interrupted once more. "How do we know that to be a fact?" he demanded. "How do we know that Masters and Johnson patients were actually cured after being discharged from the clinic? I'm told that Masters and Johnson did sloppy follow-ups on their so-called successful cures, merely getting in touch with each of their subjects five years later—and then only by telephone. Do you regard this kind of follow-up as scientific?"

Freeberg smiled. "In that regard, permit me to quote the words of William Hartman, a renowned psychologist at the Center for Marital and Sexual Studies in Long Beach, California. When asked about obtaining follow-up data on former patients, Hartman countered with this question: 'When was the last time a doctor ever called you back two years later to ask if you're still cured of that flu?' "

In response, District Attorney Lewis chuckled good-naturedly, but his companion, Dr. Ogelthorpe, remained unamused. "Let's stick to Masters and Johnson," said Ogelthorpe. "You won't deny one fact. Masters and Johnson gave up the use of sex surrogates in 1970."

"True," Freeberg admitted, "but not because sex surrogates had proved ineffective. A gentleman named George E. Calvert, in New Hampshire, sued Masters and Johnson for a million and a half dollars on the grounds that his wife, Barbara, had gone to work for them as a sex surrogate and had sexual intimacy with seven male patients. Masters and Johnson settled with her husband out of court and, after that, gave up the use of sex surrogates altogether. Because they were so famous, they were more vulnerable than other sex therapists, and there was always the possibility of further legal harassment. Without sex surrogates, Masters confessed, 'The success statistics with single impotent males have completely reversed. We now have a failure rate of 70% to 75%.' However, with this knowledge of the value of sex surrogates, dozens of therapists, myself included, continue to train them and use them in our work."

District Attorney Lewis was becoming restless. "Gentlemen, let's stop this quibbling about Masters and Johnson. They are not primarily at issue here. Our main concern is the female sex surrogate. And to me, any female sex surrogate sounds exactly like a prostitute. I see no difference."

They had come to the heart of the conflict, and Freeberg became more intense, more determined to resolve this, as he addressed the district attorney directly. "Mr. Lewis, there are major differences, believe me. The sex surrogate is guided by a licensed therapist who monitors her regularly. The prostitute is not. The sex surrogate is trained in the use of beneficial exercises involving touch. The prostitute is not. The sex surrogate is motivated by a professional desire to help a dysfunctional patient, to cure him. The prostitute is motivated only to make money, a quick buck, nothing else. The sex surrogate usually comes from a family that has at least one compassionate and loving parent. The prostitute usually comes from a devastated family, one filled with hate and abuse. The sex surrogate devotes herself to one patient as a teacher for a long period of time.

The prostitute gives herself to an endless number of men in a short period, because she's seeking a quick turnover, is interested in bringing in as much money as possible. As Barbara Roberts, the well-known therapist, once summed it up, 'Most surrogates would make very poor prostitutes and, because they haven't had training and their motivation is different, most prostitutes would make poor surrogates.' "

District Attorney Lewis placed the palms of both his hands on his knees and gazed directly back at Freeberg. "Well spoken, Doctor," he said, "but I'm afraid I'm still not convinced as to the essential difference between the prostitute and the sex surrogate."

"The essential difference?" repeated Freeberg. "Meaning what?"

"Meaning they both have the same basic function. It comes down to this, Dr. Freeberg. Let me use the language of the streets. They are both hired and paid to fuck."

Freeberg tried to remain calm. "Let me reply in kind in the argot of the streets. The prostitute's attitude is: get it in, get it off, then get away. Generally, the prostitute is not someone her partner cares about. The sexual surrogate, on the other hand, is not just an available vagina that offers relief or release. The surrogate is a professional friend skilled at making a man comfortable with his body. She's someone who can revive his ability to be a sensual being, a feeling he probably lost through his upbringing and conditioning. Let me put it another way, Mr. Lewis. The difference comes down to a matter of motivation and purpose. It's the difference you'll find between a surgeon and a mugger. A surgeon will use a knife to cut you, but his intent is to heal you. A mugger will also use a knife to cut you, but his intent is to steal your money."

The district attorney wrinkled his nose. "I still don't see any real difference between a prostitute and a surrogate. To me, when you come right down to it, they're one and the same thing, performing in the same way."

"You couldn't be more wrong," Freeberg protested. "The prostitute devotes herself totally to lewd acts and sexual intercourse. The sex surrogate may—just may—devote the last one or two of her twelve exercises to actual intercourse, to prove a cure has taken place. Less than twenty percent of a surrogate's activity with a man involves sexual intercourse. I assure you, sir, the surrogate is not a hooker."

"We may have to let a court of law determine that," announced Hoyt Lewis, coming to his feet with a wheeze. "Anyway, I'm not here to threaten you with arrest. At least, not yet. I'm here because I'm a nice guy, because you're new to this community, because even though you are misguided you mean well, and because I'd like to give you a chance to straighten yourself out. I'm here to propose to you exactly what the city attorney in Tucson, Arizona, proposed to you, before you decided to skip town. I'm advising you to give up totally the use of sex surrogates for hire and to go back to being a good, decent talk therapist, like all those psychiatrists around. Do that, and you're performing within the law and perfectly safe. But first you've got to drop your surrogates."

Freeberg rose from his chair unsteadily. "Drop them all? You mean that?"

"If you refuse to cease and desist in their use at once, I will have no choice but to prosecute you for pandering, and your sex surrogates for prostitution. On the first charge, if convicted, you would be liable to serve one to ten years in prison. On the second, your surrogates could wind up with six months in jail. In either case, you'd be out of business in Hillsdale and anywhere else in California. I repeat, I am serious about this. Give up your antisocial practices or suffer the grave consequences. If you resist this compromise, I will have you and your surrogates arrested and arraigned in municipal court. This will lead to a public hearing, and eventually to a public trial sixty days later. I suggest you decide which route you prefer to take. Let's say, within a week. During that time, you or your attorney can inform me of your decision. Understood?"

Freeberg nodded.

Taking Dr. Ogelthorpe by the arm, the district attorney

started for the door. At the door, he called out over his shoulder, "Thank you for your patience. I hope you make a wise choice."

Once the pair had gone, and Freeberg was certain that they had left, he lowered himself heavily into his swivel chair and turned it toward the telephone.

Rattled, he tried to remember the telephone number of his old friend and attorney, Roger Kile, in Los Angeles. Recalling the number, he dialed directly to Kile's office.

Getting Kile's secretary on the phone, he told her he had to speak to Mr. Kile at once on an emergency matter.

"Mr. Kile was just leaving for lunch," the secretary said, "but I think I can still catch him in the hall."

"Please do. Please tell him it's Dr. Arnold Freeberg."

He held the receiver listlessly until he heard Roger Kile on the phone.

"Roger? Arnold here. Hate to cut into your lunch, but I'm afraid it's a matter of some importance."

"No trouble at all, Arnie," Kile said. "Hey, you sound a bit agitated."

"Because I am," admitted Freeberg. "I'm afraid I'm in trouble again, believe it or not."

"What kind of trouble?"

"The district attorney of Hillsdale, Hoyt Lewis, just left my office. It was hardly a social call."

"Trouble, you said. What did the D.A. want with you?"

"If you've got a few minutes . . ."

"I've got as much time as you need. Go ahead, tell me what this is all about."

Freeberg told him. For over ten minutes, he recounted what he could remember of Hoyt Lewis's visit, his threat, his compromise offer.

"There you have it," Freeberg concluded. "What do I do? Looks like he's got me up against the wall."

"Hold it, Arnie. Not so fast. There can be a lot more to this before any decision is made."

"But why is this going on, Roger? In California yet? It doesn't make sense. What's up?"

There was silence on the other end for a few moments. At last Kile spoke one word. "Politics," he said.

"Politics?"

"Nothing less," Kile said. "I've never met your D.A., but I've heard of him, even in Los Angeles. He's popular, and he wants to be more popular. My guess is that he's on the make. Upwardly mobile. He wants to be known statewide, and zeroing in on you and the sex surrogate is a perfect case to capture media attention. He could become quite well known, even land himself a bigger job, if he could win this one."

"Sounds to me like he can win this one."

"Not so fast, Arnie. It could be lots more than just another criminal case. It can have far-reaching legal consequences. There are many ramifications."

"Can I possibly fight him?" Freeberg pleaded. "Do I even have a chance?"

"We'll see," said Kile. "I'm going to look into all aspects of the matter. Do a little research on my own. Before you hang up, I want you to give my secretary a list of qualified persons—doctors, therapists, surrogates you know and trust, persons who won't mind answering questions and giving me the information I need. Okay?"

"Okay."

"Once I have the names from you, I'll spend this afternoon and evening, as well as tomorrow morning and afternoon, talking to them, in person or on the phone. I should have everything in hand before tomorrow night. Then you and I can get together on this."

"When?"

"Soon as possible, of course. I should be ready for you by early tomorrow evening. To give me more time, why don't you drive into Los Angeles? Say, meet me at La Scala in Beverly Hills at seven o'clock. It's a nice, quiet, classy restaurant where we can talk and thrash this out."

"I'll be there," promised Freeberg. "You'll be ready to tell me what to do at dinner?"

"I think so."

"You think I have a fighting chance, Roger?"

"I don't know yet. But I should know when I see you tomorrow evening."

The following evening the two of them were seated in a striped brocade and velvet padded booth, fairly private, in the rear of La Scala Restaurant on a street known as "Little" Santa Monica Boulevard.

Driving down the coast to Beverly Hills to meet with his attorney friend, Dr. Arnold Freeberg had been nervous and obsessed with the threat hanging over him. If the district attorney, as Kile had suggested earlier, was determined to use Freeberg and his surrogates as a stepping stone to advance his political career, there would be little hope that he could be stopped. He would certainly prosecute. Yet, there had been a fair amount of give in his attitude. He had met with Freeberg yesterday to put him on warning, to give him a chance to retreat on the surrogate matter and to withdraw treatment. Had Hoyt Lewis been more hard-nosed and opportunistic and ambitious about his career, he would not have bothered to put Freeberg on warning. He would have just proceeded against him.

Yet, Freeberg had seen, there was no recklessness in Lewis's behavior. He would not undertake a legal action unless he was almost certain that he could win it. He was no fool. In politics, you had to win. A no-win case would get him nowhere. So it all came down to what Kile had been researching since yesterday, and his findings would guide them in making the final decision. If Kile decided that Lewis had a strong case, and Freeberg a weak one, then Freeberg would have to shut up shop in Hillsdale, and the aftermath would be that he'd have nowhere else to go in California. True, he could still retain his clinic, and work as one more less-than-effective sex therapist, and somehow survive, but it would be sad, very sad, to deny so many decent, needy persons a positive cure.

In their booth in La Scala, they were both drinking martinis, the subject of their meeting still unvoiced.

"I really did a lot of running around yesterday and to-

day," Kile had stated at the outset. "I'm bushed. Let's have
a pick-me-up drink first, then order, and after that, we can
talk."

They drank and talked about personal matters. Freeberg
discussed his wife and son. Kile, a bachelor, with the regular features and jutting jaw of a virile male featured in
cigarette ads, discussed a new girlfriend, a buyer at Saks,
and some corporate cases his office had undertaken. During this delaying action, the Caesar salad they had ordered
came and was served. As Roger Kile finished his salad, he
reached down to the side of the booth, hoisted his briefcase
onto the seat, and rummaged inside until he had found a
dozen or so file cards. He placed them beside his butter
plate, but before he could consult them, his breaded veal
cutlet was served and Freeberg's dish of spaghetti carbo-
nara was set down before him. Once the waiter had left
them alone, Kile took up his file cards.

"Okay, Arnie, let's get right into priority A," said Kile.
"You gave me a good list of persons to telephone and visit.
Each one was cooperative when they heard you were in-
volved and what Lewis was threatening."

"You told them?"

"Why not?" said Kile. "The medical experts and surrogates you sent me to are themselves threatened if you are
threatened. They all have a stake in what's happening to
you. They were, every one of them, indignant, then helpful."

Freeberg poked at his heap of spaghetti. "How helpful,
Roger?"

"Well, for one thing, I learned a lot more about what you
do," said Kile. He sliced into his veal and began to munch
the pieces. "It's clear to me that a female sex surrogate in
no way functions like a prostitute."

"Didn't you know that already?"

"I had to hear it again from someone else, from others
with expertise who were not immediately involved. Yes, I
have no doubt that a professional sex surrogate possesses
motivation and attitudes quite different from the average
prostitute's. And a sex surrogate's goals are vastly different

from those of a prostitute. A sex surrogate wants to repair her patients, and she feels she has succeeded only when her patient can make it normally with other women."

"Roger, I told all that to Hoyt Lewis yesterday," Freeberg said impatiently.

Kile ignored him. Chewing his veal steadily, Kile was going through his file cards once more. "You've got a lot of people on your side, no doubt about that. Here's a statement by the head of the Human Resource Developers Clinic in Chicago . . ."

"Dr. Dean Dauw," said Freeberg.

"Yes, Dauw. He says flatly, 'In no way are surrogates prostitutes . . . If a man is impotent and unmarried, how can he be treated without the help of a woman? She has to be someone who cares about helping people—but definitely not a prostitute. Prostitutes often hate men and are motivated by money.' I like that."

"It's true."

"At the same time," Kile continued, "there are an awful lot of experts, therapists, psychiatrists, not on your side. They feel, by and large, that sex surrogates are ill-trained and unregulated. And also, generally, under a constant legal cloud because their profession is so undefined. Here we have the Massachusetts Psychological Association banning the use of surrogates altogether, and for the reasons given." He shuffled through his cards. "Many therapists tend to quibble somewhat. Like Dr. Helen Kaplan, director of a sex therapy program at New York Hospital's Payne Whitney Clinic."

"She's highly respected," said Freeberg.

"Well, she seems to be on both sides—but less on your side. She says, 'Lonely people can be helped by surrogates, but I would try to work in psychotherapy to figure out why the person is so lonely. We have to get humanity and eroticism back into bed. You can't do that if you pay someone a hundred dollars to go to bed with you.' "

"Is that helpful to me or to our district attorney friend?"

Kile put aside his cards, then smiled. "I'm sure Hoyt Lewis will use stronger stuff against you, if he has to." Kile was thoughtful a moment, as if remembering something else. "There's one more factor weighted against you, Arnie. The judiciary, it seems, has an unspoken prejudice against sex surrogates."

"What do you mean?"

"I mean this. I was talking to a fellow attorney who had handled a divorce case in Burbank. My friend was representing the wife, a mother of two children, whom she had in her custody during the action. Somehow, her estranged husband learned that his soon-to-be ex-wife was doing part-time work as a sex surrogate, even though she did none of her work at home or near the children. The husband contacted his lawyer, who went straight to a judge to get an ex parte order, one without a full hearing, and the judge immediately took custody of the children away from the wife and gave it over to the husband. My lawyer friend and I felt that was a poor judicial decision, but it did show that out in the real world you don't always get good judicial practice or even legal fairness."

"You're not making me feel good," mumbled Freeberg.

"I'm just trying to tell you that some prejudice does exist."

"Roger, why don't you get down to it?" Freeberg shoved his plate of spaghetti away from him. "Where do I stand?"

"That's next on the agenda. I was right about what I guessed while talking to you on the phone. This is a political matter. Hoyt Lewis is looking for the main chance. He thinks he's found it. He has some powerful people in back of him, promoting him, no doubt urging him to proceed against you."

"Who are they?" Freeberg wanted to know.

"The best known is a prominent clergyman, the Reverend Josh Scrafield, who's against all sex education in schools and thinks a sex therapist like yourself can contaminate his fair community. We get him on the tube here in L.A. He does a big number."

"That yo-yo," Freeberg said with disgust. "Surely Lewis isn't taking him seriously?"

"I'd guess seriously in only a political sense. Scrafield

knows how to win friends and influence people. He has a tremendous audience to whom his word is gospel. Nice person to have in your corner if you want to get ahead."

Freeberg nodded unhappily. "So what does that add up to?"

"Those are intangibles," said Kile. "The only tangible to consider is the law."

"I gather."

"The law in California is very specific in defining the crimes of pandering and prostitution. But there is no hint of anything about sex surrogates. There we are in muddy waters. In certain states, like Connecticut and Arizona, any sexual interaction for pay is prostitution. But not in California. Sex surrogates are not against the law here. Nor are they specifically permitted, either. Surrogates are not licensed. If they were, that would be of help. You know, Arnie, doctors and psychologists are licensed here. If Hoyt Lewis makes that point—that sex surrogates are treating disorders and therefore practicing medicine, or performing as psychologists, without license—he would have a stronger case. Although, actually, since both medicine and psychology are so broadly defined, that point might not be meaningful if used against surrogates. Besides, railing against unlicensed practitioners is pretty dull stuff. It's nothing to capture the public eye. Pandering and prostitution are other matters, and that's why Lewis settled on them."

"So where am I?" Freeberg pleaded. "Tell me where I am."

"We've come to the crux of it, and in my opinion, you are on the safe side," Kile informed him without hesitation. "The law defines prostitution as 'any lewd act between persons for money.' Yet a trained sex surrogate, advised by a licensed expert in mental health like yourself, should not be liable to a charge of prostitution. Your surrogate could present in court real solid evidence of her intent and work. She could show documents, plans, programs, notes, all kinds of actual records to prove that she is engaged in legitimate therapy—and not in performing a 'lewd act' for money. She could prove that she is simply an adjunct to acceptable talk therapy."

Behind his spectacles, Freeberg's eyes had widened. "You mean the law is really on my side?"

Kile smiled. "No question in my mind. The law prohibits promiscuous conduct. The intent of the law is clearly to prevent commercialized vice, which could damage individuals, families, society. I don't see any of that in a sex surrogate's activities. The surrogate's intent is to rehabilitate suffering persons from clinically diagnosed sexual dysfunctions. The work includes no promiscuous conduct whatsoever. The surrogate's work is meant to be physically, emotionally, and economically constructive for individuals, families, society." He paused. "In short, my friend, the district attorney doesn't have much of a case at all. In my judgment, he has a weak one at best. You have a better case, and so do I on your behalf."

"You mean that?"

"I certainly do. Lewis can't go to court successfully without some real eyewitnesses to lewd behavior performed by your surrogates. Where's Lewis going to get those witnesses? You have a limited circle of surrogates working under your careful supervision, and a small number of patients you've thoroughly screened, and not one of them would ever consider defecting to the district attorney's side to land you and one of the surrogates in the slammer. Every possible witness is on your side."

"I'm sure of that."

Kile opened his hands and gave a confident shrug. "There you are, then. I'd say you're home free."

Freeberg's face had brightened, and the cords of tension standing out on his neck had relaxed. "You mean I can go on like before?"

"Not like before, but work even harder at it. Keep up with the surrogates. Take on more and more patients. Accumulate and build up bigger success statistics. If Lewis is ever fool enough to take us to court, you'll have this wonderful evidence to present. Actually, I think we'll want Lewis to learn of your success record sooner than that, in due time along the way. Knowledge of your work successes will probably give him pause—and probably prevent him from taking you to court."

"How do I handle Hoyt Lewis? I'm supposed to give him my decision within a week."

"You give him nothing. I'll take over with him from here. I'll let him stew up to the last minute while I sit on my hands. Then I'll phone him or call on him. Tell him to do what he wants to do but that he doesn't have a chance. You are proceeding with your practice."

"Doesn't he?"

"Doesn't he what?"

"Have a chance?"

Kile shrugged again. "I don't think so, but who knows? In American justice, there are usually two sides. Sometimes the weaker side can luck out. But if I were you, I'd go right ahead as if nothing had ever happened. No need to worry your surrogates about this. Just go right ahead . . . Now, Arnie, I recommend their chocolate sundaes here for dessert. The topping is like a celebration."

Even as she stood fully dressed outside the shower in her bathroom and reached in to test the spray with one hand to feel if it was warm enough for their next exercise, Gayle Miller's mind was not on Adam Demski undressing in the therapy room but on her brief meeting with Dr. Freeberg early this afternoon.

Freeberg had summoned her to review Demski's case again. This was odd because there had been thorough discussions of it before and after every session with Demski. Still, compulsively, Freeberg wanted to go into it all again, as if to be certain it was progressing successfully.

"So, anyway, you feel he's a little more comfortable about being unclothed?" Freeberg had asked.

"The first time, before the body imaging, he was reluctant, definitely uptight," Gayle had replied. "But he managed it and even seemed to relax a little. When he had to undress for the back caress day before yesterday, I thought there would be some difficulty, but he went through with it and he was considerably more at ease during the exercise."

Freeberg bent over his open folder. "Gayle . . ."

"Yes?"

"Any indication of some erectile movement?"

"None whatsoever, Doctor. Continues flaccid." She had paused. "Maybe it's too early."

"You're probably right," Freeberg had agreed. "What's next on the agenda? It's the shower nude, isn't it?"

"Correct. Later this afternoon."

Freeberg's gaze had fixed on her. "Don't get me wrong, Gayle. I don't want to rush this case. I'm only trying to say I want you to keep going with him at a reasonable but steady pace. The most important factor is the result. I'm hoping for a real success with this one." He had hesitated. "It would get us off to a good start in the clinic."

"I'll do my very best, Doctor."

Thinking back on that, her hand adjusting the shower's hot and cold knobs, she still sensed a feeling of pressure from Freeberg. He wanted the case to move along fast yet thoroughly. Above all, and this was the first time he had ever spoken to her about a result, he wanted the treatment of Demski to be successful. It seemed a needless request, and she wondered why it had been emphasized. She speculated on what was going on in Freeberg's life. Was he himself under some kind of pressure—either to prove himself or to put down some anticipated competition?

And the question about Demski's erectile progress. That definitely was tied up with the need for success. Never before had Freeberg posed the question this early in the exercises.

The shower spray was just right. Warm and lovely. She decided to put Freeberg out of her mind and concentrate on the exercise at hand. In the bathroom, she undressed herself until she was nude, then walked into the hall to the rear therapy room. Adam Demski was seated in a chair naked, browsing through a magazine. She was pleased to note that neither his hands nor the magazine covered his penis. It drooped there between his legs, to be seen, and his posture indicated that he was less shy with her. She felt good about that. Maybe they were getting somewhere.

He raised his head after her entrance and did not take his eyes from her body. "You're—you're darn beautiful, Gayle."

"I like compliments." She held out her hand. "Now, come with me."

He put down the magazine and came to his feet, taking her hand. "Where to?"

"We're going to the bathroom to take a sensuous shower together."

"But I took a shower this morning."

"This one will be different—you'll see. It's really a body caress standing up, using soap and water. After we're done, we'll dry ourselves, go to the therapy room again, and we'll do another back and overall caress with each other, head to heels. How does that sound?"

"Sounds fine," Demski said.

"Let's go," Gayle said, leading him into the hallway and then into the bathroom. Releasing his hands, she reached over to turn her white radio on to an FM station. The music was lazy and soft, maybe 1940s music when couples danced close together.

"I like the music," Demski said. "Now what do we do?"

Gayle opened the glass shower door. "You can see I have the water ready for us. It's warm. We're going to step in under the spray and face each other. Once we're wet, I want you to take the bar of soap and run it over me, really get me as soapy as you can. Then start caressing me, but no breasts or genitals. Try to keep your eyes closed, unless you want to see where your hands are. My eyes will be closed. I'll probably talk some in order to direct you. You soap me front and back, and then I'll do the same to you."

"The idea is to feel good?"

"The idea is to enjoy. Don't speak at any time unless you want to tell me something's bothering you or you're uncomfortable."

"All right."

"I repeat, the idea is to enjoy yourself, to get in closer

touch with your feelings. To let yourself go and daydream
creatively. This can be sensuous, even fairly erotic. Trying
to feel the sensuality of your touch and then mine. Let's
step inside."

They were in the shower, then under it. The spray was
deliciously warm.

Gayle handed Demski a bar of soap and stepped back
slightly. "Do you feel comfortable?" Gayle asked.

"I'm relaxed."

"So am I," said Gayle. "Why don't you soap me up?
Throat, shoulders, arms, hands, my thighs and legs."

"I'll have to keep my eyes open to see where—"

"That's all right," Gayle said. "But keep them closed
when you can."

As the music wafted in, he began to slide the soap across
her features and parts of her body, careful not to go near
her breasts or vagina.

Gayle's eyes were closed as he continued soaping her.
"Okay, Adam," she told him softly, "now put away the soap
and use your hands to caress and stroke me lightly, front
and back."

He followed her instructions, and his fingertips moved
across her upper and lower body, and involuntarily Gayle
sighed. "Nice, Adam, very nice."

After nearly ten minutes, she opened her eyes.

"Give me the soap," she said. "Now it's my turn to soap
and caress you. Close your eyes. No talk. Let your mind
float. You're in a harem with a thousand fingers fluttering
over you. Let your mind go. Remember, it's supposed to be
sensuous, and whatever sensations you get, I hope they're
good and you enjoy them. Turn around. Let me start with
your back."

He turned around under the spray, and she moved close
to him, absorbing the gentle warmth of the water, running
the bar of soap over his neck, shoulders, back, and buttocks
until his skin was foamy. With a free hand in the white
bubbles of foam, she massaged him gently.

After a while she guided him around until he was facing
her. Close to him, she soaped his chest, arms, hips, thighs,

legs. Then putting away the bar, she immersed both her hands in the foam and made circular motions with them, and then long strokes with her fingers until the shower spray had washed all the soap away.

She stepped nearer to him, her hands gliding down to his thighs once more, and then sliding along the inside of his thighs, her fingers going up and down on his wet skin.

Opening her eyes, to be sure she didn't touch his genitals, she saw something move.

Her eyes widened.

His small penis had filled a little, definitely swollen a bit, risen an inch or two from his crotch.

Resurrection, she wanted to cry out.

She was thrilled.

And Dr. Freeberg, she couldn't wait to tell him. Whether he showed it or not, he would be thrilled, too. For the first time, she could see a light at the end of the tunnel. It shone on one word in the distance. The word was: success.

Unable to contain herself over her achievement, Gayle impulsively stepped forward against Demski and wrapped her arms lovingly around him. She could feel him against her, really feel him pressed against her.

In her arms, Demski opened his eyes, startled. "Hey, what's going on? Was I falling?"

"I didn't have to hold you up. You are up. Didn't you know it?"

"I—I can't believe it."

"Better believe it. You're on your way, Adam. Really on your way. How do you *feel*, Adam?"

He smiled shyly. "Ten feet tall."

"All over," she said with a grin. "Just great."

In bed that evening, waiting for Tony to emerge from the bathroom, Nan Whitcomb determined to make one more effort to talk things out with him.

She had been able to fend him off for an entire week, pleading that her gynecologist insisted that she must avoid sexual intercourse while receiving her series of hormone shots. But every day of this avoidance had made him more and more sullen and difficult, and she had known she could not put him off forever. Sooner or later—sooner, she was sure—she would have to give in to his demand, and she hadn't been certain she was far enough along in her therapy to cooperate with Tony and give him what he wanted satisfactorily.

Lying in bed, she knew that she could not continue her delaying tactic. She had to face up to the life she had chosen, and wanted to hold on to, and that meant finding a way to make her physical relationship with Tony Zecca acceptable.

She thought that she had found a new approach, and she'd made up her mind to try it out on Tony. Constantly rejecting Tony would solve nothing. Changing Tony, at least somewhat, might be the solution.

The idea of educating Tony to her needs had probably occurred to her late in the afternoon, after leaving Paul Brandon's apartment. Paul . . . She had real difficulty thinking of him as a hired sex surrogate—and of herself as a needy patient. Paul had been unusually tender and kind to her. At the outset of their two-hour meeting, Paul had explained to her about their next exercise, the frontal caress without touching her breasts or genitals or his genitals. She had taken off her clothes with a mounting feeling of anticipation. The exercise had proceeded with gentle care by each of them. His fingers over her body had brought heat to her skin, and she had been seized by the desire to grab his hands and make them cover her breasts and bring them down to her vagina. She had resisted the temptation because she had not wanted to break the rules, upset the relationship between them, or offend him in any way. When it had been her turn to caress him frontally, the temptation had been even stronger. She had wanted to take hold of his penis, guide it into her. While she had not given in to this desire, Paul had seemed to have some understanding of what had been passing through her mind. He had been wonderfully sweet and thoughtful, even after they had been clothed once more.

Driving home, but more certainly after dinner and when she and Tony were readying for bed, she had determined to speak to Tony tonight, to try to transfer some of Paul's tenderness and kindness to Tony, the man she actually had to deal with.

She heard the bathroom door open and close and saw Tony Zecca approaching the bed. In the yellow light of their single lamp, she could see that he was naked. She tried to gird herself for their talk.

He tramped to the bed, tore the blanket off her, and yanked up her nightgown.

"Vacation's over," he growled. "You should be all rested by now. You can see, I'm ready for you. Come on, spread your fucking legs."

Instantly, she was horrified. All thought of reasoning with him, as well as the words she had carefully rehearsed in her mind, had fled. This was no time to reason. This was survival time.

"Tony, listen—no, not yet—"

"Come on, baby, lift it up, put the pillow under your ass."

She tried to resist. "No, Tony! No, I mustn't. The doctor warned me not to, not while I'm getting the shots. Give me more time. Let me—"

Zecca was on the bed, and over her, each of his hamlike hands on one of her knees. "No more stalling, kiddo," Zecca barked. "Enough of that medical shit. This doc says he's got a shot that's good for what ails you."

His powerful hands were pulling her legs apart. She gripped his knuckles, trying to stop him.

"Don't, Tony, *please!* Give the doctor another—"

"Fuck the doctor!" he bellowed.

He had her legs wide now, and with a grunt, he drove into her.

"Christ, you're tight," he muttered angrily.

He pressed with all his strength and finally, through sheer force, entered her.

She screamed with pain.

With her fists, she hit at his chest, crying out with the deep hurt of his abrasive pressure.

"Don't! It's killing me . . . I'm going to die . . ." She screamed again and started to moan.

"Yeah, you're beginning to like it," he cackled, plunging harder.

She whimpered, tears rolling down her cheeks, as he gasped and came.

At last he withdrew and sat back. "There, that wasn't so bad, was it?"

"It hurt, Tony. It hurt terrible."

"Aw, you fucking women, always complaining."

"Tony, let me go back to the doctor a couple of times before we do it again."

"You mean then you'll stop complaining?"

"Sure, I'll be fixed up."

He rolled over to his side of the bed, yawned, and covered up. "Awright, go see your fucking doctor, but after that, no more complaining."

"No more," she promised.

Early the next afternoon, Nan and Brandon were undressing in his apartment bedroom, in preparation for another exercise. As she removed her garments, Nan, in an undertone, was reciting her experience with Zecca last night. She spared no details. Rolling down her panty hose, stepping out of them, she said, "It still hurts down there."

Taking off his jock shorts, Brandon shook his head with disbelief. "Your Mr. Zecca is really an animal."

"Worse."

"And you're sure there's no way to split and make it on your own?"

"Like I told you before, Paul, where would I go?"

"Someplace, anywhere, as far as possible from him. I'm sure, quickly enough, you'd find a job to support yourself. As for being alone, you don't have to be. You're attractive enough to get a hundred men."

"You really think so, Paul?"

Her hopeful tone made him look up at her as he threw aside his shorts. She was standing nude in front of the bed. Dammit, he told himself, she was attractive in her fashion. No ravishing beauty, like say Gayle, but a lovely person who might make many men happy.

"I absolutely think so," he said.

"What if I meet someone, and he wants to sleep with me, and I want him to, and it's not all right?"

"Meaning what?"

"Well, I mean, if I tighten up with those muscular spasms again, like with Tony."

"It probably won't ever happen again," Brandon tried to reassure her. "I'm convinced you're perfectly normal."

"How can you be sure of that?"

"Nan, you'll see for yourself by the end of the therapy."

"Will I?"

"Nan, hopefully, before the treatment is over, I'll be able to prove to you that lovemaking can be pleasurable and fun." This was tricky ground, and Brandon tried to divert her to another route. "Meanwhile, you ought to talk to Dr. Freeberg more openly about what's going on with Zecca. Maybe he'll give you some support on going it alone. He may give you some alternatives."

"I want to be positive I'm normal, Paul."

"We're getting there. We'll get there. You'll see with the next exercise. We call it the sexological—the sex or anatomy tour."

"Oh, yes, I remember now. I'm frightened."

"No need to be. Basically, it's a modified pelvic examination. We learn about female and male genitals, how they are different, how they are similar. Most people, grown people, are ignorant about their genitals. By doing this tour together, we learn what is erogenous and what isn't. It helps make one more comfortable with the opposite sex." He studied her. "How do you feel? If you're still sore after what happened last night, we could postpone this . . ."

"No," she said with determination. "I want to do it." She stared back at him. "How do we start, Paul?"

"Would you like me to study you first, or would you like

to examine me first? We can begin with the female sexological or the male sexological, whichever you prefer. Would
you like to begin by examining me?"

"Yes, Paul." Nan swallowed. "Let's start with you. What
—what do we do?"

"We both get on the bed. I lie on my back, my legs
spread. You sit cross-legged between my legs. Have you
ever examined a man up close, really close?"

"Of course not."

"Then I'll guide you, show you what to touch or hold,
and explain each part. Think you can do it?"

"Certainly."

"Let's go, then."

They both got on the bed. He lay down on his back, full
length, legs wide. Tentatively, she settled cross-legged between his legs.

"Come closer, Nan," he ordered.

Slowly, she wriggled closer. He lifted his legs and placed
them across the tops of her thighs.

"Now, let me direct you and explain each part of the male
genitalia to you, its function, its responses, and so forth.
We'll start with my scrotal sac and testes . . ."

She held back nervously. He reached out, took one of her
hands, and drew it down to his testicles. Her quivering
hand touched them, and he closed her fingers around
them. "Now, just get the feel while I explain a little about
the testes inside the scrotum. Almost no women realize—
and few men know—that the pair of testicles are one of the
two most important parts of the male sex apparatus. What
you are holding produces the sperm that fertilizes the female egg. The testicles also produce the hormones responsible for the functioning of the penis. The testicles are
responsible for a man's masculinity, everything from his
deep voice to his muscular strength."

Now Brandon took Nan's hand and guided her fingers to
the tip of his soft penis.

"The other vital part of the male apparatus," Brandon
explained, "is the penis itself. The knob you are holding is
the tip of the penis, called the glans. Now I'm lowering your

fingers to the shaft of my penis. Inside my shaft are three columns of porous tissue. When a man is sexually aroused, these porous or spongy tissues fill with blood and become hard. Inserting this erection into a female vagina creates friction, and it's this friction that leads to the male orgasm. Now let me tell you more about the male organ."

Brandon directed her hand in each step, starting with the meatus and going upward to the coronal ridge and dorsal surface. He returned her hand once more to the knob of his penis.

"Just hold it again, feel it in your fingers, in your hand," he directed her.

Then he realized that something was happening. His penis was growing larger and larger in her hand, and becoming harder, stretching through her fingers.

He was having an erection.

He had hoped against hope it wouldn't happen, but he supposed it was inevitable.

She was staring down at him, and he could see her chest heaving, her breasts rising and falling.

He had to bring an end to this before something more happened. Rising on one elbow, he tried to smile. "Well, I guess that answers one question you had," he said. "Are you attractive to men? What do you think?"

"Paul," she murmured.

He had to act fast. "Enough of that for the moment," he said. "Now we do a reverse. It's my turn with you."

He pulled away from her carefully and sat up. "First, we change positions," he said, clinically as possible. "You lie down on your back, and I take your place. This will be the female sexological."

In moments, Nan was on her back, and he had reached out for the plastic speculum and flashlight lying on his bedside table, and with them in hand, he drew up close between her spread legs, lifted them over his thighs, and began.

"First off, I want you to relax a little more," he said. "That'll make it easier. Let me stroke your thighs for a while. You're wired up, which is natural, and I want you to feel at ease."

Little by little, he felt some of the tightness go out of her.

He reached for a small bottle on the table, uncapped it, and gradually began to apply a light oil to her vaginal opening.

"To make it painless," he said.

Nan's eyes were closed as he stroked her labia, then moved his fingers outside and up toward her clitoris. With one finger inside her again, he spoke of what he was contacting, both the bumpy and smooth parts, pushing back to her cervix, explaining each part. Realizing she was extremely lubricated, he took up the speculum and flashlight and instructed her to note in the mirror what he was showing her.

First, he fixed on her brown outer labia, then moved inside to her dark pink inner labia, explaining how each performed when excited. Deeper inside, he indicated the root of the clitoris and explained how vaginal muscles contracted during orgasm and pressed against the clitoris above. He continued to the thick soft tissue between the pubic bone and the urethra sponge, spoke of its function, and then went on to describe the added spongy tissue that ran from the anus to the opening of the vagina.

At one point, he thought he heard Nan whisper something. He thought it was, "Oh, my."

When he had finished his exploration, he realized that there had been no spasms that rejected entry nor any resistance that would indicate discomfort. It was a significant bit of progress.

Her eyes were no longer hypnotized by what she had seen in the speculum's mirror. Her eyes were intent upon him.

"That was fascinating," she said.

"No pain?"

"None at all. Only one thing . . ."

"What, Nan?"

"How will I know when I'm all right?"

"When you and I have sexual intercourse together," he said simply, "and it gives you pleasure. Then you'll know."

In the evening, undressing in her therapy room, Gayle suspected that she was about to reach a crucial moment with Chet Hunter.

Up to now the intensive therapy he had requested had gone smoothly enough, at least on the surface. There had been no problem with nudity, and none with his ability to achieve and maintain an erection. During the shower, the back caress, the nongenital frontal caress, she had observed that his penis had become erect during each exercise. She reminded herself that, after all, unlike Demski, impotency was not his problem. But there was a problem. Although she had not been able to experience it yet, and knew it only from his case history, she was sure that his accounts of premature ejaculation were honest enough.

This belief, thought Gayle, was evident in his personality. He was sturdy and solid enough in every way, yet he was high-strung and impatient. He wanted to get everything over with fast and move on. He was not interested in touching or caressing or the feelings of any of his body parts. He was interested only in his penis, to the exclusion of everything else. He wanted to get to that fast and make it work in the right way. Hunter had what female surrogates termed, among themselves, a total prick mentality.

It would be difficult to overcome, this haste in him, and she wondered if it would be possible to slow him down. With premature ejaculators, this was a key to cure. Make haste slowly, very slowly.

As she watched him remove his shorts, she wondered about the degree of his premature ejaculations. That had not been defined yet.

"Chet," she said casually, "as I recall, you do have a regular girlfriend, don't you?"

"Yes, I do."

"Want to tell me anything about her?"

He was at once guarded. "What's to tell?"

"Well, do you love her?"

"Enough to want to marry her."

"This is the same girl you were telling Dr. Freeberg about? The one you've gone to bed with several times?"

"She's the one."

"But you couldn't make it with her?"

"I'm afraid not. That's why I'm here. I have no trouble getting it up, but I come too fast."

"How fast?"

Hunter snorted. "Nosy, aren't you? I'm just kidding. You're here to help me. How fast? Well, not in my pants, if that's what you mean. Naw, it happens when we're in go position. When I'm ready to enter her."

"Have you ever entered her?"

"No, dammit. I always start coming first."

"When your penis touches her on the outside?"

"Yes," he said, suddenly crestfallen. "I don't like it. I have to do something about it. I just have to."

"We are doing something about it," Gayle said.

"Are we? I can't tell yet."

"You'll see. You'll get over it. The main thing is to do all the exercises with me, no shortcuts, and be patient. Trust me, Chet."

He shrugged. "What else can I do?"

"For one thing, you can lie down on the mat here, on your back."

"Okay. And you?"

He settled down on his back on the spacious floor mat.

"Tonight we're going to do genital pleasuring."

He appeared to brighten. "You mean you're going to hold me down there?"

Gayle knew this could be trouble. Until tonight, she had touched and caressed him everywhere except on the penis. She was concerned about his reaction and his degree of arousal.

Kneeling beside him, she gently rubbed oil the length of his penis. "To make this more realistic and get you to appreciate the vaginal environment. When we get to penetration, I'll be moist inside. So you might as well get used to it now."

"Sounds right." Hunter acknowledged.

Finished with the oiling, Gayle raised her hand to his abdomen and started to stroke it. She said, "When I hold your penis, it's not done to excite you. Remember, it's to give you nondemand pleasure. I'll be touching and caressing, with no strain on you to perform. You merely have to shut your eyes and do nothing. Simply enjoy it. Okay, your eyes closed, please."

He closed his eyes.

Reaching down, her fingertips arrived at the shaft of his penis. She applied her touch gently, then with firmness. "Is that about right?" she asked quietly. "Do you find it enjoyable?"

"You bet."

"It may not stimulate you too much, but—"

"You've got to be kidding."

She expected to give him several minutes to be fully erect. But almost immediately his penis had swollen, risen somewhat, and was rising further.

To continue might frustrate him too much. She had to slow him down, get his mind off his penis.

"All right, Chet. Enough of that. Now it's my turn." She reached for his arm, to make him sit up.

"Your turn?"

"Now you pleasure me in the same way."

"You mean between your legs?"

"Of course, Chet. Just to let me enjoy some unerotic fondling."

"Unerotic? I like that. It can never be unerotic."

"Try me. I'll show you."

Soon she was on her back, on the mat, with Hunter, raised on an elbow, beside her, touching her clitoris.

"A little lighter," she instructed him. She did not want to be brought to orgasm. "Lighter and more slowly."

He proceeded to do as he had been told. Her eyes closed, Gayle decided that he wasn't bad at it, not at all. Abruptly, the pressure on her clitoris became harder, faster.

"Honey," she heard him say.

She opened her eyes, saw him pointing down between his legs.

"Look at this."

He was pointing down at a complete erection, straight out and obviously hard.

She was at a loss for what to say. "Well, that's good . . ."

"It can be for both of us," he said urgently. "Let me, Gayle."

"Let you what?"

"Put it in. I'm ready. Why waste time?"

"No," she said. "You're not ready. We need more sessions."

He came to his knees beside her. "Honey, I've got to, I've just got to. I'm ready. I'll make it this time . . . I guarantee you."

"No, not yet—"

"Please, Gayle, while I can. It'll be great. Let me show you."

She considered his pleading. If only there were time to consult Dr. Freeberg. But as she knew, many of these decisions were left to the judgment of the surrogates. She considered further. What it came to was: just what was there to lose? If he truly could make it, he was on his way to a cure. If he couldn't, he would learn a lesson.

"All right, Chet," she said impulsively, "if you think you can complete penetration, that might be a good thing. Go ahead. I'll cooperate."

"You'll see, you'll see," he said breathlessly, hastily positioning himself between her widening legs. "Christ, you're something, you're great. We'll do it. I can make it this time."

She arched back, lifting her hips slightly as he guided his penis toward her vaginal opening. He was panting now, excited, so eager to make it.

She felt the head of his penis touch her down below, and she braced herself for his entry. But there was no entry.

She raised her head. His features were contorted.

And then she felt the wetness of his semen outside her vagina.

"Oh, Je—sus," he groaned as he finished his orgasm. "Jesus, I just couldn't hold it in. I'm sorry, I couldn't help it. I don't know—it just happened."

She put a kindly hand on his bare shoulder. "Don't worry, Chet. It's happened before. That's why we're together. But I promise you, if you do it my way, and have plenty of patience, I promise you one day soon you'll be fine."

"I don't know," he said helplessly. "I don't know if I'll ever be able to do it."

Later, dressed and bidding Gayle good night, Hunter had felt Gayle restrain him as he reached the front door.

He half listened to her as she said, "I'm confident enough to give you another piece of advice. I always give it when we get to this part of our program. At this point, when you see your girlfriend again, there is to be positively no sex. Take her to a movie or sit with her on a sofa and kind of repeat our exercises in a real-life way. I mean, hold and stroke her hand, her hair, her face. Touch her breasts, but over her clothes, not under them. Forget about your erections. Hold back. Get into your feelings and her own . . . and nothing more. Between slowing down with your girl, and with what we're doing, it'll work out soon enough."

Leaving her, Hunter was less optimistic. He trudged miserably to his car at the curb and pushed in behind the wheel.

He sat there in the darkness assessing his loss.

He had been certain he would make it tonight, and with penetration, he would have been on his way.

Christ, he thought, wait'll Ferguson and Scrafield and Hoyt Lewis learn about this. It could dynamite their whole game plan—and his future. If he couldn't make it with this dame, he could not go into a court of law and swear under oath he had done it to her, paid the little nympho for a real fuck, when he hadn't fucked her. And this Gayle dame would also be swearing under oath he hadn't gotten into her. He couldn't risk a lie.

Yes, once the truth were known, there was no case against Freeberg, no story, no job on the *Chronicle*.

Then, sitting there in the darkness behind his wheel, he realized that they didn't have to know. Ferguson, Scrafield, and Hoyt Lewis didn't have to know a thing about this night's failure. As far as they knew, he was in the middle of his therapy with a—a prostie. They had to know only when he'd made it and could honestly swear he'd made it.

That was the question.

Would he make it with her, ever?

Well, she said he wouldn't tonight, and she had been right. She said he would in the near future, she was confident. So she could be right about that, too, and then he'd come up roses. He'd have the spotlight as star witness during a winning trial. He'd have a job on the staff of the *Chronicle*. He'd have Suzy and have her for life.

If Gayle Miller were right, and he played his cards right, went along with her, he might have everything.

He inserted his key into the ignition and started the car.

Listening to the hum of the engine, he told himself he'd have to have more patience, will himself more patience, and go along with Gayle from now on. He promised himself he would do so. No more shortcuts. No more rushing it. He would do it her way. And maybe he'd get there yet.

VI

Because Gayle's bedside alarm clock had gone off while she was still in the midst of her dream, the dream involving Paul Brandon and herself was momentarily vivid.

She supposed what had triggered the dream had been her thought last night, while preparing for bed, that she must telephone Paul for a date, as she'd promised, and that she wanted to call Paul then and there about seeing him. But she had been too exhausted to attempt the call and had fallen asleep immediately.

Now, in the morning, Paul Brandon was still on her mind. In the dream, she had been on something like a South Sea island, a remote part of Tahiti maybe, and she had been running through a tropical forest, and Paul had been chasing her. She suspected that she had not been running too fast.

Squinting at her clock, she knew she could not take the time to telephone him. She could not risk being late for the Miller Analogies Test that would complete her application to the UCLA graduate school. She had already taken her Graduate Record Examination Aptitude Test and the Advanced Test in Psychology and felt she had done well with both. That left the Miller Analogies Test, and she had better be at her best with no distractions.

Out of bed, she hastened into the shower, dried, dressed, made up her face, and rushed through breakfast. Then, briefcase in hand, she started for the door as her living room telephone rang.

She backtracked, snatching up the receiver, thinking it might be Dr. Freeberg, or even Adam Demski or Chet Hunter.

She recognized the voice at once. The caller was Paul Brandon.

"Hi, Gayle," Brandon was saying. "I've been sitting beside my phone day and night, almost. I've been waiting for the call you promised to make. My phone hasn't rung once. Have you been trying to tell me something?"

She would be barely on time for her exam, but she had to explain. "I'm sorry, Paul. The road to 'I'm sorry' is paved with good intentions. I've just been so busy I can hardly turn around. You know I have two patients now . . ."

"I know, but still."

"That means two daily consultations with Dr. Freeberg. And two detailed reports for him after the sessions. Then other things, like pulling this house together. Right now I'm on my way to Los Angeles to take the MAT, which goes with my application to UCLA. Anyway—"

"Anyway, where does that leave me, Gayle?" Brandon insisted. "I can tell you. It leaves me alone, and very lonely."

"I want to see you," she answered, then with emphasis, "very much. I'll call you later this afternoon. Are you working tonight?"

"Not tonight. I'll be through with my patient by six. After that, I suppose, I'll be dining alone."

"No, you won't," Gayle said impulsively. "You're going to have company. A real flashy date. Me. How'd you like to have a home-cooked meal at my place? Do you like pasta?"

"I love pasta if you go along with it. What time do you want me to be there? Eight?"

"Closer to nine would be better."

"Nine it is. I'll dude myself up and come calling."

"Can't wait," she said, and hung up.

Dashing for the door, she remembered her dream.

She knew the outcome of the dream.

Paul would catch her.

She hoped.

Gayle's morning had been taken up by her MAT in Westwood, and then she had driven back to Hillsdale for two successive conferences, the first with Freeberg and Demski, the second with Freeberg and Hunter.

The afternoon was to be strenuous also. An exercise with Adam Demski at two o'clock. A second exercise at five o'clock, this one with what she hoped was a chastened Chet Hunter. After that, there would be just time enough to dictate her reports at the clinic and barely time to get home to prepare dinner for Paul Brandon as a prelude to what she hoped would be a long and delicious evening. She was sure that Paul would be wonderful, and she deserved some of the action. A busman's holiday, she knew, but not really, not actually. Tonight would be play without pay. Tonight would be from the heart. She flushed, thinking ahead to it.

At the moment, right now, she tried to hold her immediate thoughts on business.

It was two o'clock and Adam Demski arrived promptly, exuding more confidence than she had seen before.

Gayle was wearing a pale silk robe, chastely wrapped, but with nothing underneath.

After greeting Demski warmly, helping him off with his suit jacket, chatting with him about his day in Hillsdale, Gayle announced that she was ready if he was. Automatically, Demski started for the hallway and the therapy room in the rear. She followed him, aware that today's exercise was even more crucial than the last. If it worked, it would be a big step toward making him secure about his body and ultimately enabling him to achieve an erection.

In the familiar therapy room, Gayle had already spread her thick soft mat on the floor between the couch and the full-length mirror. There was a white sheet covering the mat, and on top of it two fresh beach towels and two down pillows. For the moment, Gayle ignored the mat, sat back on the couch, and watched Demski undress, pleased at the ease with which he was taking off his clothes.

Once he was naked, she stood up, pulled off her silk robe and was naked also.

She dropped down to the mat on the floor, patting one of the beach towels beside her. Demski lowered himself next to her.

"You want to know what we're going to do today?" Gayle asked him.

"Yes, what is it?"

"Something we have an option to use. I like to do this exercise. I've always found it pleasurable and effective. It's called The Clock."

"The Clock?" repeated Demski. "I don't remember being told about it. What is it?"

"There is no clock," said Gayle. "It's an imaginary timepiece set in my vagina."

Demski's eyebrows went up. "An imaginary clock in your vagina? How?" Then he asked, "What for?"

She explained the entire clock exercise to him in detail.

"Now that you understand it, shall we begin, Adam?" Gayle said. "Let's lie down and let me stroke your thighs and stomach and chest. Then we'll proceed."

Using a feathery touch, she stroked him very slowly and encouraged him to touch her just as slowly between the outer labia of her vagina and the clitoris.

After a little while, she helped him to a sitting posture as she also sat up. "Okay, now to The Clock," she said. "Let me lie down again, supine, bring my knees up, and spread my legs. You settle yourself between them, sit Indian-style, and gently slide your forefinger gradually into my opening, an inch, then an inch and a half, then two inches. I'll direct you around the imaginary clock inside and do a running commentary."

"That's all?"

Gayle smiled wryly. "There may be more, much more. There may be some fireworks."

He looked puzzled. "Meaning what?"

"Meaning I may react to this exercise. It may excite me. I could have an orgasm."

"What—what do I do?"

"Nothing, Adam, except wait until I've finished before withdrawing. Just sit and enjoy what you can do to me."

"How much of my finger did you say?"

"Just part of it. All right, put it in, your finger . . . Slide it in . . ."

Hesitantly, using the forefinger of his right hand, he approached her vaginal opening as she moved her thighs wider apart.

"Go ahead," she encouraged him.

She pushed his finger inside her. This would demonstrate to him that a man didn't have to have a large penis to give a woman pleasure.

"That's enough," she said. "How does it feel, Adam?"

"Soft, warm . . ."

"And tight, I hope, all around your finger."

"It sure is."

"Yes, because the vaginal barrel is actually folded down on itself, so that it totally surrounds and wraps whatever is inside it. Rather like an elastic pouch. No matter what the size of anything inside it, the vagina contracts or expands, closes up, encompasses whatever is there, short, narrow, long, wide, to offer a perfect fit."

This was finally dawning on him, she could see.

"Now, as to what I feel . . ." Gayle continued. "There are some nerve endings at the entrance to the vagina but very few down inside. Let me contract my pelvic muscles, and while you're inside you'll feel the contraction. There. Do you?"

"Yes," he gulped, "I sure do."

"All right, let's do The Clock. Lift your finger high to the upper center. Twelve o'clock. Then come down and around, pressing it against my vaginal walls. Lower, lower. Hey"—she contracted tightly—"six o'clock is terrific. See, I really react to that. Adam, Adam . . ."

"What, Gayle?"

"Go back to six o'clock. Rub the wall—press harder."

"Like this?"

"Adam, for God's sake, don't stop." Her eyes were shut tightly, her lower lip under her front teeth. "I—I'm coming apart."

Her orgasm was at its height, and it was a prolonged one.

"Adam, look what you're doing to me," she managed to choke out.

When it was over, and she slumped back against the pillow, he withdrew his finger.

"You did that to me with your finger."

He stood up with almost military bearing and pointed down to his penis. "And look what you did to me," he announced.

She looked. It was there, all right. Wonder of wonders for an impotent man. It was elevated, all of four inches.

"Wonderful, how wonderful!" she exclaimed. "Better than a B, I'd say. But next time, or the time after, we're going for a big B plus."

"You think so?"

"I know so!"

"I—I hope you're right."

When the doorbell sounded at ten minutes after five instead of five o'clock sharp, and Gayle admitted Chet Hunter, she realized that for the first time he was late.

During previous visits, he had arrived a little early. It had been part of his anxiety to get going, to get on with it. Arriving late indicated either that he was reluctant to rush things after his last failure or that he *had* slowed down. Welcoming him, Gayle decided that he wasn't reluctant. He simply was too driven to succeed and to normalize his life with his girlfriend. So his lateness most likely indicated that he was making a conscious effort to follow his surrogate's advice. Not to rush things.

As long as this was his mood, she decided to maintain and extend it. She would keep him slowed down.

"Chet," she said, "I was just brewing some tea. Would you like to join me?"

"Whatever you say." He was definitely chastened and appeared ready to oblige her every wish.

"Get yourself relaxed in here. I'll bring the tea, and we can talk a few minutes."

Hunter was slumped in an easy chair when she returned with the two cups of tea. Casually, she began to inquire about his work as a writer. He was evasive about his writing but ready to talk at length about the variety of research he was engaged in.

"What about your girlfriend?" Gayle asked. "Does she help you with your work?"

"She's interested, but she has a job of her own."

"Want to talk about her?"

"No," he said firmly. "Let's keep this strictly between us."

"Of course."

"And you?" he asked unexpectedly. "Do you have a boyfriend on the side?"

She hesitated. Did she?

She tried to be honest. "Maybe. Almost. We'll see."

"What if he turns out to be a premature ejaculator?"

Thinking of Paul Brandon, she tried to keep a straight face. "Why, I'd treat him the way I'm treating you."

"You think it would work?"

"I'd hope so."

Hunter drained his tea and set his cup aside. "Okay. Here I am. What's next?"

"We're going to do precisely what we did yesterday. I talked it over with Dr. Freeberg, and that was his suggestion. We'll undress and do nondemand body caressing including genitals all over again. But with a difference."

"What's that?"

"This time, when you touch me you've got to keep in mind you're touching me for your own pleasure in doing so, not for performance. You pleasure me, but you will be doing it not for me but for yourself. This is really what intercourse should mean. Once you have your penis in my vagina, or anyone's, you should be enjoying it for yourself.

And I should be into my own feelings and be enjoying it, too. We should both be getting pleasure from each other."

"What if you feel passive?"

"That can happen, and that's to be considered, too. Anyway, today we'll caress each other, and we'll each get pleasure from it. But the one difference from yesterday is that this time no more nonsense about your insisting on jumping into the hay with me and wanting to make love. I won't let you do it—not yet."

"Okay. Whatever you say, that's the way it'll be."

"But I will pleasure you in another way. I think we've come to that."

"To what?"

"Toward the end of the exercise," said Gayle earnestly, "I'm going to take your penis in hand and bring you close to orgasm."

"You mean a hand job?" He showed his surprise.

"Call it what you will. I'm going to bring you close to orgasm and instruct you on how to retard it."

"You think you can retard it?"

"I think so," said Gayle, standing. "Let's find out."

Presently, both nude in her therapy room, Hunter was stretched out on her mat and she was on her knees beside him, going through the nondemand frontal caress. Throughout, she had avoided his penis, which was stiffening steadily.

Briefly, Gayle considered his penis.

"Now you want to have an orgasm," she said.

"You bet!"

"You'll have one," she assured him, "but first a minilecture and the exercise that goes with it."

"I hope it doesn't take too long."

"Chet, if I did it quickly, you'd come to orgasm quickly, before you could get inside me or your girlfriend."

"Okay, okay, go ahead."

She looked at him. "Have you ever heard of the squeeze method?"

"The what?"

"The squeeze technique to arrest ejaculatory inevitability."

"The squeeze? Sure, I read about it in my researches."

"That is what we are going to do now. Premature ejaculation is the result of anxiety. Let me put it this way. When I
begin to stroke your penis, you'll have a real urge to come
right away. From need. You'll want to perform the act and
get it over with, yet another side of you is telling you that
you want to last longer and be a good lover. Isn't that
true?"

"I guess so."

"Believe me, it's true, Chet. Now, there are two tradi-
tional ways to overcome prematurity. One is the so-called
common sense approach. You take a drink or two of liquor
to dull your erotic excitement. Or you use an anesthetic
ointment or a condom. Or you try to diminish the erotic
excitement by distracting yourself, looking off at the furniture or curtains or trying to think of business. The other
approach is to solve it all through insight therapy, talking it
out with a psychoanalyst or psychologist. In this you might
learn prematurity involves your unconscious conflicts
about women that began with childhood problems. Both of
these approaches may work, but neither is as immediate or
effective as surrogate therapy. This, I repeat, involves the
squeeze technique. I know, but you don't, that premature
ejaculation is the result of your inability to focus your attention and feelings on the sensation of sexual arousal before
orgasm. You're only concerned with getting to your own
orgasm. Hopefully, the experiencing of touch and caress
will change all that. Meanwhile, in a few sessions, the
squeeze will prevent ejaculatory inevitability. Believe me, it
works, Chet."

"Anything you say, teacher."

"Okay. What we'll do is this. I'll stroke you to excite you
to the point where you feel an orgasm about to start. When
you're close to that, you tell me so—tell me to squeeze."

"How soon? When?"

"Not the second you're about to ejaculate. Maybe a half
minute or so before. In fact, I'd rather retard you early, to

play it safe, and then we can gradually try it closer and closer to your orgasm, maybe five seconds before emission."

"I hope I can tell you in time."

"You will," Gayle promised him. "The instant you tell me, I'll reach up to the glans, or head of your penis, with my thumb and first two fingers and squeeze rather hard just below the rim of the head, the two fingers on top and my thumb pressing the underside for four seconds. It won't hurt. You'll usually lose your erection and certainly any desire to have an orgasm. Your entire stress mechanism is reduced. You go limp. Then we start all over. I play with your penis until it's erect again. Don't worry about that. The penis can be brought to erection a dozen times or more, easily. Each time, I'll retard your orgasm by squeezing and then give you the pleasure of getting it up again. We'll set a goal today. We'll try to have you hold back for five minutes. We'll build that up to ten minutes. Our ultimate goal is fifteen minutes, to have you holding back orgasm outside or inside a woman for fifteen minutes. Want to try it?"

"Go ahead."

He'd lost a good deal of rigidity, and Gayle reached down and began to caress his abdomen and thighs, closer and closer to his genitals. Her hand closed around his testicles, and immediately his shaft began bulging, and soon it was standing straight out. She ran her fingers along it, placed her hand around it, and began to run her hand up and down.

Hunter, his eyes tight, his buttocks quivering, began to groan. "I—I can't hold it," he whimpered.

Instantly, Gayle moved her fingers on top of his penis and she squeezed.

"Oh!" he cried out.

But he did not come. The penis went soft in her hand and began to slip from her grasp.

"There, you made it, Chet," she said. "Erection, excitement, but no ejaculation."

"Okay," he said breathlessly, peering down at his limp member. "Now what?"

"Now I make you happy with your manhood, but don't let it get out of control."

Once more her fingers and hand pleasured his penis, and once more he was rigid. Again her hand stroked his shaft, and again his eyes closed tightly and he began to moan.

"I—I—I'm ready . . ." he whispered.

She squeezed hard.

No orgasm. Limp once more.

She continued repeating the exercise, each time retarding his ejaculation. But after five successful minutes of this, when he was at the peak of one more erection, she found a folded tissue, held it over the head of his penis, and continued with her hand.

This time, when he groaned, she did not squeeze. She allowed him to ejaculate all the way.

When it was over, he turned on his side. "Thank you, Gayle. That's it?"

"The beginning," she said. "To be really effective in retarding ejaculation, you'll have to do some homework."

"What do you mean?"

"I mean touching yourself."

He sat up. "Touching my—oh, you mean masturbation?"

"Exactly."

"But I don't—"

"Chet, everyone does, or at least has, at one time or another. You must have."

"When I was a kid, sure. All kids do."

"Now you're a man. I want you to do it again before our next exercise. It's so simple. Start masturbating. Then use the squeeze technique on yourself. Do it for five or more minutes, before release. Do that, and you'll save us both a lot of time. You'll get where you want to be."

"I still don't like that kind of homework. Not at my age. I can't see myself masturbating. If it were some kind of workout with a woman, I could handle it—"

"But you can't handle it with a woman yet. That's why you're here. Masturbation can get you with a woman sooner." Gayle tried to smile. "The homework could be worse. And it's free." She came to her feet, speaking to him seriously. "I'll tell you a secret. Masturbation is really the key to sex therapy. Believe me, Chet, the golden rule of sex treatment is: Do unto yourself, successfully, and you'll be able to do unto others forever." She searched his face. "Please take my word for it."

He shook his head slowly. "I want to, but I can't. I don't mind you doing it, but—"

"Chet, we can save a lot of time if you help me out. Masturbating isn't so awful."

"Well, I don't like it."

She studied him. "Chet, a man who's uncomfortable with masturbation may have a lot of work to do on himself psychologically. If you don't agree with me, go ask Dr. Freeberg."

"I intend to."

"I'll be waiting to hear what you find out."

Dr. Freeberg had been listening to Chet Hunter, and now he began to nod. "Basically, what Miss Miller advised you is correct. Perhaps she phrased it a bit dramatically in stating that masturbation is the key to sex therapy. I might be inclined to put it another way. Masturbation is a valuable exercise in conjunction with pleasuring and other therapeutic procedures. Why do you object to it so strongly?"

"Because lying around at home and jerking off by myself —I don't like it—"

"Why?" Freeberg persisted.

"It tells me again I can't make out with a woman."

"And intensifies your sense of failure?"

"I suppose so."

"I wonder if that's all, if your resistance to the idea didn't start much earlier? You say you masturbated when you were a youngster. How did your parents feel about it?"

Hunter sat up. "My God, I wouldn't have thought of telling them!"

"Ah, then even in your childhood you had the belief that

masturbation was wrong, and that if your father and mother learned about it, they would disapprove. So you must have already known about their negative attitude toward masturbation."

"Now that you mention it . . . Yes, I guess I did know it was considered a bad thing. I must have heard my parents at some time say it was a bad thing and unhealthy." Hunter reflected on this briefly. "My parents are hard-shell Baptists. They would have the notion that masturbation could lead to mental illness of some sort, even to insanity. I must have picked up on that."

"But at this time," said Freeberg, "you must know different. You must know there is not a shred of scientific evidence that masturbation can harm you."

Hunter agreed. "I'm aware of that. I've done a lot of research for my own writing, so I've learned that. But I guess I'm still tied down by the fears of my childhood."

"Well, childhood fears shouldn't inhibit you any longer. The old Kinsey report discovered that ninety-four percent of all men masturbate at one time or another. A more recent study shows that nearly one hundred percent of all males have masturbated at some time. I don't mind telling you that I've masturbated."

"You mean when you were a kid?" Hunter interjected.

Freeberg shook his head. "Not only when I was a kid. In more recent years, when my wife was away and I was under tension and needed relief."

Hunter blinked. "You're pretty honest, I will say."

"And pretty normal," added Freeberg. "Mr. Hunter, trust me when I tell you that masturbation isn't a sin. In your case, when we're trying to retard prematurity, it can be a virtue. Masturbation, with Miss Miller doing it for you, with you doing it for yourself, can lay the foundation for teaching a man to control himself. I'd suggest you follow Miss Miller's advice. At home, masturbate yourself to erection, and ten seconds before ejaculation, use the squeeze method."

"That's another thing I don't like," said Hunter. "I can

accept it when a young woman prevents my premature ejaculation. But I don't like to do it to myself."

"Well, there's something else you might do that can be equally effective."

"Oh, yeah? What?"

"The surrogates call it the stop-and-start method. Therapists call it the Semans procedure, after urologist James Semans, who began to use it in 1956. You stimulate yourself almost to the point of ejaculation, then stop cold and wait until your arousal subsides and your erection goes down, and then you repeat it, stop, and then start again."

"At that point, I'm afraid I couldn't stop, couldn't hold it in," Hunter confessed unhappily.

"Then go back to the squeeze method. Disagreeable as you may find it, you will always find it effective."

"I suppose if I can let her do it to me, I could somehow do it to myself."

"That's better. When you go home tonight, try it. If you are slow in getting aroused, look at something you consider erotic or pornographic . . ."

"You mean like those frontal nudity shots in the girlie magazines?"

"Exactly. Look at them, and fantasize, until you are ready for your orgasm. Don't worry about losing your erection. The erections you can have at your age are countless. You won't run out of them. Once you terminate an erection, stroke yourself until you have a new one. Do this five or six times tonight, and tomorrow resume it with Gayle Miller. Will you do it?"

"If you think it'll help me make out with a woman."

"Gayle Miller has promised you it will lead to normal intercourse. I can almost guarantee it." Freeberg rose and put out his hand. "Good luck, Mr. Hunter."

"Can't we do this together?" Nan Whitcomb asked.

She was lying on Brandon's bed, propped on an elbow, watching him take off his trousers and then shed his briefs.

"Together?"

"The nondemand genital pleasuring."

Naked, Brandon sat down on the bed, puzzled. "To be honest with you, Nan, I don't know. I only know the standard practice. You lie back, close your eyes, relax, and I caress you from head to toe. After that, you do it to me."

"But doing it together is the same thing. Aren't you permitted to do some things differently sometimes?"

"I suppose so, as long as we stick within the parameters of the exercise. Actually, Dr. Freeberg wants us to be fairly flexible when something innovative is called for."

"Then let's touch each other at the same time."

Brandon was still hesitant. "Any reason for that?"

"I don't know. It's just something that might feel good. I mean, when you touch me, and after that, separately I caress you, it's sort of like two things apart—not entirely, but somewhat. I'd like to have simultaneous contact with a man."

"Well, why not?" said Brandon suddenly. He had a few misgivings, unspoken, but the exercise seemed reasonable enough. "I'll lie down beside you. We'll both shut our eyes. I'll caress you, and yes, you can caress me, doing to me what I'm doing to you."

For a few moments she searched his face. "You're sure you don't mind, Paul?"

"I'll enjoy it," he said with a smile.

He dropped down next to her, maneuvered himself closer until their bare hips touched. He saw her close her eyes. He reached toward her head, then closed his own eyes and began passing his fingers through her hair, around her ear, down her cheek, along her neck.

At the same time, he felt her warm fingers on his face, imitating his own caressing.

Gradually, he slid his hand down to her breasts, cupping them lightly. They were soft except for her nipples, which had hardened. As he did this, he felt her fingers on his chest, rubbing the hair on his chest, rubbing his nipples, because she had not forgotten that this could be an erogenous zone for a male as well.

They continued their stroking, until fifteen or twenty

minutes had passed. At last his free hand inched down until it could feel the upper rim of her pubic hair. It was when she was about to do the same to him that his major misgiving surfaced. For he knew that he had a growing erection. Once her fingers reached it, he was concerned about his control.

Just as he felt the bud of her clitoris under his touch, he also felt her fingers encircle his hard penis.

It would take Spartan effort to hold himself in check, and he knew it would be difficult because he knew that he was swelling and rising toward an orgasm.

With greater rapidity, his fingers massaged her clitoris. A sound escaped her lips, and her strangled words broke the silence. "Oh, my . . . my, don't—don't stop!" Then her voice cracked, "Keep going!"

His massaging became more intense but so did his own desire for an orgasm in her hand.

"Ohhh!" she cried out, and as she did so, her torso arched and shook, and her fingers gripping his penis tightened hard around it.

At once, all desire to have an orgasm ceased within him. Involuntarily, she had applied the squeeze technique.

"I'm coming," she choked out.

He nodded dumbly in their self-imposed darkness. "Good," he heard himself starting to say. "Good." He was grateful to her that she had accidentally prevented him from letting go.

When they both sat up, their eyes open now, she was instantly apologetic. "I'm sorry, Paul. I couldn't help myself."

"You did absolutely nothing wrong. I think Dr. Freeberg would agree it was beneficial for you, for your therapy. You loosened up, let go—"

"Fully," she filled in. "First time."

"And that can only be helpful."

She looked down at him. "You didn't get much pleasure out of it."

"All that I needed. It was, after all, a nondemand exercise."

In his mind, he questioned the surrogate use of "nonde-mand." He supposed the usage was technically correct. It meant the man did not have to perform, could just absorb pleasuring, as well as give it back, with no sexual demand on him. This time, he had wanted to respond, and been able to, in a sense. It was something he must talk out with Freeberg. But then he realized that it was nothing he need discuss. Because deep inside he knew that while it had been Nan's hand pleasuring his penis, his mind had fantasized that it was Gayle Miller who had been stimulating and excit-ing him.

He saw Nan strapping on her gold watch. "A gift from Tony," she said, "for my birthday he forgot about. I'll have to leave soon. He'll be home for dinner."

"This early?"

"He likes to eat early, watch some television, and go to bed. I hate to go to bed early."

"You mean because you hate what happens when you go to bed. What are you going to do about it tonight?"

"I'm going to try to fight him off." She hesitated. "Paul, I've still got ten minutes before putting my clothes on and leaving. Do you mind if we just lie here together?"

"That would be nice."

After they lay back against the pillows, Nan turned her head to him. "Paul, would you hold me? I mean, put your arms around me?"

"I'd like to."

He slid an arm under her bare back and embraced her closely, letting her protruding breasts flatten against his chest.

"You're wonderful," she whispered, "the most wonder-ful man I ever met. Don't get upset if I kiss you. I'd like to kiss you."

He brought her face to his and pressed his lips to hers, and meant to keep it at that. But her moist mouth had opened, and her tongue darted out, into his mouth, search-ing for his tongue. When the French kiss was done, he gently pushed them apart as she whispered, "I really adore you."

He could not answer because this worried him.

Shortly after, she hastily dressed. Examining her hair and features in the mirror, to make sure there were no telltale signs, she carefully combed her hair and made up her face. During this she spoke only once.

"What do we do next time, Paul?"

He swallowed. "Penetration. First attempt."

She smiled down at him. "It'll work," she said. "I'm sure it will."

With that, she left the bedroom.

Nan returned to the house only minutes before Tony Zecca arrived from work.

The dinner was already on the table when Tony lumbered off to take his ritual pee and wash his hands before dinner. She went into her own bathroom to soap and wash her hands, then came back to join him across the table.

He was already in his place, gorging himself on a rare steak like a cannibal. Picking at her own dish, she cast him a covert look that mingled both distaste and fear.

"You're giving me a lot of trouble, babe," Zecca said, chewing hard on his steak, then halting to clear a hiccup with a swallow of beer.

"How?"

"By being fucking absent all the time. I hired a cashier and wound up with a fucking prima donna. You're costing me a goddamn fortune with all the part-time help I got to hire to replace you while you go running off to some god-damn doctor. The new girl at the register, the spick, is worse than the nigger one."

"Costing you what?" she said, her annoyance surfacing. "You pay them almost zero. You're using slave labor."

She hated him, among other things, for his vicious references to blacks and Hispanics.

"They steal from me, from the register," he growled, chomping at another piece of steak. "They're all goddamn crooks."

Look who's talking, she wanted to shout. She wondered

how he'd ever survived Vietnam. She didn't mean how he'd
survived fighting against the Vietcong. She meant how he'd
ever escaped being killed in the field by one of his fellow
infantrymen, black or Hispanic, that he'd abused with his
racist remarks. But maybe when they had all carried equal
weapons, he had kept his mouth clamped shut and his
attitudes to himself.

"They're not all crooks," Nan managed to say.

"What in the hell do you know? Anyway, thank Christ
that's coming to an end tomorrow. You see that you're back
on the job at nine sharp."

"I can't, Tony."

"What?"

"I have an appointment with the doctor."

"Goddammit, no way!" he roared, slamming his open
palm on the table, making his empty plate dance. "I told
you that you could go to that fucking doctor one more time
—one more shot—and that was today."

"And I told you he has to see me for a week or two more.
I told you that."

"Not on your life!" Zecca bellowed. "Why is that fucker
dragging you out to see him every day? To pile up more
bills?"

"Tony, stop it. I won't have that kind of talk. This is one
of the best gynecologists in the profession. He has to see
me a week or two more—he'll decide how much longer
tomorrow. I'm still not in shape . . ."

"Meaning you can't get in the sack with me tonight and
do what any normal woman does?"

"I can't help it, Tony. I have to wait until I'm cured. I'll
ask the doctor—"

"No, you won't," Zecca interrupted. "Me, *I* am the one
who's going to ask this doctor of yours why he's fucking me
around, and how long he thinks he can keep crapping me.
When you take off to see this doc of yours tomorrow, I'm
driving you. I'm going in with you to find out what that
cocksucker is up to. What time you going in?"

Caught off balance, she spoke the first thing that came to
her head. "Ten . . . I have an appointment at ten tomor-

row morning. Tony, please don't embarrass me. I mean, your coming in with me . . . This is a woman's doctor for female complaints—maybe sometimes he sees a man and wife, but we're not married; you're not my husband . . ."

"How the hell will he know?"

"I—I told him when I started. It's on my application. I'm single."

Zecca was on his feet. "Not tomorrow, you're not. Tomorrow you got your boyfriend with you. I'll see you at breakfast, and we'll go in to see your fucking cooze-loving doctor together. Now, no more ifs and buts. Get your ass to bed and get some rest. I'll let you off the hook tonight because I'm saving myself for tomorrow night. Because tomorrow night I'm going to fuck you until your ears bleed."

After he left the table, Nan pushed her unfinished food aside and sat shivering, wondering what she could do.

Only when she had trudged into her dressing room, and changed into her nightgown, did the answer come to her.

He was already in bed when she reached her side. She crawled under the blanket and lay there, trying to think it out. Once he fell asleep, he would sleep like a log and not awaken until daybreak. She lay very still, waiting for him to sleep.

In ten minutes, fifteen, whatever time had passed, she heard rasping sounds beside her and knew that he was snoring and would not awaken until it was light.

But just in case, she must do what was to be done silently and quickly. Almost without making a sound, she turned back the corner of her blanket and slipped out of bed. Ignoring even her slippers, she padded softly on her bare feet to the bathroom, shut the door, left the light off, and made her way to her dressing room beyond, where she turned on a green-shaded dim lamp.

She found her suitcase, unlatched it, and set it open on her dressing table bench.

With determination and haste, she dressed, then began to gather together her sparse collection of clothes—the few blouses, skirts, dresses, belts, hose, shoes, undergarments

—and packed them into the single suitcase. Inside one pair of shoes, she checked to see if the money was still there, her small savings from her cashier's job and from what she had been able to save from her household shopping allowance. The total sum hoarded would not carry her far, or for any length of time, but it was enough to survive until she found another job. Then she closed the suitcase.

One act left. Tearing a sheet of paper from her scratch pad, she scribbled a hasty note to Tony, thanking him for all he had done for her but insisting that she had to leave to pursue her life on her own. Tony's determination to interfere with her visits to her physician had been the last straw, an invasion of privacy that she could not accept. She wished him well, told him she was sorry it had come to this, and said good-bye.

With a piece of Scotch tape, she affixed her note to her boudoir mirror.

Back at the bathroom door, her ear against it, she could clearly hear Tony's uninterrupted snoring.

So far, so good.

Taking up her car keys and suitcase, she crept out of his house.

Once outside, she found that the night was chilly but somehow more hospitable than the house.

Inside her secondhand Volvo, she started it, worrying about the noisy engine, and backed out of the garage and into the street.

Quickly, she drove away. Fast.

She was free, at last. She hoped. Freedom was frightening, but at least there was someone else who cared about her. She hoped.

In the kitchen of her small house, Gayle Miller finished preparations for her intimate dinner with Paul Brandon.

She was of two minds about the evening ahead. On the one hand, she felt too pressured by haste and would have preferred a more leisurely meeting. Seeing both Demski and Hunter in a single afternoon had been exhausting,

although the progress made in both cases had been gratifying. After that, dictating two reports for Dr. Freeberg had
been time-consuming. She had rushed to a nearby super-
market to do her shopping for dinner and then had busied
herself preparing a meal she wished could be more sophis-
ticated.

With her preparations for dinner done, she glanced at
the kitchen wall clock. He wasn't due for twenty minutes.
Time enough to ready herself for him.

In her bedroom, she dressed with care. As a surrogate,
she always underplayed the attire she wore for patients. It
was her policy never to wear anything sexually provocative,
lest the garments threatened her patients into believing
demands were being made on them and they had to perform successfully.

But Paul Brandon was anything but a patient. He was an
integrated human being, a man who functioned, a man she
wanted to impress and excite, a man she desired very, very
much. Therefore, for a private and personal date, she could
behave as a female who might be in love.

Dress sexily, she told herself, and she did. A white low-
cut silk blouse that partially revealed her breasts not covered by her half bra. To this she added a short tangerine-
colored skirt, ultrasheer hose because her shapely legs
were flawless, and high-heeled brown pumps. She went
easy on the cosmetics, maybe a bit more lipstick than usual.
By the time she was completely groomed, the doorbell
rang.

Paul Brandon arrived carrying a dozen long-stemmed
red roses for her.

Thrilled and pleased, she accepted the bouquet, hugged
him with one arm, thanking and welcoming him with a soft,
warm kiss. Leading him to a chair, Gayle had almost forgotten how truly attractive he was. He had the gaunt good
looks of one of those strong silent movie stars who had won
the West. He was wearing a gray cord sport jacket, a tieless
maroon sport shirt, and well-tailored charcoal slacks.

"Let me put these in a vase," she said, indicating the

roses. "Then I'll get us something to drink. What'll you have?"

"Whatever you're having," he said.

"I'm having Scotch on the rocks."

"Make that two."

After she served him his drink, and held her own, she sank on the sofa near him.

"You know, Paul," she said, "I feel we're practically strangers. We've dined together twice and yet I've learned next to nothing about you."

"We didn't exactly dine twice, Gayle. We had coffee and whatever in a fast-food place. Hardly conducive to any conversation in depth."

"You're right. Well, at least tonight we're alone."

Brandon sipped his Scotch. "Tell me about yourself. Do you have any family?"

Gayle shook her head. "Not really. My father died when I was little. My mother is alive, but she's in a nursing home and prematurely senile. I see her once a month to make sure she's being taken care of properly. Then I have an older brother in Toronto. He's a computer whiz."

"Does he know what you do?"

"Oh, we're very open with each other in our correspondence and occasional phone calls. He knows and understands and sees nothing wrong with it. Because he knows what motivated me to become a surrogate. I told you about that before, about how the fellow I was going with suffered from sexual dysfunction and eventually committed suicide."

"I remember," said Brandon.

"I've remained single. What about you?"

"Me . . . I'm very single, too—deliberately so. I was married once . . ."

"You were? What happened?"

Brandon shrugged. "A young actress in L.A., originally from Oregon. Need I tell you more? Her real love affair was with herself, and her future. I'll spare you the bleak details. Suffice it to say, she didn't like sex in general, and I didn't like it with her in particular."

"So you divorced?"

"After a year," said Brandon. "But I remained haunted by a kind of guilt. Let's say an uncertainty. I'd had affairs. She'd had affairs. But somehow we couldn't make it good together. I was the one who was dysfunctional. But, in a sense, so was she. Anyway, I read about a sex encounter group that had a program run by two psychologists down in La Jolla. So I enrolled. Actually, very enlightening. I found out my case wasn't so unusual. Deep down I didn't like the lady I was married to. I wanted to get away from her, and my body got the message before my head did. The experience stimulated my interest in sex education once more, and I returned to Oregon to resume teaching. When I heard Dr. Freeberg was looking for a male surrogate, I applied. Here I am."

"Are you interested in it only as a way to make a living?"

"Truthfully, I don't know yet. I guess I feel now there's more to it than that."

"I'm glad," said Gayle, relieved. "Do you have a family?"

"No brother, no sister. In a sense, no parents. I have parents, but they divorced maybe ten years ago, and since then each has remarried, and mostly we're out of touch." He appraised Gayle. "You can say I'm a loner like yourself. Not that I want to be. Obviously, that's why I'm here."

She met his gaze. "Why are you here?"

"Because I don't like being without you."

She smiled. "Well spoken." She set down her empty glass and stood up, reaching for his hand. "Let's have dinner."

Brandon came to his feet. But instead of letting her take him into the dining room, he pulled her firmly to him. She did not resist.

"Dinner can wait, can't it?" he whispered into her ear.

"Do you—do you have something better in mind?" she said weakly.

"This." He brought his face down to her and pressed his lips to hers, then kissed her hard. "I'm trying to tell you I love you," he said.

Momentarily, she drew back. "Paul, I love you, too. Let's stop wasting time . . ."

"I was hoping you'd—"

"—go on from here? I can't wait." She linked an arm in his. "My bedroom's off the hall."

He followed her into a small but pretty room, with flowered chintz chairs and curtains, a pair of lamp shades in pink, and a queen-size bed, ready for occupancy.

Gayle stood silently as he undressed her, then himself. She watched him stiffen and felt herself grow damp.

He grabbed her, smothering her mouth with kisses, and slowly moved his mouth down to her breasts, tonguing and kissing each until the brown nipples were enlarged and firm.

She took him by the arm and led him to the bed. "I've been dreaming of this all day," she said breathlessly, "even while I was working."

As she dropped down on the bed, he said, "Working? Working with whom?"

"First, with the impotent patient from Chicago. It was very successful. I came."

"*You* came?" Brandon lowered himself on the bed, his eyes on her. "How did it affect him?"

"He got his first hard-on. I mean, that's the point, you know, no pun intended."

Brandon frowned. "Then what did you do?"

"I congratulated him. Wouldn't you?" Touching Brandon, Gayle said, "There's just one thing, Paul. If I'm a little slow tonight, just have patience."

"Why? Did you also see your second patient today?"

"The premature ejaculator? Yes, he's on intensive."

"What did you do with him?"

"The usual. I introduced him to the squeezing technique."

"How?"

"Paul, for God's sake, by squeezing his penis before he came, of course. It worked."

Brandon remained very still. "You don't have to be so graphic."

She was staring at his deflating penis. "I'm sorry, darling.

Let me help you. Come here." She patted the bed beside
her.

Shaken, Brandon obeyed her. "What do you intend to
do?"

"Relax you. Let me give you a facial caress, maybe a back
caress, some pleasuring—"

"Hold on there. I thought this was purely social, not
business as usual."

Gayle was confused. "But it is. I only wanted to—"

"No, none of those damn exercises. I don't want them
tonight."

"Well, let me do something else." She sat up, taking his
limp penis in her hand. She leaned down and began to
bend her head toward it.

"Hey, what are you doing?"

"I'm going to kiss you there. I'm sure that'll work."

Brandon grabbed her hair and pulled her head back.
"Kiss me there? Listen to me, I wouldn't mind that ordi-
narily, but I just have a feeling this is something you do with
your patients. Do you go down on them?"

She faltered. "I've never had to. Not once." She met his
eyes frankly. "But if I had to, I suppose I might do it if it
were necessary."

He shook his head with disgust. "Shit, you are something, you really are." He rolled sideways and left the bed.
"You're on a power trip, that's all. You don't give a damn
about love. You just want to show how great you are, how
you can dominate any man. I think that's shit."

Gayle was aghast. "Paul, are you crazy?"

He yanked on his jock shorts and was pulling on his
trousers. "Crazy to be here, to believe that a sex surrogate
could be a real woman." He stuck his bare feet into his
shoes, then swept up his socks and shirt and jacket. "No
way. You go down on your patients . . . or do anything
you like with them—but not with me. I should have known.
With two sex surrogates—zilch—never the twain shall
meet. Sorry, Gayle, my young pro. It won't work. Good
night!"

By the time she had pulled on her robe and chased into

the living room to explain it all better, to persuade him to calm down, it was too late.

The front door had just slammed. The living room was empty.

VII

When Tony Zecca awakened in the morning, he was surprised to find that Nan was not in the bed beside him. This was unlike her, since she was usually asleep when he left for the restaurant. Although, several times, he remembered, she had risen before him to do some shopping for the house.

Zecca dressed hastily, without further concern about her absence, because he had arranged to be at his office early to interview two more applicants for the temporary job as cashier. Then he would return in time to take Nan to her doctor and have it out with the bastard.

Once dressed, Zecca had gone into the dining room, calling out to his housekeeper in the kitchen that he was ready for his breakfast.

Sitting down at his place mat, he folded the morning paper to the sports section while Hilda appeared with his orange juice and hot coffee. He was finishing his orange juice and reading the box scores when Hilda reappeared with his eggs, bacon, and toast.

Attacking the eggs and bacon, concentrating on the sports results, he asked Hilda absently, "What time did my lady friend have her breakfast?"

"She didn't," said Hilda, disappearing into the kitchen. Zecca banged down his fork, then twisted in his chair. "Hilda, goddammit, come back here!" He waited for his overweight German housekeeper to return. Seeing her materialize in the kitchen doorway, he barked, "What in the hell do you mean, she didn't have breakfast? She never goes out with no breakfast."

"Who says she went out? I didn't see her go out. She must be around somewhere."

"Yeah, that's it," agreed Zecca. He shoved what remained of his eggs into his mouth, pushed away the sports section, and left his chair. He meant to head straight for the restaurant, but then he remembered he had planned to return to the house to pick up Nan and drive her to her phony doctor for a showdown. He'd give that phony doctor a piece of his mind, and then some, and once and for all make him stop stalling Nan along and interfering with their normal love life. He didn't know the time he was supposed to meet Nan for her appointment, and he decided he'd better find that out before he went to work.

Nan's bathroom door was closed. Zecca yanked it open and barged inside. No one there. Then for sure the bitch was in her dressing room. Why those fucking women always took so much time dressing up he didn't know, when all you wanted with them was to have them bare ass.

Zecca jerked open the door to the dressing room, shouting out, "Nan, goddammit!"

No answer. The dressing room was empty.

Zecca spun around. Something fishy. Her clothes rack was empty. He pivoted all round, and his eyes fell on the note Scotch-taped to her mirror.

He strode to the mirror, tore off the note, and tried to make out her shaky handwriting. Something real crazy about leaving him. Leaving him! He held the note closer and read each word carefully. He had it now. She'd walked. The bitch had walked out on him, something no woman since Crystal had ever done or even dared think about.

In a fury, Zecca crumpled her note, balled it up, and crushed it in his huge fist.

Anger wrestled with bewilderment. Why would she have
done a cuckoo thing like that? He'd been good to her, given
the homeless nobody a home and a job, yet she'd walked
off. How come? She had nowhere to go, nowhere on earth.
She knew no one else, far as he knew, except . . .

Except the fucking doctor she'd been seeing almost every day.

That knowledge and the recollection of their talk yesterday when she so desperately tried to keep him from seeing
her doctor fitted together and told him the whole story.

Nan had thrown him over, left him to shack up with her
doctor, who'd probably been screwing her regularly from
the first day.

Well, goddammit, Zecca told himself, neither of them
would get away with it. He'd find that hot-nuts doctor and
punch him out so he'd never forget not to fool around with
anyone else's woman. Then he'd get his mitts on Nan and
drag her back where she belonged. That was it. His course
was clear.

Only one roadblock.

Who in the fuck was her fucking doctor? He had to know
who deserved a beating before going to wherever they were
shacked up and dragging her back with him.

Who in the fuck was her doctor, dammit?

She'd never told him, clever bitch, as far as he could
remember. And he could kick himself in the ass for never
having bothered to ask her. He just hadn't bothered, and
now his fury mounted once more at her cheating on him.

He tried to think. To go to a doctor, you had to pay him.
Therefore, there should be bills around. But he always kept
track of her bills and filed them at the restaurant office for
his accountant and the IRS. Yet he'd never once seen a
receipt, or a bill, from her so-called doctor. Obviously, she
paid in cash always, out of the small savings she'd had when
she'd moved in, or out of her earnings or whatever she
skimmed off her household allowance.

No bills, not one.

Wrong. There had been one bill, he remembered, one
bill on an M.D.'s letterhead way back in the beginning. It

had slipped through before she got smart. And Zecca had it, and if he remembered right, it had been on the doctor's letterhead stationery.

He snatched up Nan's telephone, dialed his restaurant, and got his head waitress, who was also his floor manager.

"Marge," he said, "I'm coming in, but I have no time for those interviews with the temporary cashiers. Cancel them out for today, and let that bimbo we have stay on and keep robbing us until I throw her out. I'm coming in on something else, a tax matter, so I'll be in my office and don't let anybody bother me."

Leaving the bitch's dressing room, Zecca tore out of the house, jumped into his Cadillac, and was on his way to sweet revenge.

A half hour later, in the rear room cubbyhole office of his restaurant, he'd checked when Nan had started working for him, knowing she'd gone to fix her snatch with the doctor sometime after that.

Ten minutes passed before he had the doc's receipt in hand. He felt triumphant.

Dr. Stanley Lopez—a spick yet—and his charges for the first overall checkup.

The only receipt. No others either because she paid him in cash or, more probably, because he paid her for banging her. Some shots she was getting!

Receipt in hand, with Dr. Lopez's address on it, Zecca turned his Cadillac toward the downtown district of Hillsdale.

Fifteen minutes later he slowed in front of a six-story medical building with a parking lot underneath. Zecca drove down the ramp, left his Cadillac with an attendant, found Dr. Lopez's name on the directory beside the elevators, then took the first elevator going up.

He got off at the fourth floor.

The frosted glass door just to the right of his elevator read: Stanley M. Lopez, M.D. Zecca pushed open the door, balled up his fists, and almost bounded across the fancy reception room to where some kind of good-looking Latina gal was busy over some paperwork.

Her expression was startled when she saw Zecca.

He guessed it showed on his face, how he felt, so he tried to contain himself.

"Yes?" the receptionist asked.

"I want to consult with Dr. Lopez about my—my wife."

"She's a patient here?"

"A regular."

"Her name, please."

"Zecca," he said automatically, and then he corrected himself. "No, actually she likes to use her maiden name. Her name—my wife's name is Nan Whitcomb. She was coming in to see Dr. Lopez today."

The receptionist furrowed her brow. "That can't be, I'm afraid. Dr. Lopez had no appointments today. He has to conduct a seminar at USC. You're sure your wife is a patient who comes here regularly? I just can't seem to place her name."

"I'm sure, all right," said Zecca grimly, digging into his jacket pocket for the receipt he'd brought along. "Have a look. Here's your receipt for a bill she paid."

The receptionist took it, stared at it, puzzled, then slowly got up and made her way to a file cabinet behind her. She knelt down, pulled out the bottom file drawer, fingered through the tabs, and then pulled out a manila folder. "You're right, sir. We have a file for 'Whitcomb, Nan.' Let me have a look."

Walking slowly back to the counter, the receptionist had opened the folder and was studying the contents inside. Suddenly, she raised her head, smiling at Zecca. "I think it's all clear now. I was actually right. Your wife isn't Dr. Lopez's regular patient. She just visited him the one time for a physical checkup. She was a referral from Dr. Freeberg. He always has his patients come to Dr. Lopez for a checkup before working with them. Dr. Freeberg's the one you want to see for any consultation."

"Dr. Freeberg? Nan never mentioned him."

The receptionist stammered, looking up at Zecca's glowering face. "Maybe because she's shy. Most wives are, when it comes to this."

"Comes to what?"

"Visiting a sex therapist. Dr. Arnold Freeberg's a sex therapist who runs the Freeberg Clinic on Market Avenue. About five minutes from here. Your wife must be a patient there. I'm sure Dr. Freeberg will be pleased to arrange a consultation with you."

"Yeah," said Zecca, "I'm sure he will. Dr. Arnold Freeberg, you say?"

"Dr. Arnold Freeberg. When you leave our building downstairs, turn left, then right at the first block. That's Market. You can walk it in ten or fifteen minutes. If you're driving, five minutes. I'll write out the address of the Freeberg Clinic for you."

Jamming her card into his pocket, Zecca mumbled his thanks and left the reception room.

Waiting for the elevator, Zecca boiled with inner rage.

So Nan, his little cunt, was living it up with a sex therapist, whatever that was. He didn't have to guess. He knew. Dr. Freeberg, a kike for sure, was sticking it to her daily. And Nan was loving it. Some treatment.

Well, he told himself, as the elevator arrived, he had a more lasting treatment for both of them when he got his hands on them. He'd make mincemeat of the doc. And he'd bring Nan home on a leash and keep her there on her back where she belonged until she appreciated what she had.

The first thing to do was to find out where this Freeberg had his Nan stashed. He had to catch them in the act together. Then he'd know what to do next.

Leaving the elevator, he already knew what to do next.

Making Freeberg into mincemeat was too good for the fucking bastard. He should waste the son of a bitch—or have one of the boys who owed him do it for him.

That was the solution. Waste him.

An eye for an eye, like the Good Book said.

The telephone call from Roger Kile, who had introduced himself as Dr. Arnold Freeberg's attorney-at-law in Los

Angeles, had come to District Attorney Hoyt Lewis in Hillsdale at eleven fifteen this morning.

Lewis had speculated through the week whether the call would come from Dr. Freeberg himself or his lawyer . . . and what Freeberg's decision would be. Now he knew that Freeberg had hired a lawyer to make the call for him. And now Lewis would know what decision Freeberg had made.

"I'm calling you," Kile was saying, "to discuss the ultimatum you've given my client, Dr. Arnold Freeberg. As Dr. Freeberg's attorney, I am empowered to discuss the matter on his behalf."

"Mr. Kile," said Hoyt Lewis coolly, "I'm not certain there is much to discuss."

"Perhaps not," said Kile. "At the same time, to be positive my client has your ultimatum right, I would appreciate it if you would repeat the terms of your offer to him. I'd like to hear, in your own words, what you told Dr. Freeberg when you visited him."

"I'll be glad to oblige you. I presume you intend to record exactly what I conveyed to Dr. Freeberg?"

"I do, sir."

"Very well. In my one meeting with Dr. Arnold Freeberg, I informed him I had investigated his practice of employing sexual surrogates, mainly female, to cohabit with males for pay. I told him that, from evidence available, his present role as a therapist fell under a California statute that regards pandering as a crime. I told him that his female surrogates fell under the section that regards prostitution as a crime. I told him that if so charged and convicted, he was liable to a prison sentence of up to ten years, and the single sex surrogate I selected as an example to be charged could, on conviction, serve a prison sentence of a half a year."

"And then you offered my client a compromise," stated Kile.

"Yes, a compromise out of a spirit of generosity. Actually, Dr. Freeberg possesses no criminal record. This is a first-time offense—excluding his run-in with my counterpart in Tucson—and in the belief that Dr. Freeberg had misunderstood the law of California, I offered him another chance. Quite simply, Mr. Kile, I told him he could avoid any charges or prosecution if he ceased his use of sex surrogates and confined his practice solely to that of being a licensed therapist. On the other hand, if he elected to ignore my offer, but persisted in operating, as he has been doing, I would have him arrested, arraigned, and prosecuted."

"Let me interject something right here, and be frank about it," said Kile. "When I first undertook defending Dr. Freeberg and his surrogates, I was a bit uncertain about his work and about the law. I knew Dr. Freeberg was legitimate and sincere, and was directing his surrogates, but one possibility niggled my mind. That he was covering himself with his advice and his directions, and that the surrogates might be prostitutes masquerading as surrogates. When I began my researches, I talked to a number of sex surrogates. I learned quickly that there was a qualitative difference between a sex surrogate and a prostitute. Today I am satisfied, to a moral and legal certainty, that there is no question at all that the surrogate and prostitute are qualitatively different beings. Freeberg and his surrogates are healers. The pimp and his prostitutes are nothing but exploiters. Obviously, every other district attorney in California and New York acknowledges this difference, and that's why there has never been, in twenty-five years, a legal action against a therapist and a surrogate."

"Mainly because the moral climate in this country had not deteriorated to its present low ebb," said Hoyt Lewis. "Now it's reached a new low, and I want to put a stop to it. The process of cleansing has to start somewhere, and I've decided it should start here. I repeat, I can't see a clear distinction between a pimp and his prostitutes, and a sex therapist and his sex surrogates. This test case will prove there is no real distinction, and when I'm through, not a state in the Union will permit the use of surrogates."

"But you must acknowledge," insisted Kile, "that a vast difference in motivation and behavior separates a female surrogate from a common prostitute?"

Hoyt Lewis's voice hardened. "I acknowledge no such thing. I am familiar with the arguments. Dr. Freeberg presented them to me most eloquently. To my mind, they don't hold up, and they won't hold up in a court of law. A female sex surrogate is as unlicensed as a streetwalker—"

"Mr. District Attorney," Kile interrupted, "I see the surrogate as secondarily licensed under the law. She is, after all, serving with the continuing guidance of a fully licensed therapist and serving in the capacity as an adjunct or assistant to him."

"Sorry, Mr. Kile. I disagree. Dr. Freeberg's sex surrogates, at his instigation, are performing lewd sexual acts for hire. They are prostitutes in disguise. I won't have that in Hillsdale." He paused. "I see no purpose served in continuing this debate. I have given Dr. Freeberg a fair choice. Freedom to continue his practice in Hillsdale without the use of sex surrogates, or prosecution for pandering and prostitution if he persists in using surrogates. I assume you've called with his decision?"

"I have."

"What is his decision?"

"I am empowered to state, as Dr. Arnold Freeberg's attorney-at-law, that because we are certain he is behaving within the law, he will continue his practice and his use of partner surrogates."

District Attorney Hoyt Lewis had not anticipated with any certainty that this would be the decision. He had guessed that Roger Kile had presented his feeble arguments on behalf of his client to make Lewis think twice about prosecution, and that, when the chips were down, he would back off into the compromise. This was better than he had hoped.

"Dr. Freeberg is going on with the sex surrogates, you say?" Lewis repeated. He felt strangely elated. "That's definitely the decision?"

"Definitely."

Lewis wanted to say, "Your funeral," but aware that he was being taped, he refrained. He said instead, "I'm sorry. I guess there's nothing more to add except—I'll see you in court."

"If you have a case," said Kile mildly.

"Mr. Kile, I assure you, I very much have a case."

An hour later, District Attorney Hoyt Lewis had the Reverend Josh Scrafield across his desk from him.

"I hated to break in on your day, Reverend Scrafield," the district attorney began. "I know how busy you are, but since this concerns the matter of Freeberg and his sex surrogates—"

"There's not a thing that concerns me more than that matter. That quack doctor is polluting our community."

"I'd offered Freeberg a compromise, as you know," said Lewis. "His lawyer just phoned me with his decision."

"And?" said Scrafield eagerly, coming forward in his chair.

"Dr. Freeberg has elected to ignore my offer. He intends to continue his use of surrogates."

"He's going on with his foul practice?" said Scrafield, with delight in his voice. "He's going to continue?"

"And so are we," said Lewis calmly. "We are going to prosecute to the full extent of the law."

The Reverend Scrafield wet his lips. "Pandering and prostitution," he said, half to himself. "Mr. District Attorney, you can't lose. We'll beat the drums for you the minute you give the green light. You'll win the case and enjoy all the benefits and advantages to be derived from the victory. This is the greatest thing that could have happened to us. The case against Freeberg is open-and-shut."

Hoyt Lewis nodded. "I believe it is—that's why I'm proceeding. But it all depends on the star witness you brought me."

"Chet Hunter? Never mind about him. He's enrolled as a patient with Freeberg, busy every day at that clinic or somewhere with a young chippy named Gayle Miller."

"They're going at it?"

"Chet Hunter assures me they are. I haven't seen him

since we were all together, but I speak to him regularly on the phone."

"I'm sure," said Lewis, "he's keeping some written record of his daily—uh—activity?"

"He is. A day-by-day record, a journal. It's all on paper."

"Excellent," replied Lewis. "Now is the time to see Hunter again and find out what he has for us." Lewis rose behind his desk. "There's still that one thing to nail down, the one truth I must have." His tone underlined what followed next. "That they are actually engaged in sexual intercourse," he said. "That's the key. After they do that, we're on our way. I'll serve Freeberg and Miss Miller immediately. Until then, we'll hold off. As soon as Hunter tells us that intercourse has taken place, he's to deliver his tape recording of the payoff session to us. He *will* be using a tape recorder, won't he?"

"Of course. He knows all about it."

"I'll require that corroborative evidence on tape to support Hunter's verbal testimony in court." Momentarily, Lewis worried, "Can he get away with it? How'll he do it?"

"He uses a miniature voice-activated recorder in his research work. Keeps it well hidden in the vest pocket of his jacket. It'll pick up every word, every sound, while they're going at it."

Lewis seemed relieved. "That's all I'll need to proceed. Once Hunter has the intercourse session in his journal, and backed up by the actual tape, he should inform you, and then you should inform me. When that's done, I will then arrest and arraign Dr. Freeberg and Miss Miller. So contact Chet Hunter as soon as possible and find out where he stands."

The Reverend Scrafield was on his feet, grinning and winking. "If Chet's home I'll see him immediately. Congratulations, Mr. Lewis. As you put it, we're on our way."

A half hour later, the Reverend Scrafield had settled himself into the dilapidated uncomfortable armchair in Chet

Hunter's apartment and surveyed the cramped quarters with distaste.

"This is where you see her?" said Scrafield.

"See her?" repeated Hunter from his chair opposite the clergyman. "Oh, you mean Gayle Miller."

"Freeberg's little whore you're involved with. Does she come here?"

"No. She rents a house—more a cottage, actually—about twenty minutes from here."

"I think maybe you'd better give me her address so Hoyt Lewis will have it handy when he's ready to haul her in."

Reluctantly, Hunter jotted down Gayle Miller's address on a slip of paper and handed it to the clergyman.

Scrafield considered the address. "Where do you do it? In her bedroom?"

"Not in her bedroom. In her therapy room."

"In her what?"

"An extra room she has to demonstrate the exercises, sort of half office, half social room with a large couch and a floor mat to lie down on."

"Have you laid her?"

"Well . . ." Hunter hesitated. "Why don't you read what I've been doing?" He reached for the carefully typed sheaf of papers on his desk and gave it to Scrafield. "I've been keeping a sort of play-by-play record of our activities together. Every time I've finished an exercise, that evening I write an exact report on what happened. In fact, I also typed three more pages this morning, so those twenty-one pages you have are right up-to-date. I'd suggest you look them over, so you know—"

"All I know," said Scrafield, "is that our district attorney has ants in his pants waiting for you to finish the job. He's itching to get going, and he delegated me to meet with you and find out where we stand."

"Well, that journal of my daily encounters with Gayle Miller will give you and the D.A. a comprehensive picture of exactly what's going on."

"All right, let me read it."

"I can get us some coffee while you're reading."

Scrafield was already going over the typescript. "Yes, coffee'll be fine."

Hunter went into his pantrylike kitchen and puttered about making coffee, feeling uneasy about Scrafield's reading and concerned with the clergyman's reaction.

At last he brought the coffee out into his living room, setting Scrafield's cup on the end table beside him and placing his own cup on his desk. Scrafield had ignored his coffee and was concentrating on the journal. Hunter drank his own coffee, pretending not to watch for his visitor's reactions.

Another ten minutes went by before Scrafield finished his reading and put Hunter's journal on his lap.

He fixed a cold eye on the researcher. "Chet, I've got to tell you—this is a pile of crap."

"What do you mean?"

"I mean, it adds up to zilch. I'll give it to you like A,B,C. I once read in some book that only one crime counts. Not stealing the jewels or embezzling . . . The only crime that counts is murder. The same goes here. When you're out to prove prostitution, it's not diddling around that counts but only sexual intercourse. I don't see any sexual intercourse here."

"Well, all I've written about is part of it," said Hunter defensively.

"Not to me, it isn't, and not to Hoyt Lewis, either." Scrafield picked up the typescript once more and began to leaf through it. "What have we got here—hand caress, facial caress, back caress, body imaging, a shower, some feeling around but not touching breasts or genitals, then feeling around the genitals, and so on and on. What does it all add up to? A crock of nothing. In court, there'll be only one question. Did you lay her? Well, why haven't you? Why don't you?"

Hunter felt the perspiration on his forehead. "As you know, I got into this therapy thing by saying I had a problem."

"There's no problem a good fuck can't solve. You mean you can't get it up with her?"

"I can. I have."

"Then what's holding you back?"

"Well, Reverend Scrafield, I'm trying to follow the rules. There are rules in therapy, and you've got to follow them."

Scrafield was plainly disgusted. "Who gives a damn about rules? You've got this good-looking woman—you say she's a looker—in the nude, on her back, and instead of putting it to her, you're diddling around. She's used to having men go inside her. That's clear . . . It's her business. So get down to business!"

Hunter was sweating profusely now. He didn't want to tell Scrafield that he had tried, and it had been a fiasco. Nor did he want to discuss the squeeze technique that Gayle had found necessary to use with him.

"We're making progress," Hunter said lamely. "I expect I'll have sexual intercourse with her tomorrow."

"You're sure?"

"That's next on the agenda."

"Can you promise me?"

Hunter gulped. "Sure, I can promise you."

Scrafield's stony expression had cracked into the resemblance of a smile. He jumped to his feet. "That's more like it, young man." He waved the sheaf of typed pages. "You go right out and make a photocopy of this and drop it off for the D.A. Then, when you deliver it, reassure him he'll also have the taped evidence in hand any minute now."

"By the day after tomorrow."

"All right. The minute our D.A. has your sworn statement that you will testify in court, we'll move, and get Freeberg and Gayle Miller in custody." He patted Hunter on the shoulder. "Long as you're at it, be sure you enjoy yourself tomorrow—before we put her out of circulation."

Undressing in his bedroom, as Nan Whitcomb sat naked on the bed with her adoring eyes on him, Brandon could not concentrate on what was immediately ahead for him. His mind was totally filled with Gayle and his stupid behavior last night in walking out on her. He felt riddled with guilt and with the fear that he had ended their budding relationship and lost someone he was truly in love with. He wanted only to get to a telephone in private, call Gayle, and find out if she would see him once more.

Meanwhile, his clothes were off, and he knew Nan was awaiting his next move.

Brandon knew what his next step should be.

Penetration.

He stood unmoving, afraid to proceed. For one thing, with his mind on Gayle, he worried slightly that he might not achieve an erection with Nan. But meeting her eyes, he knew that was not what he really feared. He really feared the adoration in her eyes, and her newly acquired relaxation in his presence. He feared that if he successfully coupled with her, and they both enjoyed the experience, Nan might misread it for love. If so, that would create a real problem.

"Something on your mind?" Nan asked cheerfully.

"Just thinking what we should take up next."

"What is next, Paul?"

Should he attempt a stalling tactic until he could have more time to decide how to handle what intercourse with her might lead to?

Instinctively, he wanted more time to think out how he should handle her.

"Actually, Nan," he found himself saying, "I think it would be best for both of us if we repeated our last exercise, just once more, to see how we both feel."

Nan was unable to hide her disappointment. "We'll do the genital touching again? Wasn't there supposed to be something new?"

"Not necessarily. It wasn't bad last time, was it?"

"It was wonderful, Paul," she quickly assured him. "I wouldn't mind."

"You can let go, possibly have an orgasm again. It's not our goal, but there's nothing wrong if you feel like it."

"I'll feel like it. But I'll feel like it more if you'd have an orgasm, too. Last time, I'm afraid I shortchanged you. I'd like to make you happy, too."

"We'll see," he said noncommittally, joining her on the bed.

They moved to the middle of the bed, then turned face-to-face, their eyes open. Taking up a bottle, he applied a light oil to her body, avoiding her vaginal mound, and then he handed the bottle to her and asked her to apply the oil to his body. She did so industriously, making a careful detour past his genital area, but by the time she had covered him with the oil, he could see her breasts rising and falling more rapidly. He had wanted this to be a slow, extended session, but her obvious desire to be touched by him told him it would not last as long as he had hoped.

"Okay, Nan," he said, "let's go ahead with the exercise. Do you want us to pleasure each other simultaneously, like we did last time, or do you prefer we sensate focus on each other separately, taking turns?"

"Taking turns," she answered at once. "I can concentrate better. You can do me first, and after that, I'll do you. Do you mind?"

"Not at all," Brandon said. "Actually, it is preferable to do this in sequence. You lie back, close your eyes, and really make way for your feelings."

"Good," she said.

She was on her back, her eyes tight but her arms and legs limp.

Bent over her, he went for her head, his fingers running through her hair, then dancing over every crevice of her face, and playing along her shoulders. Her breasts were heaving when he reached them, and the nipples were points.

As he stroked her stomach, there was an almost inaudible sound. He thought it might have been a moan. His fingers touched her pubic hairline and glided over the visible bud of her clitoris. Her knees came up, and her legs spread, and he knew he would never get to her thighs.

"I want to come . . ." she sighed.

He had meant to get to her thighs, but he would never make it. After all, this was genital pleasuring, and Nan did not deserve to be deprived of it.

His fingers were going from her clitoris to her vagina and back again, and abruptly she raised her hips well off the bed.

"Paul, Paul," she cried out, and then she exclaimed, "I'm coming!"

He knew, he knew, and helped her all the way over the top.

When the prolonged orgasm ended, she sank down on the bed limp, trying to catch her breath.

Then he got to her thighs at last, caressing them, and after that her legs. Throughout the remainder of the exercise, she lay motionless, and he told himself that she was too exhausted to pleasure him the same way, which in a sense was a relief. Because he didn't want his body to subvert his determination not to get too involved with her.

Suddenly, to his surprise, she was sitting up, her eyes open. "Thank you, Paul," she said, and leaned over and kissed him. "You wanted me to have feelings," she added. "I had them, very much."

He was afraid to ask what they had been. He did not answer her.

She pushed him backward. "Now, my turn," she said. "I'm going to do it to you. I hope you have the same feelings."

He continued to avoid making any reply and dutifully lay down and closed his eyes with misgivings.

He was encompassed by the touch of her hands on his cheeks, throat, chest.

"You're gorgeous, sweet and gorgeous," he heard her whisper.

He made believe it was Gayle speaking to him . . . He could see Gayle nude and magnificent as she had been last night . . . And then he knew it was happening to him.

His swollen penis was rising, standing straight up.

There was no containing it. He was helpless now.

Her hand had curled around his rigidity, very practiced, perfect, perfect, perfect.

He did not know how many minutes had passed. Maybe

five or six. Maybe more. But it seemed an eternity of delight, and he wanted only release.

"I—I—I . . ."

Her hand moved faster. "I know, my darling," she whispered.

Her hand covered the top of his penis, and he came and came and came.

The next thing he knew was the satiny feel of her pliant body. She was lying close to him, he realized, and embracing him.

Her eyes were on him.

"You were marvelous," she said, "just marvelous."

"You, too," he said weakly.

"I felt closer to you than ever."

"I hoped you would."

He stared at the ceiling, and she was silent awhile, staring at him. At last, she spoke. "Paul, there's something I want to tell you."

He was not sure he wanted to hear. He wondered what it would be. He nodded.

"I left Tony Zecca," she said as if she were giving Brandon a present. "I couldn't take it anymore, so I walked out last night while he was asleep."

Brandon was alert now, propped on an elbow. "You left him?"

She released Brandon. "Like you once suggested."

"But I—" He didn't know how to respond. "Where did you go?"

"I called you to ask if you could suggest a hotel, but you weren't in."

"No." He remembered being with Gayle . . . and walking out on her. Oh, God, what idiocy.

"So I phoned Dr. Freeberg at home, and he was kind enough to get me a room at the Excelsior Hotel, not far from the clinic."

"I'm glad." He sat up, and then she sat up. "What are you going to do for money?" he asked.

"I've got enough for a few weeks. After that, I'll have to find a job."

"You'll find one," he said, troubled. He began to get out of bed.

"Paul . . ."

He turned toward her. "Yes?"

"If you'd like, I could stay with you here tonight. Would you like that?"

"Of course I like to be with you," he replied unhesitatingly, "but it's not allowed, Nan. I'd lose my job if Dr. Freeberg ever found out. Even if I wanted to break the rules, I couldn't tonight. I have another—another appointment."

"Oh." Her disappointment was evident.

"I'm sorry, but we'll be seeing each other tomorrow afternoon for the next exercise."

"That's right. I won't forget." She seemed considerably cheered up. "What will it be?"

The word came out with difficulty. "Penetration," he said, and quickly added, "if you think you can do it yet."

She smiled. "I can do anything with you, Paul, *anything.*"

Within minutes after Nan had dressed, hugged him good-bye, and left his apartment, Brandon was on the telephone, hoping he would find Gayle at home.

To his good fortune, she was home.

"It's Paul," he said to her, "hat in hand. Gayle, I want to apologize for my behavior last night. I was a stupid ass."

"I'm glad you called," she replied seriously. "I was thinking about us all day. I almost called you. I don't think I behaved very well, either. I wasn't very sensitive. I wanted to tell you that."

"Gayle, when can I see you again? The sooner the better."

"Yes, I want to see you, too. Why don't I come up to your place?"

"When?"

"Not until after dinner. I promised to have a bite with two of the other surrogates. I could make it around ten o'clock. Or is that too late?"

"It's never too late."

"I'll be there. Give me your address. I look forward, Paul. I really do."

Arriving at his apartment, Gayle was greeted by Brandon with a hug and kisses.

Stepping back, she surveyed his living room. "Not bad," she said, "for a struggling male sex surrogate. I like those Giacometti lithos on the walls."

"I try to think thin."

"Are they real?"

"Who can afford real? They're reproductions. I'm so glad you're here, Gayle."

She dug into her purse and extracted something.

"I brought you a present, a peace offering," she said, smiling. "I think we've made our peace, but I'd like you to have it anyway."

"What is it?"

Handing it to him, she said, "A key to my house. When we have our next date, and you get there before I do, you can go inside and get ready for me." She took him in. She gestured to the terry cloth bathrobe he was wearing. "I see you *are* ready. What's underneath?"

"Just me. No camouflage."

"I'd better catch up with you." She pecked a kiss at him. "Show me your bedroom."

He led her off to his bedroom.

"Be it ever so humble," he said.

She studied it. "Do you use the bedroom here?"

"For what?"

"For your patient. I use a special therapy room. I reserve my bed for the likes of you."

"Yes, this is where we do the exercises."

Gayle started unbuttoning her blouse. "How are you doing with her—whatever her name is?"

"Nan."

"Are you making progress with Nan?"

"I hope so. She was suffering from vaginismus. I have the feeling she's relaxing somewhat."

Gayle pulled off her blouse. "But you don't know yet."

"I should know after our next session."

"Penetration?" asked Gayle quietly.

"Yes. But there's a problem that makes me a little nervous." He wrinkled his brow. "I'm not sure how to handle it."

"What's the problem?"

"Well, to be honest, I believe my patient is falling in love with me. She left her boyfriend—no loss, he was a bastard —and today she offered to move in with me."

"That's a no-no, Paul."

"I told her so."

Gayle reached behind to unhook her brassiere. "I mean, the rest of it, too. You can't allow a patient to fall in love with you."

"I'm not encouraging it, believe me. Still, I can see it happening. It's making me uncomfortable. She's a nice woman. I don't know how to deal with her."

"Maybe you're not being professional enough?"

"I'm trying, Gayle."

"Maybe not enough. Maybe you're sorry for her and got too involved." She paused. "How come your Nan left her boyfriend?"

"I can't say I objected. In fact, I may have encouraged it. From what she tells, he's an animal. He could be the cause of her trouble. Anyway, she turned her back on him."

Gayle had not taken off her bra yet. "Because you encouraged her? Paul, it doesn't sound like you're handling her right. Maybe this is something Dr. Freeberg should know about."

"What could he do?"

Gayle said firmly, "He'd take you off the case. Knowing Dr. Freeberg as I do, he would never permit a surrogate to become seriously emotionally involved with a patient."

"I'm not the one who's involved," said Brandon patiently. "Nan is."

"Then it's Nan, okay. But you let her fall for you without taking steps to prevent it. Dr. Freeberg would not allow that

to happen or certainly would not let it go on. Have you told
him about this?"

"No."

Gayle stepped nearer to Brandon. "You must tell him.
It's your duty to tell him."

"You think he'd actually take me off the case?"

"In ten seconds flat."

"But the therapy isn't completed."

"He'll find someone to complete it."

"Gayle, I'm the only male surrogate in his stable."

"I guarantee, he'll find your Nan another one."

Brandon shook his head. "I don't like it. My quitting,
someone else coming in—it could hurt her deeply."

"Dr. Freeberg would know how to manage it. You owe it
to yourself, to Freeberg, and to her to report the whole
thing."

Brandon shrugged. "I guess you're right. It makes me a
little sad to have to do this, but I will."

"That's better," said Gayle cheerfully. "Well, here's
something that'll maybe cheer you up."

She drew off her bra, and her breasts almost jumped out
at Brandon.

With one arm immediately around her, he bent to kiss
the nipples of each breast. "You're fantastic," he exhaled.
He started kissing and tonguing her breasts again, and as
he did so he pulled her up against him.

She clung to him a moment, then pushed away. "Hey,
mister, I don't feel anything. From you, I mean. Take off
your robe."

He complied, and they both looked down at his flaccid
penis.

"Dear one," Gayle said, "what gives? Don't you feel like
it?"

"Of course I feel like it. I—it's just that—"

Gayle was eyeing him carefully. "Just what, Paul?"

"Well, I won't lie to you. The fact is I had an orgasm
earlier, but give me a little while . . ."

Gayle's hands flew up to her breasts, covering them.

"You had an orgasm—when you were with Nan?" she said incredulously. "With Nan?"

"Let me explain, Gayle. We were doing nondemand genital pleasuring—"

"Some nondemand!"

"And we were stroking each other. We were just following the rules, and it got a bit out of control . . . I mean, she'd orgasmed when she was with me yesterday, and she wanted me to, so—"

"So you let her get you off!"

"I didn't want to. I couldn't prevent it."

"The hell you couldn't. What you wanted was the girl who loves you to make you happy, because maybe you love her."

"Gayle, stop it. You're way off base, I swear. I don't care for her . . ."

Gayle snatched up her bra and was putting it on. "And as for me, I don't care for you. You allow another woman to get you off, and now you expect me to line up and follow her." She pulled on her blouse. "No way, my friend! Not in a million years!"

Brandon grabbed her arms. "On my word of honor, Gayle, there's no one to be jealous of."

"Who's jealous? I'm just an old-fashioned monogamist. One man, one woman. That's the way I intend to live my life. I don't need a polygamist to mess things up. As for you, tonight you can play with yourself! Good-bye!"

And with that, Gayle Miller stormed out of the bedroom and out of the apartment.

For Gayle, it had been a bad night.

Once she had returned to her house and bedroom, and gone to bed, she had been unable to sleep. Fantasies about this affair—she could only imagine it as an affair, not therapeutic sessions—that Paul was having with the woman named Nan filled her mind. Gayle had no idea what this Nan looked like, or how she behaved, but repeatedly she conjured up a picture of a young woman more attractive than herself and more spontaneously giving.

Lying in bed, trying to find sleep, Gayle was enveloped by the fantasies. Nan's genitals were beautiful, perfect, more lovely than her own. Paul worshipped them. Nan's orgasms were probably better than her own, as was the orgasm he enjoyed that had been induced by her, and there was no way Gayle could compete with such love.

As the night wore on, Gayle tried to banish the fantasies and replace them with reason. This Nan wasn't a normal woman like herself. Nan was there with Paul because she had to be treated for things that were wrong with her. Gayle did not have those things wrong with her. Paul liked Nan, was caring about her, as he should be, but he had unreservedly professed his love for Gayle herself.

Her fantasies had been senseless, she decided. She knew better than that. Love and commitment were not in the crotch but in the heart. Paul loved her from his heart, as she loved him. The problem was not Nan, nor Nan and Paul, but her own jealousy. Yes, Paul meant enough to her to make her feel jealous if he gave any part of himself to another woman. From her earlier sessions with Dr. Freeberg, Gayle knew that jealousy came from a basic insecurity, a therapeutic issue she had thought she had worked out. To expect a totally monogamous relationship was unrealistic. Because total monogamy couldn't exist. Men looked at other women, and women looked at other men. Were flirtatious, and even more. But this did not invalidate their dominant love for one mate. Paul could be allowed his minor side thing with Nan, yet keep Gayle close in his heart as someone he cherished the most.

Having thought that out, she felt more at ease and drowsy. And finally, before dawn, she slept.

When she awakened to the bright sun from behind her curtains, and she saw the hands on her bedside clock, she knew that she had overslept. Not by much, but she was an early riser. Once her head had cleared, she was glad she had caught up on her sleep. She needed rest because she needed all her strength.

There was a trying day that lay ahead of her. First, Adam Demski in the late afternoon. Then, Chet Hunter in the early evening. With each of them, the scheduled exercise was initial penetration. It was crucial and important.

But, she reminded herself, what was also important was to straighten things out with Paul Brandon.

He was, she knew, usually a late sleeper. So the odds were that he might still be home.

Gayle sat up, took the telephone in her lap, and dialed Paul.

Happily, after a few rings, he answered the phone. His voice was fuzzy, but he was there.

"Paul," she said, "it's Gayle. Did I wake you up?"

"Yes. I'm glad you did. I—"

"Let me say something right away, Paul. I am abjectly apologetic. I behaved like a fool last night. Now I can admit why. I *was* jealous. Green, unalloyed jealousy. I think I was wrong to be. Was I?"

"Gayle, I love you more than anyone and anything on earth."

"The same for me. Paul, will you come over here tonight? Let me make it up to you."

"Can't wait."

"Nine thirty," she said. "I can't wait either."

They were stretched out on the broad mat together, both nude, and Gayle propped herself on an elbow and decided to be direct with Adam Demski.

"If you're wondering what's next, Adam, it's penetration."

She saw concern cross his countenance.

She went on easily. "This will not be the only attempt, Adam. There'll be another—maybe two more. I don't want you becoming nervous and starting to look at yourself as a performer."

"Do you think I can do it?"

"I feel you can. That's why we're going to undertake the

exercise. I'll be the dominant partner, the one on top. The exercise is called stuffing and quiet penetration."

"Stuffing?" he said. "What does that . . . ?"

"Let me explain, Adam. Most men think that to achieve intercourse they have to have an erection that is rock hard. Well, that's not true, not true at all."

"It isn't?"

Gayle resumed earnestly. "I'll let you in on a secret, Adam. Intercourse can be accomplished with an almost flaccid penis. If you get only five percent swollen, not one hundred percent, it's enough. Most men prefer the missionary position, themselves on top, because it's more macho. But with this exercise, with me on top, I'll be better able to direct and control what follows. With myself above you, I can use gravity, instead of working against it. We'll start with this soft penetration. Next time or the time after, we'll do the harder penetration, with the male superior and thrusting. But for this time it is me on top."

"I don't know . . ."

"*I* know. I know you've solved your impotency because I've seen it. I know you can feel pleasure, feel sensuous, and make me feel good, too. Let's not be grim and serious. Let's be playful, have fun. I'm going to ask you to kiss my breasts and run your hands over my body, and then I'm going to caress you all over, including your genitals. I'll tell you when you're ready."

Resignation left Demski's face and made way for interest and curiosity.

Gayle fell back against the pillow. "Adam, touch my breasts, kiss them and the rest of me."

He half rose and began to oblige her.

After minutes of this foreplay, Gayle gently pushed him down on his back and began to run her fingers over his face, his chest, allowing them to play across his upper thighs. Then at last she began to play with his testicles and stroke his penis.

She could feel his penis enlarging, not to a fully erect position, but definitely enlarging.

It was enough, she decided. "Lie quietly, Adam, and don't move."

Gracefully, she mounted him, taking his barely swollen penis in the fingers of one hand and directing it to her vagina. Slowly, easily, she began putting the penis into her vulva, and she could feel his small shaft inside her. "Remember The Clock, Adam? When you used your finger inside me? Now it's your penis inside me."

"I'm not sure I'm in you."

"Okay, I'll prove you are." Astride him, Gayle tightened her inner vaginal muscles. "Did you feel that?"

"And how!"

"No moving, Adam. No thrusting or trying to perform. This exercise should accomplish no more than prove to you that you can get inside me. The real purpose is not to perform but to get you used to being potent enough to enter me, to have your penis in a woman's vagina in a nonthreatening, nondemanding situation. The whole idea is to let you know that you can get enough of an erection to enter a woman and to sustain that erection inside her. How does it feel?"

"Good, very good."

Although she tried to teach her patients not to be detached, Gayle made herself become detached in these moments. She wanted to be a spectator to his reaction.

They had been motionless for some time, and inside her vulva, she could feel him softening and receding slightly.

So as not to let him lose what had been gained, not undermine his confidence, she whispered, "Okay, Adam, you can move a little if you want to."

"I want to."

"Go ahead. Back and forth a few times. It may make you come. If it does, don't worry. That would be natural."

Her thighs closed on him as he began to move inside her. For an instant, she felt his penis grow more rigid, and he moved faster, and then he came, gurgling with pleasure.

Later, when he was showered and dressed, and she had her robe on, she saw him to the door.

In the doorway, he turned and pecked a kiss at her. "I think you made me do it. Or sort of do it."

"Oh, *you* did it, all right. You got a solid passing grade. Definitely a B plus." She kissed him in return, lightly. "Next time, look for something much more."

"An A?"

"Adam, I promise you an A."

After she had douched and bathed, Gayle slipped into a fresh robe, in time to show Chet Hunter inside.

As they walked through the hallway to her therapy room, she could see that Hunter was more nervous and tense than usual.

Settling on the mat while he undressed, Gayle asked him if he had done his homework.

"Just like teacher told me." He took off his jacket carefully and placed it on the couch. "It's not much fun alone."

"Immediate fun is not the purpose," Gayle told him, "but it'll get you ready for fun."

"I hope so."

"Well, did it work?"

"Sure it did. I got myself to an erection, and when I felt I'd ejaculate, I stopped and squeezed. I did it maybe four or five times."

"Very good," said Gayle.

Hunter had taken off all his clothes. "What I want to know is, When does the real thing happen?"

"Now."

His grim expression disappeared. "You mean right now? You mean we're going to have sexual intercourse?"

"Penetration," Gayle corrected him. "What we call soft penetration—meaning not that you'll be soft, but we'll go at it slowly, to get you used to being inside me but holding back."

"Great."

"As long as you can hold off from prematurely ejaculating, we'll continue the squeeze technique together. You'll see how effective it is."

"I'm ready when you are. Can we start now?"

"Certainly. Let's lie down together and take turns caressing each other until you get an erection."

"That won't take long, honey." He was staring at her breasts. "Once I touch those boobs, I'll be sky-high."

"Fine. Then you remain on your back and let me get on top."

"Wait a sec! I'm not used to having a woman on top. What's the idea?"

"The idea is to make it easier for you to hold back. Less chance for you to move and ejaculate."

"I don't see that," he protested.

"You will, Chet, believe me. Once you have your erection, just stay put while I straddle you. If you feel you can't restrain yourself, let me know at once. I'll apply the squeeze and retard your ejaculation, and then I'll caress you until you're ready again."

"That doesn't sound much like penetration to me."

"We'll get to your kind of penetration when I tell you. For starters, after you're inside me, and you feel like having an orgasm, let me know, and we'll keep applying the squeeze technique and letting you penetrate until you can stay inside me for five minutes. Remember, once inside me, if you feel like ejaculating quickly, don't wait—tell me, and I'll prevent it."

"Whatever you say."

Gayle took him by the arm. "Now, let's lie down together and touch each other, taking turns."

Once they were side by side on the mat, Gayle began to stroke him, moving her fingers past his genitals to avoid exciting him too soon. After a while, she lay back and indicated that Hunter could caress her.

When Hunter's hand reached her breasts, and as he had predicted, his erection was instantaneous. She could feel it against her.

She peered down. Full erection. No problem there.

What happened next would confront the problem. But Gayle was experienced with such cases, and confident.

"All right, lie back, Chet, and let me do the rest."

Obediently, he dropped into a supine position, and Gayle rose to her knees and gently mounted him. She inched closer to him until the top of his penis brushed her pubic hair.

"How do you feel?" she asked.

His eyes were shut, his expression distorted. "Like coming . . . I feel like—"

Immediately, her hand darted down to the head of his penis, catching it between three fingers and pressing.

"Dammit," he said as his penis went limp, "I could have made it."

"You wouldn't have," Gayle counseled him. "But you will."

"When?"

"Be patient. Tonight. Now, let's start over."

Still astride him, Gayle's fingers fluttered around his face, neck, chest. Automatically, he reached up for her breasts over him. At once, his penis began to swell and rise.

Again she directed his penis toward her vagina, and once again he warned her he was about to ejaculate.

She caught him and squeezed and retarded his orgasm.

The process started all over again and went on for at least ten minutes. Each time she brought him closer and closer to her vagina, and each time she prevented a premature ejaculation.

Lying there, she could feel him relax, his muscles loosening. "I'm about wiped," he said. "I'm beginning to think I can't—"

"You can," she interrupted quietly. "You will, Chet."

Slowly, she caressed and stroked him once more. This time it took longer to revive his flaccid member. After ten minutes, after massaging her breasts, he began to grow larger below.

When he had achieved a full erection, she lowered herself on it, let his shaft glide completely into her vagina. She could almost hear the seconds ticking by . . . Four, five, six, seven, eight, nine, ten. "Don't move," she whispered, "and be sure to let me—"

But that moment, he moved, and his body began shaking

and trembling beneath her, and she sat still, feeling his orgasm explode inside her.

When it was over, and he stretched beneath her, spent, she slipped to his side and she smiled. "Well, I'd say it was a good start, Chet."

"I was actually in there all the way, wasn't I?"

"Penetration for real."

"But not long enough. I got too excited—I couldn't hold back, didn't have time to tell you."

"Still, you did what you couldn't do before."

He looked up at her. "Sexual intercourse."

"Yes, and it will get better, be of greater duration, if you continue to do your homework."

Sitting up, he asked, "What's our goal, Gayle?"

"The average male—the average—usually has intercourse before orgasm for five to seven minutes. We're going to keep on until you can do ten minutes. After that, you graduate. You'll make someone very happy."

"Yeah, someone," he said, nodding, "someone'll be very happy, that's for sure."

At nine thirty that evening, after there had been no response to the doorbell, Paul Brandon used his key to enter Gayle's house.

Going into the bedroom, he found Gayle in bed and sound asleep. He bent closer to her to make sure, and heard her shallow breathing. She was gone for the night.

After studying her beautiful face in the innocent repose of sleep, Brandon shook his head. It was hopeless, he told himself, being in love with a female sex surrogate. Why couldn't it have been someone average he'd fallen in love with, like a woman spy or a marathon runner or another man's wife?

Why a female sex surrogate, of all things?

She spelled only trouble.

With a sigh, he put down the box of candy he'd brought her, left, and went out into the darkened night.

VIII

It was while Nan Whitcomb was wrapped in his bathrobe awaiting her crucial exercise—penetration—that Brandon, entering the bedroom to remove his clothes, was startled by the ringing of the telephone.

Usually, Brandon turned down his phones before an exercise was about to begin, but unaccountably he had forgotten to do so before Nan's arrival. Well, accountably, perhaps, he told himself, because his mind was still occupied by thoughts of his failure to make contact with Gayle last night, and by his apprehension of what immediately lay ahead with Nan.

The phone was still ringing, and since Nan had just gone into the bathroom, Brandon felt safe in picking it up.

The voice on the other end was Gayle's. "Paul? Am I disturbing you?"

"Not at all."

"I'm just waking up completely, and my head's a little cobwebby—but I found the candy and have a feeling that you were here last night. Were you?"

Brandon smiled to himself. "Well, as they say, if a tree falls in a forest, and no one hears it, did that tree really fall in the forest? Well, my dear, I fell at your feet last night, but no one heard me. Was I there? Yes, I was there."

Gayle sounded stricken. "You were? Oh, dear God, forgive me. I'm truly sorry. I dozed off on you."

"You were exhausted, so it's understandable."

"Do forgive me. I wanted to be with you. Paul, how can I make it up to you?"

"By being with me tonight. Why don't I pick you up for dinner? That is, if you won't be too tired?"

"I won't be tired tonight. I'm just having my hair done this afternoon."

"Let's say I come by at seven thirty. I'll have a reservation at Restaurant Lapin Agile. French, but still casual."

"I'll be ready."

"Can't wait."

He hung up, turned off the sound on the telephone, then quickly turned off the sound on his two extension phones and hastened back to the bedroom to get ready for the reappearance of Nan Whitcomb.

He had taken off the last of his clothes when he saw Nan, still wearing his terry cloth robe, standing in the bedroom doorway observing him lovingly.

Slowly, almost teasingly, she unbelted the white robe and slipped out of it. Casting it aside, briefly allowing him to take in her nudity, she advanced toward him. As she approached him, he became aware that she had sprayed herself with some kind of exotic-smelling perfume. She kissed him on the cheek and proceeded to the bed, where she sat down.

"Today's the day, isn't it?"

Momentarily, Brandon felt unnerved. She was treating this session like a long-awaited honeymoon night.

"Yes, it is."

"Penetration," she said softly.

He tried to strengthen his resolve to remind her, after it was over, that they were not lovers but teacher and patient, and that soon her therapy would be finished and their relationship would end.

"Nondemand penetration," he emphasized. "You are not expected to respond."

She didn't pout, but the movement of her bony neck and shoulders had the effect of pouting. "Why nondemand?"

"Because this exercise is to prove to you that you can again be entered totally and without pain, and nothing else has to be proved."

She blinked at him. "I hope I'm all right, Paul. I can't imagine having that awful tightening with you."

He tried to maintain some kind of professional stance. "If our exercises have gone well—and I think they have—there should be no problem."

Nan lifted her legs onto the bed and pushed herself against the pillows at the headboard. Brandon walked to the bed and lowered himself beside her.

"What do I do now?" she inquired innocently.

"We'll start with frontal caressing, taking turns, to get ourselves into the mood."

"I *am* in the mood, Paul," she said simply.

"That helps."

"I'm wet down there." She offered a shy smile. "Not difficult. I've been looking at you."

Somehow, he sensed, he had to slow her down. "Fine. But before we start, I'd like to say a few things."

"Whatever you want."

"Your only prolonged relationship with a male has been with Tony Zecca. As a result, you may still have some negative body images about yourself."

"I think maybe you've helped me overcome them. I feel more attractive now."

He concurred. "You are attractive. At the same time, with Tony you had no pleasure, only pain, and no orgasms."

"That's true."

Brandon went on doggedly. "With Tony you turned off all your physical receptors, experienced no joyous physical sensation. My goal, in our program, has been to get you in touch with your own sensuality."

She smiled less shyly. "I'm positive you've succeeded, Paul. I've never felt ours was an artificial relationship only. Even though this is paid for, and we talk to a therapist, I felt from early on that what's between us is something more.

I've stopped thinking of you as a surrogate." She hesitated. "That's good, isn't it?"

Brandon wasn't sure if he was perspiring, but he felt as if he were. He wanted to let her know, in these moments, that a vital part of their therapeutic relationship was disengaging themselves from each other soon and being able to say good-bye to all that had been happening between them. This was the time to tell her that, and yet in observing her vulnerability, he could not bring himself to do so.

"Yes," he said weakly, "that is good, and I appreciate it." He paused. "All right, Nan, let's get into our feelings and relax and have pleasure in our relationship. Close your eyes and let's begin."

Brandon began to stroke her, and after that, she stroked him. She was extremely receptive to his touch and had become expert in her caressing of him.

There would be no problem with his erection. He was ready for her.

He looked at her. "All right, Nan. Let's try penetration. Nondemand penetration. I'll lie here, flat on my back. You lift yourself up and get on top of me. Then, very gradually, lower yourself down on me, until I've entered you fully. I won't move. Don't you move either, once I'm inside you. If you have any pain, let me know at once."

Nan nodded eagerly and climbed above him. His erection held, and he braced himself for their first contact.

"Remember, Nan, no thrusting from either of us. Even if you feel like it, don't. Just get used to my being inside you."

She had his penis in one hand as she arranged herself over it and moved it until it touched her vaginal lips, and then she eased herself downward. When his penis slid into her, she continued downward until she engulfed him.

"No pain?" he asked.

"It's wonderful," she said breathlessly. "I feel ecstatic. Let me move a little, Paul."

"No."

"Please . . ."

"Absolutely no."

"But I'm marvelous now. I'm all well. Paul, darling, I love it . . . I love it more than anything . . ."

With his hands firmly on her arms, he lifted her off him and withdrew, and she fell beside him, hugging and snuggling and kissing him and whispering, "And I love you even more. I'll love you forever."

He tried to respond, without being too responsive, and as quickly as it could be done, he brought their exercise session to an end.

Once she was dressed, and at the door, she halted briefly. "The same time tomorrow?"

"Yes, Nan."

"Will it be more, more of the same?"

"Yes."

"But closer to the real thing? I mean, moving?"

"Yes," he said almost inaudibly.

She kissed him. "I *do* love you," she said.

Peering through the living room window, he saw her drive off. Troubled, he went through his apartment, turning on the volume of the telephones again.

The resolve to overcome his problem—Nan's obvious emotional involvement with him—now had become an urgent necessity. Lingering over his bedroom phone, he lifted the receiver and dialed the Freeberg Clinic. He asked to speak to Dr. Freeberg. He learned that the therapist was out on a business call but would be back in an hour or so. Brandon left word for Freeberg to phone him as soon as he could.

Pacing about his living room, puffing away at his pipe, Brandon brooded over the matter. He tried, in his mind, to clarify every instance of Nan's involvement with him, its seriousness, her determination to block out their professional relationship and regard him as her real-life boyfriend. This could not continue, he knew, and yet he was incapable of telling her it was a professional relationship that would be over within a week. He knew that, much as he hated to do so, he would have to allow Dr. Freeberg to take him off the case and replace him with another male surrogate to wind up the therapy with Nan.

An hour and a half passed before Dr. Freeberg returned his call.

"How are you, Paul?" Freeberg wanted to know.

"Never better."

"Your message says you wanted to consult me about something."

"There is something I wanted to report, Doctor. I—" And then what he had prepared himself to say, what he had rehearsed, became stuck in some recess of his throat.

He pictured Nan being summoned by Dr. Freeberg tomorrow and being told that Paul Brandon had to be taken off her case and that a substitute would appear in his place.

He could imagine Nan's consternation at this unexpected turn of events. Somehow, she would perceive that the man she loved had rejected her. Somehow, she would be frightened by the idea of starting all over with a stranger. It would surely set her therapy back by weeks, if not end it altogether.

Brandon realized that no matter how well Freeberg managed it, this would be a brutal blow to Nan, as brutal as anything ever inflicted upon her by Tony Zecca. Brandon knew that he could not be the one responsible for inflicting more pain on Nan.

"Please go on, Paul," Brandon heard Freeberg say.

"Actually, I didn't want to consult you," Brandon said, "but merely report something to you. It's good news, and I didn't want to hold it back."

"What is it, Paul?"

"Nan and I had our initial nondemand penetration today. I'd say her vaginismus is cured. There were no obstructions. It went well. I'm sure she's cured."

"You're positive?"

"Just about."

"But you haven't tried penetration and thrusting yet, have you?"

"Not yet."

"Try that tomorrow, and let me know. If that comes off well, then we'll be positive she's cured, and you'll deserve congratulations. Good luck."

Good luck, he thought bitterly, hanging up the phone.

He was worse off than before. He hadn't the faintest idea of how he would handle Nan Whitcomb tomorrow.

At least tonight with Gayle he'd have no problem. He wouldn't even hint to her about his fainthearted and evasive talk with Freeberg.

Gayle didn't have to know.

If a tree falls in the forest, and no one hears it, did the tree actually fall?

It had been a happy evening for Brandon and Gayle.

For one thing, Lapin Agile was a cozy restaurant, providing the perfect background for easy conversation. The pianist across the crowded room softly played popular songs of old Montmartre. Three of the walls surrounding them were covered with colorful framed Toulouse-Lautrec posters representing many of the artist's friends from May Belfort and Jane Avril to Aristide Bruant and the Troupe de Mlle. Eglantine.

Most of all, adhering to a promise he had made to himself when he had gone to pick up Gayle, Brandon saw to it that there had been no discussion of their therapy activities. Any references to their jobs as surrogates or to their patients were strictly avoided. He would not allow himself to fall into that trap again. And instinctively, Gayle had gone along with him.

At their rustic wooden table, they had talked about their pasts and their futures, about music, books, movies, about politics, sports, television programs. They had talked, and laughed, about his adventures as a substitute teacher. They had talked about each other, how they felt about each other and what they wanted from their relationship.

Neither could remember, by dinner's end, what they had eaten, only that it had been delicious.

By the time they had finished their desserts, they had fallen into silence, holding hands across the table and speaking only with their eyes.

Tonight, Brandon told himself, was finally the night so

long postponed. He was eager to have this breathtaking young woman in his arms and make her a part of him, as he would be a part of her. At last he broke the silence to tell her so.

She nodded. "It's what I've been wanting, too, Paul. Let's go back to my place."

Once in his car, he drew her closer to him and headed toward her house.

Throughout the drive, both were quiet. Brandon could feel his heart quickening with anticipation, like that of an excited schoolboy.

Parking in front of her bungalow, Brandon brought her to him, kissed her avidly, and whispered against her ear, "Let's go inside."

While Gayle was straightening her dress, and smoothing her hair, Brandon went around the car to open the passenger door and help her out.

As she stepped down beside him, Gayle said offhandedly, "There was something I meant to ask you. That patient of yours, the one who has a crush on you—I keep forgetting her name—"

Brandon squirmed uncomfortably, took Gayle by the hand, and started her up the walk. "Nan," he said, barely audible.

"Did you say Nan?"

"That's right."

"I wanted to ask how you made out with her. Was it difficult to break the news to her, that you had to terminate her?"

Playing dumb, Brandon guided Gayle up the three steps to her porch.

She stopped before her door to hunt inside her purse for the key. "Did she take it badly?" Gayle resumed.

Brandon decided he would have to face up to the inevitable and admit the truth. "Gayle, I just couldn't tell her we were winding up."

"Oh, no?"

"I couldn't do it one on one, Gayle. It would have been

like executing someone. I just couldn't get around to it, so—"

Gayle, key in hand, was ominously still. "So you reported what was going on to Dr. Freeberg?"

"I started to. In fact, I called Dr. Freeberg to discuss the matter."

"Well, what did he say?"

Brandon was finding this even more difficult than he had expected. "He didn't say anything . . . because I didn't tell him anything."

Gayle's expression was one of incredulity. "You didn't tell Dr. Freeberg that your patient has fallen in love with you and expects to have a real-life romance with you?"

"Gayle, I couldn't. I simply couldn't. It would have been inhumane. To have reached the point I have with her, and then back off and let Dr. Freeberg tell her another man would take my place—it was impossible for me to do."

Gayle stared at him.

"And exactly what point have you reached with Nan?"

"I—we—I think we've overcome her vaginismus."

"You mean you're fucking her?"

"Not really. It was only nondemand penetration."

"You're fucking her," Gayle persisted with rising anger, "and you're loving it, and she's loving it and in love with you. And you're doing nothing about it."

"I'm not loving it, and I don't love her," he said heatedly. "I'm just trying to be decent."

"You call that decent? Leading her on when you tell me you don't love her? If that's what you're doing, I think that's rotten. I have an idea that's not what you're doing. I have an idea you like what you're getting from her, and you don't want to give it up."

"Gayle, for Christ's sake, then what am I doing here?"

"That's what I'd like to know. What *are* you doing here, and what am I doing here with *you?*"

She jammed her key into the front door and turned it.

Brandon reached out and gripped her arm. "Gayle, will you stop this nonsense and be reasonable? I can under-

stand someone being jealous, but when they're jealous
without any cause—"

Gayle yanked her arm free. "I *am* jealous, damn you! And
with good cause. It's just not fair!"

"Gayle, please let me come inside and—"

"And what? Let you fuck me the way you're fucking her?
No way!"

"Gayle, give me a chance to talk to you."

"I'm not talking to you again until you've broken up with
your little Nan or you have Freeberg insist that you do.
Until then"—she pushed her door open—"fuck off!"

With that, she ran into the house, slamming the door in
his face.

Brandon sat dejectedly behind the wheel of his car in
front of her house, trying to decide what to do.

For many minutes, he sought to focus his resentment
against Gayle on her. She was being a fool, a childish fool,
he kept telling himself, allowing immature jealousy to in-
tervene in their relationship. Her jealousy was so displaced
as to be unbelievable.

But to Gayle it was believable, and for some minutes, he
tried to see his involvement with Nan from Gayle's point of
view. He could see that although she was a professional sex
partner, she was not a professional female. Perhaps she
knew more about the mechanism of sex than the average
woman, just as a physician knew more about the mechanism of health than the average layman. But a physician
could not heal himself any more than Gayle could overcome the insecurities of an ordinary woman.

Examining Gayle's anger, Brandon even considered the
possible validity of her feeling. Did he enjoy making love to
his patient and being loved by her in return? Could Gayle
have intuitively hit on some truth there? He examined and
reexamined this possibility, and what he emerged with
were two stark facts. One was that he was sorry for Nan and
wanted to help her but was absolutely not in love with her.
The other was that he was deeply in love with Gayle—and

was seriously on the verge of losing her for now and forever.

There was only one way for him to prove to Gayle that
she—and not a patient named Nan Whitcomb—was his
true love. Gayle had spelled out the one proof she would
accept. He must personally be forthright with Nan and
remind her that their relationship was purely a professional
one and would terminate with their next encounter. Or he
must in all candor inform Dr. Freeberg of his problem and
seek Freeberg's guidance in solving it.

As a so-called professional, he had been performing his
work amateurishly. He must speak to Dr. Freeberg at once
and be totally honest with him.

Brandon snapped on his dashboard light, held his wrist
near it, and peered at his wristwatch.

The time was close to ten forty-five. He half remembered
hearing somewhere that Dr. Freeberg kept late hours, writing and reading until midnight at least. If this were true, Dr.
Freeberg would still be awake. Brandon had to take a
chance. The sooner the better.

With determination, Brandon started his car and began
to drive around the neighborhood until he found a shopping area. When he located it, he could see a filling station a
block away, its lights on. He drove toward it and saw that
the lone attendant was closing down the station but that the
door to the glass-enclosed telephone booth nearby was
open.

Brandon guided his car past the pumps and parked in a
vacant slot near the telephone booth. Getting out, feeling
in his pocket for change, and then for his miniature address
book, he started for the glass booth.

Inside it, he closed the door and the light went on. Finding Dr. Freeberg's home phone number, Brandon sorted
out his change, dropped the required coins into the slot,
and dialed Freeberg's number.

There were no more than two rings before Freeberg
himself answered the phone.

"Dr. Freeberg? This is Paul Brandon. I hope I didn't
wake you."

"Not at all, not at all. I'll be up for hours. Just puttering around with some research for a paper I was planning to write. What's on your mind, Paul?"

"It's something I think is rather important, something regarding my relationship with my patient, Nan Whitcomb. I do need your advice."

There was a pause. "Is this something you meant to discuss with me when you phoned me earlier today?"

"Yes," said Brandon, surprised. "How did you know?"

Freeberg chuckled. "Because your afternoon call was uncharacteristic. It was obvious you had something important on your mind but found yourself unable to get down to it. I'm pleased you've decided to discuss it now. You want to tell me what this is all about?"

"My patient, Nan Whitcomb, she's fallen in love with me," Brandon blurted out.

"Ah, so that's it," Dr. Freeberg said. "You're doing the right thing to tell me. I'd suggest you let me hear it all, omitting nothing. So Miss Whitcomb's in love with you? You'd better give me every detail."

For over ten minutes, Brandon spilled out every detail of his series of sessions with Nan. He placed special emphasis on those moments when he perceived that Nan was falling in love with him—from her offer to move in and stay overnight with him to her declaration of love for him this very afternoon.

"I should have discussed this earlier with you, Dr. Freeberg," Brandon concluded, "but I was afraid you'd want to take me off the case and replace me with someone else. I worried that if this happened, it might wound Nan deeply and set her back, after we've made so much progress."

"I can understand your concern," said Dr. Freeberg. Then he inquired, "How many sessions do you have left with her?"

"Two at the most. Possibly, if all continues to go well, I might wind it up with the exercise we have scheduled for tomorrow afternoon."

There was silence on the other end of the line. Dr. Freeberg was thinking this through, Brandon knew, and he waited anxiously.

"All right," said Dr. Freeberg, "I believe I know what must be done. I'm going to call Nan Whitcomb at her hotel right now. I'm going to postpone her session with you tomorrow and set it for the day after. Then tomorrow, I'll see her."

"See her about what?"

"Paul, under no circumstances, at this stage of the therapy, would I see fit to remove you from the case. You're right—it could be a rude shock to her, set her back, and it might take a long time for her to establish a bond with someone else, even if I could find another male surrogate quickly. No, that's out. What I intend to do is tell Miss Whitcomb I want to discuss her case with her. Then I'll"— he paused—"I'm looking through my engagement book here, and I'm tied up until late afternoon . . . so that's it —I'll arrange with Nan Whitcomb to see her late tomorrow. I'll have a good grandfatherly talk with her."

"What can you tell her?"

"Basically, I'll try to get it through to her that her relationship with her surrogate is not a personal one but a professional one. I think I can manage this without doing her any harm. Once this is done, I feel certain it will make it easier, more comfortable, for you to wind up your last exercise with her without further involvement."

"Thanks, Dr. Freeberg. Thank you very much. My fingers are crossed. I hope you'll succeed."

After he had hung up on Dr. Freeberg, Brandon remained standing in the telephone booth. At last he dug into his pocket for more change. Once he'd found the change, he inserted the coins in the phone, and cheerful again, he began to dial Gayle Miller . . .

Late the following afternoon, Tony Zecca sat tensely and watchfully behind the steering wheel of his Cadillac parked less than half a block away from the Freeberg Clinic. His eyes, as they had been for the last three days, remained fastened on the entrance to the clinic, watching for every person who entered and departed.

Still boiling inside at Nan's deceit, Zecca's real rage was directed toward the man who had seduced her and taken her away from him.

Zecca had been obsessed by the need to find out who Nan's seducer and lover was—and to make the bastard pay for it. So far, Zecca had not succeeded in uncovering the bastard's identity for sure. He had suspected, from the outset, that Dr. Arnold Freeberg, the doctor she had always been visiting, was the culprit, but so far, as of this minute, Zecca had not been able to prove it.

The first day of his clinic watch, Zecca had thought he'd had Freeberg nailed down. Parking at his post, across and not far from the clinic, he had gone inside to case the joint. Luckily, at the receptionist's desk, he had found a stack of brochures describing the function of the clinic, and these had included a biography and photograph of the eminent Dr. Arnold Freeberg.

Once he had learned what Freeberg looked like and what he did for his dirty living, Zecca had gone back to his parked car to watch for him. It had been a long and grueling wait, but just before nightfall of that first day, Zecca's patience and endurance had been rewarded.

He had seen Freeberg leave the clinic, lock the front door, and get into his car in the adjoining parking lot to drive to wherever he was shacking up with Nan. In his Cadillac, Zecca had followed the fucking doctor, trying to decide what he'd do with the bastard once he arrived at wherever he was keeping Nan. Freeberg drove up to a new house at the edge of town, drove into the garage, and was greeted at the front door by a plain, plumpish woman, obviously his wife, whom he was cheating on as far as Zecca could make out. This meant that Freeberg had Nan stashed away in some hot love nest somewhere else.

Yesterday, Zecca had grimly waited once more for Freeberg to close up the clinic and leave, and once again Zecca had followed him when he drove off. And for the second

time Zecca had seen the two-faced bastard go into his
house to join his wife.

Somewhat discouraged, Zecca continued his relentless
vigil all the long afternoon of this third day.

Suddenly, through his car door window, he recognized a
very familiar figure walking toward the entrance to the
Freeberg Clinic. He saw her from behind as she went to the
door and then went inside.

Nan herself, on the way to her lover and her daily shot.
The bitch. But the hell with her. It was the old bastard he
was going to get.

Zecca's instant response at the sight of Nan was to leap
out of his car and confront her. He started to open his door,
and then did not do so. Getting his hands on Nan right now
was pointless. The smart thing to do was to wait and see if
she came out of the clinic with a man, and if that man were
Freeberg.

Zecca huddled in the driver's seat, alertly watching and
waiting.

It was more than twenty minutes, this wait, and it was
getting dark when Zecca's patience finally paid off.

He saw Nan herself emerge from the clinic, someone
holding the front door open for her to leave. Next, the
someone who had held the door for her emerged, too. It
was a man, all right, *the* man, the old prick who was her
doctor, none other than Dr. Arnold Freeberg, the very one
Zecca had suspected from the start as the sonofabitch who
had wooed her away from him.

Locking the clinic door, Freeberg joined Nan, took her
by the arm, and started her down Market Avenue, in the
opposite direction from where Zecca was parked.

Zecca contained himself. When he was sure that there
was a safe distance between the frigging couple and himself, and he could keep them in view without being spotted,
he leapt out of his car.

Hugging the darker areas alongside shut-down buildings
and store fronts, Zecca tracked the pair.

They walked together only a short distance, then crossed
the street, and disappeared into some tall building. Once

Nan and her doctor had gone inside, Zecca quickened his step, hastening to find out their secret place of assignation.

Zecca stood before the building now. It was a hotel. The Excelsior Hotel. So this was where Nan was hiding out, and where her doctor friend was going every day to fuck her.

Zecca's first temptation was to go inside also, learn Nan's room number, and burst in on the two of them locked on her bed, then to beat up on old Freeberg until there wasn't an unbroken bone left in the old shit's body, and then to slam Nan around and take her by the hair and drag her back to his home where she belonged.

Eager as he was to have a go at them, some survival instinct inside Tony Zecca restrained him from the act.

If he burst in on them, and beat up on Freeberg, there could be trouble. Zecca might find himself arrested and in the morning headlines. It was the last place anyone high up in the mob would want him to be. Zecca was only on the fringe of the mob, a lesser light financed by it, doing occasional favors for it, but still one of their boys. The mob did not like any of its own being in the hands of the police or on the front pages of papers. Definitely not.

The getting even, he decided, should be done in a quieter and safer place. The getting even should be done by one of the mob's hit men, more expert in these matters than he himself was.

Maybe.

He started back to his Cadillac. He would think about it.

There were two pull-up armchairs in Nan Whitcomb's hotel room, and Dr. Freeberg waited for Nan to occupy one before he took the other. After refusing Nan's offer of white wine, and gaining her permission to allow him to smoke, Dr. Freeberg lighted a cigarillo and sat back.

"I wanted to speak to you," Dr. Freeberg began, "and intended to do so in my office. Then I thought what I had to talk over with you could be discussed most easily in the privacy of your own hotel room rather than in the clinic or downstairs in the hotel bar. I hope you don't mind?"

"Not at all," said Nan, her curiosity clearly evident.

Dr. Freeberg gestured at the room. "I hope you find this comfortable. It was the best I could do when you called."

"I'm grateful you could get me anything."

"Does Mr. Zecca know that you're here?"

"God no, he'd be the last person I'd tell."

"Do you think he'll try to find you?"

Nan shrugged. "I'm not sure. When he found my note, he may have said good riddance. But knowing his ego, I suspect he'll try to find me and drag me back. Even if he traced me, I'd never go back with him, never. Not now."

Dr. Freeberg nodded understandingly. "I can't say that I blame you. You've suffered a particularly brutal experience. But don't think you're alone in that. Your experience, in a way, was not dissimilar to what so many women go through with their husbands or lovers."

Nan seemed surprised. "Really?"

"Usually women with an incompatible mate don't suffer physical brutality, but rather they endure emotional brutality. This is probably because many men get too used to their women and begin to take them for granted. Such men gradually regard their women not only as servants but as someone to service them sexually—someone to have intercourse with—without an exchange of loving and caring, with no time for caressing and enjoying foreplay. These men want only to have their own orgasm and feel better. Such men don't see women as individuals with feelings of their own. They're out of touch with their mates as sensitive human beings to be nurtured and loved."

"You can say that again, in spades, when you speak about somebody like Tony Zecca."

"Mr. Zecca is an extreme example. I simply wanted to reassure you that you are not alone. On a more civilized scale, his behavior goes on all the time everywhere. But soon you'll find there are more thoughtful and sensitive men you can have relationships with . . ."

"I've already learned that, Dr. Freeberg," Nan said, "ever since I met Paul Brandon."

"Yes, of course, Paul Brandon," said Dr. Freeberg, puffing on his cigarillo. "Actually, it's Paul I want to talk to you about."

Nan showed genuine bewilderment. "Talk about what? I've told you all about him, our relationship, in my sessions with you. Haven't I told you everything?"

"Not quite, Nan. Not quite." Dr. Freeberg stamped out the butt of his cigarillo and leaned forward on his chair. "You recall, Nan, don't you, the first meeting we had after you became my patient? The first meeting Paul and I had with you, all three of us together? At that time we made a verbal contract, an agreement. You had a problem, hardly entirely your own. So we set a goal. Through therapy and exercises, we laid out a program that we were confident would help you reach your goal of complete sexual enjoyment. We held nothing back from you. We laid out every aspect of the treatment and exercises. That's true, isn't it?"

"Yes, you did."

"One thing I told you in complete candor. Under my direction, Paul Brandon would professionally help you, be a surrogate partner to teach and direct you. You were paying for Paul's expertise, not for his emotional caring for you. From the start, you knew that your relationship with Paul, while it would become an increasingly intimate one, was a professional relationship, a temporary partnership for a limited number of weeks. You were made to understand that once your surrogate had succeeded in solving your problem, he would have finished his work and would return to his own private life and own personal relationships, and you would have concluded your therapy and would go on with your own private life and your own relationships."

Dr. Freeberg saw that Nan was staring at him, a pained expression on her face. He paused, and waited for her to speak.

"I think I know what you're trying to tell me," Nan said slowly. "You're trying to tell me you think I've fallen in love with Paul, and I shouldn't have."

"That's what I think, Nan, listening and reading between the lines of Paul's reports."

"And you think I've made a mistake?"

"Yes, it's a mistake," Dr. Freeberg said without equivocation. "As your surrogate, Paul cares for you very much—he's developed a bond with you. This is the relationship we hoped would develop between you. It had to develop. But it also has a beginning and an end. Paul is really only a stepping-stone to what is waiting for you in the outside world. Now you both must sever that bond, he to go his way, and you to go yours. He has a private life, and this is merely his work. I repeat, you are paying for his expertise, not for his caring. It would be wrong to expect anything more. Can we discuss it further, Nan?"

She sounded tearful. "No, I don't believe that will be necessary."

"My dear Nan, for everyone the reality of a situation is sometimes difficult to face. I am positive you can do it and be happy soon again." He paused. "Now, how about that glass of wine? Will you pour for both of us?"

In his office in city hall, District Attorney Hoyt Lewis, conscious of the Reverend Scrafield's tense presence across the desk from him, still made an effort to skim the photocopy of Hunter's log a second time.

The journal that Hunter had kept of his exercises with Gayle Miller was meticulous in every detail, and when Lewis finished his hasty second reading he was basically satisfied with the report. Nevertheless, he gave himself a half minute to ponder every aspect of the evidence.

But Scrafield, opposite him, was finding it difficult to contain his own eagerness to proceed. "Hoyt," he demanded, "tell me what you think. It's all there, just like I told you, isn't it?"

"I think so," said Lewis.

"Is anything bothering you?"

"Not really. Perhaps one thing." Lewis dropped the photocopy of Hunter's journal on his desk. "What Hunter refers to here as 'penetration.' It hasn't happened yet. When you depend on one witness, you want everything as explicit as possible."

Scrafield was impatient. "I told you, you don't have to worry. Chet Hunter assures me he'll be humping Gayle tomorrow. He guarantees it and will report to us personally when it's happened."

District Attorney Lewis scratched his nose, lost in thought, and his head made a motion of assent. "Yes, Hunter appears reliable enough. I had him checked out again. His record as a member of the police reserve is perfectly clean, and he's well motivated to come through, according to Ferguson over at the *Chronicle*. But what's keeping him from screwing the lady? That's not the worst assignment in the world."

"All in due time, Hoyt. He's got to follow their rules, that's all. Don't upset yourself. He'll come through. You can bet on that."

Hoyt Lewis sat up. "I intend to bet on that."

"What's the next step?" Scrafield wanted to know. "How are you going to proceed?"

"The usual way. I'll start with a press release—notify Ferguson what my office plans to do . . . tell him I'm readying a criminal complaint against Dr. Arnold Freeberg for pandering."

"What about Gayle Miller?"

"Not yet, not until she's actually committed her act of prostitution. But we already have sufficient evidence to announce the forthcoming complaint against Freeberg on the pandering charge. So the first announcement will concern Freeberg alone."

"Can I make it the subject of my broadcast tomorrow night?" asked the Reverend Scrafield eagerly.

"No objection, as long as you confine any fire and brimstone to what's contained in my announcement."

"When can I mention the prostitute?"

"As soon as Hunter scores with her," Lewis promised. "That'll be immediately after tomorrow. Then I'll proceed against them jointly, issue arrest warrants against Freeberg for a felony and against the Miller woman for a misdemeanor. I'll have them brought over to the jail to be booked and their bail set, and have them arraigned before a judge in forty-eight hours."

Scrafield was smiling. "And then what?"

Hoyt Lewis also smiled. "Then they go to trial, and both wind up out of business and in the slammer."

"And you'll wind up on every front page," said Scrafield, grinning.

"And so will you, my friend," said Lewis, standing. "If Freeberg and Gayle Miller do their part, we'll do our part. It's in the bag, I promise you."

IX

"Gayle," he asked, "is this exercise my graduation?"

Adam Demski and Gayle were nude in her therapy room, seated beside each other on the edge of her floor mat.

"It could be," Gayle replied. "I expect it will be."

"If I rise to the occasion," Demski said with amusement.

"You'll rise to it," Gayle promised.

Observing him, she liked what she saw, contrasting his demeanor with the rigid, frightened person she had first laid eyes on a few weeks ago. Beside her was a young man who appeared confident and relaxed enough to make jokes and to smile. His attitude pleased her, and she could not imagine that he would suffer a relapse into his old impotency.

"Gayle," he said, taking her hand, "when we do penetration . . ."

"Yes?"

"I'd like to be on top this time."

Gayle considered this but only briefly. She decided that he was ready for the more usual position. That he would never consider himself a success until he could consummate sexual intercourse from the male superior position. The missionary position was the way of the world for most men, what they believed was expected of them.

Now Adam Demski wanted to prove, to himself, that he was ready to have a real encounter in the real world. That meant thrusting from the top. Success in that way would fully reinforce his new feeling of potency.

"Of course," Gayle found herself saying. "I see no problem."

She wanted to add that there were many other positions that might be better for him, more comfortable for him, even more effective, with some future mate, but she did not want to confuse him at the moment. There would be time to discuss variations when he met with Dr. Freeberg and herself for their final talk.

Right now he wanted to prove himself in the popular male position, and she'd made up her mind to do everything possible to make it work for him.

"Shall we begin, Adam?"

"I want to."

Gayle eased herself down on the mat, and Demski followed her. Then she swung her legs around and adjusted her body until she was stretched out fully on her back. Immediately, he was on his knees on the mat, hovering over her.

"Not so fast, Adam," she cautioned him. "I think we both could use some preliminary play. I want to lubricate naturally, and I want you to achieve a complete erection before penetrating me."

"Of course," Demski said apologetically. "I guess I got a little eager."

"No hurry. Let's enjoy every moment of this, from our foreplay to the climax."

"I'm for it," Demski agreed, dropping down next to her and stretching his body alongside hers.

"Can we keep our eyes open?" he inquired.

"Whatever you like."

"I'd like."

He snuggled close to Gayle and began brushing the tips of the fingers of his right hand across her forehead, around her eyes, across the bridge of her nose, and giving feather-like touches to her mouth and her lips.

Soon he reached her breasts, was stroking them gently, and leaning over to kiss her nipples.

She could feel his effectiveness. Uncontrollably, she could feel her nipples stiffen and the moisture beginning to grow between her legs.

Then she became aware of something else against her thigh.

She glanced down between them and made out his small flaccid penis lifting toward a real erection.

She reached down and curled one hand around it as her other hand massaged his shoulders and back.

Suddenly, without a word spoken, Demski was on his knees above her.

The sensation was pleasure mingled with triumph as the head of his penis probed briefly and began to slide into her.

She could hear his heart as he began thrusting forward and backward. What surprised her was how strongly he had her impaled, and how steady and unremitting his thrusting was. Somehow, she had expected him to come to a quick orgasm, and then she realized she was confusing him with Chet Hunter. This had not been Demski's problem, and it was not his problem now.

Glancing fleetingly at an end table clock, she saw that seven or eight minutes had passed since they had begun.

Still he was over her, going steadily, and involuntarily she found herself lifting and lowering her buttocks in rhythm with his.

It was going on and on, and she was beginning to think he was a retarded ejaculator who might never come—or indeed that she might come before he did.

Then she heard a hoarse cry, and he was going at her wildly, and she knew he was climaxing.

As he stopped, and remained on his elbow panting, she caught the clock in the corner of her eye.

Twelve minutes.

Not bad. In fact, very good.

As he withdrew from her, she saw that his mouth had formed into a wide smile.

She reached up and brought his mouth down to her own

and kissed him. And then she hugged him tightly, enjoying the perspiration on his face and body.

Happily, he whispered into her ear, "Well, teacher, do I graduate?"

"Adam," she whispered back, "today you are a man, ready to go out and delight a population of receptive females. Yes, you graduate with honors."

"With honors?"

"I'll sign your report card. Look closely at my face and you'll see what I gave you."

"What did you give me, teacher?"

"An A plus. Definitely. You'll have the world at your feet. Congratulations!"

They were in the bedroom of Paul Brandon's apartment.

"Well," Nan Whitcomb said with a sigh, "I guess this is the last time." She was naked except for her nylon panties. She drew them down and stepped out of them.

For a while she gazed down at her vaginal mound, and absently she began to smooth her curly pubic hair as she seemed lost in thought.

She raised her head to take in Brandon, who was still undressing.

She spoke. "I want to say one thing, Paul, before we go on to the last time."

"Maybe it won't be the last time if it turns out you still have a problem."

"I don't expect a problem, Paul. I'm pretty sure I'm going to be all right. But I want to say something else. I— I'm ashamed of myself for giving you so much trouble."

"What trouble? You didn't give me any, really."

"Yes, I did. You're being very sweet. But I did. Dr. Freeberg was frank about it. Quite open, thank God." She paused. "You know, he talked to me about our relationship."

Brandon nodded, taking off his trousers.

Nan went on. "Dr. Freeberg was right to speak to me about what was happening, to show me how I was putting you on the spot. He brought me to my senses." She stared wistfully at Brandon's naked body. "It's true I was foolish. I did sort of fall in love with you. I couldn't help it. I did give you a terrible time, when you were only doing a job, a professional job to cure me—"

"Don't be harsh with yourself, Nan," Brandon broke in. "It wasn't a one-way street. I can see now that I got emotionally involved with you, too, maybe unconsciously encouraged your love. I shouldn't have. It was unprofessional of me." He reached out for her hand. "I want you to know that I really did—and do—care for you, even as I tried to guide you."

She pulled him toward her. "You're the kindest man I've ever known." She smiled wryly. "True, I haven't known many, and those I did know were all downers until I met you." She took his face in her hands and kissed him. "I won't say I love you anymore, but I do love you. The difference is that I've faced the fact that it'll be over."

He returned her kiss, running his fingers across her cheek. "You'll do better from now on, much better," he promised her.

"At least I'll know what to look for—someone kind and caring and intelligent . . . just like you." She rubbed her body against his. "But since I have you here now, why don't we go ahead and enjoy the last time?" She tightened her hold on his hand. "I want to prove to you that I'm ready." With her free hand, she touched his rigid erection. "I know you are."

"I certainly am . . ."

He led her to the bed, and when she was supine, he climbed on after her, then rose above her.

Nan raised her knees. Her legs were apart.

Brandon lowered himself between them and slowly, slowly entered her.

He did not have to inquire whether she felt any pain. Her grateful expression told him all he needed to know. There was no longer any pain. There was only pleasure.

"Oh, my," she choked out once as he continued to thrust inside her.

At last she reached up to hold on to him. Her face contorted, and he could feel she was in the throes of orgasm,
and he let go, too.

After an interval, he withdrew and dropped down on the
bed beside her. He could see from the motion of her hips
that she wanted more relief. He reached for the bud of her
clitoris and passed his fingertips back and forth over it.
Quickly, she had her second orgasm, and soon after, she
had her third. And then she lay there inert, spent.

After a while, she turned her head toward him. "Was I
okay?"

"Perfect."

"You were delicious. Thank you for making me able to
say that."

They lay quietly, and then because of his genuine concern, Brandon asked her, "What are you going to do next,
Nan?"

She thought about it briefly. "I think I'll leave town. I
don't want to stay here and risk running into Tony Zecca
again. Maybe I'll go to the Midwest. I have a cousin in Des
Moines. Another in Chicago. Wherever I go, I'll find a way
to support myself, any job, and I'll use what extra money I
have to take a secretarial course on the side. That should
help me find better work and maybe help me meet somebody as nice as you. What do you think, Paul?"

"That's a fine idea. But don't leave immediately. Dr.
Freeberg would like us to join him for dinner the day after
tomorrow. It's his custom whenever his patients and their
surrogates have concluded their exercises successfully.
Will you come along?"

"I'll be there. And Paul, Dr. Freeberg told me you had
your own personal life to live. I'd like to meet her."

It was early evening in Gayle's therapy room.

Gayle, stripped down, fell back on the couch, waiting for
Chet Hunter, watching him divest himself of the last of his
clothes.

"Did you do your homework?" she asked.

"With dedication."

"How do you feel?"

"Like I can make it."

"You *did* make it last time," she reminded him. "We had penetration."

"Not by my book, sweetie. You were on top, treating me like a fragile object. You managed to get me in you, sure, but not for very long—less than a minute, maybe . . ."

"More than that," Gayle assured him.

"Whatever. I'm afraid I was still premature. You want me to hold back five minutes—"

"Ten, Chet. I said ten minutes."

"Well, I don't know. Maybe." He approached the couch, and his countenance was drawn and serious. "Gayle, I've got to make it work. There's too much at stake for me. You know I have a girlfriend. I'm crazy about her. I want to be with her and be married to her. I can't until I'm cured. Do you think I'm cured?"

Gayle bobbed her head in assent. "I think you will be, after tonight."

"What happens tonight?"

"Your valedictory performance."

"I thought I'm not supposed to perform?"

"You won't actually be performing. You'll just have a good time, Chet . . . Maybe a memorable one."

"Doing what?"

"You know what. Penetration the way you've always wanted it. Male superior position and you engaging in complete intercourse. I may have to hold you back once or twice, and squeeze, but we'll keep going until we're both satisfied."

As he listened, she could see his excitement growing.

"I'm starting to feel like it, Gayle."

She lowered herself to the mat on the floor. "Come here, Chet. Lie down with me."

"But I'm ready. You can see."

"Not so fast, Chet. We're not getting this over with fast. We're going to take our time, build up the pleasure, and when we're both ready I'll let you know. Now, lie down next to me and let's relax with some preliminary touching."

"If you say so," he complained, settling down on the mat.

"I say so. Your partner knows best."

Hunter stretched out beside her. "Hi, partner," he said. "I'm really ready to go."

"I know. But don't. Take your mind off your penis and concentrate on sensuality all over. Stroke me. After that, I'll stroke you."

Hunter grunted and began to move his fingers across every expanse and nook of her body. He was soon absorbed in caressing her, and taking pleasure in her reactions.

"You're something," he said. "You're great. I can't get any bigger down there."

"You don't have to. And please forget your penis. Now, let me touch you."

As she ran her hands about his face and abdomen, he became less urgent and he began to emit soft sighs of pleasure.

"I need you, Gayle," he whispered, trying to control his breathing.

"What are you waiting for?" she asked.

He was over her.

A moment's hesitation as his penis slid inside her. There was no ejaculation.

Automatically, he began moving up and down inside her.

"Slowly," she said, "slowly. Very good, Chet. Do you feel like coming?"

"Not—not yet."

She felt like grasping his buttocks, and assisting him, but she did not want to overexcite him. She rested her palms on his shoulders.

"Good, very good," she repeated.

"The hell it's good," he exalted. "It's great!" He began thrusting faster and harder. Gradually, she could see his face growing strained.

"What is it, Chet?"

"I'm afraid—"

She twisted loose from him, grabbed hold of his moist

penis head, and using her forefinger and middle finger on top, and thumb on the side, she squeezed firmly.

"Oh, Christ, I want to . . ."

"Never mind. You will, you will."

She squeezed again until he'd gone limp.

With a peek at the clock, she concentrated on him once more, settling him back and playing her fingers over him.

She could feel his penis beginning to fill once more. It was swelling and rising. It was upright.

"Now, enter me again," she said, and directed his erection inside her once more.

He began to move inside her steadily, deeply.

"Keep going, Chet."

He kept going.

"Gayle, I—I—"

"You're allowed," she called up cheerfully.

It was a noisy and extended orgasm.

He fell off her like he'd been shot. "That was a beaut," he said breathlessly.

She grinned. "We call it a mature ejaculation. Now, let's rest."

After a short time, she crawled off the mat and threw on her robe. "I'm going to wash up, then go to the kitchen and get us something refreshing. Will tea do?"

"Anything will do, sweetie," he replied.

When she returned with tea for both of them, he sat up on the couch to sip from his cup, and she sat beside him. He was bubbling with enthusiasm. "I actually don't need any refreshment," he said. "I already had mine. You're really a wonder, Gayle. You actually made me go all the way. How long was it before I came?"

"Seven minutes."

"Think of that! Fantastic." Abruptly, his expression darkened. "Only I wish I could have done it without the squeeze."

"You're going to, my friend," she said with a smile, setting down her teacup and rising to slip out of her robe. "Because this time we're going to do it—no hands, see. All the way without a squeeze."

"You're not satisfied with seven minutes?"

"I am, sure. But I'm not letting you out of here, on your own in the cruel outside world, until you've penetrated me for at least ten minutes. You will. And then I'll let you go, much to my loss. So let's get started, Chet."

About to turn on her shower that evening, still high over her twin triumphs this day, Gayle thought she heard the doorbell. She saw that it was close to ten o'clock, the time that Paul Brandon was due to arrive.

Momentarily abandoning the shower, Gayle pulled on her silk robe and started out of the bathroom.

She was filled with anticipation. For days their relationship had misfired. Until now, each of them had been occupied and preoccupied with the needs of others. The others had been repaired. Tonight, unfettered, they would at last be able to fulfill themselves.

Outside the bathroom, Gayle could hear the key turning in the lock of the front door.

She could see Brandon entering the living room, and her excitement mounted. She waited for him. They met in the hallway and embraced lovingly.

"How are you, my darling?" she wanted to know as she led him to the bedroom and helped him discard his jacket.

"Thrilled to be alone with you at last." While he unbuttoned his shirt, she unbuckled and unzipped his trousers. "A bit bushed, though," he added. "It's been a long day."

"For me, too," she admitted. "How did it go with Nan? Did Dr. Freeberg make it easier for you?"

"Oh, yes, she was no real problem." He sat on the edge of the bed, taking off his shoes and then his socks. "Actually, she was reasonable throughout."

"And you?"

"Totally professional throughout," said Brandon, taking off his trousers. "And you, what about you? Did you graduate both your patients, or just one?"

"Both."

"They succeeded with you at last?"

"They did, thank God."

Brandon eased off his jock shorts. "You must be tired by now."

"I'm all right."

"After four hours with them? I'm surprised you can still stand."

"Not that strenuous. Remember, they're patients. At best they don't have that much endurance. If I'm tired at all, it's because of the stress. After all those sessions, well, when you come to the last one, you keep worrying whether all you've done will work out. That's where the tension is for me."

"But it worked out. You're finished with them now?"

"Completely." She studied him. "You're the one who's bushed. You're bushed from one patient?"

"Don't forget, Nan was my first patient. It's like you said, there's a lot of tension. Look, Gayle, let's forget about the others. We're done with them. Let's concentrate on loving each other."

"You're right."

He reached out his arms to take her in them.

She backed off. "Get into bed, Paul, and wait for me. I've got to go back in the bathroom to take my shower. It'll just be a jiffy." She turned away. "Wait for me, Paul."

"Hungrily. Don't be long."

She smiled. "It won't be long, and it'll be worth it."

She saw him stretching out on the bed as she left the room.

The shower was wonderful, like a ritual beginning of a new life. Once she'd shut it off, and dried, she busied herself applying cologne to her body; and after that, she dabbed matching perfume behind her ears and in the cleavage between her breasts.

Leaving her robe behind, she walked to the bedroom. His lean body was still stretched on the bed.

She couldn't wait to arouse him, to have him, to love him at last.

Hastening to the bed, she swung onto it and dropped down beside him.

He did not move.

She lifted herself slightly to peer down at him. His eyes were closed in sleep. He was snoring intermittently, and the sounds were hardly audible. But they were there.

Poor dear, she told herself, he's fallen sound asleep.

Yet she did not mind because she understood. He'd had a draining and exhilarating day, and so had she, and she wanted to rest and sleep, too.

She cuddled down beside him, her arm over him, enjoying the warmth and closeness of his smooth skin.

She yawned and felt herself sinking into sleep.

There was time enough for them to make love in the morning.

They would be refreshed. They would be ready. They had the next day. And the day after. Countless days.

She knew it would be the most memorable lovemaking in her entire life. She only wanted to make him happy. She only wanted to . . .

Right now she only wanted to sleep, and she slept.

Returning to his apartment, after his final session with his surrogate, Chet Hunter felt like he was walking on air.

He wanted to call and report to Suzy, but he knew he was too tired to undertake such excitement and the possibility that she might want to come right over to be with him. In his condition, exhaustion underpinned by exhilaration, he wanted only to cap off his success by having a strong drink of whiskey alone.

But even before he could go into the pantry for his bottle, he realized that there was something else he must do first. There was one call he *must* make. The Reverend Josh Scrafield would be waiting impatiently for the results of the last session, waiting to hear if penetration had been achieved with Gayle. Scrafield would be dying to know if Hunter had fulfilled their agreement and if they were finally in business.

Hunter sat down by his living room telephone and

quickly dialed Scrafield. A woman answered, and seconds later the minister was on the phone.

"It's you, Chet?" Scrafield asked edgily.

"It's me."

"Well?"

Hunter pressed closer to the mouthpiece of the telephone, and he said in a confidential voice, "I made it, Reverend. I just now made it."

"You put it to her?"

"Twice. Positively."

Scrafield seemed unable to believe the good news. "The play-for-pay girl, you stuck it in her?"

"I sure did."

Hunter heard Scrafield exhale into the phone. Scrafield said, "As a bona fide police reserve officer, you'll swear to what you're telling me?"

"I'll swear on a stack of Bibles. I've even got the tape."

"Good boy!"

"I haven't got it on paper yet," said Hunter, "because I'm whipped."

"She gave you a workout, did she?"

"And how. Anyway, I'll write it all up the first thing in the morning. I guess I should call Hoyt Lewis and Ferguson—"

"Never mind, I'll take care of them," Scrafield interrupted. "I'll call Ferguson first—and then I'll call the D.A. at home, even if I have to wake him. I'll let him know you did it, you have the proof, and we're in go position."

"That should do it for Hoyt Lewis, shouldn't it?"

"There'll be no stopping him from now on. You finish your part of it the minute you get up in the morning. Write down the whole story, every juicy detail, complete your journal on Freeberg and the Miller woman, and bring everything you have to Hoyt Lewis as soon as possible. Good work, Chet. Glad you got it up when it counted. We'll have that pimp Freeberg, and his little hooker, behind bars before you know it. Stupendous!"

Hanging up, Hunter knew he had suffered one twinge. When Scrafield had referred to Gayle as a hooker. The viciousness of it gave him a moment of discomfort. But what the hell, business was business.

He could hardly wait for morning, when he'd finish his story, tell Suzy what had happened, and then deliver the goods.

In a self-congratulatory mood, he lifted himself out of his armchair and started for his pantry to mix himself a strong, strong double Scotch and soda.

Brandon awakened first, trying to clear his head and recall what had happened last night, and then he was aware that he was not alone. There was Gayle, snuggled beside him and coming awake.

He drew her tightly against him. "At last—" he began.

The telephone behind her began to ring loudly.

"Let it go," he whispered.

She stretched to squint over his shoulder at the bedside clock. "I can't," she said regretfully. "It's eight thirty. Only Dr. Freeberg calls this early. I have to answer, Paul."

Reaching behind her, she found the receiver.

The caller was Dr. Freeberg. "Gayle," he said, "I have to speak to you . . ."

"Do you want me to come to the clinic?"

"No. I mean, right now. Are you free to talk?" He paused. "Are you alone?"

She glanced at Brandon, his expression a frown, and she said hesitantly, "Not—not quite, Dr. Freeberg. I'm with Paul—Paul Brandon."

"No problem. He's family. I have something I must tell you."

"You sound upset," said Gayle, sitting up, covering her breasts with the top of the blanket. "What is it?"

"I am upset, and with good reason," Dr. Freeberg went on. "Listen to me, and listen carefully. I've just been arrested. The police are outside waiting to—"

Gayle was astounded. "You—you what? Did you say arrested?"

"Yes, for pandering. It's something that was a possibility,

and I should have told you about it, but I didn't because I
was assured it would go no further. I didn't want to unduly
alarm you or the others. But it happened just now, and I
thought I'd better tell you before—"

"They're taking you to jail?"

"To be booked first."

Brandon was shaking Gayle's arm. "What's going on?"
he demanded to know.

Gayle covered the mouthpiece of the phone. "Dr. Free-
berg's been arrested for pandering," she told Brandon.
She took her hand off the mouthpiece and spoke to Dr.
Freeberg. "Who on earth is doing this?"

"District Attorney Hoyt Lewis. Let me explain. It all began some days ago. Lewis came to my office to tell me that
my use of surrogates was really an act of pandering and
against the law in California. He threatened to take me to
court unless I gave up the use of surrogates. I contacted my
lawyer, Roger Kile—you've met him—and after some research into California law, Kile assured me that Lewis had
no case. Kile told me to proceed as I had been doing. I'm
sorry . . . I should have warned you . . ."

Gayle stiffened. "Warned me? Warned me about what?"

"Gayle, you're going to be arrested, too."

"Me? For what?"

"Prostitution. Me for pandering, which is a felony
charge, and you for prostitution, a misdemeanor, because
you are working for me."

"I don't believe it!" said Gayle. "What about the others
of us, the other women and Paul?"

"No, just you and I are being charged. Obviously, if they
win the case against you, they can charge everyone else
later."

"But why me?" Gayle wanted to know.

"I tried to find out. The best I could learn at this point is
that the prosecution's chief witness was one of your patients."

"One of my patients? That's impossible. You know both
of them as well as I do. Adam Demski's from out of town.
He's a stranger here. Besides, he wouldn't hurt a fly. And

Chet—Chet Hunter. He wouldn't claim I was a prostitute, not in a million years. Dr. Freeberg, I saved him. I put him together again."

Dr. Freeberg's voice was implacable. "One of them fingered you, and me as well, and is going to be a witness against us in court."

Gayle shook her head. "It still makes no sense. What—what's going to happen to us?"

"There are arrest warrants out for each of us, but they're charging us with different offenses. We'll both be taken to the city jail to be booked . . . You know, fingerprints, mug shots . . ."

"Oh, no."

"And bail for each of us will be set. I've already notified Roger Kile, and he's rushing up from Los Angeles to have a bail bondsman take care of our bail. So we'll be released immediately."

"For how long?"

"What follows will be different for each of us. I'm to have a preliminary hearing in ten days, where a judge will decide if there is a likelihood that a crime has been committed. If he decides there is, I'll be bound over to the Superior Court, arraigned again, and then go on trial in about sixty days."

"What about me?" Gayle asked in a quavering voice.

"Your misdemeanor arraignment is simpler. You'll go before a judge with Roger Kile accompanying you, and he'll enter a plea of not guilty on your behalf. Then you may or may not be put on trial, too."

"Is all this going to be in the newspapers and on television?"

"I'm afraid so, Gayle. But don't be frightened. Roger will be defending us."

"Don't worry? I'm damned worried, Dr. Freeberg. I'm scared as hell. When are the police going to arrest me?"

"In about ten minutes. I have to hang up now."

Gayle slammed down the telephone receiver and turned to Brandon. "Paul, the police are going to be here any minute." Then, as Brandon grabbed hold of her, trying to soothe her, her eyes filled. "Dammit to hell, there goes everything. It'll be made public. Can you see someone arrested for prostitution getting a scholarship to UCLA? Everything ruined . . ."

"Not everything, Gayle. There's still the two of us."

"Yes, but one of us'll be in jail!"

And she burst into tears.

X

The first thing on Chet Hunter's mind, when he awakened in the morning, was to get in touch with Suzy Edwards and break the fantastic news to her.

Still in his pajamas, he telephoned Suzy at the Freeberg Clinic.

"Suzy, I've got to see you today," he said excitedly. "When can you get here?"

"Why, you know, soon's work is done. I can be there a little after six."

"No, before. I must see you before."

"You make it sound like something important," said Suzy, bewilderment in her voice. "What is it?"

"Not on the phone," replied Hunter. "There's something I want to show you. And yes, it *is* important."

"Well, I suppose I could drop by at my lunch break—"

"Your lunch break? That would be great. You can grab a sandwich here while we talk."

"About what?" Suzy persisted. "Can't you even give me a hint?"

"You'll see. I'll be waiting for you at twelve fifteen."

The minute he hung up, Hunter thought of another call he must make. He lifted the receiver once more, and he dialed city hall. When he had it, he asked the switchboard operator to put him through to District Attorney Hoyt Lewis's office.

The district attorney was out on business, Hunter learned. "But," Lewis's secretary went on, "I know he was expecting to hear from you. Also, he said he'd be meeting with you."

"That's why I'm calling," said Hunter. "Give him this message. Tell him it's about the Reverend Scrafield's talk with him last night. Tell him I'm getting it all down on paper, and I'll make some copies and messenger one to him before noon. I'll come by to see him between two and three, if it's okay. Will you tell him that?"

"I certainly will, Mr. Hunter." The secretary giggled. "I gather you made out yesterday."

"Hey there, how do you know . . . ?"

She giggled again. "You forgot. I'm Mr. Lewis's *private* secretary. I typed out his criminal complaints two hours ago."

"So that's it." Hunter grinned to himself. "Yes, my dear lady, I made out yesterday."

After hanging up again, Hunter's good cheer persisted. He had almost two hours to get ready for this momentous day. He would shower, shave, dress, eat a full breakfast, and then have more than enough time to complete his journal for Hoyt Lewis.

He moved through all the acts of the morning briskly and on schedule. In fact, ahead of schedule, because he wanted to wind up his journal with care—to impress Suzy, when she read it, then the district attorney, and finally the *Chronicle*'s managing editor, Otto Ferguson.

At his electric portable typewriter, Hunter tried to recall, as vividly as possible, and in fairly accurate detail, what had occurred yesterday evening in his final session with Gayle. While he had the dialogue on tape, only his mind could reconstruct the background and color.

She had been sitting on her couch, stark naked, waiting for him to finish undressing.

She had inquired how he felt.

He had said, "Like I can make it."

She had admitted, "You did last time. We had penetration."

Hunter began to type it all out. The part about his fear of prematurity, he decided to skip. Such details weren't necessary. Hell, he wasn't trying to be James Joyce or Henry Miller, either. He decided to concentrate on what was relevant, and still true.

"You told me your goal was to get me to go five minutes," he had said.

"Ten minutes, Chet, ten minutes," Gayle had replied.

Hunter resumed typing.

He wrote faster as he neared the good parts, omitting only a few lines of what had happened.

"You'll just have a great time, Chet," Gayle had promised him. "Penetration the way you've always wanted. Male superior position and you engaging in complete intercourse."

He was writing even faster now.

"What are we waiting for?" Gayle had asked.

She was a hot little cookie, that one, he mused, maybe not what Suzy could prove to be but not bad for a paid sex partner.

Recalling entering her, Hunter swallowed hard and spelled out the details of their coupling.

He remembered what followed. "How long was it before I came?"

"Seven minutes," she had said. And later she had said, "But I'm not letting you out of here until you've penetrated me for ten minutes. You will."

And he had, the second time better than the first, and he wrote it all down.

Tearing the last page out of the typewriter, he reread what he had written. He was a clean typist and had to make only three corrections.

When he finished reading, he sat back aglow.

Wouldn't this light a bonfire under the district attorney? And Scrafield? And more important, Otto Ferguson?

But most important of all, there would be Suzy Edwards's thrilled reaction.

Gathering the final pages together, Hunter hurried downstairs to make two visits. One was to the Copy Shop, where he had three copies run off. Then he crossed over to the Ultra-Speed Messenger Service and arranged for the copies to be delivered to Hoyt Lewis at city hall, to the Reverend Scrafield at his church, and to Otto Ferguson in his office at the Hillsdale *Chronicle.*

It was exactly noon when he completed his chores and returned with his original typescript to wait for Suzy's arrival.

At fourteen minutes after twelve Suzy arrived, kissed Hunter, then held him off to see whether she could read anything in his face to satisfy her curiosity.

"What's this all about?" she wanted to know.

"This," said Hunter, handing her the original of his final typing and leading her with it to his armchair. "Sit down and read about my last therapy session."

Although they had seen each other regularly during the last two weeks, Hunter had avoided two things: any attempt at sex with her, which Dr. Freeberg had cautioned all patients about (and besides, Hunter had been too fearful of another failure with Suzy); and discussions of his activities with his sex surrogate and his progress, because he had been uncertain if anything good would come of it.

Now, at last, she would know all about it.

Hunter hovered near her as Suzy, her curiosity quotient rising, began to read, slowly and then faster.

Toward the end of her read, she kept murmuring, "Wonderful . . . wonderful . . . wonderful."

Suddenly, she was done and on her feet, hugging Hunter ecstatically. "Honey, you made it!" she exclaimed. "Oh, honey, it worked and you're all right now!"

Her enthusiasm unnerved him slightly. "Well, I think so, Suzy. It worked, sort of . . ."

She held him off. "What do you mean 'sort of'? You did it with that marvelous woman not once but twice, actually three times. Why are you so hesitant?"

"Because I'm not sure what lasting effects I'll have from my surrogate. Gayle proved I could do it with her. With her, somehow, it worked. But now that she's turned me loose, how do I know I'm cured with anyone else? It might not work without her."

Suzy gripped his arms and eyed him closely. "Chet, were you in love with her? Are you in love with her?"

"Of course not! I'm in love with you. She was only a teacher. You're the one I love."

Suzy's arms went up around him. "Then show me, Chet. Prove she cured you enough to do it with me. That's all you want to know, anyway. Let's do it."

He appeared startled. "Right now? I—I have to go out soon. You have to go back to work." He added lamely, "And what about your lunch?"

"Oh, Chet, that's silly. There's still enough time to prove to yourself . . . and to me—"

He embraced Suzy tightly. "Hey, don't get me wrong. I want to go to bed with you any time, all the time—"

"Then right now's the time."

"You bet," he said, starting to loosen his tie.

She'd yanked her blouse off, dropped it, and headed for the bedroom. "Follow me, Chet!"

"Hey, kiddo," he said, "you've given me a hard-on a mile long."

He was trying to get out of his trousers when she took him by the arm. "Then hold on to it, save it for me."

At the bed, they were undressed in a half minute flat.

For a moment, she gaped at him. "I've been waiting for that one a long, long time, honey."

Suzy threw herself on the bed, bouncing, as Hunter fell on top of her. It was difficult for him to restrain himself, but all the exercises he'd learned in the past days danced through his head. Slow down. Caress, touch, stroke. Slowly, slowly, get to feelings and pleasure, and don't try to prove anything.

After about five minutes of foreplay, he had had enough, and from the throaty sounds Suzy was making, so had she.

Her thighs were apart to receive him, and he was over her.

No thought of premature ejaculation or possible failure even crossed his mind. He had entered his surrogate all the way, last night, not once but twice, and maintained his erections and withheld his orgasms for what had seemed to him eternities.

There was no thought he couldn't do it with Suzy, his own gorgeous Suzy.

His penis was touching her velvety vaginal cleft.

Yet, no spasm, no sperm, just the body-hungering desire to enter her, to be one with her.

Without hesitation, he plunged into her, deeply into her, feeling only the heat of her body and his own as they locked together in their first coupling.

It was the dreamed-of consummation at last, and the greatest high he had ever enjoyed in his entire life.

They went on together. Neither was aware of the time. They were aware only that no premature ejaculation had thwarted their pleasure.

When ejaculation did occur, it was at the peak of their enjoyment, and for the first time, it was normal.

After it was done, they clung to each other, both in relief and in celebration of what the future held for them.

Once they had rested, and gone to the bathroom to shower together, they dressed themselves.

"Now I'll make sandwiches for us," Suzy announced.

"Make one for yourself," said Hunter. "I'll eat later. Right now I've got an appointment."

As he hurried into the living room, Suzy followed him. "What's the big rush, Chet? Don't you want to relax and—"

"I can't," he said, retrieving the final pages of his journal. "I'm meeting with the district attorney at city hall."

"The district attorney? You doing some research for him?"

"I already did." He waved his pages. "He's going to arrest Freeberg for pandering and Gayle Miller for prostitution, and he needs this for evidence, so I—"

Suzy's expression was appalled. She darted in front of

Hunter, blocking his way. "Wait a minute, Chet. Don't tell me you don't know . . ."

"Know what?"

"Freeberg and Gayle were arrested this morning. Freeberg wasn't quite so worried after his lawyer, Kile, convinced him no patient would be willing to provide real evidence against them. But"—she stared at Hunter—"you mean you're the one who is going to give evidence that Freeberg is a pimp and Gayle is a hooker?"

"It was just a job, Suzy. Somebody had to be a witness, so I came up with the evidence."

Suzy was stunned. "*You* did that? I don't believe it!" Her fury was beginning to mount. "You're supposed to be the man I love. But looking at you now, I see a horrible weasel, a shitface of a weasel!" She caught her breath. "I sent you to Freeberg and Gayle to fix you up, and instead you used the opportunity to investigate them, to turn it into a sting operation."

"That was incidental, a side thing," Hunter explained uncomfortably. "Of course, my real purpose was to get some help and normalize our relationship. But along the way, I picked up this evidence." He waved the papers in his hand once more. "Do you know what this means for us, Suzy? It means this is now a political issue, and I'm guaranteed a job on Ferguson's paper. It'll put us on our feet."

He tried to get past Suzy, but she stood in his way. "You're not going anywhere. If you try to, don't come back. I never want to set eyes on you again. I'd regard you as the lowliest thing in the universe. Not good enough to come out from under a rock. Chet, do you know what you're doing to them—to Dr. Freeberg, to Gayle Miller—after what they've done for you? Your evidence could put them both behind bars, put Freeberg out of business, ruin Gayle's career."

"Listen," pleaded Hunter, "I don't make the laws—"

"But you're going to be the one to try to prove they broke the law. You're their only evidence. How can you be against them? How can you go in there and destroy Gayle Miller, that wonderful woman? I just read what she did for

you. I just found out what she did for you in your bedroom.
Now you're going to try to prove she's a criminal."

"You know that was never my intention."

"That's what it comes down to. Chet"—Suzy had him by
the shoulders—"you can't . . . You can't do it."

"I'm sorry, Suzy, but I'm committed."

"Then get uncommitted." She snatched the story from
Hunter. "Chet, did a low-down prostitute do this for you?
Or was it a legitimate surrogate working for a licensed
therapist?"

"Suzy, please don't stand in my way. The court will decide what's right or wrong. All I know is what's right for me,
for us. I want to get someplace."

"Chet, you are no place! As a human being, you are
nowhere! You're behaving like a rat!"

"Suzy, stop that!"

"You can go on with the work you've been doing. A
decent opportunity will come along, and you'll go further.
But don't do it this way. Right now you have to live with
yourself and me. How can you even consider turning on the
people who did so much for you? Please think about it,
Chet. Think about it!"

Tony Zecca sat behind his desk in the backroom office of
his restaurant, waiting for the telephone at his elbow to
ring.

He had placed the call to Big Manny Martin in Las Vegas
nearly a half hour ago. He had been told that Manny was
out of his suite but would be back soon and would return
his call. He had been advised to sit tight for it.

He had been sitting tight all this while, wondering if he
had done the right thing, and wondering what he should
ask of Manny when he phoned back.

There was little doubt in Zecca's mind that Manny would
do whatever was requested of him. Zecca had always had a
smooth working relationship with Manny and the mob.
With his restaurant chain, Zecca had set up a perfect cover
for them to launder loose money and give themselves an

acceptable legitimacy in the eyes of the IRS. They'd helped him get along, and get along well, of course. But he'd helped them more and in a more crucial way. Beyond the business, he had done many other favors for the mob, allowing his chain to perform as a safe conduit for their drug smuggling from South America. There was no question in Zecca's mind that the mob owed him one, and Manny was the person to ask for a repayment.

What was confusing to Zecca was exactly what repayment he should request when Manny's call came through.

What was not confusing to Zecca was his ultimate goal. That was clear. Get rid of that fucking Dr. Freeberg, by one means or another. Freeberg had seduced Nan and was keeping her on the side for some daily nooky. Once Freeberg was put out of commission, Nan would be alone and lost. Zecca would have no trouble bringing her back under his control.

Zecca's first instinct had been to take care of Freeberg himself. Though he was careful to conceal the fact from Nan, he always packed a .45 wherever he went, and turning the doctor into a corpse would be easy. Somehow, something made Zecca hesitate about going after the doctor on his own. Not that he was adverse to killing anyone who had harmed him or stood in his way. But the fact was he had not killed anyone since his Vietnam years, because his facade and value to the mob had been respectability. If he ever caused a scrap, and had a run-in with the police, it could end his usefulness to the mob and even put his own life in jeopardy.

Zecca had finally decided that what he wanted done should be done by the faceless mob. They were expert at this, and no clue would be left to trace the act to them. He himself would remain in the clear—hands clean—and free to bring Nan back into his life.

So Zecca had buzzed Manny in Las Vegas.

Now, waiting for the return call, only one uncertainty existed. Exactly what did he want to ask of Manny? Did he want Manny to assign a hit man to waste the fucking doctor and dump his body? Or did he want Manny to send down one or two strong-arm hoods to rough up Freeberg, beat him to a pulp, and tell him to get out of town fast if he wanted to hold on to what was left of him?

Trying to determine what should be done, what he should tell Manny he wanted when the call came, he glared impatiently at the telephone and reached for his unopened copy of the day's Hillsdale *Chronicle.*

Opening the newspaper to turn to the sports section, a headline on the lower half of the front page caught his eye. Actually, what caught his eye was the name of Dr. Arnold Freeberg in the lead paragraph of the story.

Curious, Tony Zecca hastily read the story.

Finishing it, he lay back in his swivel chair, a smile of satisfaction on his face. So, District Attorney Hoyt Lewis was charging a local sex therapist, Dr. Arnold Freeberg, with using female surrogates to cure patients. So, Lewis was arresting and booking Freeberg and an as yet unnamed surrogate for the criminal offenses of pandering and prostitution. So, Lewis was going to place Freeberg on trial and end his practice in Hillsdale.

Tomorrow, the district attorney would hold a press conference outlining details of his prosecution against Freeberg.

Zecca's smile broadened.

His dilemma was over. A means of getting rid of Freeberg had been neatly resolved by the law. Zecca would not have to ask anyone to get rid of Freeberg. The D.A. was doing it for him. The D.A. would, in effect, waste the fucking doctor, and Zecca would have the faithless bitch Nan back in his bed for as long as he wanted her.

That moment, the telephone rang.

It was Big Manny Martin himself on the line from Las Vegas.

"Hiya, chum," said Manny. "You have something important to discuss?"

Zecca swallowed. "Not really important, boss. Maybe I overdid it in my enthusiasm. More routine, really."

"What is it, Tony?"

"Uh, the shipment—the shipment from Colombia—

came in a week early. Thought you'd want to arrange a pickup."

"Is that all? We'll catch it on the regular pickup. Thanks for staying on the ball, Tony. See you soon."

After he hung up, Zecca settled back, relieved.

Just as well to have District Attorney Lewis do Manny's job for him. Tomorrow, Zecca resolved, he'd be on hand to keep an eye on the D.A.'s press conference.

Only a second before being shown into the district attorney's office did Chet Hunter feel any unsteadiness in his legs. This, he was sure, came not from nervousness about the momentous step he was taking but from the exhaustion engendered by his second roll in the hay with Suzy Edwards. It had been better than the first, far more prolonged, and much better.

Now, his shoulders back, feeling strong and certain, he walked into the district attorney's office.

The Reverend Josh Scrafield was there, of course, off to one side, beaming at him. Hunter detoured to shake Scrafield's hand, then continued on to the district attorney's desk.

Hoyt Lewis was standing, his hand extended. Hunter took it briefly.

"Congratulations!" Lewis boomed out. He tapped the copy of the last installment of Hunter's journal lying on his desk. "A great job, an absolutely perfect job."

"Thank you," said Hunter.

"I've been eager to see you, Chet," said the district attorney. "I want to map out our strategy with you, before my press conference tomorrow. Sit down, sit down. Let's talk it over."

Hunter remained silently standing.

Lewis settled in his leather chair. "The main thing is that you testify on the stand just as you wrote it all out for me. We can't lose. You're going to make a magnificent witness for the prosecution. You're going to be an unimpeachable witness."

Hunter cleared his throat. "I'm afraid I won't be," he said simply.

Hoyt Lewis raised his head with a jerk, as if he hadn't heard right. "What?"

"I'll repeat it for you," said Hunter. "I'm not going to appear as a witness for you. I've come to the conclusion that Dr. Freeberg is not pandering and Gayle Miller is not engaging in prostitution. They should not be prosecuted. They're performing legitimate therapy. I participated in a cure with them, and it worked. They're good people, and they deserve to be left to continue their work."

Hoyt Lewis shook his head in disbelief. "Have you lost your mind, Chet? I can't be hearing you right."

From behind him, Hunter heard the angry shout. "Are you crazy or what?" bellowed the Reverend Scrafield. He strode across the office. "Did Freeberg pay you to do this?"

Hunter remained calm. "On the contrary. I paid Freeberg to put me together, and he did."

Scrafield had his hands on Hunter's lapels. "You back off, play turncoat, and I'll have your neck, I *swear* it!"

"Let go of him," ordered Lewis. The district attorney studied Hunter. "Chet, this may have been a momentary aberration on your part. I don't know what's behind it, but you deserve another chance. Are you going to stick to the script and be my witness?"

"No," said Hunter. "I absolutely refuse to testify for you."

"You can't refuse to testify," said Lewis evenly. "That's a crime in itself. If you won't testify voluntarily, then I'll have you subpoenaed to stand as a witness."

"You can do that, and I'll comply," said Hunter. "But the one thing you can't do is make me be a friendly witness for the prosecution. In fact, I'd be a very bad witness for you. The defense would be happy to have you put me on the stand. Need I say more?"

The district attorney sat silent and fuming in his chair.

"I guess that's all there is to say," concluded Hunter. "I'd better go now. Hope to see you again one day—but it won't be in court."

With that, Hunter turned and left the office.

As Hunter entered the city hall corridor outside the district attorney's office, he felt a vast sense of relief. He had not known how he would stand up under the pressure from Hoyt Lewis and the Reverend Scrafield, and now he felt that he had stood up quite well. He had not been craven. He had shown courage. He suspected, as Suzy had suggested, that he owed Gayle more than merely his repaired sexuality. In restoring his manhood, Gayle had somehow restored his morality and his confidence in his future. He was pleased he had not sold her out.

Proceeding up the corridor, he thought that he heard his name called out. He halted, then whirled about to see if either Lewis or Scrafield was calling to him.

The person leaving the men's room, who was trying to get his attention, was neither Lewis nor Scrafield but someone else he had not expected to see again.

"Chet," said Otto Ferguson, approaching him, "I've been waiting for you."

"Waiting for me?" said Hunter with surprise.

Ferguson came before him. "I wanted to have a few words with you. I tried to find you and then guessed you probably came here. When I verified with Lewis's secretary that you were indeed here, I hurried straight over to stand by until you came out. I suspect you were having a heavy meeting in there."

"You're right," said Hunter, still confused by the editor's presence, "it was a very heavy meeting."

"What happened?" asked Ferguson, his gaze fixed on Hunter. "Did you tell them you'd be their witness, or did you change your mind?"

Hunter blinked at the editor. "I changed my mind. I refused to cooperate with them."

"I'm mighty glad," said Ferguson. "If you hadn't I wouldn't be here speaking to you."

Hunter was now thoroughly bewildered. "What are you talking about, Mr. Ferguson? You're the one who got me into this whole thing in the first place."

"That's before I knew what Dr. Freeberg and his surrogates were really up to," said Ferguson. He pulled a roll of pages out of his jacket pocket and waved them at Hunter. "Now I know."

"What's that?" asked Hunter.

"Your own pages. The journal you sent over to me earlier today. Chet, when all this started, naturally I was suspicious of Freeberg's operation, but still I thought your story might be too raunchy for family reading. That's why I advised you to make it into a political issue. I felt that as a political issue it would be valid for me to run all the sex stuff, especially if the D.A. brought up charges of pandering and prostitution. But I was wrong. I was misguided by my lack of facts."

Hunter's bewilderment was total. "What do you mean?"

Ferguson shook the story under Hunter's nose. "I mean this. I read every word of it, and it really shook me up. You come through sounding like a decent, compassionate creature who desperately needed help, and Gayle comes out like an angel of mercy."

Hunter stared at Ferguson with disbelief. "You—you liked what I reported on the surrogate treatments?"

"I loved it! It has all the elements of a perfect story—a suffering hero filled with inner conflicts and defeat, a beautiful heroine who will do anything to save him, then boy meets girl, and after weeks of suspense, the boy is saved and we get a happy ending." Ferguson paused. "It's all true, isn't it?"

"Every word, Mr. Ferguson."

"Well, there are thousands and thousands of people out there, silently and secretly suffering from sexual disabilities, and your personal account could give them a chance for happiness."

Hunter's mouth had gone dry. He found breathing difficult. "What are you saying, Mr. Ferguson?"

"I'm saying I'm going to run your surrogate story almost in its entirety as a series of articles under your own byline. I may ask you to edit out a bit of the overt sexuality—some judicious cutting, a few euphemisms, might make it more acceptable without distorting or compromising the honesty of your narrative."

"You're going to let me edit it?"

"Of course, once you're behind your desk at the *Chronicle.*" He grabbed Hunter's hand and shook it. "Congratulations, Chet."

"I can't believe it."

Ferguson winked. "As you grow older, my son, you'll learn that virtue is sometimes rewarded. Be in my office at ten tomorrow morning. We'll discuss your salary." He started away, then stopped and turned. "I hope you have someone who's going to benefit from all your newly acquired sexual wisdom."

"I have! We're getting married!"

"I hope Gayle gets to catch the bouquet thrown by your bride."

After Ferguson had left, Hunter stood in the corridor, dazed by the turn of events.

Then he started to run in search of a phone, to let Suzy Edwards know that they could now get married as soon as possible.

Inside the district attorney's office, Hoyt Lewis sat bent over, his elbows on his desk, his hands holding his aching head, a picture of utter dejection.

Only an hour before, he had never been happier. After reading what Hunter had uncovered and was ready to stand witness to, Hoyt Lewis's wildest dreams of his glorious future had seemed close to reality.

And now, because of a mushy-headed witness who had refused to testify for him, Lewis's ambitions had all gone up in smoke.

"Disgusting, absolutely disgusting," he muttered.

The Reverend Scrafield, who angrily continued to stride back and forth in front of Lewis's desk, agreed.

"I could kill that dumb sonofabitch," Scrafield growled.

Lewis took his chin off his hands and tried to straighten up. "Well, there's nothing we can do. Hunter's got us by the balls, so to speak. We'll have to call it quits."

"What about your press conference?" Scrafield wanted to know.

"I'll go through with it but make only a brief announcement stating that we were misinformed about Dr. Freeberg's operation and that we are dropping our charges. I'll have to say that although Freeberg and Gayle Miller are presently under arrest, we will drop the charges against them immediately."

Hoyt Lewis realized that Scrafield had stopped abruptly before his desk and was looking down at him. "Wait a minute," said Scrafield slowly, "I think I've got an idea that can resurrect our case."

"Yes?"

"You reminded me of something," Scrafield said, "that Gayle Miller is still under arrest for prostitution. She is under arrest, isn't she?"

"Of course, but we can't proceed against her. Without a witness, we have no case."

"Hold it," Scrafield said. "I have an idea. What if I came up with a perfect witness, a witness twice as good as Hunter might have been?"

Lewis became alert. "Meaning whom?"

"Meaning none other than the little whore herself, Gayle Miller."

"Gayle Miller? I don't get it."

"You said that she's still under arrest for prostitution. She doesn't know you're not going to put her on trial."

"She'll know tomorrow after my press conference, when we drop charges."

"This is today," insisted Scrafield, "and she still doesn't know. I've seen your file on her. I remember one thing. She's applied to UCLA for a graduate scholarship. If word gets out that she's being tried for prostitution, she'll lose any chance of getting that scholarship. That girl's got a lot at stake in being tried."

"Reverend Scrafield, just what are you driving at?"

Scrafield came around the district attorney's desk and stood hulking directly above him. "Hoyt, this Gayle knows only that she's been arrested and is about to be tried as a hooker. She must be trembling in her boots. I bet she'd give anything to be unarrested, cleared, freed. Well, what if I go to her and offer her a proposition? Give her a chance to be free?"

"How would you manage that?"

"By going to see Gayle tonight and presenting her with this proposition: 'You're arrested, about to be put behind bars and your reputation ruined, but there happens to be one way you can save yourself and come out looking like Miss Purity. Turn state's evidence, Gayle—join our side and become our leading witness against Freeberg and his surrogate whores. Claim you were misled into living that kind of life, that Freeberg is pandering and the other girls are behaving as prostitutes, and you want no more of it. Turn state's evidence, Gayle, be our witness for the prosecution, and the district attorney will dismiss all charges against you.' What about it, Hoyt? Would you make such a deal with her?"

"I sure would. Having her as a witness would make it for us."

"Okay, tonight," said Scrafield, "I'm going to see our friend Gayle."

"Do you think she'll go for it?" asked Lewis anxiously.

"She'll go for it," Scrafield replied grimly. "I'll see to that."

XI

It was not quite eight thirty in the evening when the Reverend Josh Scrafield, having discarded his clerical collar for a blue knit tie and white shirt and conservative dark blue suit, reached the front door to Gayle Miller's house. He noted that the overhead porch light was on.

For a moment, Scrafield remained immobilized, considering carefully what approach he would take with Gayle Miller. Getting in to see her was the major hurdle. Once in her living room, he was certain that there would be no problem. His approach, of course, had to be elastic. So much depended on what kind of person this Miller woman proved to be. He had never seen her, and except for the information Hunter's journal and Hoyt Lewis's dossier had given him, he knew not a thing about her personally. There had been some indication, in Hunter's account, that she was attractive and forthright. But then, Scrafield assumed, all women in this line of work must be attractive and forthright—at least attractive, to be sure.

Getting into her house was the main step, and Scrafield began to feel more certain that he had the means to accomplish this.

His hand went to the doorbell, and he pressed it three times and waited.

He thought that he heard someone approaching from behind the door, and then a muffled voice inquired, "Who is it?"

The Reverend Scrafield pressed closer to the door. "I'm here to see Miss Gayle Miller on a business matter. Are you Miss Miller?"

The door opened a crack, just enough to make a portion of Gayle visible.

"I'm Gayle Miller," she said. "What do you want to see me about?"

For an instant, at the sight of her, Scrafield was too taken aback to speak. He had expected someone attractive, true, yet by the nature of her calling and from the fact that she had been arrested for prostitution, he had expected someone whose good looks would be cheapened and coarse. What he saw, instead, through the slit of the doorway, was a fresh and lovely young thing, startlingly lush and beautiful, gowned in some kind of pale green silk robe that indicated her body was a match for her face.

"There's some important business I have to discuss with you, Miss Miller," Scrafield said.

"I can't imagine what . . . But whatever it is, can't it wait until tomorrow? I have an appointment, and I have to get dressed."

"I'm afraid this is something that has to be settled tonight."

Gayle opened the door a little more and peered at Scrafield. She seemed to recognize him but couldn't quite place him.

"Who are you?" she wanted to know. "What kind of business?"

"I'm the Reverend Josh Scrafield."

"The evangelist? I've seen you on television. I thought you looked familiar." She paused. "What do you want to see me about?"

"About your arrest this morning."

She appeared surprised. "How do you know about that? Besides, why is that any business of yours?"

Scrafield felt more confident now. "I've been asked to

serve as an intermediary between District Attorney Hoyt
Lewis and yourself. It has to do with the district attorney's
planned prosecution of you. He sent me over tonight to
offer you a proposal concerning your arrest. May I come
inside?"

She opened the door wider. "All right, I guess I should
listen to what this is all about. Come on in."

With a pleased and grateful smile, Scrafield entered her
modest living room.

Gayle waved him toward the sofa, but Scrafield lingered
briefly where he stood, unable to take his eyes from her.
The delicacy of her features, the ample curves of her youth-
ful figure, utterly belied what he had read about her in
Hunter's erotic journal. This girl resembled a vestal virgin,
not the shocking and experienced sex surrogate he had
envisioned from Hunter's account.

She had tightened her silk robe in front of her, but its soft
folds could not hide from Scrafield's stare that she was clad
only in a half bra and the tiniest of bikini panties beneath it.
"I was about to get dressed. I have an appointment pretty
soon," she said. "Please be brief. Sit down and tell me
what's going on."

"Thank you, Miss Miller." Scrafield sat on the edge of the
sofa cushion, wondering what assignations had taken place
here.

He watched while she adjusted a pull-up chair to face
him, crossing her shapely legs beneath the silk robe, careful
not to let her knees be exposed.

"So the district attorney sent you to see me?" she said.
"He has some kind of proposal about my arrest?"

Scrafield cleared his throat. "Exactly."

"Well, do you want to tell me about it?"

"Yes, of course. The district attorney has looked into
your background and activities, which you understand is
normal procedure. He knows, for one thing, that you performed as a sex surrogate for Dr. Arnold Freeberg in Arizona when it was against the law. You were both forced to
leave Arizona."

Gayle bristled. "That's not quite the story, Mr. Scrafield.

Dr. Freeberg was given the opportunity to continue practicing sex therapy without the aid of surrogates. He thought that would be ineffective and chose to leave the state. I volunteered to follow him. We came to California, where we thought the attitudes were more liberal." She shrugged her shoulders. "Obviously, we were mistaken." She met Scrafield's gaze. "Anyway, what's that got to do with what?"

"Perhaps it's not precisely relevant to your current case," Scrafield admitted, "but I mention it to give you an idea of the kind of information that the district attorney has been able to obtain about you. What is more relevant is your current status and activities. For example, we know just what you've been doing as a surrogate here in Hillsdale."

"It's hardly a secret," Gayle flared. "Surrogate procedures have been well publicized." She studied the clergyman. "About me, what I've been doing—who told you about me?"

Scrafield shook his head. "That's not a matter for me to disclose. That will be revealed when you stand trial. But there is other information the district attorney has that may be of even more interest to you."

"Like what?"

"You wish to enter graduate school at UCLA. You can't afford it without a scholarship. Recently, you applied for a scholarship."

"Is there anything wrong with that?" said Gayle belligerently.

"Not from the district attorney's point of view. Only from yours. Because once your arrest for prostitution has been disclosed, and once you go on trial so charged, it seems unlikely that you will be a successful candidate for a scholarship." Scrafield paused. "This could hurt your future. District Attorney Lewis made it clear to me he does not wish to hurt your future."

Gayle seemed to slump. "All right, what are you leading up to?"

When Gayle slumped, her breasts moved, and Scrafield was mesmerized. Her breasts were full, ripe, the best he had seen in years. No wonder Hunter had been able to get it up, Scrafield thought, and no wonder Hunter had not wanted to testify against her. He was probably hoping for an encore with this lush creature.

Scrafield had hardly heard what Gayle had been saying. Distracted, Scrafield said, "Uh, Miss Miller, do you have a drink in the house? I find this assignment a bit difficult, and a shot of whiskey might make it easier."

"I have some Scotch, but I don't have much time." Reluctantly, she came to her feet. "Oh, all right, I'll get you a shot."

She started off to her kitchen. Her ass undulated. Scrafield felt the stirring between his legs. This was unseemly, and he tried to ignore his reaction.

"Uh, Miss Miller, make it a double, if you don't mind."

"Okay."

She returned with the double shot, no ice, handed it to him, and sat right down.

As Scrafield swallowed the whiskey in two gulps, Gayle asked steadily, "What are you leading up to? You say the D.A. doesn't want to hurt me. Then what does he expect to do, putting me under arrest?"

Scrafield savored the effects of the Scotch. "That's better. Thank you. What does the district attorney want to do? He arrested you to throw a scare into you, to bring you to your senses. But he has no desire to try you in court, make a public spectacle of you. He would rather make you into a useful member of our community."

"How?" Gayle asked suspiciously.

"By offering you a deal that would enable him to drop the charges against you, not reveal your name, and to offer you freedom from further prosecution."

Gayle's suspicions mounted. "What kind of deal?"

"He has authorized me to inform you that if you will turn state's evidence, all charges against you will immediately be dropped."

Gayle's face displayed an expression of hope. Yet she remained cautious. "Turn state's evidence. What does that mean?"

Through her thin robe, Scrafield could discern the outline of her thighs and the lines of her panties. He tried desperately to concentrate. "State's evidence, a great opportunity, would give you a chance to join the prosecution as a firsthand witness for the district attorney."

Gayle stiffened. "Witness against whom?"

"Why, against the other defendant in the case," Scrafield went on smoothly. "You need only take the witness stand for the prosecution and admit you committed all the acts you did under the direction of the other defendant."

Gayle glared at the clergyman. "The other defendant being Dr. Freeberg?"

"Yes, Dr. Freeberg, of course."

Gayle was on her feet. "You want me to testify against Dr. Freeberg? Are you crazy?"

"I'm simply trying to help you," said Scrafield innocently. "Only trying to get you out of trouble."

"By putting a wonderful, decent man in jail, a man who's done nothing wrong ever? You want me to turn against the man who's done so much for so many people, myself included?"

Scrafield came to his feet quickly, imploring her. "Miss Miller—Gayle—be reasonable. The district attorney and I are offering you a chance to be free. In court you won't have to accuse Freeberg of anything. Simply, under oath, relate how he paid you to perform sexual acts with strange men."

"You expect me to crucify Dr. Freeberg? Have him found guilty of pimping?"

"Pandering," Scrafield tried to correct her.

"You want to turn me against one of the finest human beings I've known in my life? You're plain out of your mind. I wouldn't do that in a million years. I'd rather go to jail forever than turn against Dr. Freeberg."

"Gayle, he's a panderer," Scrafield repeated evenly. "Don't sacrifice yourself for a—"

"And you, you're a fucking Holy Joe!" she interrupted angrily. "Now, get out of here with your goddamn propositions! I don't want to see you or hear from you ever again! You fucking bastard, get out of here!"

Scrafield trembled with excitement at her sluttish language. Underneath the virginal facade, she was a hooker through and through, a real piece of ass who had handed it out, for pay, even for free, to dozens and dozens of men.

"You heard me!" she shouted at him. "Get out and leave me alone!"

Scrafield walked slowly to the door, with Gayle at his heels.

"Please reconsider," he mumbled.

"Beat it!" she cried out, and as he put his hand on the doorknob, she pivoted angrily away and rushed toward the entrance to her bedroom.

Scrafield opened the door to leave, then looked over his shoulder, and what he saw in the bedroom made him slam the door shut, while he remained inside the living room.

He could see her in the bedroom, pulling off her silk robe and throwing it aside. Between her lace half bra and her abbreviated transparent panties, her body was silkier than her robe had been. As she turned to survey herself in a mirror, he had a full front view of her, and even from this distance, he believed he could make out the long dark triangle of pubic hair at the crotch of her panties.

Scrafield felt his heart beginning to hammer. He'd had women through the years, many of them, often some of his unhappily married parishioners who worshipped his golden voice and obvious virility. He'd also enjoyed the favors of Darlene Young regularly for several years. He accepted Darlene's servicing him, although lately he had begun to think her too fat and just a little too far along in years to provide him any real titillation.

But this sexy slut in the bedroom . . . She was the most desirable female he had ever seen. He could not leave. He had to have her. In the end, it would mean nothing at all to her. She'd had a thousand men before. He'd merely be the thousandth and one.

Blindly, Scrafield moved nearer to the bedroom.

He was inside the bedroom, not many feet from her. She had turned and her bare back was to him. She was moving toward a chair to pick up a skirt.

"Gayle," he called out quietly.

Startled, she froze, then spun around, her eyes wide. "You!" she exclaimed. "What are you doing here?"

"Trying to plead with you one last time. Gayle, please reconsider . . . Agree to work with me."

"I wouldn't help you for anything in the world! Get your ass out of here!"

He was hypnotized by the dark triangle hardly hidden by her bikini briefs. "Gayle." He found it difficult to speak. "Gayle, forget everything I said—this is something else— I've never seen anyone like you . . . I can take care of you right now, the way you've never been taken care of before." He was moving closer to her. "I'll treat you like a queen, Gayle. You'll be a queen. You won't have to be a whore with me . . ."

"I'm not a whore, goddamn you!" she screamed. "You get away from me!"

But Scrafield was upon her, his arms uplifted.

Gayle swung her hand at him, trying to slap his face. But he caught her by the wrists, bringing her hands down to her sides.

He held them tightly against her thighs, breathing against her contorted mouth. "You are a little whore, you know that? You whored with those men your pimp kept handing you. I can prove it. I can prove you handed it out every day. Now I'm going to give you a chance to be with a real man who knows how to treat a whore . . ."

He released her wrists, and before she could fend him off, he had her by the shoulders. He drove her up against the side of the bed and down on it on her back. Desperately, she tried to rise, but he hit her with his fists until she fell back half conscious, moaning.

Never taking his eyes off her, he removed his jacket, let down his trousers, and unbuttoned his shorts. His erection, which she eyed with terror, sprang straight out.

His fingers fumbled for her bra, ripping at it, tearing it off her body. His big hands went down to the elastic band of her bikini briefs.

"Don't . . ." she begged him. "Don't, don't . . ."

She tried to rise and fight him off, but with one fist, he slammed her against the head again and down flat on the bed.

She tried to press her thighs together, but it was no use. He had each leg in a powerful grip. She tried to resist, but his uncontrolled strength was too much for her.

He'd managed to get her legs wide apart, and for an instant, he savored the length of the dark pubic hair covering her vaginal mound.

He had taken his pole of an erection in one hand, ready to direct it into her—when they both heard a metallic click in the living room behind them.

There was definitely the sound of the front door opening.

"Paul!" Gayle screamed at the top of her lungs. "Paul, help me!"

At the sound of the running footsteps, Scrafield straightened and swung about, just as Brandon burst into the room. In a second, Brandon saw what was happening, and he threw himself at Scrafield.

Brandon had Scrafield by the throat, but Scrafield's strong hands loosened Brandon's hold.

"You dirty bastard!" Brandon bellowed, clutching the clergyman by the shirt, spinning him toward the living room, then swinging a roundhouse punch at him, catching him on the side of the head and driving him to the floor of the living room.

Gayle had rolled over, snatched at her phone, was dialing 911, crying into the mouthpiece, "Emergency! Rape! He's still here! Get the police, get the police!" She was shouting out her address as Brandon disappeared into the living room after Scrafield.

But Scrafield, scrambling to his feet half naked, was waiting for Brandon.

They went at it toe to toe, battering each other across the room, overturning small tables and lamps, grunting and hammering at each other.

Round and round the room they went, swinging at one

another wildly, sometimes landing, sometimes missing, but going at it without pause.

Although breathless, Scrafield, better trained, stronger, began to recover his poise.

He saw the younger man come at him once more, ducked, parrying his blow, and then with all his might he hooked an uppercut to the side of Brandon's jaw. Brandon's arms dropped, and he reeled backward, with Scrafield atop him, fists crunching again and again into Brandon's bleeding face.

Brandon went down to his knees, dazed.

Scrafield madly kicked out at his head and sent him flat.

Wasting no more time, Scrafield pulled up his trousers as he hobbled to the door.

He yanked the front door open in time to see two men in blue uniforms leap out of a patrol car and come racing up the walk.

The two policemen had him by the arms.

"Wait a minute, buddy!" the taller policeman yelled at him. "Where in the hell do you think you're going?"

"I—I—" Scrafield couldn't find his voice.

"We have a report there's been a rape," the other policeman was saying.

"The rapist, he's inside," Scrafield coughed out.

"Well, let's all go inside and see . . . ."

"No!" shouted Scrafield, trying to tear away.

"If not inside, you're going to the station," the taller policeman announced, and that instant Scrafield realized that the second policeman had drawn his hands behind him and had clamped handcuffs around his wrists.

Scrafield went limp, gave up.

Early the following morning, when District Attorney Hoyt Lewis entered his reception room on his way to his office, he found Dr. Freeberg, as well as Gayle Miller with a young man he did not know, already waiting for him.

Lewis halted with an apology. "Forgive me for awakening

you so early, but I felt it important that all of us get together before the day got too busy. Please come into my office."

They all rose and Gayle, who was holding the young man's hand, said, "Mr. Lewis, this is my boyfriend, Paul Brandon. Do you mind if he comes in with us?"

"Not at all," said Lewis affably. "Let's go inside."

Once they were in his office, Lewis gestured for them to find places across from his desk, and after they were seated he settled into his leather swivel chair.

Lewis concentrated on Gayle. "I'm sorry about what happened last night, Miss Miller. It must have been terrible."

"It *was* terrible," Gayle snapped. "I'm just lucky that Paul —Paul Brandon—came in at that moment. What's going to happen to that dreadful preacher?"

"We'll talk about that shortly," Lewis said. "I have something else on the agenda first." He picked up his briefcase, set it on his knees, unlocked and opened it, and pulled out two manuscripts.

"Do you know what this is?" he asked Freeberg. "It's a journal, two copies of a journal, that one of your patients kept during surrogate therapy. It was the basis for my prosecution against you, Dr. Freeberg, and you, Miss Miller. Do you want to know who kept this journal and turned it over to us?"

"Who was it?" demanded Freeberg.

"A patient of Miss Miller's named Chet Hunter," said Lewis.

"Chet Hunter?" said Gayle with disbelief. "But he couldn't—he wouldn't . . ."

"He did it," said Lewis.

"The bastard," Brandon interjected.

Lewis held up a placating hand. "He's not entirely to blame. He had the idea, but it was I who gave him—with support from the Reverend Scrafield—the go-ahead to pull off this little sting operation. With this evidence in hand, I authorized your arrests."

Gayle was furious. "What about us? Are you actually going to put us on trial?"

"That, too, can wait a bit, if you don't mind," said Lewis.

"Before answering you, I must know something else." He leaned across his desk, handing one copy of the Hunter manuscript to Dr. Freeberg and the other to Gayle Miller. "I want you both to read the journal Chet Hunter kept and to let me know if it is entirely accurate in its account of your surrogate therapy."

"One minute," said Freeberg. "If this is evidence against us and you want us to verify it, I want to have my attorney present."

"You won't need your attorney," said Lewis. "You have my word that whatever you say will not be used against you. All I want you to do is read it and tell me if it is accurate." He stood up. "I'll be making some calls from my secretary's office. I'll be back in a half hour."

Hoyt Lewis left his office, and in a half hour, he returned to his own office and desk.

"Well?" he said to the others.

"The part about me, my own role, is perfectly accurate," said Freeberg.

Gayle threw the journal back on Lewis's desk. "Yes, he's got it just right about me, too."

"Thank you," said Lewis. "Now, let me tell you why I brought you here. When I first read Hunter's report, I read it hastily and with prejudice. My mind was searching only for evidence for a headline case, not for the truth. Last night, before the chief of police called to tell me of the Reverend Scrafield's violent attack on you, Miss Miller, I began to have second thoughts about Hunter's report."

"What do you mean, Mr. Lewis?" Freeberg wanted to know.

"To be truthful, I became ashamed of myself," said Lewis, "of my role in this action. Hunter was to have been our star witness against you. But he was so moved by what Miss Miller had done for him that he backed out of the case, and I was prepared to do the same thing. Still, when Scrafield suggested that he himself go to Miss Miller with that wild proposal, I did agree to let Scrafield do this. Later, when Scrafield had gone, I began to feel uneasy about the whole thing. That's when I reread Hunter's account of your

therapy with him—I reread it with care. It gave me a better
insight into your work, a better understanding, and I
wished more than anything on earth I could recall Scrafield,
but it was too late. He was already with you." Hoyt Lewis
paused. "Again, I'm so sorry about what happened last
night. I'll take my share of the blame. Therefore, I think
you should have a voice in the disposition of the Reverend
Scrafield. Once that's settled, I'll go on to discuss your
futures. But first, since I'm seeing Scrafield in a half hour,
what would you have me do with him, Dr. Freeberg, and
you, Miss Miller, and yes, you, too, Mr. Brandon? What
would you have me do with the Reverend Scrafield?"

For ten minutes after Dr. Freeberg, Gayle Miller, and
Paul Brandon had left, District Attorney Hoyt Lewis remained seated alone, waiting for his next guest. Now his
eyes were fixed on the door to his office as it opened and
the Reverend Josh Scrafield stepped inside.

Lewis had expected the clergyman's bearing to be erect
and his manner aggressive, that of an innocent victim who
had been put upon, and Lewis was not surprised that
Scrafield's deportment was exactly as he had anticipated.

"I'm glad you could see me," said Scrafield, crossing the
office, moving vigorously.

Lewis neither rose to greet him nor offered a handshake.
The district attorney merely jerked his head toward the
empty chair beside him and waited for Scrafield to be settled. "I wanted to be the first to tell you this," said Lewis.
"Scrafield, you're a stupid fool."

Scrafield's composure didn't waver. "Listen, Hoyt,
there's more to it."

"I read the charges you're booked on," Lewis said. "I've
talked to the two witnesses, Miss Miller and Mr. Brandon,
at length—"

"You don't really think I tried to rape her?"

"No, you were only trying to tell her you were sorry for
harassing her."

"You've got to hear my side of it."

Hoyt Lewis nodded. "That's why you're here, Scrafield. To let me hear your side of it before I put you away."

Ignoring the last threat, Scrafield gathered himself together, and with the earnestness so well known to his television viewers, he proceeded to expound his defense in a winning and melodious voice. "Hoyt, in all fairness, hear me out," he began. "You may not believe me, but I went to see Gayle Miller with the sole intent of performing the mission we had agreed upon. The instant I made our offer, Miss Miller lost her head, reverted to type. Not only did she vehemently decline our offer, but she began cursing both of us in a stream of the foulest invective I've ever heard. I suppose I shouldn't have expected anything better from her, but somehow I did, and I was taken aback, to say the least."

Momentarily, Scrafield examined the district attorney to assess what effect his account was having on the official, but Hoyt Lewis's expression revealed no reaction.

Hastily, Scrafield resumed his account. "When I realized that I'd get nowhere with her, I decided to leave. I was just getting ready to go when the little chippy changed her tactics. She began to act provocatively. She was wearing next to nothing, and she was clearly shaking her ass at me. I told her she was acting like a whore and it would get her nowhere. Then she sidled up to me and said, 'I have a better idea if you want to talk it over.' She led me to her bedroom—of course I should have known better than to follow her in there—and then she said that she still wouldn't turn state's evidence against Freeberg, but there was something she could do on her own. She said she had a counterproposal to make. If I could convince you to free her, she said she'd give me a free fuck on the house. I was astounded, believe me—"

Hoyt Lewis interrupted. "Scrafield, I don't believe you. I don't believe you at all. If she was giving you one on the house, why was she fighting you tooth and nail when her boyfriend pulled you off her? Why did she call the police for help? And how come the police found you running into the street without your pants fastened?"

The clergyman's poise began to dissolve slightly. "Hoyt, I'm telling you, Gayle's a lying slut, and her boyfriend's in collusion with her."

Hoyt Lewis considered Scrafield coldly. "In short, four people lied while you alone tell the truth?"

"Hoyt, for God's sake, you're not taking that little roundheel's word over mine? You yourself agreed with me that she was a prostie—"

"And I was wrong, absolutely wrong from the start, and I'm prepared to admit it," said Hoyt Lewis. "You're a great talker—I'll give you that—and you're clever about people —I'll concede that as well. From the outset, you were clever enough to play up to my one weakness, my ambition. Yes, I allowed myself to be lulled by you and drawn into this mess. I began to regret it fully when I sent you to see Gayle Miller last night. I've regretted it ever since. You may not like what she does for men, to cure them—maybe it makes me a little uneasy, too—but that's my problem, not Gayle's. She's trained. She's honest. She believes in what she's doing. What she does is useful to many people who need help. She is anything but a prostitute, and I'm going to admit that to the press this afternoon." Lewis caught his breath. "You and I were the real prostitutes, trying to use her body to further our ambitions. I'm ready to confess that publicly. Are you?"

"There's not a thing to confess."

Scrafield's obstinance annoyed Lewis further. "Scrafield, you're a goddamn hypocrite, and you were caught with your pants down. I'm going to prove that in court."

Once again, Scrafield took on his familiar persuasive tone. "Hoyt, I don't want to go to court. Even if I win, it'll destroy me for life."

Lewis shook his head. "I never thought I'd hear myself say this to a man of the cloth. Scrafield, I don't give a shit what you want."

Scrafield's persuasive tone did not change. "Hoyt, you've got to show some kindness," he said smoothly. "You confessed to a weakness. All right, I'm willing to confess to mine. Sometimes, like all human beings, I suffer lust." He came forward in his chair. "Hoyt, don't forget we were in this together. You owe me one."

"I don't owe you a damn thing. But if you think I do, you name it."

"Just don't force me to go to court," he persisted.

Lewis stared at him. "You want me to let a potential rapist run around loose in Hillsdale?"

"You know I'm not a rapist. I had a fleeting aberration, but I'm not a rapist."

"I doubt if a jury would agree with you."

"Hoyt, I'll do anything not to stand trial."

Lewis studied Scrafield thoughtfully. "Anything?"

"Yes, anything."

"Perhaps, then, there is an alternative, one I'm considering just to save the city an expensive trial and to prevent disillusionment to your flock." He was lost in thought once more. "I'm willing to drop the charge against you if you not only leave Hillsdale forever but leave the state of California for good."

"Hoyt, that's like telling me my alternative is the guillotine. My life is here! Everything I have is here!"

"Suits me. You can put it in trust until you get out of jail."

Scrafield gazed down at the carpet, silent. When he raised his head, he said flatly, "You'll drop the rapist charge if I leave town?"

"I'm advising you to skip town, forfeit your bail."

"You won't try to have me brought back?"

"Frankly, I don't want to see you again, ever. You can reconstitute your life somewhere else but not in my bailiwick. I might say that this alternative was not volunteered by me. When I had my two witnesses as well as Dr. Freeberg in to hear their stories, I asked each of them what they thought I should do with you. I was simply for tossing you in jail. Dr. Freeberg went along. Gail's boyfriend, Brandon, thought you should be hung up by your balls. Gayle was more charitable. She suggested you be exiled. She felt it was punishment enough. She had some compassion. She said she knew men. Too many would be prepared to sell their souls, give up anything, to have sex with a woman they coveted. Understanding this, Gayle was ready to forgive and forget. She's a true Christian. You're a fraud. So I'm going along with her wish."

Scrafield sighed. It sounded more like a croak. "Well, I suppose I have no choice but to comply."

"No, you have no choice. What you have is forty-eight hours to pack your belongings and get out of town."

"All right, Hoyt"—Scrafield nodded—"I'll do just that." It was no use.

He could only do what he was ordered to do—get out of Hoyt Lewis's sight. But rising heavily, Scrafield knew that he was not through. He was not quite ready to leave town.

There was still one bit of unfinished business. A rage welled up inside him. Gayle Miller and Paul Brandon, they had done him in. Scrafield was not through with them. One of them had to pay for this.

One of them would.

That was all that obsessed him as he turned his back on the D.A. and left the room to obtain his vengeance.

Because it was a warm, sunny afternoon, and because the morning newspaper had carried an announcement of District Attorney Hoyt Lewis's impending press conference that gave promise of scandal, a goodly crowd had gathered before the Hillsdale City Hall.

Six broad stairs led down from the glass entrance doors of the city hall to a wide concrete terrace embraced by two semicircles of green planters, one on either side. At the center of the terrace stood a wooden lectern with a microphone attached to a public address system. Off to the left were four rows of folding chairs already filled with reporters from the print media throughout California and various other states in the West. Behind them rose an outcropping of manned television cameras and radio representatives carrying their own microphones and portable recorders.

Stretching down from the terrace were twelve more wide steps that reached the sidewalk and street. A dense gathering of at least two hundred curious citizens filled a portion of the thoroughfare, all kept orderly by a half-dozen blue-uniformed policemen spread out at attention in front of them.

The press conference had been called for two o'clock.

At exactly one minute before two, District Attorney Hoyt Lewis emerged from a lobby door of the city hall, holding two sheets of paper in his hand, and slowly descended to the terrace.

Squinting up from the street at the D.A., Tony Zecca shifted restlessly from one foot to the other in the second line of spectators. This was the moment Zecca had looked forward to with grim satisfaction. Obviously, the press conference was being staged to allow the D.A. to announce that the slimy Dr. Freeberg, already under arrest, was to go on trial for a felony charge. Soon Freeberg would be out of the way and, probably after his jail term, would be forced to leave Hillsdale. And Zecca would have Nan Whitcomb to himself for his very own purposes. Zecca's mind had quickly gone to their reunion and reconciliation. Zecca wondered if he should first punish Nan in some way, as a lesson to her before taking her back, or if he should be magnanimous and forgiving of her waywardness. For the time being, he leaned toward the latter course. It meant better fucking the first night she was again in his bed.

Once more, Zecca focused his attention on the D.A., who had arrived at the lectern and was adjusting the microphone to a comfortable height.

Before beginning his statement, Hoyt Lewis glanced about him and seemed to acknowledge several persons whom he knew.

Briefly distracted, Zecca searched the crowd for a glimpse of Nan. As far as he could see, she was not present.

Hearing the tinny reverberations of the microphone on the terrace above, Zecca again gave the D.A. his full attention.

District Attorney Hoyt Lewis was speaking at last.

"I had originally summoned you all here," said the district attorney, "with a different intent in mind. Since that time, certain facts have come into my hands that now force me to alter the content of my announcement. I had considered canceling this press conference altogether, but then I decided to proceed with it to clarify a certain matter and not allow false rumors to run rife.

"As many of you are aware, word was released through the media that my office had undertaken an investigation of a new medical establishment that recently opened in this city. This establishment was and is known as the Freeberg Clinic. Dr. Arnold Freeberg, the founder and head of the Freeberg Clinic, is a licensed psychologist, specializing in sexual problems. He undertook the use of partner surrogates or sexual surrogates—mostly female surrogates—to give guidance and firsthand instruction to his unhappy patients.

"After a preliminary investigation of his activities, I came to the conclusion that Dr. Freeberg and his surrogates had committed a crime under the state's law against pandering and prostitution.

"As some of you know, the day before yesterday I placed both Dr. Arnold Freeberg and one of his female sex surrogates under arrest.

"However, since yesterday, other facts previously unknown to me have come to light. As a result, I have come to realize that the arrests were a huge mistake. My mistake. Perhaps I acted against the defendants too hastily, in my zeal to keep this city clean and orderly.

"At any rate, I am now satisfied that both Dr. Freeberg and his surrogate assistants are engaged in work valuable to our community. I therefore wish to tell you that neither the activities of Dr. Freeberg nor those of his surrogates fall under the criminal provisions of our laws against pandering and prostitution, and all charges against them have been dropped.

"I cannot adjourn this press gathering without making a public apology to Dr. Arnold Freeberg."

With that, he turned around and raised a hand to beckon someone standing in the city hall entrance above.

Dr. Freeberg came forward briskly and joined Lewis at the lectern.

Smiling, Lewis shook hands with the therapist. "Dr. Freeberg, I want to acknowledge publicly the disservice I have done you, and right here and now I make an apology to you and your staff."

Dr. Freeberg smiled back. "I want to thank you from the bottom of my heart for your gracious effort to right a wrong. I appreciate it and I thank you."

Waving to the crowd amid the spattering of applause, Dr. Freeberg started down the steps to join the spectators.

Having heard what he had heard, seen what he had seen, Tony Zecca froze and his features reddened in fury.

What was taking place before his eyes was the greatest crime he had ever witnessed.

Wildly, almost out of his mind with rage, Tony Zecca knew only one thing.

Justice . . . justice must be done.

Zecca's right hand darted into his bulging jacket pocket.

Justice *would* be done.

It was Paul Brandon, in the front row of the crowd, who was the first to become conscious of some kind of altercation occurring almost immediately to his left.

Just as Dr. Freeberg neared the bottom of the last flights of steps, Brandon saw a short, stocky, powerful man, a very angry man, roughly elbow two spectators in the front row aside, burst out between them, and raise his right hand.

Gripped in his hand, Brandon was horrified to see, was a black revolver.

Apparently, others saw what was happening, too, because there was a shout from people crowded nearby, and then a woman's voice cried out shrilly from behind, "Nooo! No, don't do it, Tony!"

The hand on the gun had taken aim, and a finger tugged at the trigger.

The gun exploded once, twice, three times.

The first shot hit Dr. Freeberg. His hands clutched up at his chest, he swayed, his legs buckled, and gradually he collapsed to the edge of a concrete step, tried to rise, and then rolled down the remaining three steps to the sidewalk.

Before Brandon could join the others in reaching Dr. Freeberg, a shocked young woman broke out of the crowd, spotted Brandon, and stumbled toward him, tearing at his arm.

"Paul, stop him!" she screamed. "It's Tony! He did it!" As Brandon looked off, Nan cried out to him, "Be careful, be careful, he's gone crazy!"

Brandon whirled away, plowed through the shocked mass of spectators, pushing and shoving until he was in the open, and then he saw Zecca.

Zecca was in the open, too, twenty yards ahead, fleeing down the middle of the street.

"There he is!" shouted Brandon at the nearest policeman, pointing to the street.

But already, Brandon saw, two other policemen were on the run, racing after Zecca.

Glancing over his shoulder, Zecca saw that he was being pursued. Abruptly, he stopped, pivoted, held his gun high, and fired at the policemen.

Zecca's shots went wild.

The two policemen, crouching, fired back with more care and deadly accuracy. One, two, three, four shots targeted in on Zecca. The impact of the bullets lifted him into the air, stumpy arms flailing, and then he came down like a limp rag doll and lay sprawled on the pavement.

By the time Brandon reached the body, both policemen were bent over Zecca, examining him and shaking their heads.

"Did you get him?" Brandon wanted to know.

"Dead," said the first policeman to rise. "Stone cold dead. Some nut, eh?"

"Some nut," Brandon agreed.

It was ten minutes before Brandon returned to the foot of the city hall steps where the crowd had parted to let the ambulance through.

Paramedics had Dr. Freeberg on a wheeled gurney, very still on the gurney, as they slid it into the ambulance.

Brandon realized that Gayle had found him, had her arms around him, and was weeping and sobbing.

Brandon held her and tried to make out Freeberg's condition.

"How is he?" Brandon asked. "Will he live?"

"I don't know," Gayle moaned. "He looks awful, just awful."

XII

The third-floor physicians' conference room of Hillsdale Central Hospital had been turned over to the members of the press, who were standing by for the first report on Dr. Arnold Freeberg's condition since he had been rushed into surgery after the Zecca shooting.

Having circulated among his new colleagues briefly, Chet Hunter decided to leave the press watch and return to the visitors' waiting room at the far end of the hall. He had been there earlier, and Suzy and Gayle had introduced him around. Now, feeling he had some business among Dr. Freeberg's closest associates, he was going back to the waiting room.

Approaching the surgery, with a sign reading NO ENTRY on the door, he saw that three persons were seated in folding chairs across the way. Two of them Hunter recognized as Dr. Freeberg's wife Miriam and son Jonny. The third, a well-attired middle-aged man, Hunter guessed to be Dr. Freeberg's onetime college roommate and present attorney, Roger Kile. Passing along, Hunter was tempted to interrupt them to learn if there was any news yet. Kile was speaking to Mrs. Freeberg in an undertone, and from Mrs. Freeberg's intent and fretful expression, Hunter thought

that this was no time to approach them. They would get the
first news, and those in the waiting room would get it immediately afterward.

Reaching the entrance to the spacious visitors' waiting
room, Hunter stood in the doorway briefly to survey it.
Every cushioned wicker chair and the two sofas were occupied, and the television set in the corner was still. Unno-
ticed, Hunter took in the various occupants. Seated in
chairs at one side of a sofa were a man and a woman he
knew to be Adam Demski and Nan Whitcomb, and they
were deep in conversation. Right next to them on the sofa
were Paul Brandon, Gayle, and Hunter's own Suzy Edwards. Briefly, Hunter gave his attention to Brandon and
Gayle, once more. Brandon, Hunter remembered, was also
a surrogate like Gayle. According to Suzy, they were a close
number. How odd, Hunter thought, two surrogates going
steady. How could two professional surrogates make it together? Did they go through all those caressing and touching exercises first? Probably. Then again, probably not.
Anyway, Hunter thought, they might make a fascinating
follow-up feature story for the *Chronicle* one day.

His eyes continued to scan the room. There were the
other female surrogates he had met earlier, and with his
excellent recall, he remembered their names: Beth Brant,
Lila Van Patten, Elaine Oakes, and Janet Schneider. Everyone in this grouping seemed anguished, doubtless concerned about the fate of Dr. Freeberg.

Hunter decided to check in with Suzy.

Entering the waiting room, he crossed it until he came to
Suzy. He leaned over to kiss her, then gave her a questioning look. "Anything yet?"

"Not a peep," said Suzy. "I overheard a nurse say it may
be another half hour. It depends on where the bullet is
embedded."

"Fingers crossed," said Hunter quietly.

"They'll save him, Chet. God won't let a man like that
die," said Suzy.

"Your word in God's ear," Hunter said. "I think I'll hang

around a little while. I want to have a private talk with Gayle, if it's okay by you."

"You know it's okay."

Hunter took two steps along the sofa until he was confronting Gayle Miller, who had just stopped saying something to Brandon.

"Mind if I cut in?" asked Hunter. He addressed Brandon. "Do you mind if I take Gayle away from you for a few minutes? I'd like to have a personal word with her."

"Remember, she's only on loan-out," replied Brandon good-naturedly.

Hunter extended his hand and helped Gayle up from the sofa. "Just something between us," Hunter whispered. "There's an empty laboratory next door. It seems like a safe place to talk."

"Sure," said Gayle.

Hunter led Gayle into the hallway, then opened the door to the deserted laboratory and gestured for her to precede him.

At the nearest formica counter, he drew two high stools from under it, helped Gayle onto one, and seated himself on the other opposite her.

"I wanted a few words with you, Gayle, before whatever happens . . . happens."

"What is it, Chet?"

"You know now that Suzy is my girl, the one who sent me to Dr. Freeberg."

"That was a real surprise," said Gayle. "You're a lucky man. We all adore her."

"So do I, but that's not what I want to talk to you about. If not for her, I'd be the mess I always was. Anyway, she loved me as much as I loved her, and she is the one who encouraged me to go into therapy with Dr. Freeberg. When she told me about the clinic and what was going on there, about you, and the other sex surrogates, that's when I forgot her real purpose in confiding in me. That's when I went haywire."

"Chet, what's on your mind?"

He gulped. "You know, I'm responsible for your arrest as well as Dr. Freeberg's."

"I know, Chet. The district attorney showed me your journal."

Hunter shook his head. "I'm sorry, Gayle, I really am. I meant neither you nor Dr. Freeberg any harm. I just wasn't thinking ahead. I couldn't see what my machinations might lead to. I could think only of myself and my immediate future. I was totally the victim of an all-consuming ambition. All I could see was the chance to get the inside story on the clinic and its operation, on Dr. Freeberg and one of his sex surrogates, because I knew the exposé would land me a job as a writer on the staff of the Hillsdale *Chronicle*." He paused. "I simply got too involved with getting someplace."

Gayle nodded. "We all do sometimes."

"After Suzy read the report, she got mad and pounded some sense into my thick skull. Luckily, she found a few brain cells containing decency and morality. She made me see you for what you really are—and I wanted to tell you . . . and beg your forgiveness."

"All's long since been forgiven." Gayle smiled at Hunter. "You saw me for what I really am—what *am* I, Chet?"

"A guardian angel."

"Oh, come now." Gayle eased herself off the stool. "You know what I really am?" She pulled open the laboratory door. "I'm someone who knows how to use the squeeze method."

Hunter laughed. "The angel of squeeze."

"Exactly," said Gayle, and she left the laboratory.

Paul Brandon was slouched on the sofa, his cold pipe in hand, wishing he could smoke, when he saw Gayle come back into the waiting room. Observing her cross the room, he once more admired her feline grace, and he desired her again.

He jumped to his feet when she reached him, then settled down on the sofa with her.

"Any news yet?" Gayle inquired.

"Not a thing."

"Oh, God, let him be all right."

Brandon nodded toward the hallway. "You and Chet Hunter, what was that all about?"

"Confession. Expiation. Cleansing the soul. Chet just wanted me to know he was sorry. And grateful to me for you know what." She eyed Brandon. "What have you been doing while I was next door? Ogling the other surrogate ladies to find someone prettier?"

"How did you know? As a matter of fact, yes. Look at that Lila's legs. But to be honest, I have a preference for women with fat legs, like yours."

"Beast."

Brandon had become serious. "To tell you the truth, I've been eavesdropping." He was seated with his back to Nan and Demski, who were sitting in chairs to one side of the sofa, and he indicated them with a movement of his head, lowering his voice. "I wondered if they would be too shy to make contact after they were introduced."

Gayle glanced past Brandon. "Clearly, they're not too shy."

"Did you see how the first half hour they sat alongside each other like two wooden Indians? I was nearby when Nan became aggressive. She mentioned something about the weather."

Gayle continued to watch them. "They're talking a blue streak now. I wonder what they're talking about?"

"Maybe about us."

"Maybe about themselves," Gayle guessed. "I wish we could hear."

Nan Whitcomb had moved her wicker chair a few inches closer to Adam Demski, so that she could address him without being overheard.

"No," she was saying in an undertone, "I don't mind telling you how I got to Dr. Freeberg. I had some trouble and an M.D. recommended him. I had what they call vaginismus."

Demski, puzzled, mouthed the strange word. "What's that?"

"Muscular spasms in the vaginal area that make sexual intercourse difficult and painful."

Demski blushed. "I—I guess I never heard of it. Uh, how —how did it happen?"

"It can have many causes, according to Dr. Freeberg," explained Nan. "One cause can be some bad experiences with men. In my case it came from a terrible experience with a man named Tony Zecca."

Demski looked blank for a second and then seemed to recall the name. "You mean the fellow who shot Dr. Freeberg? I'm sorry about his being killed."

"I'm not," said Nan. "He was an animal—and dangerous."

"Why did he do such a terrible thing?"

Nan was silent, and then she spoke. "I can tell you why. Maybe I shouldn't, but—"

"You can tell me."

"I lived with Tony briefly. It was horrible. He gave me such great physical pain that I went to see an M.D., and that's how I was referred to Dr. Freeberg. I finally saw there are decent men in the world, so I walked out on Tony. Just left him. I guess he figured I'd run off with another lover. Somehow he traced me to Dr. Freeberg. He must have thought Freeberg was my lover—or at least that he was responsible for my walking out. Tony wasn't used to that. He was terribly possessive. I don't know what happened next, but I guess Tony decided to get even by killing Dr. Freeberg." Nan emitted a sigh. "I feel responsible for what happened to poor Dr. Freeberg."

Spontaneously, Demski patted Nan's forearm, then quickly withdrew his hand. "It wasn't your fault," Demski reassured Nan. "If he could, Dr. Freeberg would be the first to tell you that."

Nan sighed again. "Maybe you're right. Dr. Freeberg's a

wonderful man." She gazed directly at Demski. "What
brought you to him? Or shouldn't I be asking?"

"You've been frank with me. I don't mind saying." Demski's Adam's apple moved. "I—I'm from Chicago—an accountant . . . And I am—was—"

Nan touched his hand. "You don't have to—"

"Impotent," Demski blurted, hastily adding, "but I'm
cured now. Thanks to my surrogate."

"How wonderful. Who was your surrogate?"

In an almost hidden gesture, Demski pointed to Gayle on
the sofa.

"Gayle Miller?" Nan whispered, her eyes holding on the
attractive brunette. "No wonder you're cured. I'd give anything to look like that."

"You do," Demski said, gulping. "Even—even better."

"You do know how to flatter a girl."

"I mean it," said Demski. "Who—who was your surrogate?"

Nan put a finger to her lips and with her thumb indicated
Brandon on the sofa.

Demski took in Brandon and whispered, "He sort of
looks like a movie star."

"Oh, he's nice. But I find an accountant easier to talk to
than any movie star type." This time she blushed, then
glanced off toward the doorway. "I wonder when we'll hear
about Dr. Freeberg?"

Five minutes later a nurse poked her head into the waiting room. "The surgeon is on his way here."

She disappeared.

An immediate hush fell over the waiting room, all eyes
converging on the entrance.

Seconds later, a tall, lean, bespectacled physician, still
garbed in his green cap and green gown, materialized in the
doorway, kneading his fingers together.

He took a few steps into the waiting room.

"I'm Dr. Conerly, the chief surgeon at Central, and I'm
sorry to have kept you this long, but the news I have for you

was worth waiting for. Dr. Freeberg is fine—couldn't be better, considering his ordeal."

It was as if a single exhalation of relief permeated the waiting room.

Dr. Conerly went on. "We've just rolled Dr. Freeberg out of surgery and will place him in the intensive-care ward briefly, just to be certain his recovery is complete. Without going into clinical detail, I can tell you that Dr. Freeberg's wound was not life-threatening. It was his good fortune that the bullet that lodged under his left clavicle missed his heart and lungs—in fact did no damage to any vital organs. In surgery, we removed the bullet. No permanent damage, not even serious damage aside from his trauma. We were able to patch him up nicely. We'll want him here several days, just to keep an eye on him. If everything goes as we expect, he will probably be able to be back at his desk—on a much shorter work schedule for a while—in ten days. You can all relax now and go home."

The visitors were beginning to rise when Dr. Conerly called out, "Oh, yes . . . Are Miss Miller and Mr. Brandon here?"

When Gayle and Brandon stood up and moved toward him, Dr. Conerly said, "I want to speak to you for a minute before you leave."

Dr. Conerly waited for Gayle and Brandon at the door. "I have a message for you from Dr. Freeberg. He wanted me to tell you he'd made a table reservation for tonight at eight thirty at Mario's Gardens. Since he can't be the host, he asked if you two would invite the other guests and sit in as hosts for him. Do you understand?"

"We do, and we will," said Gayle.

"Oh, yes, Dr. Freeberg asked me to tell you—'have yourselves a great Tom Jones dinner.' Well, good luck."

After the surgeon had left, Brandon looked down at Gayle, puzzled. "What was that about a great Tom Jones dinner?"

Gayle winked, slipped her arm through Brandon's, and said, "You'll find out."

* * *

After supervising the removal of the last piece of padded furniture, the Reverend Josh Scrafield watched from the doorway as the shippers loaded it into the van to put it in storage until they heard from him in St. Louis.

Scanning the street without success for the return of Darlene Young, Scrafield wheeled back into his empty quarters and began to gather together some of his smaller personal effects.

After about ten minutes, Scrafield heard the front door open, and he hurried into the living room to make sure that it was Darlene who had returned. She was carrying a small paper bag and frowned at him as she handed him the bag.

"Here's the pickup you wanted," she said, "from Hanover Hardware Store. Mr. Hanover wasn't there, but he left this with one of his clerks, a young guy named Charles. As it turned out, Charles gave me more than this bag."

"What are you talking about?"

Darlene moved closer to Scrafield. "He gave me some information I didn't know. Said a couple of policemen are his customers, and they passed along a tidbit of gossip. That you were arrested last night for trying to rape one of Freeberg's sex surrogates named Gayle Miller."

"What kind of bullshit is that?" snapped Scrafield. "Rape her? Hell, I'd like to kill her for coming on to me the way she did. A really cheap whore. She tried to blame me, and I was arrested by mistake. But you see me here now, quite unarrested."

"Then why are we going to St. Louis tonight?"

"Better offer. Just came up. Don't worry, you'll even get a raise. Are you all packed, ready to go with me?"

"A job's a job," she shrugged.

"Just remember that," Scrafield said sourly. He busied himself removing a small bottle with yellowish liquid from inside the bag. He began to loosen the cap that had been screwed on.

"Hey, you better be careful with what you're doing," Darlene said. "That's sulfuric acid. If it gets on your skin,

the hardware clerk told me, it can disfigure you for life."
Darlene hesitated. "What do you need sulfuric acid for?"

"It's the best-known drain cleaner around. I want to see
that our new place is clean. Now, enough of this crapping
around. Let's get going. You drive." He paused. "By the
way, one brief stop before we head out of town. You know a
restaurant called Mario's Gardens?"

"Everyone does."

"Okay, stop in front of the place for a minute and wait for
me. I have to see someone inside, and then we'll be on our
way."

"Whatever you say."

"That's what I say," growled Scrafield as he headed for
the front door.

They went out to Scrafield's Buick, and Darlene settled
behind the wheel, waiting for her preacher to get comfortable beside her.

Then she drove off.

Their round table at Mario's Gardens was near the dance
floor.

As host and hostess, Brandon and Gayle dominated the
group. To one side of them sat Nan and Demski, at the
other sat Hunter and Suzy, and the seventh chair meant for
Dr. Freeberg was removed.

They'd been finishing their drinks, as well as their
chopped Italian salads, when a busboy took their plates,
and two waiters appeared and served them their hot pasta
main courses.

Observing Gayle twisting her spaghetti around her fork,
Brandon said, "You still haven't told me something."

"Told you what?"

"The meaning of a Tom Jones dinner."

"This is it, right now," said Gayle. "Remember that old
movie *Tom Jones?* There was a terrific eating scene in it. The
hero and heroine were eating together, eating food out of
each other's plates and staring at each other. It was the
sexiest scene in the whole movie. Somehow, the therapy

surrogates, from the very onset of their treatment, adopted this eating scene as their graduation ritual."

"Why?" asked Brandon.

"Because there's a pretty close link between food and sexuality," said Gayle. "What we're doing here this evening is merely symbolic of an actual Tom Jones dinner. The real Tom Jones, if it's scheduled to take place, occurs in the last exercise between surrogate and patient. Each brings finger food, and you don't talk but sit side by side and feed each other and maybe have some wine. It's not a sex session, but it is lusty. A way of being intimate and saying good-bye. Eventually, there is talk, of course. The surrogate and partner review their close relationship, what went well in it, what went poorly, what was funny, what was sad, and what they could do to make things better in the future. They recollect their original fright and nervousness, and the high points of the days behind them. Talking, we know we may never lay eyes on each other again as long as we live, but what we experienced together can never be taken away from us as long as we live. We talk about how we're closing our relationship with each other and setting out to form new relationships, always retaining a fresh view of the sweetness and richness of life. We pleasure each other by exchanging food and remembrances. And symbolically, that was what Dr. Freeberg wanted us to enjoy together tonight. So let's enjoy our Tom Jones dinner."

Gayle held her forkful of spaghetti up to Brandon's mouth, and he nipped and sucked at it, eating and swallowing, and then speared a fork of fettuccine and fed it to Gayle.

Chewing, she looked around the table.

"All of you, get into it. Chet, you feed Suzy, then let her feed you. And Nan and Adam, you do the same. You'll see what fun it can be."

They busied themselves with the ritual, and halfway through their main courses, they started to engage in conversations, recollecting the best and the worst of times of their therapy and all agreeing that on this night they all felt happy and exulted.

Eventually, the music from the five-piece orchestra resumed, and Gayle and Brandon could see that Suzy and Hunter were already in each other's arms on the dance floor, and that Nan and Demski were leaving their chairs, holding hands and dreamily beginning to dance together.

For a while, Gayle and Brandon, their fingers entwined, silently watched the two couples swaying and moving about the partially darkened room.

"Want to join them?" Brandon asked quietly.

Gayle shook her head. "I just want to join you, as soon as we can leave here."

Brandon nodded. "I'll see that it's very soon."

Darlene and Scrafield drew up before the ivy-covered exterior trellises of Mario's Gardens.

"Here we are," said Darlene. "What next?"

"You stay behind the wheel, double park, keep the engine idling. I'll be out in a minute."

Inside, in the foyer of the restaurant, Scrafield accosted the short, slick-haired maître d'.

"I'm looking for someone who is dining here tonight," said Scrafield. "Miss Gayle Miller. She's at Dr. Freeberg's table."

"Oh, yes . . ." As the maître d' started away, he paused. "Who should I tell her is asking for her?"

"Tell her Mr. Lewis. She'll know. Tell her I have something I want to give her."

Observing the maître d' leave, Scrafield smiled to himself. He was getting adept at using other people's names and voices. When he had hit upon his scheme, he had called Dr. Freeberg's secretary and told her that he was Otto Ferguson and he wanted to know where he could talk to Gayle Miller. The secretary had told him that Dr. Freeberg had reserved a table at Mario's Gardens for this evening, and that Gayle Miller would be among the guests.

That had been easy. So was this, using Hoyt Lewis as bait.

Scrafield fingered the bottle of sulfuric acid in his pocket. When he gave Gayle what he intended to give her—what she deserved—she would look like the Phantom of the Opera—even worse. No man would ever again be enticed by the little whore.

That instant, he saw the maître d' returning, and a step behind him—one last look at that beautiful face, those wiggling hips—was Gayle Miller.

The maître d' gestured toward Scrafield, then turned away to his reservations.

Puzzled, Gayle approached Scrafield. "It's you! The man said Mr. Lewis was here. What do you want?"

Scrafield took a step closer to her. "I wanted to leave you something to remember me by."

"What do you mean?"

Scrafield dug into his pocket for the sulfuric acid, unscrewing the top as he tugged it free.

Holding the uncapped bottle in his hand, he swiftly raised his right arm, pointing the mouth of the bottle at Gayle's face, about to fling its contents at her.

As his arm came back slightly to spew the contents over her, another arm suddenly came from behind Scrafield, under his throwing arm, smashing up hard beneath his arm, lifting it and the opened bottle toward his own face.

The jarring upward blow sent the sulfuric acid splashing out across Scrafield's startled countenance and into his mouth, which was agape. The acid had the searing effect of a flamethrower. Scrafield scratched at his forehead, cheeks, mouth, and shrieked.

At the same moment, Gayle screamed for Paul.

As the maître d' went down on his knees before Scrafield, now writhing and moaning on the floor, Gayle stared into the face of Darlene Young.

"I'm Miss Young, his assistant," Darlene said quietly, watching as Brandon arrived to take Gayle into his arms. "I had an idea he wanted to get even with you, Miss Miller. Now he's the one who'll be disfigured."

"Better beat it before the police come," Brandon urged her.

Darlene shook her head. "No. I want to tell the police

what happened." She smiled wryly. "Sorry to have spoiled your dinner." She paused. "But maybe I didn't after all."

Three hours and three cognacs later Brandon was slowly driving Gayle to her home.

As they turned the corner and approached the house, he glanced down at her as she moved closer to him. Placing an arm around her, he asked, "How do you feel?"

"Recovered, Paul. Never better."

"It could have been horrendous."

"But it wasn't. I hardly remember that it happened. In fact, I remember just one thing. You forgot to offer me dessert."

"I didn't forget it at all. I thought this was a Tom Jones dessert. Something we should share together at your house. Do you approve?"

She tightened her hand over his. "What are we waiting for?"

Gayle was fitting her key into her front door when Brandon started removing her black sequined sweater and then unzipping her long skirt.

In the dimly lighted living room, they embraced and clutched each other, then silently came apart and began to undress each other.

His arm around her shoulders, her arm around his waist, they padded barefoot into the bedroom illuminated by a single lamp.

Arm in arm, they moved to the side of the bed. Then Brandon lifted her up and lovingly placed her on her back on the bed and lowered himself beside her, very closely, until they were flesh to flesh, bodies contacting each other.

His fingers ran over her forehead and mouth, and her hand moved across his abdomen.

"Paul . . ."

"Yes?"

"I—I hope you don't mind, but since Dr. Freeberg's not

looking over our shoulder . . . can we go short on the
touching and caressing?"

"You want me to break the rules?"

"No rules tonight, please. No patients tonight. Just you
and me, on our own time. And in love. So let's—"

Her legs had opened wide and he was over her.

"Paul, I'm ready. Very. And you're—"

"Very."

"It's going to be fun," she said breathlessly.

He went into her slowly, slowly, deeper and deeper, to
the very hilt. It was moist, her vagina, and soft as down, and
it engulfed him like a frantic hug. He began moving inside
her, back and forth, still slowly.

"Ahhh," she moaned, "I love it."

"I love you," he gasped.

They were going steadily when her hands gripped his
ribs, slowing him even more.

"Paul . . ."

"Yes?"

"Do you talk when you make love?"

"Sometimes. Maybe. I don't know."

"I do, Paul. I talk."

"That's fine."

"Because usually I don't talk doing it with patients. We're
not supposed to."

"I know."

"But this is just you and me alone, and I like to vent my
feelings. Also, maybe—"

"What, darling?"

"—because I'm enjoying myself so much with you that it
keeps me from being embarrassed. Besides . . ."

"Besides?"

"I—I hope you don't mind if I'm noisy. I like to let go."

"Let go. I will, too."

"Ahhh, good, good. Faster, Paul, faster. Not so slow.
Faster."

He quickened his movements. Downward, upward. He
accelerated their coupling faster and faster.

"Paul . . ."

He could hardly hear her, with her head going from side to side on the pillow, and her pelvis rocking to and fro.

"Paul . . ."

"Yes?" he gasped.

"You know a woman takes maybe fifteen minutes longer to come than a man does?"

"I've heard."

"Not me, Paul."

"No?"

"Not me. I get ready much quicker—maybe as quickly as you . . . Do you mind?"

"Can't wait," he gasped.

For minutes, they were lost in each other, totally fused, all sense of time gone.

"Oh, Paul . . ."

"Yes, darling?"

"I'm almost there. All I need is—"

"Is what?"

"—for you to rub my clit a little harder . . . No, not that way . . . I didn't mean your hand. I want your body to rub my clit when you go in and out . . ."

"Like this?"

He clasped her by each cheek of her buttocks and drew her up against him. Pressing hard together, they caressed each other.

"Oh, yes, yes . . . That's—yes—just right . . ."

"Just heavenly," he gasped.

On and on, clamped tightly together, on and on, both breathing hard.

"Paul—"

"Darling?"

"—those, those books, novels, where the hero, heroine, they're making it, and near the end she screams, 'More, more, more . . . Don't stop . . . Do it harder, please harder.' You know?"

"What—what about them?" he gasped.

"They're not phony, not fantasy; they're real, they're realistic. I know."

"Know what?"

"It's true . . . I'll prove it." Silence, only heavy breathing, body writhing, and then from deep in her lungs came an outcry, "Don't stop . . . More, more, more . . . Harder, please harder . . ."

He was blinded by perspiration, his chest heaving, his arms trembling, as he went berserk inside her.

She was holding on desperately, her heart hammering, her skin flushed, her breathing irregular, her nails raking his flesh, as her pelvic mound wrenched upward, "Paul, my God, I'm coming, I'm coming, I—"

She screamed out words unclear, and then, panting, she said, "I came."

He could not hear her. He was erupting inside her. The eruption continued and continued and then it was spent.

"I came," she repeated from far away.

"I came, too, my darling," he gasped, "like never before."

Gradually disengaging, he fell back on the pillow close to her, his matted hair against her disheveled hair. After a long interval of regaining their equilibrium, she finally turned her head and looked at him. "Hey, where have you been all my life?"

Their arms went around each other, and after a little while, they were sound asleep in their embrace.

Brandon awakened first at shortly after nine o'clock in the morning, his head clear and his muscles loose and rested.

He shifted his head on the pillow to see if Gayle was asleep. Her eyes were closed, and one of her breasts, not covered by the blanket, lay in repose and slightly spread out.

Realizing the blanket covered them both, he guessed that she had briefly awakened in the night to draw it over them.

Feasting on her gentle profile, the happy memory of last night suffused him. He wondered if she, too, upon awakening, would still feel the sensual aftermath of their lovemaking.

As his gaze held on her, he saw her eyes flutter open. After an instant, they opened wide. She seemed to know where she was, and who was with her, because she searched for him at once. She found him regarding her so lovingly that her lips curled upward, and she stretched her arms out for him.

Brandon went into her arms, pressing his mouth to hers, and then working his kisses down her neck to her breast, where he circled the nipple with his tongue.

"I know what I'd like before breakfast, darling," he whispered.

She reached down beneath the blanket and put her hand between his legs, taking hold of him. "I think I know what I'd like, too," she said softly.

His hand grabbed the top edge of the blanket and stripped it away from her.

That moment their passion was interrupted by the sound of a distant thunderclap. Or what sounded as loud as a thunderclap.

It was the telephone on her bedstand, ringing insistently.

"You don't have to answer," Brandon said. "This time it can't possibly be Dr. Freeberg."

"But it has to be something important. No one else ever calls at this hour. I must answer, Paul."

She snatched up the phone receiver and brought it to her ear.

She listened, then replied to someone, "Yes, this is Gayle Miller."

She listened some more, and from the intent expression on her face and her half of the conversation that he could hear, Brandon guessed it was someone important about something important, after all.

"Oh, how wonderful!" she exclaimed.

The receiver was pushed tightly against her ear, and her expression had become one of unadulterated pleasure.

"That's the best news in the world I could have heard," she was saying. "How very kind of you to call me. I'm absolutely thrilled. I'll look forward to your mailing the details, and I'll be there, all right. You *bet* I'll be there. Thank you a thousand times, Dr. Wilberforce."

Gayle dropped the receiver on its hook and spun about on the bed, her arms upraised as she gave a great whoop, her face totally wreathed in a smile.

"Listen to this, Paul, listen. That was the head of the Admissions Committee for the Graduate Program in Psychology at UCLA. They're sending a letter telling me that of the more than five hundred applicants to the Psychology Department this year, I'm one of the sixty students to be accepted. And also, I've been given a Chancellor's Fellowship—a full one-year's scholarship. They were kind enough to call and let me know without my having to wait for their admissions letter. Isn't that fantastic!"

Her arms came down and encircled Brandon, hugging him to her.

He kissed Gayle. "Congratulations, darling. It *is* fantastic, absolutely."

"Now I'm going to quit surrogating, much as I hate to, and go full steam ahead. I'll be another Freeberg, sooner or later—you watch and see."

"I know you will. I'm sure you will."

Brandon reached for her again, but she held him off briefly and, cocking her head at him, considered him with special seriousness.

"And you, Paul, you should be, too. You should also get a graduate degree in psychology, and then we can both be on campus and afterward have our own clinic and work together. We can work together and love together. What on earth could be better? You must do this, Paul. You must try it."

Brandon grinned at her. "I already have."

"You have?"

"From the moment I met you, Gayle, I knew you'd get into graduate school, and I wanted to get in, too. So I applied, went through the whole routine, and prayed."

"And then what?"

"My prayers were answered. I received my preliminary notification of acceptance last week."

"You bastard, not telling me! With me worrying about your future?"

"I couldn't tell you, Gayle. I had to be sure you'd be accepted. Because if you hadn't been, I might have withdrawn from the whole thing and gone on to do something else with you. Thank God, I don't need a scholarship. I've saved enough along the way to manage."

She took his face in her hands. "Congratulations to you, too, Paul!" She smothered his face with kisses. "Now I'm really on cloud nine."

He cupped his hands under her breasts. "Ever think of trying for cloud ten?"

"I'm beginning to think of it seriously this second."

They both heard the front doorbell ringing.

"Who can that be?" Gayle wondered.

"I'll take this one," Brandon said. He leapt from the bed and tramped out of the room. In the living room, he picked his trousers up off the floor, pulled them on, and fastening them, marched to the front door and flung it open.

A delivery boy stood on the porch with a bouquet of yellow roses in his grip.

He handed the bouquet over to Brandon, who signed for it.

Closing the door, carrying the roses, Brandon tramped back through the living room to the bedroom.

Gayle was on her knees on the bed, curious.

"Flowers. Who can they be from?"

"I don't know," said Brandon.

"There's a little envelope attached to one of the stems. I can see it. Come closer."

He did, and she tore off the envelope. "It's addressed to Miss Miller and Mr. Brandon. Let's see who sent them." She slit the envelope and pulled out a card. She read it aloud: " 'We spent last night together and we did it. It was divine. We want to thank you both for making this possible. We don't know what's ahead for us, but last night—wow!' "

Gayle squinted down at the bottom of the card and gulped. She raised her head. "It's signed, 'Nan and Adam.' "

Brandon had put down the bouquet of flowers. "Gayle, fun and games may be all right for them," he said, "but not for me. I want to marry you."

"When?"

"Don't rush me, lady. First, a little premarital love, my last fling at being sinful. After that, some eggs and bacon. Then back to bed until dinner. After that, some nocturnal love. We'll be ready to sleep, and when we wake up we can get married. Or do you have anything else on your mind for today . . . and for the rest of your life?"

"Only you, Paul. Forever."

He climbed on the bed and rolled over next to her. He took her in his arms to begin the first day of Forever.

AN ACKNOWLEDGMENT

Of the numerous sex surrogates who gave me assistance—there were nine in all, six of them female—I want to credit two in particular who made this book possible.

I want to thank Maureen Sullivan, the best-known and busiest of all female sex therapists, and I want to thank Cecily Green, the articulate training administrator for the International Professional Surrogates Association.

These two deserve credit for the accuracy in this novel. On the other hand, they should be held blameless for those few instances when I used author's license to depart somewhat from the facts in order to make a work of fiction possible.

Irving Wallace